KATIE FLYNN

THE GIRL FROM SEAFORTH SANDS

arrow books

Published by Arrow Books in 2001

8 10 9 7

First published in Great Britain in 2001 by William Heinemann

Arrow Books
20 Vauxhall Bridge Road, London SW1V 2SA

www.randomhouse.co.uk

Addresses for companies within The Random House Group Limited can
be found at: www.randomhouse.co.uk/offices.htm

The Random House Group Limited Reg. No. 954009

A CIP catalogue record for this book
is available from the British Library

ISBN 9780099416548

The Random House Group Limited supports The Forest Stewardship
Council (FSC), the leading international forest certification organisation.
All our titles that are printed on Greenpeace approved FSC certified
paper carry the FSC logo. Our paper procurement policy can be found
at: www.randomhouse.co.uk/environment

Mixed Sources

Product group from well-managed
forests and other controlled sources
www.fsc.org Cert no. TT-COC-002139
© 1996 Forest Stewardship Council

Typeset by Deltatype LTD, Birkenhead, Merseyside,
Printed in the UK by CPI Bookmarque, Croydon CR0 4TD

For Florence Walker, whose excellent memory of her father's work as a shrimp fisherman enabled me to write this book.

My most sincere thanks go to Heather and John Cross for introducing me to 'Auntie Flo', aged 102, whose delightful reminiscences gave me the idea for this book, and thanks, also, to the Liverpool Local History Library for finding me the ancient – but incredibly useful – book on Liverpool fishermen in the early years of the twentieth century.

Chapter One

1902

It was a cold day, although June was well advanced, and Amy Logan, cowering in the doorway of a shop on the corner of Berkeley Drive, wondered whether she had been wise to leave the house in such a hurry that she hadn't even put on a coat. She had peeped out of her shelter hoping that the rain would have begun to ease but it seemed to her, she thought sourly now, that it was pelting harder than ever.

Drawing back into the shelter of her doorway, Amy remembered that today should have been Coronation Day, but two days ago King Edward VII had been and gone and got appendicitis, whatever that might be, and the whole thing had had to be cancelled. Amy had supposed, vaguely, that it was an ailment only suffered by royal personages, but her mother had disillusioned her. 'Kings and princesses!' she had scoffed when Amy had aired her views. 'No, no, it's a thing anyone could have. Your stomach blows up and you get awful pain; your Uncle Reggie had his appendix out years ago when he was just a lad. Still and all, I reckon it's a nastier business when you're a man grown.'

Amy's mam was deeply interested in the royal family. She admired Queen Alexandra greatly and often said that she and the Queen had a good deal in common, though she had never deigned to explain exactly what she meant. Perhaps it was the fringe, Amy thought now, or the regal bearing, for Isobel

1

Logan always walked as though she had a poker up her back. At least, that was what Amy had heard her elder brother Edmund saying one day, his tone half laughing, half admiring. But in any event Amy had swallowed her disappointment over the loss of a day's holiday, because she had been told that as soon as King Edward recovered the date of the coronation would be fixed once more. And let's hope it won't be a day like today, Amy thought grimly, peering out at the downpour. It wouldn't help to have all those fine clothes and fancy hats dripping down royal necks. She grinned to herself. Suppose the colours ran? The Muspratt family who lived in Seaforth Hall would look really good with their faces streaked with purple or green. Amy, who saw members of the Muspratt family in church every Sunday, could just imagine their chagrin if their smart clothes were ruined, even in such a good cause as a coronation.

But right now, great cloud-reflecting puddles filled the road and when a vehicle came by the cart was preceded by a bow wave of water where, just opposite her doorway, two large puddles had joined to form a veritable lake.

Amy thought, a trifle wistfully, of the room she had left in such a hurry twenty minutes or so earlier. The kitchen had been warm and bright, and she and her sister Mary had been knitting and chatting happily enough when she had heard the rattle of a handcart over the rough cobbles which paved the jigger. Immediately Amy had known what this meant. Her father, Bill Logan, was a shrimp fisherman and the rattle of his handcart meant that he was bringing in his catch to be cleaned, shelled and prepared for potting. Potted shrimps were a great

favourite with the Liverpool housewives who shopped in the St John's fish market on Great Charlotte
Street, so shrimps potted today would be sold to the
stallholders, making the Logan family a fair sum.
The Logans had six children, although Edmund no
longer lived at home, and any money they could
earn was welcome.

But however much Liverpool people might enjoy
shrimps, both potted and plain, Amy absolutely
loathed them. When she had been small she had
simply disliked the smell and taste of the little pink
creatures, but as soon as she was seven or eight and
deemed old enough to help, she had had to join Gus,
Charlie, Mary, Albert and her mother round the big
kitchen table in their work of preparing the shrimps
both for market and for the potting. The shells of
shrimps are spiteful to small, soft fingers and Amy
very soon had the criss-cross, paper-thin cuts on her
hands – as had all the Logan children – caused by
the spiny carapaces of the little shrimps. There was
always a risk, furthermore, of being stabbed by a
spine of a yellow weaver fish, if one of them had
been netted accidentally. These small yellow fish had
poisonous spikes all over their bodies that could
cause agonising wounds, which would remain painful and swollen for many days despite the most
rigorous attention.

Amy very soon realised, what was more, that only
the swiftest possible withdrawal from the scene
would enable her to elude the job. A quick visit to
the privy in the yard might get you out of the way
for ten minutes, but then a brother or sister would be
sent to rout you out and return you to the kitchen to
do your share.

Amy, the youngest of the Logan family, had come

3

later to the shrimping than most, because her father spoilt his little girl and knew how she hated the work, but Isobel was adamant that all the children should do their share. 'Just because she's the youngest that does not mean she can shirk jobs she doesn't like,' she had said severely, staring at Bill over the top of her small half-glasses. 'She's young and quick with keen eyesight; that means she won't miss bits of weed and shell, and she'll be helping to earn her keep the same as the rest of us. Being the youngest isn't anything special. Why, if I were to have another littl'un, she wouldn't be the youngest any longer. You'd expect her to work then, I dare say?'

Bill had seen the justice of this – even Amy had realised it was fair enough – and had stopped trying to get her excused from the work, so now it was in Amy's own hands. If she heard the rattle of the handcart returning and could make herself scarce before Bill got into the yard, then she was safe so long as she stayed clear for two or three hours, for it took that long for the family to work through a batch of shrimps. Then, when she did return home, the chances were that her mother might not realise she had deliberately bunked off and Amy would be safe again – until the next time.

But right now, with the rain being blown almost horizontally across the front of her doorway, Amy was beginning to wonder whether she might have been better off picking shrimps. The kitchen would be warm and cosy, the family chatty and her father, if he had had a good catch, would be expansive and talkative, encouraging Amy's elder brothers Charlie and Augustus to talk about the fishing and their various adventures. There might be a cup of tea if one worked fast and neatly, producing perfect shrimps with no stray legs still attached or tiny bits of transparent shell still in place.

On the other hand, though she had skipped out of the house before anyone else had heard the cart, mumbling an excuse about visiting the privy, Isobel was becoming suspicious of Amy's frequent absences when work was on hand and might easily extract a penalty if she guessed that her daughter was skiving off once more. Only a week previously Amy had returned to the house to find a quantity of shrimps still unshelled. 'Ah, Amy,' her mother had said with a narrow smile, 'just in time, chuck. You can finish off that lot while Mary helps me with the tea and the boys have a rest. I know you wouldn't want to see your brothers and sister do your share as well as their own.'

Amy had been mortified and had vowed to herself that next time she disappeared she would be sure to stay away until the hateful work was finished. She did not mind if she was given extra work about the house, so long as it was not preparing shrimps. Isobel could get her peeling spuds or mending nets or even cleaning creels, so long as she avoided the shrimps.

Having decided to stay out until the danger was over, however, did not mean that this miserable doorway was a good place to be. Amy peered out once more, trying to decide just what to do with her time. Her friend Ruth lived a couple of streets away and Ruth's mam would probably welcome Amy in, despite the fact that Ruth was the eldest of five children and their little house was always crowded. But Amy was barefoot – it was summer, after all – and the thought of splashing through perhaps a

5

quarter of a mile of chilly puddles and then having to retrace her steps a short while later did not really appeal. Besides, Ruth's mother would expect Amy to help amuse the little ones and to give Ruth a hand with whatever her friend was doing. It might not be as bad as preparing shrimps, but Amy was not overfond of helping to make a meal which she would not be eating, so going all the way to Ruth's was not a good idea.

If I had some money I'd go and buy a bun at the baker's on Rawson Road, Amy thought longingly. But Isobel did not give the children pennies for peeling the shrimps or doing other household chores. 'Earn money away from the house,' she was fond of telling her children. 'Don't take money out of it. Fisherfolk need every penny they can get.'

Having decided against a visit to Ruth's, Amy bent her mind to alternatives. It wasn't the weather for a stroll around Knowsley Road looking at the shops and there would be few games of ollies or skipping going on in such weather. Even her favourite place, Bowersdale Park, would not provide much amusement on such a day. It was a shame that Seafield Grove was, by and large, an elderly neighbourhood, so that there was little choice of companionship with children of her own age locally. The small terraced houses were largely inhabited by fishermen, most of whom had grown-up families. The two exceptions on Seafield Grove were the Logans and, at the far end of the street, the Keagans. Suzie Keagan had been widowed shortly after the birth of her son Paddy, and had moved in with her widowed mother-in-law and aunt. Isobel did not like the younger woman and disapproved of young Paddy who, despite being the same age as Albert,

6

was rarely in school and was clearly more than his mother could cope with. Bill, however, said that Paddy's heart was in the right place and felt that, in the circumstances, the boy had to take paid work whenever he could get it. He never made any comment when Isobel said that Suzie was a bad manager, making little effort to see that the money she earned got spent wisely, and Amy thought that this silence was a reluctant agreement. Left to herself, Isobel had once been heard to say that Suzie would seldom have cooked or cleaned, for she disliked housework, and this meant that their neighbour had all the makings of a slut. But Suzie's elderly mother-in-law and aunt kept the place reasonable, and though Paddy wore shabby, too-small clothing and did not seem to possess a pair of boots, at least he was fed most of the time and had, what was more, plenty of spirit, most of which he bent to mischief, Amy thought now.

So the two old ladies did the housework and cooked for the family, and Suzie worked, somewhat desultorily, at any job she could find, seldom keeping the same employment for very long. The money Paddy picked up through running messages and selling firewood and, Amy suspected, nicking from the stallholders on Scotland Road, was a very real help in keeping their little boat afloat. And Amy knew that her father did his best to keep the Keagans supplied with odds and ends of fish whenever his catch was good, despite what his wife thought of their neighbours.

Bill was prejudiced in favour of the Keagans because Abe Keagan, Suzie's dead husband, had been a fisherman like himself and had been lost at sea during a violent storm, which had sunk his boat and drowned every man aboard. Bill thought Suzie was more sinned against than sinning, Amy knew, but her father would never have dreamed of saying so in front of his wife. Bill had once told her that, until Abe's death, Suzie had been a good wife and mother, working hard to sell the fish her husband's family caught. If things had been different, if only Abe had not died, Suzie, Bill seemed to think, would have been every bit as sensible and reliable a housewife and mother as his own wife. Isobel was a good woman, but narrow-minded and strict. She had made up her mind to disapprove of the Keagans and that included Paddy. Nothing would change that, even though Albert and Paddy, both aged twelve and pupils at the same school, were bezzies and, during the school holidays, seldom apart.

Now, peering out into the rain, Amy saw a small figure sloshing through the puddles. It was a boy, coming up the street towards her, and even at this distance she recognised Paddy Keagan. Thinking about him had sort of conjured him up, she told herself crossly. Why on earth had she wasted a single thought on the Keagan family when they were far from her favourite people? In fact, she disliked Paddy intensely for several reasons. The most obvious one being that he disliked her and never lost an opportunity to tease, taunt, or even to bully her. He had divined that his family were disapproved of by the Logans, although clearly not by Albert, and because of this he was all too ready to find something wrong with her in his turn.

Another reason for disliking him was that he had a crush on Mary. Mary was lovely, Amy was very fond of her, but she thought that Paddy had a cheek to hang around their house hoping to catch sight of the older girl. Not that Mary encouraged him – she thought him Albert's friend and no more than a kid anyway – but Amy still resented his liking Mary, particularly as it went hand in hand with disliking her. Of course, Mary was a blue-eyed blonde and very pretty, whereas Amy had red hair and greenish-hazel eyes and was not, she acknowledged ruefully, pretty at all. But her mam was always saying it was character that counted, not looks, so Paddy had no right to like Mary because she was pretty and dislike Amy because she wasn't.

However, Paddy was getting nearer by the minute and although Amy shrank into the back of her doorway she had little hope of eluding his eyes. Paddy would spot her, and would probably guess why she was there and what she was avoiding, and would make it his business to tell Mary and Albert, even if he would not dare to tale-clat to her mam. Accordingly, Amy turned her back on the roadway and shrank into the corner, knowing that Paddy was less likely to see her if the pallor of her face was hidden.

For a moment she thought she was safe but then, while she was still considering turning round to see where Paddy had gone, someone screamed 'Yah boo, Shrimpy!' right into her ear, at the same time gripping her shoulders and twisting her round to face him. 'Don't know why you were hidin' your face – I could tell it were you by the smell o' fish.' It was Paddy, of course, his grimy face split by a broad grin. Amy gave him a shove and then, when he continued to hold her skinny shoulders, turned her head sideways and, with some disgust, bit his filthy fingers as hard as she could.

Paddy let go of her as though she had been red

hot. 'You bleedin' little cat,' he said on a gasp. 'Oh, you wicked little slut, you've near on chewed me finger off! Oh, if you wasn't a girl I'd give you such a clack around the ear your head'd ring for a week. If you wasn't a girl I'd swing for you, so I would!'

'Well, me being a girl never stopped you from screeching in my ear and nigh on giving me a heart attack, let alone grabbing me hard enough to bruise,' Amy said crossly, rubbing her sore shoulders. 'What are you doing here anyway? It's perishin' wet and cold, and you've got no coat.'

'Huh! And you'll notice I aren't askin' what you's doin' out in the rain,' Paddy observed, giving her a malevolent glare. 'Your dad's barrowed in his catch and you're skivin' off as usual, leavin' the dirty work to someone like your Mary, who does more'n her share anyroad.'

'So what?' Amy said belligerently, stepping towards him, hands on hips, and then retreating hastily into the shelter of the doorway once more as the rain caught her. She might occasionally do bad things, she told herself now, but she was not a liar and did not intend to become one, even to spite Paddy. The way to hell began on the slippery slope of telling lies, Isobel often remarked, and since the Logan children knew their mother and father to be both truthful and honest, they tended to follow the parental example, even when it did not much suit them to do so. Of course, swearing around the house was inadvisable, to put it no stronger, so the young Logans watched their language within doors. But a child who did not occasionally use a bad word when in company with their friends would soon be picked out as different and Amy had no desire for such a doubtful honour. Therefore she said, 'Bugger off,

Keagan!' before setting off at a smart and splashy run in the direction of her home. Doing the shrimps might not be much fun, but when you compared it with being taunted and terrorised by Paddy Keagan, while at the same time getting soaked to the skin, it did not seem so terrible after all.

'What's the marrer, Shrimpy?' Paddy taunted, easily keeping pace beside her and making sure that everyone of his footfalls splashed her as well as himself. 'Changed your mind, eh? Goin' to do your share after all, tatty-'ead?'

'Mind your own bleedin' business,' Amy said breathlessly, then tightened her lips and put a spurt on. Small and skinny she might be – well, she was – but she knew from past experience that she could outrun most boys. Paddy's constant attacks had indeed proved this more than once, so now she speeded up and fairly flew along the wet road, swerving into the jigger several lengths ahead of him. She ran up the jigger, bounded through the backyard and was in the kitchen and across to the table very probably before Paddy had turned off the road. Breathlessly, with her heart still thumping from her run, she grinned at Mary, then slid on to the bench next to her sister and, without a word, began to attack the shrimps.

Paddy, foiled of his prey, slowed to a walk and sauntered passed the Logans' front door, casting a wistful glance at the house as he did so. He could never understand why he was not truly welcomed by Mrs Logan when he came calling. He acknowledged that she was a good woman and kind to him in her way, for during school time she quite often gave Albert a double carry-out. She must know that

Paddy's mam, who seemed to find it difficult to hold down a job for more than a few days together, was often hard pressed to find food for them all, let alone the time to prepare him butties. Yet though Mrs Logan might feed him without even being asked, she never encouraged him with so much as a friendly word or look and seldom allowed him to cross her threshold.

Therefore Paddy, aware of this, did not linger by the Logans' dwelling but continued to the tiny house on the end of the row where the Keagans lived. He went down the back jigger and in through the door, not remembering until he entered the room that he had been sent on a message and that Gran, stirring a large black pot over the fire, would be expecting him to return with a sack of the tiny potatoes, which the greengrocer on Elm Road sold off cheap at the end of each day's trading. But Paddy had no scruples about wrapping up the truth when necessary and said breezily, before his Gran could open her mouth, 'They ain't got enough yet to sell off; what's there is mainly earth and stones, to tell the truth. I's to go back in an hour or so. He reckons he'll have more stock in then.'

Gran gave a loud sniff and moved briskly across the kitchen, catching Paddy quite a painful blow around the ear with the long wooden spoon in her hand. 'You're a tarrible liar, Patrick James Keagan,' she said resignedly. 'Why, you ain't been gone long enough for the cat to lick her ear. You can't have reached the end of the road, you lazy little bugger. Comin' back, full of lies, 'spectin' me to believe some old tale . . .'

'Sorry, Gran,' Paddy said humbly. He might have known it didn't pay to try to pull the wool over

12

Gran's sharp old eyes. 'But it's mortal chilly out and wet as well; I've come back for me coat.'

'I t'ought as much,' Gran said, turning back to her cauldron. With her thin, greying hair made lank by the steam of her cooking, she looked more like a witch than a respectable householder. 'What was you really doin', young Paddy?'

Paddy took a deep breath; Gran was remarkably astute and probably had a fair idea of his 'goings on'. 'I were on me way to the shops when I spotted young Amy, hidin' in a doorway. I knew her dad had just brought in his catch – heard his barrow turnin' into the jigger as I passed it – so I guessed young Amy were bunking off, leavin' Mary to do all the work as usual. So ... so I kind of walked her home, saw her indoors. Well, you know what you've always said, Gran, it pays us to be nice to the Logans even if they ain't nice back. Then we's in the right and they's in the wrong, you said.'

Gran sniffed again. Despite the fact that she hardly ever left the house, she kept her ear to the ground and rarely missed a trick, Paddy knew. Still, the story was as near the truth as damn it. So now he took his ragged jacket off the back of the door and struggled into it. 'Sorry I forgot meself, Gran,' he said humbly, pulling open the back door. 'I'll get down to Evans's and be back with the spuds before you've missed me.'

'Who says I'll miss you?' Gran said pertly. 'Oh, you ain't a bad boy, Paddy. I've known worse.'

Out in the rain once more, Paddy hunched his shoulders and prepared for the dash round to Elm Road. He was grinning to himself as he jogged along. His gran was a good old girl so she was. She was seventy-six years old and had come to Liverpool from Connemara as a bride over fifty years ago. Michael Keagan and his family had been one of the many Irish smallholders who had lost their livings when the second potato famine had struck. Despite the hardships the young couple had encountered in Liverpool, they were both hard workers determined to make a success of their new life. They had worked their way up from doing any odd jobs they could get, until Michael owned first a handcart and then a stall, selling for a few pennies more, anything he could buy cheap. Their business enterprise had thrived until he was able to take a share in a longshore fishing boat, while his wife sold their catches to anyone eager to buy.

The time came when Michael and his brothers were all working on the boat, which by now belonged to the Keagan family. They had enjoyed several successful years, often taking good hauls of fish when other boats could not find. And then, when Paddy was eighteen months old, disaster had struck. A storm at sea had taken not only the lives but also the livelihood from the Keagan family. In one blow Paddy's mother, grandmother and great-aunt had been widowed, and had moved from their respective homes into the tiny end-of-terrace house in Seafield Grove. With no catch of their own to sell the women had taken what work they could get. Great-Aunt Dolly, even then in her seventies, had undertaken the household duties. Paddy could not remember those early days but he gathered, from the way Suzie talked, that they had been hard indeed. She had worked for the odd day or so in the market when Christmas came around and she cleaned for anyone who would employ her, usually small shopkeepers or one of the many pubs which abounded in the area. Gran cleaned too and was famous for her scrubbing, but once Paddy was able to earn a little by his own efforts she was not sorry to take over the running of the house from Dolly who burned, Gran said, more potatoes and fish than ever she cooked. Aunt Dolly was childless and had never been much of a housewife.

As Paddy gained Elm Road the rain, which had seemed to fall unceasingly, began to ease. Paddy turned thankfully into the shop and dug a hand into his pocket for the pennies Gran had given him. Mr Evans, standing behind the counter in his stained brown overall and surreptitiously smoking a dog end, hastily pinched it out and shoved it behind his ear as he came forward across the empty shop. 'Afternoon, Paddy,' he said jovially, 'I dare say you'll be after spending a few bob, ain't that right?' He chuckled wheezily. 'Oh aye, did you back the winner of the Grand National, our Paddy? What'll it be, then? A couple o' dozen oranges and a nice pineapple? Or how's about some of them black grapes, eh?'

Paddy chuckled as well, although the joke was an old one. 'I wish,' he said. 'Two-penn'orth of small spuds please, Mr Evans.' He looked hopefully at the older man. 'Gorrany messages or little jobs for me today? The rain's easin' off and me gran's stewin' fish. I wouldn't mind bein' out o' doors for a bit.'

Mr Evans pulled a doubtful face. 'Well, I dunno as I've much in the way of messages,' he said slowly, 'unless you'd like to sort sacks o' spuds for a penny?'

Paddy sighed. Sorting spuds was tiring, dirty work but you could do a lot with a penny. There was the magic lantern show at the village hall, for instance. A boy could see the whole show, sitting on a wooden bench with his pals on Saturday mornings, and buy himself some sweets to suck during the performance, for a penny. But Paddy was not a bad boy and he knew what he would do with the money really. He would take it home to Gran, who needed a penny even more than he did. That way, the next time he earned himself some money he would probably be told to keep it, or at least the majority of it.

However, his gran wanted the small potatoes now and Mr Evans would not be too pleased if he went off without sorting his spuds. Paddy was still mulling over the point when a figure darkened the doorway and, turning, Paddy saw his friend Albert, cap on the side of his head, both hands shoved into the pockets of his grimy kecks. Rescue, Paddy thought thankfully. Albert was a bezzie worth having. When he had done his own messages, whatever they might be, he would be happy to deliver the bag of spuds to the Keagan household.

'Wotcher, Paddy,' Albert said cheerfully. 'How you doin', Mr Evans? Me mam sent me along for a couple a pounds o' carrots, a turnip – a nice big 'un – and some onions.' He smacked his lips. 'She's gorra neck o' lamb so she's makin' Irish stew – me favourite.' He turned to Paddy. 'What's you here for, Paddy? Don't say you's havin' Irish stew an' all?' He glanced down at the large bag of spuds by Paddy's feet. 'Blind Scouse?' he ventured.

'No, I think it's fish,' Paddy said rather gloomily. 'But I say, Bertie, could you run a message for me? I'd do the same for you if I wasn't so pressed for time. Gran needs the spuds, you see, but Mr Evans here could do wi' some spuds sorting, so . . .'

16

'That's all right by me,' Albert said breezily. Mr Evans had been weighing up Albert's purchases and putting them into the string bag which he had slung on to the counter. Now he totted up the prices on one of his brown paper bags and named a sum. Albert paid, picked up Paddy's spuds and his own string bag, bulging with vegetables. 'Will you come round to our place when you've done sorting spuds?' he asked hopefully. 'Me mam might give us a jam buttie, tell us to play out 'till supper's ready,' he ended.

'Sure I will,' Paddy said gratefully. He heaved one of the enormous sacks round into the back room behind the counter and began, methodically, to form the potatoes into three piles, large, medium and small. Albert was a good pal, he reflected. Two penn'orth of tiny spuds were heavy, but Albert hadn't hesitated. Odd, really, when you thought about it, how different the Logans were, one from another. Bill was a nice old bloke who would do anything for anybody, but Isobel was sharp as they came, while Mary was an angel – there was no other way to describe her – and Albert as good a bloke as ever breathed. And then there was the detestable Amy. She had ginger hair when the rest of the family were all blonde, and she was sharp and spiteful when the others – Mary, Albert and Bill at any rate – were all good-hearted and generous. Paddy knew full well that, had he asked Amy to carry spuds for him, or to do him any other favour for that matter, he would have received a dusty answer, probably laced with invective. Like mother like daughter, I suppose, he told himself, diligently sorting spuds with hands that were very soon as earthy as any potato. In a way, you could say us Keagans were

17

all different, too. Mam's easygoing and soft as marshmallow, while me gran is sharp as a needle, like what I am. Oh, well, Gran always says there's nowt so queer as folk. And with that philosophical thought, Paddy gave all his attention to sorting the spuds as quickly and neatly as he could.

Much later that evening Suzie came out of the canny house on Scotland Road, where she had worked for the past eight weeks, and looked, a trifle apprehensively, up at the sky overhead. It was full of scudding grey clouds but, although the road and pavements were still generously puddled, the rain seemed to have ceased, for the moment at any rate. Suzie only had a light shawl cast over her arm but she didn't bother to put it on, for it was warm despite the recent rain. Besides, she usually caught a tram home and on such an evening a shawl was not needed; the tram, though draughty, was a good deal warmer than the street. Added to which, the shawl was hiding something she would far rather her employer did not see in her possession. Mrs Hathaway, mean old cat, would not be best pleased to discover that her cleaning woman had managed to possess herself of a number of currant buns and the best part of a nice bit of ham. It wouldn't hurt her to give me some leftovers, the way she makes me slave, Suzie thought righteously, tucking the shawl securely round the purloined food. Anyhow, it ain't often us Keagans see meat; this'll be a rare treat for everyone, so it will.

There was a tram stop opposite the canny house where Suzie worked, so she crossed the road and joined the short queue of people waiting for the next vehicle. Other people might walk the five miles home, but Suzie did not believe in overexerting herself. The tram ride was only tuppence and she had some tips jangling in her apron pocket. The staff were supposed to share out their tips at the end of the day but Suzie, neither cooking nor serving but merely skivvying, rarely got tips. Instead, however, as she cleared tables and cleaned floors, walls and chairs, she whisked any pennies or halfpennies she might find into her apron pocket and outfaced anyone who suspected that she was feathering her nest instead of passing on the largesse to those who had earned it.

Mrs Hathaway was a marvellous cook, though, which was why Suzie had stayed in the job for so long, despite the pay being on the mingy side. She was employed to clean the room where the customers ate and the kitchen, of course; to do rough work such as scrubbing potatoes, cleaning vegetables and scouring pans, but when the main midday rush was over she sat down to a good meal with all the other employees. Work officially finished, for Suzie, at six in the evening, but she usually stayed later, despite not being paid to do so. There was the big dinner which Mrs Hathaway served to her workers when the place began to empty of regular customers, and there were what Suzie thought of as the 'leftovers'. Some people were given leftovers, but they were staff who had been with Mrs Hathaway a long time, not here-today-gone-tomorrow cleaners, who might well turn out to be no better than they should be. So Suzie nicked anything she could get away with, ate heartily at mealtimes and wondered how long she could stand such extremely hard work, for hard it most definitely was. Mrs Hathaway would not have kept her on for eight days, let alone eight weeks, if she had skimped her work.

However, all good things come to an end. Suzie had noticed, this very evening, that Jimmy, who did some of the cooking and a good deal of the waiting, had begun to look at her with a sort of wary closeness. She had no way of telling whether he had realised she took tips left for the serving staff, or whether he had counted the remaining currant buns that remained on the big dishes behind the counter, but she thought it possible that her job could finish abruptly. Hence the prigging of the bit of ham. It might be her last chance and, since it was summer and therefore not always easy to hide her 'leftovers', she might as well take what she could when the weather made a shawl a necessity and before Mrs Hathaway told her not to come in again.

The tram rumbled round the corner and came to a splashy halt, deluging the waiting people with water. Suzie sprang back and cursed with the rest, then climbed wearily aboard. She sat down on one of the hard wooden seats and reflected that it felt soft as goosefeathers to one who had been slaving for Mrs Hathaway all day. Still, she had a lot to be thankful for. The joint of ham and the currant buns would make more than one meal, and she reminded herself that a lot of widowed women in her position went home to a cold and empty house, and had to start lighting a fire and cooking a meal for their family. Suzie knew that Gran would have a warm room and a good meal ready to welcome her, that Great-Aunt Dolly would wash up and clear away after that meal, and that Paddy would have spent his day as usefully as he knew how. Yes, she told herself gazing out at the greying streaks, there were many worse off than herself.

The tram pulled up at another stop and several men climbed aboard. Suzie glanced incuriously towards them, then brightened. 'Mr Logan! Where've you been, then? I thought the Caradoc was your local?'

Bill sat down on the seat beside her and gave her a friendly smile. 'Who's to say I've been boozin'?' he asked cordially. 'I might've been to a Bible meeting for all you know.'

'You can't fool me, Mr Logan,' Suzie said, grinning. 'If you'd been to a Bible meeting you'd have had Mrs Logan with you. Besides, you wouldn't come into the city centre for no Bible meeting when there's St Thomas's church just around the corner. Anyroad, you aren't usually on this tram. Come to think, you don't catch trams much, do you?'

'Norra lot,' Bill agreed, shifting on the hard seat. 'No, I've not been to a Bible meeting nor yet to the boozer. Well, I did have a bevvy after seeing Arthur Stokes, but don't you go telling my wife. She doesn't understand a feller can like a drink without being wedded to the stuff.'

'Your wife's Temperance, isn't she?' Suzie enquired. 'Well, I ain't, but I might just as well be. There's no money for drink in our house. Not that I miss it,' she added. 'Never did take to it meself. And I'm hopin' young Paddy will steer clear as well. Me old father and me brother Tim could be violent when they'd had a skinful, and nothing breaks up a family quicker than a feller who abuses the drink and his own strength.'

'Aye, that's right enough,' Bill agreed. 'Your Paddy's a good lad, though. He and Albert are

21

bezzies, and there's no one I'd rather me laddo went about with. Mrs Logan agrees with me, I know, even though she don't say much.'

Suzie, who had been staring straight ahead of her, turned to gaze at him, her eyebrows arching in surprise. 'Mrs Logan approves of our Paddy?' she asked incredulously. She put up a hand, stroking the rich, golden-brown hair back off her forehead and giving Bill the benefit of a teasing, provocative glance. She remembered Abe telling her once that it had been a teasing glance from her big blue eyes that had first caught his attention and his interest. 'I thought all Keagans were bad through and through in your wife's book,' she added.

Bill took off his cap and began to turn it round and round in his hands. There was a flush on his weather-beaten cheeks, but presently he looked up and grinned sheepishly at her. 'You mustn't mind Mrs Logan,' he said softly. 'It's just her way. Me wife's a good woman you know, Mrs Keagan, none better, even if her mind is a trifle set. Her old mam made all her children take the pledge when they were six or seven and taught them that pleasure of any sort was sinful. Mrs Logan knows better than that now, of course, but it's coloured the way she looks at life.' He sighed, giving Suzie a straight look out of his round, golden-brown eyes. 'Many's the time I've told her to be more tolerant and I know she does her best, but it's uphill work when you've had narrowness and self-righteousness preached at you since you was a kid.'

'Aye and I know she's been good to our Paddy often enough,' Suzie agreed, remembering the times her son had been fed by Isobel Logan. 'As for yourself, Mr Logan, you know how grateful we are

22

for the fish. I won't deny if it wasn't for that we wouldn't always make ends meet. I does me best, but I find it hard to hold on to a good job even when I manage to get one. It's 'cos I mainly goes for cleaning or domestic work of some sort, where there's women in charge. Me old ma-in-law says I should tie back me hair and tek good care not to look too pretty, but ... well, I say self-respect's worth a bob or two.'

It was an invitation to Bill Logan to tell her that she was a good-looking woman, that other women would obviously be jealous of her, not want to employ her, but Bill did not respond in the way Suzie had hoped he would. Instead, he just nodded briefly as the tram drew to a shuddering halt and got to his feet. 'Don't you go worrying over such things,' he said. 'No point. As for the bits o' fish an' that, what's that to a feller in my trade?' He began to make his way down the tram, speaking to her over his shoulder as he did so. 'I'm gerrin' off here so's I can go to me aunt's house for half an hour, to see that she's all right and have a jangle. Goodnight, Mrs Keagan.'

Suzie smiled to herself as Bill Logan disembarked and the tram began to move once more. She guessed he would go to his aunt's house and chat and drink tea until not even the most suspicious would smell beer on his breath. Bill Logan was far too canny a man to make bullets for his wife to fire at him. Far too nice a man, Suzie's thoughts continued, for such a straight-backed, tight-mouthed wife. But he and Isobel must have been married for thirty years and a woman could change a good deal in that time; as, indeed, could a man. The girl that Bill Logan had fallen in love with could have been gay and amusing, but thirty years of bringing up kids and making every penny do the work of two could change anyone. Suzie knew it was changing her. There had been a time when her main aim in life had been to have fun and to get herself a decent man who would take her away from the miserable court off the Scotland Road where she had been born and brought up. Then she had met Abe and he had taken her back to the neat house in Seaforth and introduced her to his family, told her all about their boat, their trade. She had seen at once that marriage to Abe was bettering herself, especially when they had moved into a terraced house of their own and begun to furnish it nicely, to plan their future lives together.

They had wanted children and, although Suzie had been no fonder of housework then than she was now, at least she had found it bearable in a new little house, surrounded by nice things. She had cast off her family – had been glad to do so – and had entered wholeheartedly into the life of a small fishing community where the name Keagan was respected and where she herself had been totally accepted.

When Paddy had been born she had agreed with Abe that their boy should better himself, get an education, work at his books. In those days, selfish though she had been, she had not wanted Paddy to be forced into working as soon as he was able to hold down a job. She had dreamed of seeing her son the owner of a fishing vessel, as his father had been. But somehow the harsh reality of living in poverty in a big city had whittled away at her resolution until she found herself glad of every penny the boy could bring in and was no longer concerned when he sagged off school, so long as he was not caught.

Thinking it over now, she remembered also that she had been honest enough when Abe had been alive. Or was it just because there had been no need to prig joints of ham, to take tips left for others, to let her mam and her aunt do all the housework? She remembered life in the court, where she had had to fight for every mouthful of bread, every penny. Yes, in the old days, before she had met Abe, she had been as sly and on the make as anyone else.

The tram stopped once more and Suzie noticed that it was beginning to rain. Damn! She would have to put her shawl over her head and shoulders or folk would think it mighty odd. If only she had brought a shopping bag, but Mrs Hathaway would not let casual staff bring bags on to the premises. Too crafty, Suzie thought crossly. She was surprised that they let her bring the shawl – come to that, she wouldn't put it past old Ma Hathaway to insist that the staff removed their drawers before starting work, in case they stashed away food in them.

The tram lurched forward again just as a man came up the aisle, giving Suzie a grin as he passed her. Suzie cast down her eyes and pretended not to notice. She often thought about marrying again, for Abe had been dead now for more than ten years, but somehow she couldn't be bothered with all that courting business and she had no intention of taking a feller unless it was in marriage. Her ma-in-law was a tartar and wouldn't put up with any funny business, to say nothing of Aunt Dolly, who was in church five days a week and always telling her what happened to bad girls.

Still, marriage would be a way out of her difficulties; after all, it had been marriage that had got her out of the court and away from her dread

25

family in the first place. Then death had robbed her of her pleasant life and had forced her to become a breadwinner once more. If she were to marry . . . but the trouble was she seemed to attract the wrong sort of man, or otherwise the right sort of men were married already. Take Bill Logan, for instance. He was twenty years or more older than she, but a reliable, strong sort of man and, she acknowledged to herself now, very attractive. If only he were not already wed. But he was and somehow the thought of marrying someone she did not know very well, only to discover that the new husband had feet of clay, was not one which appealed. Some day, Suzie told herself, Mr Right will come along and then I shan't have to work for bad-tempered old women who sack me because they're jealous of me looks. What's more, I shan't have to purrup with Gran and me Aunt Dolly bossing me around and telling me how I ought to behave. One day, one day . . .

The conductor rang the bell and people began to surge towards the rear of the vehicle. Suzie joined them and climbed down off the tram at the Seaforth Sands terminus, thankful that the rain had stopped once more, though the road and pavements were still puddled. She crossed the road and went under the Rimrose Bridge, just as a train passed overhead. The Caradoc Hotel looked most inviting on the corner opposite, but Suzie decided she must step out for home and pressed on down the Crosby Road. She passed the Royal Hotel, which at other times might have tempted her, and soon came abreast of the massive bulk of Seaforth Hall, set back from the road in enormous grounds. She crossed over the end f Shore Road and glanced to her left down to the ach. The sand was dark and the sea glimmered whitely as the waves crashed on the shore, but there was nothing else to be seen and soon she reached Seafield Grove on the right, lined on either side with terraced houses fronting directly on to the pavement.

She passed the Logan house with its brightly lit windows and wondered, enviously, what the family were doing. Waiting for the head of the household, no doubt, though perhaps the younger ones were already abed. She hoped that by now Paddy was sleeping soundly and told herself for the hundredth time that she really must begin to look for work that paid rather better than cleaning for Mrs Hathaway. Only she was so tired. Tired of trying to make ends meet, tired of the endless round of work and managing the money, tired of her boring existence, in fact.

Shocked at her own thoughts, she turned into the jigger, telling herself all over again that at least she was going home to a meal and a warm room. And no man. The thought popped into her head, shocking her by its forthrightness. She reminded herself how the thought of remarriage frightened her – had she not just been thinking so on the tram? She knew she was still an attractive woman but she knew also that she was lazy. The sheer effort of beginning a relationship with some young feller who might turn out to be more trouble than he was worth daunted her. It must be because I was so deeply in love with my dear old Abe she told herself, conveniently forgetting the way she had leapt at his proposal as an escape from the court. Once again she thought of Bill Logan, his friendly, open face, his generosity in often passing on some of his catch to the Keagar family. He was a handsome man, despite his fift~ three years. Any woman would be . . .

But Bill Logan was, so to speak, spoken for and the other men she met tended to want a woman for almost anything but marriage. Suzie knew herself, despite appearances, to be less interested in the physical side of marriage than most women. In the ten years of her widowhood she had never been tempted to leave the straight and narrow for a bit on the side. She had had a difficult time giving birth to Paddy and had decided, quite coldly, that she would not have any more children. For the best part of a year she had kept Abe to his own side of the bed by pretending illness; then an old gypsy woman had sold her a little brown bottle, full of an evil-tasting draught . . .

The wretched stuff had worked, though it had made her almost as ill as she had pretended, she remembered now, slopping along the pavement. She had been told to take a tablespoonful of the stuff whenever her monthlies were due and since she had not fallen pregnant in the six months before Abe had died, she supposed it must have been the gypsy's concoction. But if she had had her way there would have been no need of medicine, for she could cheerfully have dispensed with having Abe all over her, especially when he'd had several pints of ale and was inclined to be rough with her. Odd how most women seemed to think that going to bed with a man was something special; Suzie simply considered it dangerous. Babies, after all, turned into children, into more mouths to feed. No, she did not think, somehow, that she would marry again. Of course, it would be different if she met someone really first-rate, someone who would support her, take care of her, keep the worry of Paddy and the ol women off her mind. Someone like Bill . . .

But thinking like that never got anyone anywhere, Suzie told herself, as the back door opened under her hand. There was no point in coveting another woman's man, quite apart from its being a sin, particularly a man who's married to a plaster saint like Isobel Logan. She supposed, vaguely, that even if Isobel went and died on him, Bill Logan would look around for another prim, prissy-mouthed woman, who was prepared to work all hours and sell shrimps door to door without a word of complaint. And have ten kids, she reminded herself, wincing at the very thought. Oh, no, she did not mean to go through *that* again, she was better off a widow, much better off.

On this thought she emptied the contents of her hawl on to the kitchen table and grinned triumphantly across the room at Gran, who was dishing up stewed fish and potatoes into a cracked pottery plate. 'I'm home, Gran,' she said. 'Got some currant buns for Aunt Dolly to soak in a nice saucer of tea, so's she don't have to chew, and a nice joint o' ham for tomorrer's dinner. Mr Logan pop by wi' some plaice? Thought so. Honest to God, I'm wore out, but I'm still hungry as a horse after workin' like a slave all day.'

Gran sniffed. 'I suppose you'll say that hard-faced Hathaway woman give you the meat and them buns?' she said tauntingly. 'Well, so long as you don't expect me to believe you . . .'

'Believe what you like.' Suzie cast the shawl in the rough direction of the hook on the back of the door and sat down at the table before the plate of food. 'I don't suppose it'll stop you eating them wherever they come from. That right?'

'Beggars can't be choosers,' her mother-in-law

admitted, coming over to the table with a mug of steaming hot tea and setting it down before her daughter-in-law. She picked up the joint of ham and looked at it critically. 'There's good eatin' on this, I'll say that for you. But how long will you last there, eh? A few currant buns is one thing, but a whole joint o' ham . . . well, they'll soon have your measure at that rate.'

'I'm sick of it anyway,' Suzie said, her mouth full of floury potato. Gran was a prime cook, she had to admit that. 'I were going to move on soon enough.'

'Oh aye? Before you're pushed, you mean? Oh, go on, don't bother to tell me no more lies. I'm tired, I want me bed. Wash up when you're done, gal.'

She left the room and Suzie continued to eat the fish and potatoes, and to sip at the scalding hot tea. Gran wasn't a bad old stick, a lot easier to get along with than Aunt Dolly with her religious mania and her spiteful tongue. Suzie finished her meal and stood up, the mug of tea in one hand. She would take it up to bed with her and drink it while she took off her outer clothing. She had no intention of doing the washing up and clearing away. Aunt Dolly, self-satisfied old fool, could do that. She might be eighty-two or three – Suzie was never quite sure of her aunt's precise age – but she wasn't helpless yet and she ate enough for two. She could do the washing up. Suzie doused the lamp and wandered across the kitchen and up the short flight of stairs to her room. Here, in her muddled and unmade bed, she settled down to sleep. Drowsily she considered Gran's words. Perhaps the joint of ham had been a little unwise. She would go back to the canny house next day, and if she was accused of thieving then, naturally, she would hotly and indignantly deny it.

Meanwhile, she could go along to the Caradoc Hotel, or the Royal, or even the International Marine and see if they had a vacancy for an evening barmaid, just in case she got the push. The Caradoc had advertised just such a position on a board outside the pub; she had seen it a couple of days earlier. She supposed she could stand working there for a few days, just until she found something better.

Soon Suzie slept, her conscience untroubled by thoughts of the day to come.

Bill Logan said goodnight to his aunt and set off on the walk home, glad that the rain had not restarted. He had had a good day and had concluded a nice little business deal with Arthur Stokes. He and Arthur had been at school together and though they had gone their separate ways – he to the fishing and Arthur into the retail grocery business – they had remained good friends. So when he and the other man had met up at the St John's fish market it had been natural for Arthur to suggest that he might come round one evening for a drink and have a chat. Bill had agreed, though he had guessed that there was more in Arthur's invitation than met the eye and so it proved. Arthur was keen to find a supplier of potted shrimps and had immediately suggested that he and Bill might work out a deal which would satisfy them both, and such indeed had been the case. The Stokeses were prepared to pay the Logans a very fair price since Arthur's shop, being well out of the centre of Liverpool, catered for customers who rarely got into the city and would be prepared to pay an extra penny or so for the convenience of buying potted shrimps from their own corner shop. Arthur, for his part, knew that the potted shrimps would bring the customers in, so was happy to cut his profit to a minimum for the sake of the extra business.

It had been a bonus, meeting Mrs Keagan on the tram, Bill thought now. She was a beautiful young woman, hard-working and good-hearted, if a little sloppy, and he often felt ashamed of the way Isobel regarded her. The girl had done nothing to deserve his wife's constant criticism – unless being younger and beautiful was a sin, which Bill sometimes thought Isobel must believe. His wife said that Suzie nicked stuff from her various employers, that she changed her jobs a good deal more regularly than she changed her underwear, that she put all the work of the house on the two old ladies, using her various jobs as an excuse for sluttishness. Yet when he thought about it, it did not seem likely that Isobel disliked Suzie merely because she was pretty, because such a view scarcely agreed with Isobel's feelings for Mary. Mary, her favourite daughter, was blonde and extremely pretty, very like Isobel had been when they had first married. Was that the reason for Isobel's partiality? Would this also account for the fact that his wife did not greatly care for plain little Amy and was as constantly critical of her small daughter, as, indeed, she was of Suzie Keagan? Bill reached the back door of his home and pushed it open, stepping thankfully into the warmth of his kitchen. It didn't do to start thinking too hard, he reminded himself. All parents have a favourite child – he was very fond of Amy – and there was nothing obvious to account for such feelings, it was simply the way one felt.

'Still raining?' Isobel asked, from her seat by the fire. 'Call itself summer? Well, I should think the

32

poor King is downright grateful for his appendix blowing up the way it did, for this is no weather for a coronation. They would probably have had to swim up the Mall, getting all those lovely robes soaked. I've saved you some tea if you're still hungry, or did you eat with the Stokeses?'

Bill walked round the table and dropped a kiss on his wife's thick, greying hair. 'Aye, it's grand weather for ducks, not dukes,' he said, chuckling. 'Still an' all, the coronation's only postponed, not purroff for ever. Likely it'll be fine for the real thing when the King's better.'

Isobel ignored the caress but smiled up at him, shaking her head. 'Oh, you, Bill Logan! There's been a lot of disappointment over the King's illness, you know it as well as me. Now what about some food, or have you already eaten? It's Irish stew if you'd care for some. What did Mr Stokes want?'

'I did eat with the Stokeses,' Bill admitted, reaching into his jacket pocket for his pipe and then, with a sigh, putting it back once more. Isobel did not approve of tobacco any more than alcohol, and would grow tight-lipped and silent if he tried to smoke in the house. 'But that was a good while ago. I could just do with a plate of your Irish stew.'

'Right,' Isobel said, leaving her chair and crossing the room to the stove. With her back to him she added conversationally, 'You know our Amy lit out when the shrimps came in? Well, she came back after no more'n ten or fifteen minutes. I think maybe that young lady is learning at last that everyone's got to do their share in this world. She worked well, I'll say that for her. She helped with the potting as well.'

'Glad to hear it,' Bill said, going over and sitting down at the table. Isobel placed a brimming plateful of Irish stew before him and he picked up his spoon and began to eat. 'This is grand, queen,' he said appreciatively presently, reaching for a thick slice of home-baked bread and dipping it into the gravy. 'I'm a lucky feller, so I am.'

Isobel, seating herself opposite him, smiled. 'Aye, you're right,' she agreed. 'I'm a good cook, though I say it as shouldn't. And I'm not doing so badly myself, for there's many a worse husband in these parts.'

Chapter Two

As Bill had predicted, no sooner had the King recovered from his operation than the date for the coronation was fixed once more, this time for 9 August. Isobel read pieces out of the paper to the children as they sat peeling shrimps, telling them all about preparations for the celebration. There had been the great feast the King had given thousands of Londoners the previous month and, though his bounty had not stretched as far as Liverpool, everyone agreed it was a generous gesture. Then there were the decorations. Wonderful arches which spanned the widest of roads, monuments decorated with artificial flowers and brilliant illuminations, while enormous bouquets and garlands of real flowers wreathed the major buildings. Amy, Mary and Albert listened to these tales of wonder, and envied Londoners and anyone else fortunate enough to be going to the capital city for the great event. In fact, the children all knew that there were people in Seaforth who would go up to London, not perhaps for the coronation but to see the decorations, which would remain in place for several days after the King and Queen were crowned. Seaforth was home to several families who, while not as rich as the Muspratts, were still very well-to-do. The Grim-shaws, for instance, went to St Thomas's and were very rich indeed. During the summer holidays and usually at Christmas, too, they had their grand-children to stay. Philip was fourteen and Laura twelve; the children knew that much since Isobel sometimes sold fish at the big house on Crosby Road, but they scarcely saw the Grimshaws during the services, for the Grimshaws had a closed-in pew with high wooden walls, which hid the occupants from ordinary worshippers. Laura was not allowed much freedom, not nearly as much as Amy, but Philip, being a boy and also older, frequently made his way down to the shore to fish. A couple of times he had begged an illicit ride in the shrimp boat, and both Bill Logan and Amy's brothers said he was a decent young chap and not a bad fisherman either.

However, Amy was not particularly interested right now in the Grimshaws or, indeed, in the coronation itself. She considered it thoughtless, if not downright selfish, of the King to rearrange his coronation so that it was during the school holidays instead of in term-time, but no one was perfect. Isobel was a keen royalist, knowing every detail about the royal family and she was a great admirer of Queen Alexandra, so when the papers reported the great event Isobel would be in her element. Indeed, she would be too busy reading all about it to worry overmuch what her daughters were up to. But Coronation Day having dawned at last, Amy and Mary had obtained permission to take their midday meal down to the sands and to spend their time on the beach, digging for cockles if they felt inclined but otherwise having a lazy day. So now she and Mary skirted Seaforth Hall and made their way past the Grimshaws' big house, heading for the particular spot where they had decided to spend their holiday. 'For it is a holiday,' Mary told her sister as they left the house, their carry-out in the string bag that swung from Mary's hand. 'It isn't often our mam let's us off for a whole day, let alone gives us a picnic.'

'It's not often the King and Queen get crowned,' Amy pointed out, skipping along beside her sister. 'Oh, but isn't it a lovely day, our Mary? I wonder what Albert's doing – something he shouldn't ought to, I reckon.'

'He's not a bad lad,' Mary objected. 'Not like Paddy Keagan. He leads our Albert into more mischief than a cartload of organ-grinders' monkeys. But there's no real harm in him, our Dad says. And he offered to carry my basket last time I did the messages for our mam.'

'I think there's harm in that Paddy. And anyway, Albert needn't do as he says,' Amy pointed out righteously. 'Mammy would say he could choose the good road or the bad, same as the rest of us. I say, Mary,' she added as a thought struck her, 'why don't we call Albert Bertie, same as Paddy does? Come to that, Mam always uses full names, even for Augustus. Everyone else calls him Gus.'

'Mam doesn't like nicknames,' Mary said as they reached the sand and began to walk along it, scuffing their bare feet in the warm, golden grains. 'She'd call Dad William, if she could, only he told her when they were first married that he wouldn't stand for it. That's why we girls have short names which you can't muck about with. You can't shorten Amy or Mary, can you, chuck?'

'No-o-o,' Amy admitted after some thought. 'But why choose Augustus or Albert? They are names which everyone shortens, wouldn't you say?'

'Dad chose 'em,' Mary said briefly. She plonk

herself down in the sand and pushed the straw hat she was wearing to the back of her head. 'Phew, isn't it hot, though? And it can't be more than ten o'clock, if that. Shall we start on our drink? Just a sip or two each, mind.'

'That's fine by me.' Amy rooted for the bottle in the string bag. 'Oh, Mam put in a bottle of water and one of ginger beer. Shall we start on the water and save the ginger beer till later?'

'Yes, that'll be best,' Mary agreed, taking the bottle of water from Amy's hand, uncorking it and lifting it to her lips. She took several thirsty gulps, then replaced the cork and handed the bottle back to her sister. 'Do you want a drink, Amy?'

Amy took a mouthful, but she was not particularly thirsty, and quickly replaced the cork and carried both bottles down to the edge of the waves. Here she dug a hole with her hands as a dog might and, when the water had crept halfway up the sides, she put both bottles in it, knowing that the sea would keep the drink cool. Then she kilted up her skirt and waded into the water. Mary, after a moment's hesitation, followed suit and for some time the two children simply revelled in the water, splashing backwards and forwards and trying to spot shells, seaweed and tiny crabs, which they could see through the waves but could not pick up without getting soaked.

After half an hour of this rather frustrating game, Amy went ashore and took off her white cotton apron, her long grey skirt and the two petticoats beneath it. Then she rolled up the legs of her frilled drawers and took off her blue blouse. While Mary was still gaping at her, wide-eyed with horror, she marched back into the water until it was up to her chest, gasping at the cold but thoroughly enjoying the sense of freedom that her near-nudity gave her.

'Amy!' Mary squeaked. 'Whatever are you doing? Mam would half kill you if she saw you now! You should know better, indeed you should. Mam would say no decently brought-up girl would kilt her skirts up, let alone take them right off. Remember we're on a public beach, our Amy, and though it's early still, folk are going to start coming on to the sands any minute now. Why, anyone might come along and see you and think you a nasty, common sort of kid. Come out of that at once, do you hear me?'

'No, I shan't,' Amy said defiantly, splashing with her arms and pretending to swim. Indeed, when each of the little waves came inshore it lifted her up and carried her with it, making her feel as though she really was swimming. 'I don't see why you're making such a fuss, anyhow, because no one's here yet. Besides, ever such smart ladies and gentlemen go swimming these days, you know they do! Don't you remember the pictures in that old copy of the *Sketch*, which Mam brought home from the Grim-shaw place? I'm sure what they were wearing wasn't nearly as respectable as my drawers and chemmy.'

'The folk who go swimming have proper costumes and ... oh, Amy, someone *is* coming, honest to God they are! Now will you come out and stop shaming me? I do declare, if I were to tell our mam ...'

'But you won't,' Amy pointed out. Mary might disapprove, but she wouldn't go tale-clatting to Mam, not she. Nevertheless, she glanced along the beach and saw that someone really was approa ing. Two – no, three – figures, one of which what she took to be a fishing rod in one hand and a basket of some sort in the other. 'Oh, damn,' Amy muttered. But she knew her sister was right. Seaforth Sands was a popular venue with half Liverpool when the weather was fine and today was to be a holiday for a good many people, though schoolkids, already on holiday, were missing out. Accordingly she began to wade out of the sea, though her tilted chin and defiant glare would tell her sister, she hoped, that she was coming because she wanted to do so and not because she was afraid of the consequences.

Indeed, the little wavelets were no more than lapping at her ankles when she took another glance along the beach and realised, with considerable dismay, that she recognised at least one of the small advancing group. The detestable Paddy Keagan, hair on end, ragged jersey tied round his waist, kicking a round pebble before him and singing what was probably a very rude sea shanty, was approaching, thankfully at a saunter. And it stands to reason, Amy told herself, hastily splashing ashore, that if Paddy's here, Albert's with him and that could mean . . . oh, all sorts of trouble.

The far worse trouble, that of being soaked with salt water and without so much as a handkerchief with which to dry herself, did not occur to poor Amy until she was approaching their bag of food. Then, glancing down at herself, she saw how far from glamorous one looked in a sodden chemise with drawers which had managed to trap, in their one plain frill, a quantity of grey-looking sand. 'Oh, God ѕve me, I'm in a pickle this time,' she muttered ѕder her breath. 'Oh, oh, they're getting awfully ѕe, so they are, and that pig of a Paddy is starting to grin like . . . like an ape!' She seized her skirt and pulled it on all anyhow, then began to struggle into her blouse, which was too small for her anyway. Her long hair was dripping down her back, soaking her all over again, and Mary was expostulating, telling her that she couldn't possibly put dry clothes over soaking underwear and wasn't she the stupidest, naughtiest kid ever to disobey her elders, now.

But Amy was past caring what Mary might say. What worries me is what that bleedin' Paddy would put about if he sees me in my drawers, Amy told herself, continuing to struggle into her – by now – damp clothing. Oh, he would jeer at her, he would scoff, he would . . .

A great guffaw of laughter interrupted her thoughts. Paddy stood not six yards distant, grimy hands on hips, his belongings cast down, a grin from ear to ear splitting his horrible, dirt-smeared face. 'Ooh, look at ole sainted Shrimpy, Mammy's good little darlin', a-wearin' of frilly kecks an' soaked right through to her miserable speckled skin,' he shouted. 'And she's been a-swimmin' in her bare skin just like us fellers does, only she can't swim for toffee-nuts, bein' a stupid, brainless *girl*, acourse.'

The three boys were grinning but the eldest of them, who must be Philip Grimshaw, Amy supposed, suddenly stopped smiling and said, 'Oh, come on, Paddy, there's no need to be rude, is there?'

'I's always rude to her,' Paddy said airily. 'She's a tale-clat an' a nuisance; she thinks she's someone special. She's rude to me so I's rude to her.'

'Fellers shouldn't be rude to girls,' the boy, Philip, pointed out. Not self-righteously, Amy thought, but rather as a matter of course. 'And you can't blame her for taking a swim on such a grand day. I wouldn't mind a swim myself.'

Amy, having struggled at last into her clothing, turned to face the boys. She glanced rather shyly up at Philip, thinking him handsome and much older than he looked, for she knew from Albert that he could not be more than fourteen or fifteen. He was a good deal taller than either of his companions, however, with crisp, taffy-brown hair and matching eyes, a firm chin and a mouth with a good deal of humour in its swift, curling smile. Accordingly, she gave him a quick grin, to show she appreciated his championship, then faced up to her old enemy. 'I can swim then, Paddy Keagan, I taught myself just this minute, so I did! And I may be freckled, but I'm not clarted up with dirt like you are.'

'Swim! All you did was flap like a stranded plaice an' come in on a wave – I saw you wi' me own eyes. Aw, you're a great ole fool, Amy Logan, to think you can swim the first time you try.'

If it had not been for Mary's restraining hand, Amy would have hurled herself back in the water, clothes and all, just to prove to Paddy Keagan that she could indeed swim, but Mary hung grimly on to her and Amy realised that this was a good thing, since she knew, in her heart, that Paddy was right. She could not really swim at all; it was the sea which had been kind and lifted her up just for a moment. Had she been out of her depth, however, she suspected that she would have gone straight down into Davy Jones's locker no matter how she might flail around.

'Paddy, do leave off,' Mary said, as she clung to Amy's arm. 'As for you, our Amy, just you ignore him. He's out to annoy you, that's all, and don't you rise like a fish to a fly? I told you it was very wrong to go right into the water and now you know for why. Oh, and look up the beach, girl! There's a heap of folk walking along the sand, so maybe our Albert and Paddy and their pal just about saved you from making a real cake of yourself.' She turned to the boys. 'Do you have a carry-out?' she enquired. 'If so, why don't we all sit down and have it right now, and forget our differences? It's a special holiday, after all, our mam won't expect us back until this evening.'

'I've gorra bit of food,' Paddy said gruffly. He could never argue with Mary, Amy knew that very well. 'And some water in a bottle. You've gorra stack of stuff, though, haven't you, Albert?'

'Same's the girls, I guess,' Albert said. 'Phil?'

'In the basket,' Philip told him. 'The housekeeper packed it so I don't know what it is, but she said it'd stop me from starving until dinner time. Oh, and there's a bottle of raspberry syrup. We can all share.'

'Right,' Albert said. 'And no more snipin' at the girls, Paddy, 'cos it makes for awkwardness. I'm goin' to set up me fishin' line first, though. We can watch it as we eat, the girls too. Good thing we came right up this end o' the beach, the other end's thick wi' folk already.'

It was true. Amy, glancing along the way they had come, could see family parties, groups of young people and children already industriously digging in the wet sand at the edge of the waves. What was more, she knew from experience that as the day went on, even the less popular part of the beach where the marram grass grew and the shoreline tended to be muddy at low tide would grow crowded with people. Therefore it behoved them t get as much pleasure from the day's holiday as they could while a large area of sand around them remained empty of people. Amy had never gone fishing with her brother, because Albert almost always went with Paddy. The older boys, most of whom fished for a living, preferred to take a rod into Wales or the Wirral for a day's sport. As for the fishing boat, she had never asked her father to take her shrimping and thought she probably never would. Even had she done so, she doubted that Bill would want her on board. She imagined he would think it unlucky to take a woman out fishing and was devoutly glad of it.

However, fishing with Albert and the others might be quite fun, so she watched with interest as the boys set up their lines. Her brother and Paddy had short hazel wands, which they stuck in the sand after they had thrown out lines baited with what looked like grubs of some sort. Philip, however, had a proper rod with a line and a float and bait, which looked more professional somehow. He cast expertly, too, sending his baited line a good deal further out to sea than either Albert or Paddy had managed, but then he, too, stuck his smart, cork-handled rod in the sand, and strolled back to where Mary and Amy were watching.

'There, that didn't take long, did it?' he asked, sitting down on the sand beside Mary and reaching across for the basket he had been carrying. 'It's early still, but I could do with a snack.' The basket lid was cunningly closed with two loops and a wooden peg. He unfastened it and threw back the lid, revealing several compartments filled with interesting-looking packages as well as an oddly shaped bottle full of a dark-red liquid, neatly corked. Amy was fascinated

44

to see that the lid of the basket held cutlery, a couple of enamel mugs and plates.

'There's all sorts in here.' Philip fished out two of the packages and began to unwrap them. 'My grandmother's cook is an awkward old blighter, but she has a soft spot for me. Besides, if she packs me a decent picnic, she knows she'll be rid of me all day, which makes her life easier, I suppose.' He held out the package towards the two girls. Amy, looking at the chunks of cheese, slices of thick bread and cuts of ham, found that her mouth was watering already. If this was the cook's idea of a carry-out, what sort of meals did Philip normally enjoy?

'Cor!' Amy breathed reverently. 'Your cook must've thought your sister was going to share your carry-out, eh? No one could think one feller needed this lot.'

Philip laughed. 'My sister's gone to the city centre to visit our great-aunt,' he said. 'She and Grandma will get a grand luncheon at Great-Aunt Betty's. Laura loves iced puddings so Great-Aunt's cook always makes one for her.'

The Logan family had ham at Christmas, but iced puddings? She'd never even heard of such a thing, let alone tasted one. They had cheese from time to time, but it was still very much a treat. And fancy having plates and mugs on the beach, where such things were virtually unknown. It must be wonderful to have so much money and so many possessions that one could risk the loss of cutlery or even plates and mugs. The Logans guarded such things with jealous care. Isobel would never have dreamed of letting so much as a teaspoon leave her neat kitchen.

But if the rich had many possessions, the poor could have good times too. Amy remembered one of her brothers telling her once how Dad had taken the older ones on an expedition to New Brighton. They had dug cockles, boiled them in an old Glaxo tin over the driftwood fire they had built and eaten them as the sun began to sink. Gus had never forgotten the trip, and now Amy felt dimly that though it was wonderful to have loads of money and a picnic basket full of delicious food, there were compensations in being poor. She did not think that even the most succulent ham could ever be as delicious as food you had won from the sea, cooked over your own fire and eaten in the sunset's glow. She remembered some of Isobel's favourite sayings, that money was the root of all evil and that riches gave only the delusion of pleasure, and for the first time she thought she saw some meaning behind her mother's words. For all the Grimshaws' money, they would not know the intense pleasure that Amy and her family – and the Keagans come to that – got from the small excitements in their lives. Ham at Christmas, cheese when the money stretched to it, a trip on the ferry, a ride on the overhead railway and cooking your own supper on a sunset beach. To the Logans and the Keagans such things were the very stuff of pleasure, something to be treasured all the more because of their rarity and remembered in the years ahead.

'What'll you have, young Amy? Cheese or ham? Only better take a bit of bread first, so you can make a sort of sandwich.'

'Thanks,' Amy breathed, delighted by such generosity. 'Can I have a bit of both? Just a little bit you know.'

'Amy!' Mary was scandalised. 'It's greedy to have

46

both. Besides, this is Philip's dinner. We shouldn't . . .'

'Oh, let her have both, there's plenty for us all I should think,' Philip said airily. He watched while first Amy and then Mary selected their food, folding the bread over the meat and cheese, and then did likewise, while Albert and Paddy, as a matter of course, helped themselves. The five children sat on the sand, munching in companionable silence, until Amy happened to notice that one of the hazel wands was being tugged almost out of the sand by some movement in the sea. She grabbed Mary's arm. 'Look, Mary! Does that mean someone's caught a fish?'

'Bejaysus, that's my stick – rod, I mean – so it is,' Paddy exclaimed, jumping to his feet. The other two boys promptly followed suit and very soon Albert and Paddy were up to their knees in the waves, both attempting to catch hold of the slippery line and draw it in by hand, for only Philip had a proper reel. Amy went as far as the edge of the waves and watched the struggle, which ended with Paddy and Albert drawing the fish so close to the shore that Paddy fell upon it and presently staggered from the waves, bearing in his arms a sizeable codling. 'Will you look at that!' he wheezed, as he reached Amy's side. 'Isn't he a fine aargh . . .'

The fish, wriggling and flapping wildly, had momentarily escaped from Paddy's grasp, but the three children – for Amy did not intend to be left totally out of the chase – fell upon it in the creaming waves and Paddy dispatched it, chiefly by falling upon it and driving it into the sand. Scrambling to his feet, he grinned triumphantly at his fellow fishers. 'Gorrim! And he's dead as a Dodo,' he said, holding up the limp and sandy grey body. 'Shall us cook him for our dinners?'

'Oh, we've got our dinners,' Albert said. 'We have fish often. Paddy, you take him home for your mam.'

Amy was relieved when Paddy, having considered the size of his fish, nodded agreement. 'All right. Me mam'll be glad of it,' he said. He began to slosh the fish to and fro in the water until, Amy thought, you could almost have believed it alive again. 'Do you reckon there's enough on this 'ere for me gran to have some as well? Still, you never know, if I rebait me hook I might get another. They's bitin' well today, wouldn't you say?'

'That one certainly did,' Albert said appreciatively. He looked up to where his own rod stuck up out of the sand. 'Tell you what, Paddy, if I gets a bite you can have that 'an all. But we'd better get your hook rebaited and into the water, to give your fish's pals a chance to join 'im.'

'Right you are.' Paddy shoved his fingers into the fish's mouth and withdrew the hook, examining it with a grunt of satisfaction. Clearly its sojourn in the fish's gut had done it no harm, Amy concluded.

The three children emerged from the water and made their way to where Albert's rod stood in the sand. Amy watched with interest as Paddy rooted around in an old tobacco tin and produced a wriggling grub, which he impaled upon his hook. He ran down to the edge of the sea and cast his line as far as he could, before returning to stick his hazel wand into the sand once more. Then, for the first time it seemed, he looked long and hard at Amy. 'Oh, Gawd,' he said in an awestruck voice. 'What'll your mam say to this, 'eh? She'll think I baited me

48

hook wi' *you* instead of one of me grubs. 'Cept you'd better not tell her it were my fault, 'cos I never asked you to go jumpin' in the sea and interferin' wi' me day's sport.' Still staring at Amy, he began to giggle. 'I wish you could see yourself, girl, you're enough to make a cat die laughin'.'

Amy, recalled to reality by these rude remarks, glanced down at herself. She was soaked and sandy from halfway down her blouse to the hem of her draggled skirt and knew that, in the excitement of the chase, she had somehow managed to get her hair wet and sandy too. Despite herself, she began to grin. Paddy might be a horrible boy who teased and tormented her, but at least he was honest. It had not been his fault and she did look a sight, she acknowledged the fact. It would be bad enough when she went up the beach to rejoin Mary – she could not imagine what her mother would have said had she been present. However, Isobel was safe at home, no doubt eagerly awaiting news of the coronation. The hour of reckoning, therefore, might be decently delayed until evening. By then, with a bit of luck, she would have dried off and have been able to brush away the sand and to appear at least moderately respectable. She glanced up the beach towards where her sister sat and decided that Mary must have seen what had happened, so hopefully would not chide her for the state she was in.

Albert, beside her, gave her skirt a tweak. 'Take it off, queen,' he suggested. 'If we swish it in the water like Paddy did his fish it'll get rid of a deal of sand. Better do it now, afore any more folk come walkin' past.'

Amy, with a sigh, agreed. She began to struggle out of her skirt and presently she and Albert swished it through the water and then squeezed it as dry as they could before Amy replaced it upon her person. 'It won't make much difference,' she said with a sigh, 'because when I sit down to have my dinner the sand'll stick like glue. Still, no one can say we didn't try.'

When the younger ones went roaring into the sea, Mary and Philip walked back up the beach to where they had left their possessions. As Mary had anticipated, the beach was already filling up and, with so many people about, she did not think it safe to leave things unattended. So she sat down by her string bag and Philip, after only the slightest of hesitations, sat down beside her.

'I wonder what they've hooked?' he said idly after a moment, looking back towards the sea where the three younger ones seemed to be having a private fight of their own against some monster of the deep. 'Surely it shouldn't take three of them to tackle one little plaice?'

'It might not be a plaice,' Mary objected, wincing as Albert fell to his knees and was immediately up again, though clearly drenched. 'I should think it's a shark, or a whale, judging by the commotion. Oh, Lord save us, Amy's forgot to kilt up her skirt; she'll get soaked to the skin all over again! Honest to God, that girl should've been a lad, she just doesn't know how to behave and that's the truth.'

Philip glanced at her; Mary saw that he had golden-brown eyes with very thick, fair lashes and a dusting of freckles across his rather aquiline nose. 'Your sister's a spunky kid. There aren't many girls who'd jump into the water like that just to save a pal's fish.'

'Well, I wouldn't, for one,' Mary admitted. 'I like paddling all right and I might like swimming, if I had a swimming costume, but I wouldn't go jumping in with all my clothes on.'

Philip turned and looked at her again, his mouth quirking into an engaging grin. He nodded slowly, still smiling at her. 'No, I guess you wouldn't plunge fully clothed into the briny,' he agreed. 'But if you'll excuse me saying so, Miss Mary, you're a young lady, not a kid. And you've had responsibilities as the elder, which young Amy won't ever have. I'm older than Laura and when we're together I'm responsible for her, so I behave in a more serious fashion, I suppose. Do you feel freer when Amy's not with you? I'm sure I do when Mother takes Laura off my hands.'

'I don't know about that,' Mary said, having thought the matter over. 'It's just that . . . that Amy doesn't think before she acts. She's not a bad girl, just a thoughtless one. And Dad encourages her. He thinks she's a spunky kid, too, but Mam doesn't agree. She'd like Amy to be a real little girl; she says Amy's neither one thing nor the other. And she's a real worry to me, acting the way she does. I never know what she'll do next and that's the truth of it.' She had been facing Philip, but now she turned to glance once more at the sea and gave a shriek. 'Oh, my Gawd, she'll be drowned for sure. Oh, oh, oh!' She jumped to her feet and would have run down the beach, but Philip seized her arm and pulled her into a sitting position once more.

'She's up again and I think they've got the fish,' he said, as Mary settled herself by his side. 'It's a codling, by the looks, and a decent sized one at that. See? Paddy's got it in his arms, just as though it were a baby. Oh! It jumped clear back into the sea. Well, will you look at that.'

For several moments the two young people sat and watched, fascinated, as the three children collapsed on the edge of the sea in a whirl of foam, and flailing arms and legs. But fortunately for Mary's nerves, the battle was a short one and presently Albert, Paddy and Amy came dripping up on to the beach and clustered round Paddy's fishing gear. 'They're rebaiting the hook,' Philip said wisely. 'They'll try for another one now, after such a good start. I say, d'you fancy an apple?'

At six o' clock, tired but happy, the Logans and Paddy trailed home. Paddy carried, slung over one shoulder, a string of three decent-sized codling and was in a boastful and triumphant mood. He had caught two of the three fish himself, despite his inferior fishing tackle, and could hardly wait to show off his catch. Amy guessed that he did not intend to tell anyone that Philip had caught the largest fish but would take credit for all three. Though she would have liked to sneer, she thoroughly understood how Paddy felt; in the circumstances she knew she would have done the same herself.

They had parted from Philip some time earlier. He had taken his own catch of two fine plaice back with him, though he had tried to persuade either the Logans or Paddy to take them as a gift. Albert had pointed out that the Logans had all the fish they needed and Paddy, who was a realist, had also refused the offer – three codling was praiseworthy, but add two large plaice to his bag and even the fondest relative might show some incredulity. So

Philip had taken his catch home, along with an empty picnic, for the goodies which cook had packed so carefully had been eaten long since.

Mary remembered the meal with awe and pleasure. It was the first time she and Amy had met Philip, and now, making their way home, she turned to her sister. 'Well, Amy? Enjoy yourself?' she asked.

'Oh, I did.' Amy sighed. 'That Philip's all right, wouldn't you say, Mary? He handed out his grub like a right one and wasn't it grand grub, too? I'm sure none of us have eaten like that, except at Christmas. Why, he thought no more of cold ham than if it'd been bread!'

'Oh, Amy, you don't judge a fella by his carry-out,' Mary said reproachfully. 'He liked you, though. He said you were a spunky kid.'

Amy giggled. 'I'm a wet one,' she observed. 'But I'm drying out nicely.'

Mary gave a little smile and then, rather adroitly she thought, changed the subject but inside her head she went on thinking about Philip. She thought he liked her – for they had talked easily and pleasantly while they waited for the young ones to return for their dinner – though he had not called her a spunky kid. He had called her a young lady and Mary, just beginning to be conscious of her pretty looks, thought this a far more valuable compliment. Secretly she thought him easily the nicest boy she had ever met. He had talked gravely, too, in a way which was somehow so friendly and pleasant that she was sure he liked her more than he could possibly have liked Amy, who was still a child, after all.

Glancing ahead of her at Paddy's lopsided figure, weighed down by his string of fish, Mary reflected that to have Philip's friendship would be a good deal more welcome than the obvious admiration which Paddy often showed. The younger boy was always hanging around their house, bringing Mary small, unwanted gifts. She knew he constantly praised her to Albert, while equally constantly running Amy down, for there was no doubt that Paddy Keagan truly disliked her small sister. Unfortunately this dislike seemed totally irrational and, though Mary had attempted to reason with him once or twice, Paddy persisted in being horrid to Amy whenever an opportunity occurred. Philip, Mary reminded herself now, had teased and laughed at Amy that very afternoon, but it had been the teasing of one friend to another with none of the malice Paddy showed towards the younger girl.

All the while Mary's thoughts had been busy, Amy had been chattering blithely away, but now she turned to her older sister and asked curiously, 'What did you really think of Philip? What did you talk about when we were catching fish?'

'I thought he was nice,' Mary said cautiously. She did not intend to tell her small sister that she thought Philip quite as handsome as any of the stars she saw at the Rotunda, acting their parts on the wide stage. 'He's a good friend for Albert and Paddy. I've seen him in church, of course, but we've never talked before. And it was ever so interesting, Amy. They live in an even bigger house in Manchester than the Seaforth one. The Grimshaws have heaps of money. Philip goes to boarding school – a really expensive one – and they have maids and servants and ponies of their own. They've got relatives in London who have them to stay whenever the Grimshaws want to visit the capital. Why, Philip told me that his grandparents are taking them up to London to see the coronation decorations. They're going tomorrow on the train and staying for two nights with his Uncle Richard and Aunt Mabel. His mam and dad go off to foreign parts most summers – aren't they lucky, Amy? I'd give a lot to see all those arches and lights and stuff, wouldn't you? And I'd love to go to foreign parts. He said something about Paris.'

'Oh aye,' Amy said indifferently. Happily skipping down the jigger beside Mary, it was clear that the younger girl had forgotten the state of her clothing and the row that would probably follow her appearance in the kitchen. She had had a lovely day, Mary thought indulgently, and hurried to catch up with her sister so that they both entered the kitchen together. Isobel would be brimming with talk of the celebrations and, with a bit of luck, the girls could get up to their room and change into clean clothes before their mother noticed Amy's dishevelment. If they hurried across to the stairs . . .

The ruse worked, Isobel merely turning from the range to tell them to hurry for the meal was almost ready. Mary, getting out clean calico aprons and fresh gingham skirts for them both, reminded herself that dreaming about a friendship with Philip really wasn't practical. Apart from the fact that he only came to Seaforth during the summer holidays, their different circumstances would, in any case, keep them apart. So she put him firmly out of her mind, changed into her clean clothes and went downstairs to help serve the meal.

Philip entered the big house by a side door. In the small cloakroom he kicked off his boots and took off his jacket before taking his fish through to the kitchens. Cook was standing by the sink, supervising one of the kitchen maids who was scrubbing potatoes with zest and throwing the cleaned ones into a large enamel saucepan which stood on the draining board.

'Well, you *have* had a good day, Master Philip,' Mrs Darwin said, staring admiringly at the large plaice. 'Pity you're off t' London tomorrow or I could have fried them for you and Miss Laura to have for your dinners. You can't have 'em tonight 'cause I'm roastin' a couple of nice capons, since your gran's asked the Frobishers to dinner.'

The maid, standing at the sink, turned and looked from Philip to the fish and back again. 'You could have 'em for a fish course, Mrs D,' she suggested. 'Cut 'em into strips and curled round the way you do, wi' a bit o' lemon on the top and a nice white sauce. That always goes down well.'

'No, I'm doing raspberry sorbet,' Mrs Darwin told her. 'Never mind, Edie, gal, we'll have 'em for staff supper with some fried potatoes. That'll make a nice change.' She eyed Philip closely, suddenly seeming to notice his dishevelled state. 'You'd best get upstairs, Master Philip,' she said, holding out her hand for the fish. 'Dinner's in an hour and your gran will want you to look neat and smart with the Frobishers here. I know their kids is grown, but I remember in the old days, when they were your age, and they were always smart as paint.'

Philip sighed but handed over the plaice and turned back towards the kitchen door. He was never allowed to forget the Frobisher twins. They were three years older than himself and were always held up by his grandma as a shining example of how young gentlemen should both look and behave.

Philip thought them a couple of boring milksops but it would never have done to say so – not to his grandparents at any rate. So he left the kitchen and thundered across the hall and up the long flight of stairs to his room where he washed and changed briskly, throwing his sandy clothing into the linen basket outside his door as he made his way to his sister's room. He was about to knock on the door when it opened to reveal Laura in her new evening frock. 'Philip, you're back,' she said in a relieved voice. 'No one told us, but the Frobishers are coming to dine and you know what a state Grandma gets in if we're late or untidy.' She eyed him critically. 'Oh, you've already changed – you look very smart – so that's all right. We'd best go down to the drawing room, though, Grandma will want you to do the pretty, especially since those wretched boys will be coming with their parents.'

Together the two children began to descend the stairs. 'We had iced pudding for luncheon,' Laura told him, 'and Aunt Betty gave me the prettiest hat for London. What did you do? Get any fish?'

'A couple. Well, more than that, actually. I met up with two of the boys and their sisters that we've seen around and we went fishing together. We had a good time, but I gave the little one – his name's Paddy – most of my fish, his need being greater than ours, as they say.'

Laura sighed. 'Sometimes I wish I were just an ordinary kid, like the ones you've been off with today. They might never get to see the decorations in London, but they wouldn't have to put up with the Frobisher boys being held up as an example the way we do. What were their names – the girls, I mean – were they nice?'

'They were all right,' Philip said indifferently. 'Mary's the older of the two – she's a bit prim and goody-goody, but I dare say she can't help that. Amy, the little one, was a real little devil. She went into the water with all her clothes on and got soaked. But did she mind? Not her. Plain as a boot, though,' he ended regretfully.

'Fancy going into the water in your clothes.' Laura was wide-eyed. 'I bet I'd like that Amy from what you say, better than I like the Frobishers, anyway.'

'You can guess why they've asked the Frobishers,' Philip said as they neared the end of the flight. 'It's because Mr Frobisher is something important in newspapers and will have all the latest news on the coronation.' A thought occurred to him. 'Dear God, you don't suppose they're going up to London tomorrow as well? The Frobisher twins, I mean. That really would be too bad.'

'I'm surprised they didn't go up for the coronation itself, seeing how important they are, or think they are,' Laura said with a giggle. 'Desmond thinks he's the cat's whiskers and Darcy is even more pleased with himself. Oh, I do hope they're not coming to London with us. It would ruin everything.'

Philip thought about Amy in her salt-stained, sandy clothes and about Mary, beautiful as a rose, both thinking themselves lucky indeed to be given cold meat and some fruit. He knew vaguely that the 'ordinary kids' of whom his sister had spoken were not really enviable. Their lives might seem free from the restrictions which bound him and his sister, but they were trammelled by their own parents' conventions, just as he and Laura were. And for the Logans and Keagans, treats such as the trip to London on the morrow were out of the question. What was more, when he and Laura grew up, their lives would continue to be cushioned by their parents' wealth, whereas the Logans and Keagans would have to fight hard just to keep food on the table and clothes on their backs.

But it was no good saying any of this to Laura, who mixed very little with the local children. Indeed, though Philip knew of the hardships suffered by the poor in theory, in practice he was as ignorant as his sister. He had never been into one of the tiny houses in Seafield Grove, never visited the fish market in Great Charlotte Street nor been with his friends when they were earning a few coppers by running messages, chopping up boxes for firewood, or selling bags of shrimps from door to door. He could not really imagine these pastimes and though he knew most of the kids went barefoot in summer it had not previously occurred to him that this was not from choice.

The front-door bell pealing, as they were crossing the hall, made Laura give Philip a dig in the back. 'That'll be them, arriving,' she hissed. 'Get a move on, Philip, so we can greet them with Grandma and Grandpa in the drawing room.'

'Damn,' Philip muttered, but nevertheless obeyed his sister's injunction. He wondered wistfully what Paddy and Albert would be doing now, but then he caught a whiff from the kitchens of roast capon and Cook's home-made stuffing. Despite Mrs Darwin's generous lunch he realised he was starving hungry and was already looking forward to the meal ahead. Perhaps having money and a position in life weren't so bad after all, he concluded, as he and Laura entered the drawing room.

Paddy and his fish were welcomed home by Gran who told him briefly that his mam was off searching for another job. When Paddy asked why she had left the canny house, Gran mumbled something about other members of the staff being agin her but she looked away from him as she spoke and Paddy, well used to putting two and two together where his mother was concerned, thought ruefully that it probably had something to do with the leg of mutton which Gran was even now slicing on to three tin plates. 'Makes a nice change from fish,' she remarked, as she saw her grandson looking at the meat. 'Though fish like them you caught, what was swimmin' in the briny an hour ago, are a rare treat an' all,' she ended hastily.

Paddy carried his catch over to the sink and began to clean and gut them. 'Shall you eat the fish now, Gran, and save the mutton for tomorrow?' he asked tactfully. 'Fish is best served fresh.'

'No, its all right, I'll wrap the fish in cabbage leaves and stick them on the cold slab; they'll keep fine there until tomorrer,' Gran said, continuing to slice mutton on to the plates. 'The spuds is almost cooked and there's a grand big cabbage steaming on the back of the fire, so the King ain't the only one to be havin' a coronation feast.' She jerked her thumb at the door. 'Go and tell your Aunt Dolly we's about to eat. She's rare fond of a bit of mutton, though she'll have to cut it up terrible small to get it down, her not likin' the new teeth they made for her up at the Brougham clinic. They cost her a pretty penny an' all.'

'What about me mam?' Paddy asked, turning back as he reached the door. 'Aren't we waitin' for her?'

Gran, now draining the potatoes over the low

stone sink, shook her head. 'You know what your mam is,' she said resignedly. 'She'll be goin' up and down the Scotty, poppin' into all the pubs, tryin' to get a bit of work. If she don't get an offer she'll be that down, she'll mebbe take a drink or two to cheer her up, and if she does get a job she'll take another drink or two to celebrate. I doubt she'll be home before closing time.'

Paddy, who knew very well how his mother would behave when either depressed or elated, nodded and went through to give a bang on Aunt Dolly's door. 'Grub up, Aunty Dot,' he shouted cheerfully. 'Me mam's brought in a leg o' mutton.' There was an answering squeak from within the room and presently Aunt Dolly emerged and made a beeline for her place at table. She was a tiny, mouselike woman, bent into a 'C' by rheumatism, so that Paddy often thought that the heavy crucifix which hung on the rosary round her neck might easily trip her up. But despite her disabilities she liked her food. She watched keenly as Gran served potatoes and cabbage, then glanced round the room. 'Where's the gal?' she demanded. 'Ain't she home yet?'

'No, not yet, Aunty Dolly,' Paddy said, since his gran was still serving the food. 'She's after a new job, Gran says.'

Aunt Dolly gave a sniff and delved into the pocket of her shabby black skirt, producing a gleaming set of dentures, which she scrunched into her mouth before beginning to tackle the meal. 'She'll turn up again, like a bad penny,' she mumbled through a mouthful of potato. 'She's no better than she should be, your mam.'

61

'Mam's all right,' Paddy said defensively, beginning to eat his own food. The mutton was delicious. 'She has to earn for all of us, Aunt Dolly, or we'd likely starve.'

'Aye, but she thieved this 'ere mutton an' well you know it,' Aunt Dolly said. 'She were never taught right from wrong. She was spoilt rotten as a kid.'

Gran, beginning to eat her own meal, shot her older sister an accusing look. 'If you're so high and mighty, Dolly Pringle, you'd best not eat the mutton,' she said. 'Otherwise the sin's on you as much as on our Suzie.'

It was the right thing to say. Dolly gave her sister a malevolent glare, but she continued to eat the mutton, and presently Paddy told the old ladies about his day on the beach with the other kids and about Philip's wonderful lunch basket. This turned the talk away from morality and mutton into safer channels, and by the time the meal was finished all three were in good charity with one another, and Aunt Dolly washed the dishes and sang hymns as she did so, always a sign that she was happy with life.

Suzie had still not returned from her job search by the time Paddy went to bed but this did not worry her son in the slightest. If Mam had got bar work she would not return anyway until after closing time for she would be required to clean down, wash glasses and make all respectable for the next day. But, Paddy thought drowsily to himself as he curled up under his ragged blanket, Mam being out late was a good sign; it meant she had almost certainly got work of some description. Money therefore would continue to enter the Keagan house for a while longer at least.

On this happy thought, Paddy slept.

Chapter Three

Amy was standing in front of the sink, scrubbing potatoes, when the back door burst open and Albert, lugging a heavy shopping basket, entered the room. He went over to the table and piled the contents of the basket upon it, giving vent to a relieved whistle as he put his burden down. 'Phew! Them's heavy,' he said, as Amy turned away from the sink to grin at him. 'Me arms is as long as a gorilla's. How come the older I am the heavier the shopping gets? Do you think it's 'cos we eats more as we get older, queen?'

'Well, you bleedin' well eat more, I can vouch for that,' Amy said. 'I never knew how hard our Mary worked till she left school and went into service.' Mary had gone to what their mother had described as 'a good family', who lived in Manchester but had had connections with Seaforth and so had advertised for members of staff locally. 'Now that I'm doing what she used to do I'm fair wore out, honest to God I am. You don't know you're born, our Albert. You want to give our mam a hand with the fish stall, or go from door to door with bags of shrimps, before you moan about a few messages.'

'That's women's work,' Albert pointed out, throwing himself on to one of the hard kitchen chairs and reaching into a bag from which he produced a large purple plum. He saw Amy looking at him and hastily bit into the fruit. 'It's all right, Mr Evans give it me, seeing as I bought up half the bleedin' shop,' he said, holding out the remains of the fruit to his sister. 'Halves is fair, though, wouldn't you say?'

'Thanks, Albert.' Amy bit gratefully into the sweet flesh. He wasn't a bad boy, she concluded. It wasn't his fault that Mammy worked her so hard and seemed to expect more of her than she ever had of Mary. The truth was, Amy knew, that Isobel had grown used to Amy's habit of doing a bunk whenever the opportunity occurred, almost always when work was in the offing. Consequently she worked Amy twice as hard, in the certain knowledge that Amy would do her best to get out of at least half the tasks she was set. What Isobel did not appear to realise was that, with Mary gone, there was no one else to do the work. If Amy only delivered half the shrimps she was given to sell, then only half the money would arrive home when evening came and since Mary was no longer able to finish off the selling for her sister, Amy's slackness would be immediately discovered – and punished.

Albert, on the other hand, was still treated as someone who would one day have to earn his own living at that toughest of all trades, inshore fishing. Therefore, as with her other sons, Isobel seemed to think that his childhood should be relatively untrammelled except, of course, when he went to sea with his father to help with the fishing, which he did from time to time.

Amy finished the plum and threw the stone into the rubbish pail under the sink. Then she went over to the table and began to unpack the shopping, since Albert, with his feet up on another chair, was reading an elderly copy of the *Echo*, which had been wrapped round a couple of fine cabbages, and seemed to have no intention of finishing the work.

'Do you know what we were doing a year ago today?' she asked, carrying some of the groceries over to the pantry. It wasn't a proper pantry, it was a cupboard which was floored and shelved with slabs of slate, and because the outer wall had a northern aspect it was the easiest part of the kitchen to keep cold. 'Or can't you remember that far back, puddin' head?'

'A year ago today?' Albert said vaguely, not looking up from the paper. 'How the devil should I know? Trust a bleedin' girl to ask a bleedin' silly question like that!'

'It's not a stupid question at all,' Amy protested indignantly. She carried the last of the shopping into the pantry and slammed the door shut, turning back to Albert. 'I called you puddin' head but I should think even a puddin' has more brains than you,' she went on derisively. 'What's the date, you stupid clunch?'

'Dunno. This is an old newspaper.' Albert grinned at his own wit. 'I think it's yesterday's, or tomorrer's, I ain't sure which.'

Amy heaved a deep, dramatic sigh and returned to the sink. 'It's the ninth of bloody August,' she said over her shoulder. 'Doesn't that mean anything to you, puddin' head?'

By way of answer, a plum stone whizzed passed her ear and disappeared through the open kitchen window. 'I knew all the time, eejit,' Albert said breezily – and untruthfully, Amy guessed. 'It were the coronation, o' course, and we went fishin' on the shore wi' Philip and Paddy. You and Mary come along too, as I remember. Eh, we had a grand day! Us fellers got a grosh of fish.' He laughed raucously.

'And you gals got soaked to the skin and sent to bed early, as I recall.'

'It was a lovely day.' Amy ignored the slur on her good name. She distinctly remembered hurrying up the stairs and changing her clothing before her mother had had a chance to comment upon the state of her. Supper, she recalled, had been liver and onions, followed by marmalade pudding; a feast which had been eaten in the King's and Queen's honour. But it was no good reminding Albert of that; he'd likely say she'd made it up. 'Do you remember, Albert, how the sun shone and there wasn't a cloud in the sky? The King had a grand day for his crowning, Mam said, and the pictures were prime. I know the King's children aren't kids any more, but they all looked pretty happy. Well, it must be a bit of all right to have a king and queen for your mam and dad, wouldn't you say?'

'Not bad,' Albert said. He leaned back in his chair so that it stood on its hind legs, like a rearing horse, then lifted up his feet so that the chair crashed to the ground once more. 'What's for supper, eh?'

'Belly on legs,' Amy muttered. 'We're having white fish, boiled spuds – I've just finished scrubbing them, I'll put them over the fire presently – and some of those carrots you got from Mr Evans. Mam's upstairs; when she's ready I'll go up and change.' She looked down at her fish-stained apron and the skirt, draggly from pushing the handcart through the dust of the warm August day. 'I don't envy Mary being in service, doing someone else's housework and so on all day, but it must be grand not to smell of fish. Coming home, a feller shouted out as he passed me, "Two penn'orth o' cod, miss – and go easy on the bluebottles." I could have died it was so

67

humiliating. Why, even when I'm working on the market stall and could afford a tramride home I usually walk, on account of the pong. It's awful when folk move away from you on the tram, or young women give up their seats just to get away from the smell.'

'I don't see why it bothers you.' Albert returned to his perusal of the paper. 'After all, it ain't as though you can smell it yourself . . . and when you wash it goes.'

'Ye-es, but I hate people shouting at me in the street. I don't know how our Mary stood it, honest to God I don't.'

'She never helped Mam wi' the gutting,' Albert said briefly. 'She just sold the stuff. But I'm sure I remember her saying there was a sink at the fish market and she sluiced herself down there before she came home. And didn't she keep a fresh apron there, too? I suppose that's how she got rid of the pong.'

'Did she? Well, I'll ask Mam if I can do the same, then.' Amy brightened. She had put the cleaned potatoes into a large pot and now staggered with it over to the fire. As she passed Albert she kicked him neatly on the ankle. 'Cor, this bloody thing weighs a ton; if you were a real gentleman, Albert Logan, you'd offer to lug it across for me. Fellers are meant to help ladies with the heavy work.'

'If you were a lady I might,' Albert said, prudently removing himself out of Amy's range, however. 'Where *is* Mam anyroad? She's usually in here by now, getting the supper ready.'

'Oh, she's having a bit of a lie-down,' Amy informed him. 'I dare say it's the heat, but she's ever so tired. And we didn't do as well as we might have,

68

what with Dad bringing back a record catch yester-day. We sold all the shrimps, mind; the ones left over from the door-to-door went like hot cakes on the stall. But we had some plaice left over and a few haddock as well, and you know Mam. She won't put them on ice for tomorrow; she says our reputation is for fresh fish and she won't jeop ... jeopa ... oh, well, she won't put it at risk by using ice.'

'She's right,' Albert said authoritatively. He might not work on the stall nor sell shrimps door to door, but he did go out in the fishing boat, *Mersey Maid*, and knew how important it was to bring the catch in and sell it as soon as possible. 'Well, since I've done the messages, I might as well take the scraps round to the Keagans and then go and see if Dad wants any cleaning up done. How long to supper, our Amy?'

'Say half an hour.' Amy had glanced up at the big clock over the mantel. 'I'm going to take a cuppa up to our mam. It's not often she has a lie-down and I thought she looked downright peaked by the time we'd walked home. She could have caught the tram,' she added, 'but it was that hot she said she'd rather walk.'

'Half an hour it is, then,' Albert said, crossing the kitchen and throwing open the back door. 'And don't you be late, because us fellers'll be rare hungry by then.'

Amy snorted. She was busy filling one of the enamel mugs with tea and, after a moment's thought, added a spoonful of sugar. Isobel only took sugar in her tea when she was feeling what she usually described as 'a bit cagged, like', but Amy knew she was not the only person to notice her mother's unusual pallor that day. Mrs O'Brien, who was a regular customer, and Mrs Kelly, who usually visited the market late in order to buy as cheaply as possible for her large family, had both remarked that Mrs Logan looked poorly and ought to rest more, now she'd a daughter earning and another helping out.

Rather to Amy's surprise, her mother had seemed more embarrassed than pleased by the attention and interest in her health. She had said gruffly that she was just tired, that it took some getting used to having Mary gone, that the heat got her down. And on the walk home, when Amy had tried to ask her mother what was the matter, she had been quite short. 'I said, didn't I?' she had asked crossly, putting a hand up to her head as though it ached, then changing the action to push back the fringe of grey-blonde hair which curled crisply across her forehead. 'I'm just pulled by the heat, nothing more.'

But now, when Amy entered her bedroom with the mug of tea and a cut off the fruit cake which she kept in a tin in the pantry, Isobel looked up and actually smiled at the sight of the tea and the round tin plate with the slice of cake on it. 'Well, isn't this nice?' She hauled herself upright so that she was propped against her pillows. 'My daughter's looking after me – aren't I the lucky one? I thought Mary was the best of daughters, but you're running her close, young Amy. Before I know it you'll be as useful as our Mary was.'

The somewhat sideways compliment made Amy blush with pleasure, however, for it was a sign that she and her mother were getting on better. Before Mary started work, Amy had received plenty of slaps and very few kisses from her strict and strait-laced mother, but now it appeared that there was a softening and this thrilled Amy. Everyone wants to

70

be liked, she told herself, putting the cake down on her mother's knees and holding out the mug of tea. If Mam is going to try to like me the way she likes Mary, then I'll work my fingers to the bone for her, so I will. It's just when she criticises and finds fault no matter how hard I try that I get to think I can't do right, so I'll stop making the effort. She handed her mother the mug of tea and perched on the side of the bed. 'I'm glad you think I'm a bit useful, Mam,' she said earnestly as her mother took the first sip from the mug. 'I do try – but I'm not naturally good, neither can I cook and clean like our Mary.'

'I'll teach you,' her mother promised. She blew on the tea, then looked out of the small window, avoiding her daughter's eye. Amy saw that Isobel was in her nightgown and felt the first stab of genuine fear. She must be really ill; she had said she was going to lie down for a few minutes while the meal cooked, not that she intended to go to bed. No one in the Logan family went to bed during the day unless they were very ill indeed; even the kids tended to be rousted out after the first flush of some childish ailment – measles, chickenpox, a septic sore throat – had run its course. 'Umm . . . Amy, I've got something to tell you.'

Amy's heart gave a lurch. Mam was going to tell her that she was really bad, perhaps dying. Mothers did die. Aggie French's mam had died last year and now the family was ruled by an old and irritable grandmother, who spent most of her time telling the children that it wasn't fair or right that she should be bringing up a young family at her time of life. Aggie was Amy's age but the rest of the French kids were all younger; Aggie said she couldn't wait to get a job and leave home, so her gran wouldn't be able to nag and whine at her so much.

However, it wouldn't do to let her mother know what she was thinking. 'Oh . . . I've got the supper on the go, Mam,' she said, gabbling a little. 'I've done the spuds, and I've gutted the fish and it's all ready to go in the pan. And Albert's done the messages, he's brought back some good, long carrots and . . .'

'I don't know whether you've noticed owt, Amy.' Isobel's voice rose resolutely above her daughter's. 'I should have told you some time back – Mary knows – but somehow I couldn't bring myself . . . a woman my age . . . I hate to think what young folk like that Suzie Keagan will say . . . and you and me's not known each other all that well, queen, for all you're my youngest child. But I said to your father that it wasn't fair . . . I'll be asking more of you even than I did of Mary, especially when I get near my time.' She looked at Amy with the air of one who has told all and now expects a reaction.

Amy stared straight back. What on earth did her mother mean? Mary knew? And her dad must know too, but he had been more than usually cheerful lately, not at all like a man who has received bad tidings, who has a sick woman on his hands. But her mother was sipping tea again, even taking a nibble of cake, looking at her with a little half-smile. It was no use, she would have to say she didn't understand or the most awful complications would result. 'What d'you mean, Mam? Are . . . are you ill? Is that why you've put your nightdress on in the daytime?'

'Oh. Well, I'm not ill, but I'm old for . . . women of my age don't . . . I mean, you're my youngest child and you're all of eleven years old . . .'

'You aren't old, Mam,' Amy said quickly. 'My dad's older than you and so's heaps of the women in the St John's fish market. What d'you *mean*?'

Isobel stopped glancing out of the window, down at her hands, around at the whitewashed walls, in fact, at everything but Amy. She then looked squarely into Amy's eyes. 'Oh, chuck, I'm expecting a . . . a baby,' she said and, to Amy's astonishment, tears came into her mother's eyes. 'I've not told the boys yet, nor my friends, but as I said, I told Mary and . . . and I thought you ought to know. As I get – well – get bigger, I shan't be able to bend so easily, nor I won't be as quick with the gutting and filleting, so you'll be doing all sorts and if you don't know, don't understand . . .'

'Oh, Mam, I'm that relieved, I thought you must be dying when you looked so pale and chucked up your breakfast the other morning,' Amy said. 'And what's wrong with having another baby, anyway? I'd be right glad to have a little brother or sister, even if it does mean a bit more work. I've often envied Ruth, having all those young 'uns about the place. When will it come, Mam? Will it be soon? When will you stop working?'

Isobel laughed. She looked relieved, Amy thought, as if she had been dreading telling her daughter of the expected arrival, though why she should feel like that Amy had no idea. A baby is a delightful thing, Amy told herself, taking the empty mug from her mother's grasp and watching as Isobel finished off the last crumbs of cake.

'I bet Dad's pleased as pleased can be,' she said and was rewarded by the look of delight that crossed her mother's face. 'Do you want a girl, Mam? You wouldn't want another boy, surely?'

'It doesn't matter whether it's a boy or a girl, so long as it's healthy,' Isobel told her. 'Your dad's going to tell the boys, now I've broken the news to yourself. But if you like, queen, you can tell Albert, seeing as how he'll be wondering what we've been talking about up here. Maybe he'll wonder what I'm doing in bed, too,' she added.

Amy, halfway to the door, stopped for a moment to smile back at her mother. 'You know what today is, don't you, Mam? The King and Queen were crowned a year ago today. So if it's a boy you could call it Edward, and if it's a girl . . .'

'. . . Alexandra.' Isobel returned the smile. 'What a mouthful for a little girl, though, queen. Maybe I'd best stick to the ordinary names and leave the long ones for royalty. D'you know, I'm feeling more rested already? If you give me a shout when the food is on the table I think I'll join you downstairs. I won't start interfering with what you've done, but I might give you a hand with the washing up. And we'll plan the meals for tomorrow between us, shall we?'

Amy, agreeing, went downstairs with a full heart. She felt that an understanding was growing between herself and her mother, perhaps for the first time in her life. She had always thought it would be a grand thing to be friends with your mam, as Mary had been and indeed still was, and now it looked as though she, too, was beginning to share in their friendship. Suddenly the hard work at the fish market and the slog of door-to-door selling no longer seemed such a weary way to spend her spare time. Summer holidays from school might never be the same again, but to be friends with her mam would make losing the freedom of the streets and shore almost worthwhile. Besides, it was the first real sign that she was growing up, becoming a woman. What was more, mam had said she would need a deal of help when the baby came and this might well mean she would keep Amy by her until the child was four or five. She would be unable to cope with all the housework, the preparing and selling of the shrimps, and with a young child without help from someone. Why should it not be Amy? Amy, who had always loathed the idea of going into service, found she was delighted at the thought of being a real help to her mother. She had no idea whether she would be paid a wage for such work, but found this scarcely seemed to matter. Mam will do right by me, she told herself, descending the narrow stairs. And though three months earlier she would have doubted this statement, she now realised it was true. Isobel was as fond of the new, grown-up Amy as she was of Mary.

Amy entered the kitchen feeling that her cup of happiness was full and beamed across at Albert, who was struggling to pull the heavy pan of potatoes to the side of the fire. He looked up as she entered the room and cursed as hot water splashed out of the pan, narrowly missing his feet. 'Where the hell have you been?' he enquired caustically. 'These bloody spuds have boiled over twice already and I've near broke me arms heavin' them off the fire. What was you doin', for God's sake? You've been gone *hours*, Amy Logan!'

Amy went over to the fire and pushed Albert to one side so that she might move the pan without scalding either of them. 'I've been talking to Mam,' she said importantly. 'She's been telling me we're going to have a new baby, what about that, eh?'

Albert stared at her, round-eyed. 'A *baby*?' he said, his very tone incredulous. 'She can't be havin' a baby, queen, women her age is grannies, not mams. Why, our Edmund's twenty-one.' Edmund was working the trawlers now and sailing from Fleetwood, and what was more, was courting a local girl whom Isobel had disliked on sight. Consequently they saw very little of him, though Bill, Amy thought, visited his elder son from time to time.

'It doesn't matter how old you are, if you're a woman,' Amy said knowingly. 'Anyhow, our mam isn't old and she *is* having a baby, she told me so this minute, so that's one in the eye for you, Albert Logan.'

'Well, I think that's disgustin',' Albert said morosely, slouching across the kitchen and throwing himself into his chair once more. He picked up the paper and flung it down again with a groan. 'What'll I tell me pals? Damn it, I'm thirteen goin' on fourteen – I'll be in work soon. The fellers will laugh their heads off, I'm tellin' you.'

'Well, none of my friends will laugh,' Amy said stoutly. 'Women don't laugh about babies, they like them. And don't you go telling our mam that you aren't thrilled, because she'll be mortally upset if you do. She . . . she said something about being too old herself, so the last thing she'll want is to hear you talking such rubbish. Now, shift yourself, Albert, and give me a hand for once. Mam's coming down when the grub's on the table and I know Dad would say we've all got to show her a cheerful face. So start grinning and stop scowling or I'll give you a clack. And when I dish up I'll make sure you get the smallest plateful, so there!'

Albert got to his feet and went over to the dresser.

He pulled open the drawer which contained their meagre supply of cutlery and selected a handful, then reached up for the enamel plates. 'Right you are, I hear you' – to lay the table – 'but it'll mean a deal of work for you and me, chuck. Babies always does. Still an' all, it's better than if Mam had been really ill. I were beginnin' to wonder, to tell you the truth.'

Amy, sliding the floured fillets into the frying pan, nodded her head in violent agreement. 'Aye, you're right there,' she admitted. 'I was really worried, Albert, and that's the truth.' The fat in the pan started to spit as it heated up and she flinched away from the flying droplets. 'Gawd, these perishin' dabs are fighting back! I never knew fish could be so fierce.'

'You oughter try catchin' them, heavin' the net up when it's loaded with slippery, snappin' critters from the deep,' Albert said with relish. 'That's man's work if you like, gal. Fancy moanin' about fryin' a few fillets.'

'Then you do it, if you're so clever,' Amy said briskly. She tilted her head as her ears caught the sound of the back gate clicking open. 'Hey up, here comes Dad and the boys. We'd best get a move on, Albert, or we won't have the food on the table by the time they've washed up.'

Amy woke and lay for a moment staring into the dark and wondering what had roused her. She glanced towards the window but could tell that it was not yet morning by the grey glimmer of light showing round the curtains. In fact, from the heavy feeling of her head and limbs it was probably no more than one or two o'clock. She had been lying on her side, but now she rolled on to her back and listened. Nothing. No one talking or moving in the house, no traffic passing by in the street below. Yet something must have woken her. The scratch of a mouse as it emerged from beneath the skirting board? A sparrow's sleepy chirrup as a cat passed by? Sometimes she was woken when the weather was rough by the sound of waves crashing on the shore, but it was a calm, still night in mid-February. Nothing, in short, should've brought her so annoyingly wide awake, so she had best curl down under the blanket again and try to recapture some sleep.

She obeyed her own instructions and closed her eyes firmly, curling her left hand under the pillow while her right held on to several strands of hair. This was how she always slept, but tonight the familiar magic did not work and she remained awake.

She had just decided that she had better begin to count sheep when she heard the mewing. It wasn't loud or particularly close, she thought, but somewhere out in the cold dark, a cat was in trouble. The Logan family had never owned a cat, or indeed any other pet; Mam and Dad said they had their work cut out to feed the family without stretching their meagre resources to cover animals as well. But Amy knew that stray cats did hang around the premises and that Bill sometimes fed them odd scraps of leftover fish. If one of those stray cats had got shut into the wash-house there would be all sorts of trouble. For a start, it might devour and generally mess up a quantity of the fish that would be sent to the fish market the following day, or – horror of horrors – it might fall into the copper, which her father usually kept full of water, and drown itself.

On that thought Amy jumped out of bed. One of the stray cats she had seen in the yard was little more than a kitten; she doubted that it would survive long if it did fall into the copper, which was slippery from the shrimps cooked in it and probably very attractive to feline appetites. She slung her shawl round her shoulders but did not bother with her boots. It took ages to lace them in daylight, heaven knew, so what it would be like in the dark she could not bear to contemplate. Instead, she padded across the room, out on to the tiny landing and began to descend the stairs.

Halfway down the flight, however, the mewing sound came again and this time she was sure it had come from behind her. Immediately, before she had time to think, she had whipped round, run up the stairs again and hurled herself at her parents' door. The baby! The baby must have come, although she had heard no sound of a nurse arriving. She no longer believed in the fairy tale of the stork, flapping in through the window and leaving the baby on the fortunate mother's bed, because Ruth had long ago disabused her of this fanciful notion. But she still had very little idea of how a baby actually arrived and thought, in her innocence, that its journey from the parental tummy into the light of day was a quick and simple matter. She knew the nurse would come but had very little idea why this was necessary and assumed, vaguely, that it was another of the adult mysteries into which her parents were so reluctant to admit her.

She shot the door open, bounded into the room and stopped short, both hands flying to her mouth.

Her mother lay on the bed, scarlet-faced and sweating profusely, with her legs drawn up and the covers pushed down to her waist. The nurse, a local woman by the name of Mrs Scott, was sitting in a chair by the bed. She had obviously been chatting to her patient but stopped suddenly at Amy's abrupt arrival.

'Oh! Oh, I'm sorry,' Amy stammered, feeling the hot blood rush to her cheeks. 'I . . . I thought I heard a baby cry. I thought it'd come already and I wanted to help.' She glanced nervously from face to face. 'Where's my dad? Is there anything I can do?'

At the sound of her voice Isobel had heaved the covers up over her stomach and breasts, and now she gave what Amy imagined was meant to be a reassuring smile. 'It's all right, queen,' she said huskily. 'The baby won't be here for a while yet, but as soon as it arrives, nurse here will let you know. As for your dad, he's downstairs making Mrs Scott and me a cup of tea. If you'd like to go down and give him a hand, I'm sure he'd be grateful. Unless you think you might be able to go back to sleep?'

'I'll go and give Dad a hand.' Amy, ignored the last question as not worthy of comment. How could she possibly sleep when such momentous events were taking place? Albert, Gus and Charlie, of course, would be sleeping straight through all the excitement, but that was fellers for you. No soul, Amy thought disgustedly, assuring her mother that she would bring her and Mrs Scott a cup of tea as soon as it had brewed.

Isobel was beginning to thank her when there was a movement beneath the sheet and her face became contorted with pain. She bent forward and grasped her own knees with both hands, and Amy left the room, hastily closing the door behind her. She realised that the mewing noise she had heard must have been small cries of pain and found she had no desire whatever to see her mother suffer. Instead, she decided to go down to the kitchen and do whatever her father bade her, so that the time would pass quickly until the baby's birth.

The baby was born almost forty-eight hours later, after what the nurse described as a really difficult labour, and was a tiny but perfect girl, with lint-white hair and big, dreamy blue eyes. Amy saw her for the first time before breakfast, only a few hours after her birth, and was delighted with her, though she thought her mother looked drained and exhausted, and quite twenty years older than she really was. Despite her hopes, the baby had not been called Alexandra but was to rejoice in the name of Jane. And she isn't a plain Jane, Amy thought to herself, timidly stroking the baby's cheek. Still, it's Mam's choice when you come down to it. Liverpool folk always add a bit to a short little name and chop off a bit from a long one, so if she had been named Alexandra she would have ended up being called Allie, which isn't all that special.

Mary had come home as soon as their father had got a message to her telling her that Isobel was in labour. She had been a tower of strength both to Amy and to their mother, and seemed to know by instinct what best to do for the baby. Like Amy, she was disappointed by the plain name Isobel had chosen and had managed to persuade her mother to give the child a second name. She and Amy put their heads together and it was finally agreed that their new little sister would be christened Jane Rebecca when the time was ripe.

To Amy's disappointment, Mary was only able to stay for two days, helping to look after her mother and the baby, but at the end of that time she had to return to the family who employed her. They lived at too great a distance from Seaforth to allow Mary to spend her day off with them, so having her home for two whole days was a real treat. The two girls gossiped endlessly during the day while they were working, for Amy was being kept off school while her mother was still in childbed, and at night, lying close together in the bed they had shared for so many years, Mary told Amy all about life as a housemaid. She had done her best to explain how she felt. 'I thought I'd hate being in service and so I did at first,' she told her sister. 'But it's a bit like school – ordered, sensible, so you know just what you should be doing all the time. You brush and polish, wait on the family, lay tables, clear away. You don't have to cook your own meals, answer doors, clean fish, or sell shrimps, because your tasks are laid down and once they're done you're free. It's wonderful to have time to yourself, your own little room, and friends who work beside you. And best of all, no smell of fish, no icy hands and feet, no . . . no responsibility for anything but your own work and your own pleasure. So I wouldn't want to leave Manchester to come back to . . . to *this*.' Her gesture encompassed the little house, the family – their entire life Amy thought, rather dismayed. Mary had indeed changed, grown away from them.

It did not sound much fun to Amy, but Mary clearly enjoyed the life. She had made a great many friends, both among the staff at the Cottlestones' house and the neighbours, and was much in demand as a dancing partner when she and her friends had an evening off. She seemed to be doing well in her work, too. She was a good seamstress, clever with her needle, and actually enjoyed polishing the silver until it shone like a mirror, and dusting in every nook and cranny until the rooms she had been set to look after were spotless. She did not seem to miss the small house in Seafield Grove, nor to hanker after the beach and the park where the girls had spent what little time off they had had. Mary was expected to serve the family wholeheart-edly, to attend church with them on a Sunday and to obey the wishes of the upper servants who could, and did, order her about. She told Amy that when she wrote a letter home she couldn't even take it down the road to the nearest postbox without getting permission from one of the upper servants to leave the estate house. This would have irked Amy terribly, but the placid and sweet-tempered Mary actually seemed to prefer what she termed 'an ordered existence' to the rather more haphazard life of the family in Seafield Grove.

'But you're enjoying helping with the baby and with our mam,' Amy pointed out, as she and Mary prepared for bed one night, 'and you seem to like cooking and cleaning up after the boys well enough. How will you feel, Mary, when you have to go back to being bossed around all the time? Won't you miss being able to walk down to the shore when you want to? And visiting your pals now and then?'

'It's grand being home all right,' Mary agreed, 'but how often have I had a moment to myself after I got back, eh, queen? And although I've met a pal or two when I've been doing the messages, I've never had time to stop for a jangle. In fact, there's not a lot of time for anything, the way we live. At the Cottlestone house things are more ordered, more tidy, like. When you're free you really are free. No one asks you to run messages or clean fish or bake a pie. But at home there's only us to do everything. Can you understand that?'

'Ye-es, I know what you mean,' Amy said grudgingly, after some thought, 'but I'd still rather have my life than yours, Mary. It's because I'm untidy by nature and you're the opposite. What about marrying, though? You'd like to do that one day, wouldn't you?'

'I might,' Mary said guardedly. 'And then again I might not; I do have a particular friend, but folk don't get married when they are barely fifteen, chuck. I wouldn't want to be a housemaid for the rest of my life, but marriage changes everything. What about you, Amy? I know you're still in school, though it's a bit off and on, isn't it? Mam was saying what a help you'd been to her, and that must mean you're missing school every now and then I suppose. And of course, if you're missing school you'll miss playing out as well. So your freedom isn't what it was, wouldn't you say?'

'Yes, I've been missing school on a Friday,' Amy acknowledged. 'But the rest of the week Mam manages pretty well. I help after school, of course, and I do miss seeing my pals in the long summer evenings, but I'm getting on ever so much better with our mam, Mary. Now you aren't here, she relies on me, you see, and I like that. I never thought I would, but I do. Dad says it's all part of growing up and I dare say he's right. And Mam says once she's up and about she'll be able to do a good deal more. She'll take the baby with her when she goes door-to-door selling.'

Mary pulled a face. 'Well, it might work out,' she said thoughtfully. 'But it'll come hard on you, Amy. Mam's never expected the boys to do anything she thinks of as woman's work and there's a deal of that in this house, with potting the shrimps and all. It'd be fairer on you if Mam were to pay a woman to come in and give a hand three or four times a week. After all, if you go on sagging off school there'll be trouble.'

Amy sighed. 'I dare say you're right.' She climbed into bed. 'I might as well blow the candle out; we can talk just as well in the dark.' She suited action to words and cuddled down. It was so nice to feel Mary's familiar warmth beside her in the bed. It was odd, she thought, how she had not really missed Mary until she returned home; only now did she recognise the gap that the loss of her sister's company had left in her life. Mary was due to return to the Cottlestones next morning and Amy knew she would miss her terribly. But at least I'll know she's truly happy being a housemaid and living away from home, she told herself drowsily, as sleep began to claim her. We would neither of us want the other's life, as we're very different people. It's a good thing that Mary is the older, though. Imagine how awful it would've been if I'd ended up in service and Mary had had to stay at home. On this horrid thought she fell asleep.

Two days after Mary and Amy had kissed each other goodbye under the clock on Lime Street Station Isobel woke, feeling hot and feverish, and aching in every limb. Bill roused Amy and told her to give an

85

eye to the baby and to fetch her mother a cup of tea. He was off to have a word with Mrs Scott. The old woman still came in twice each day and would continue to do so until Jane Rebecca was three weeks old, but she had told Bill to call her at once if either his wife or the baby ailed. 'Your missus ain't exactly a chicken,' she had said bluntly. 'Better to be safe than sorry.'

Amy got out of bed, dragged her jumper over her nightdress and padded down the stairs to the kitchen. The room was empty, apart from the baby in her cradle – Bill must have brought her down before he had woken his daughter. A glance at the back door showed Albert's cap and coat were missing, so Amy guessed that her brother had been sent to fetch Mrs Scott, while Bill himself had gone back upstairs to Isobel. Amy shivered a little, for the kitchen was chilly, but she knew it would soon warm up once she had stirred up the fire, which had sunk to a bed of ashes with only a red glow in its centre to show that it had not done the dirty on her and gone out.

Amy got the poker, stirred up the fire, riddled the ashes and then put fresh fuel on to the embers. In a moment it was blazing and quite hot enough for Amy to pull the kettle over the flame. While she waited for it to boil she got the loaf from the bread bin and cut a couple of thick slices. It was nowhere near breakfast time, but she found she was hungry and guessed that Albert, when he returned from his errand, would be hungry, too. She would toast the bread in front of the fire while waiting for the kettle, then she and her brother could have a snack as soon as he came back with the midwife.

The toast was made and the tea poured when the

back door opened to admit Mrs Scott, with Albert close on her heels. 'Mornin', young 'un,' Mrs Scott said breezily. 'My, that toast smells good. I'm that clemmed I swear I could eat a horse.'

Silently Amy handed her a round of buttered toast and watched, enviously, as the older woman devoured it in three enormous bites. Then, without being asked, she handed one of the mugs of tea over, but Mrs Scott, though she gazed at it wistfully, shook her neat grey head. 'Not now, chuck,' she said, heading for the stairs. 'Just you bring up an extry cup when you bring your mam's. I wouldn't let a patient wait above stairs whiles I drank tea in the kitchen.'

'She's norra bad old stick,' Albert remarked, taking the remaining slice of toast and beginning to eat. 'Some of them old women what call themselves nurses drink gin and leave your mam to gerron with it, the fellers at school say. Was that your bit of toast, gal? If so, I'll make you another while you take up the tea.'

But in fact, Amy did not get a chance to take the tea to the bedroom. Halfway up the stairs, carefully balancing two mugs of well-sugared tea, she met Mrs Scott thundering down. 'Thanks, chuck, I'll take that,' Mrs Scott said briskly. 'But I want you to go straight downstairs and tell young Albert to fetch Doctor Payne. Tell Albert to say Mrs Scott says as it's urgent and he's to come right away, if he pleases.'

Amy, thoroughly frightened, pushed the mugs of tea into the nurse's hands and fled down the stairs again, entering the kitchen with the message already on her lips. Albert was sitting in front of the fire with a round of bread on a stick held out to the flames, but to do him credit, he wasted no more time than

Amy had. 'Take this,' he said brusquely, thrusting the stick into her hands and grabbing his coat and cap. He jammed the cap down over his unbrushed hair and headed for the back door, saying over his shoulder, 'Where's me dad? What's happenin' up there?'

'I dunno,' Amy said with equal brevity. 'I only got halfway up when I met old Ma Scott coming down. Oh, Albert, do hurry! I think our mam must be awfully bad.'

The rest of that day and all the next were a nightmare, which Amy knew she would remember for the rest of her life. She longed for Mary's comforting presence, but knew better than to suggest her sister might be fetched; things were too desperately bad for that. It would've been a comfort to her had Bill been able to explain what was happening, but on the only occasion when he left Isobel's side for a moment to come downstairs and take a drink of tea he looked so grey and ill that Amy hadn't the heart to cross-question him. 'It's milk fever, only some specially bad sort,' he said in answer to Amy's one timid question. 'She's mortal bad, chuck.' He got to his feet and headed across the kitchen. 'Nurse will be down in a minute,' he added over his shoulder. 'She'll tell you what to do about the baby.'

Mrs Scott did indeed tell Amy what to do about the baby, though it was not welcome advice. 'Is there anyone hereabouts nursin' their own young 'un?' she enquired, busily making a brew of some description in a small pan on the stove. She tutted. 'Why am I asking you when I know better than anyone who's had a baby recently? You tek young Jane Rebecca

88

along to Mrs O'Hara, on Holly Grove, an' ask her to give it suck for you.'

Amy looked doubtful. 'But we hardly know Mrs O'Hara,' she objected. 'Couldn't we make her up a milk feed with conny-onny and water? Lots of women can't feed their own babies, Mam told me. Why, she couldn't feed my big brother, Charlie, when he was born, on account of getting influenza and being right pulled down by it. She said he throve on conny-onny, honest to God, Mrs Scott.'

'We-ell,' Mrs Scott said doubtfully. 'I dare say you're right, chuck. I were thinking your mam might be feedin' her again in a day or two and forgettin' it weren't likely, not with puerperal fever. We'll try the conny-onny, then, see how she takes to it.'

So Amy mixed condensed milk and water in a little jug, warmed it through and then offered the baby a tiny spoonful when next she awoke. Since the baby made no objection to the mixture Mrs Scott advised Amy to find a feeding bottle and teat, and see whether she would accept it. Amy knew where there was an old bottle – she had used it for her doll Betsy – but the rubber teat proved to be perished beyond recall, so Amy wrapped the baby in her shawl, got Albert to tie the shawl securely round her person and set off for the shops. She bought two rubber teats, returned home, and boiled them and the bottle on the stove, meanwhile nursing an increasingly indignant child to her breast, and at last, she was able to offer the baby the milk she was badly in need of. Despite the fact that Jane Rebecca had never before drunk from a bottle, let alone tasted conny-onny, she drank quite half the contents of the bottle, burped immensely and fell deeply asleep.

All this had taken some time, what with changing the baby's napkin and bringing up her wind, but at last she was restored to her cradle and Amy started to worry about her mother once more. The doctor popped in three or four times, looking worried. Mrs Scott appeared and disappeared from the kitchen, and occasionally a neighbour popped in to ask how Mrs Logan did, for Isobel was a popular figure in the neighbourhood. Nevertheless the day dragged, with Amy feeling she was the only person in the house who was completely ignorant of what was happening in the bedroom upstairs. When teatime arrived the doctor came down and bade Amy boil up his instruments, tipping a number of wicked-looking objects into the small pan she offered him. When the water had boiled for five minutes Mrs Scott came down, drained it from the pan and carried it upstairs, telling Amy as she did so in a falsely jovial voice that things were beginning to look up at last. 'Doctor Payne knows what he's doing,' she assured the anxious young people sitting around the kitchen awaiting some news, for by now the older boys had returned from their fishing trip. 'Doctor Payne is going to let out some of the badness, so soon your mam will be right as rain, you just see.'

She disappeared up the staircase and the terrible waiting started once more. Amy could imagine only too well what must be happening in the bedroom upstairs; she had been appalled by the sharpness and number of Dr Payne's instruments, and despite her best endeavours ghastly pictures of those knives and probes entering flesh would keep popping into her mind.

But for a long time nothing whatsoever happened. No one came down and, although Gus tiptoed to the bottom of the stairs and stood, head cocked, listening, when he returned he could only report a soft murmur of voices coming from the bedroom and no sign of either doctor or nurse. In fact, Amy had begun to cut them some sandwiches and the kettle was on for yet more tea when Bill Logan came heavily down the stairs and into the kitchen. He stood in the middle of the room, staring straight in front of him and not appearing to notice any of them until Charlie, as the eldest present, went over and pushed his father gently into a chair.

Charlie was very like his father, tall and broad with soft, dark hair flopping over his forehead and a gentle, patient expression, but now anxiety was creasing his brow into a frown and his voice, when he spoke, was sharper than usual. 'Well, Dad? What's happening to me mam? ... Is she ... is she ...?'

Bill Logan put his elbows on the table and his chin in his hands; for a moment he said nothing, then raised a haggard face and his eyes, full of pain, met those of his son. 'She's gone,' he said huskily, his voice breaking. 'They did all they could, it weren't no one's fault. Doctor Payne told me it were pretty well hopeless right from the start; her temperature went sky high and he couldn't get it down, nohow.'

Albert broke the silence that followed. 'Are you sayin' our mam's *dead*?' he asked. He got to his feet and, leaning across the table, actually seized his father's hands and shook them. 'Is that what you're telling us, Dad? That she's dead?'

For a moment Bill didn't speak. Amy, staring at his bent head, was horrified to see tears trickling down his face. Then he gave a gulp, nodded his head and said, 'That's right, son. I can't believe it meself and that's the truth, but she's gone. Presently, you can go up and see her, I suppose that's best, but ...'

As his words died away Amy jumped to her feet. 'It isn't true, it can't be true!' she shouted into the sudden silence. 'It's that doctor's fault, he hurt her with those shiny tool things and now ... and now ...' She bolted for the back door as a babble of sound broke out behind her and was halfway across the yard when Gus caught up with her. He put his arms round her and gave her a hard hug, then walked her slowly back into the kitchen, one arm still across her shoulders. 'We've got to face it, queen,' he said gently. 'Mam's gone, and because she ain't here no more we'll need to hang together and take care of one another, because that's what she would want. No one can run away from sorrow because it runs faster than any of us can. As for casting blame, that's norra very Christian attitude, is it? Our mam made us go to church because she believed in it, not because it was the thing to do. And don't forget the baby. You'll have to take special care of her now, queen. Be brave, Amy, and help us fellers to help Dad, because Mam would've wanted that, too.'

Mary came home, but she was a very different girl from the one who had shared Amy's bed after Jane Rebecca's birth. She was wide-eyed and white-faced with shock and misery, as they all were, but after the first few days were over it occurred to Amy that her sister was also rebellious. To be sure, she did whatever work was demanded of her, but never willingly or with good grace. February was a bad time for the fishing, but because of a sudden spell of mild weather catches were not as bad as they might have been, so there was fish to sell both in the Great Charlotte Street market and from the handcart. Amy understood her sister's reluctance to start selling fish again, but she saw no reason why Mary should baulk over looking after the baby or cooking the meals.

Fortunately, Mary's reluctance was not as obvious to the rest of the family as it was to Amy. In front of her father and brothers she managed to put on a good face over whatever tasks were to be done, but Amy could read the signs of her sister's reluctance in Mary's tight lips and impatient, jerky movements.

It did not make things easier that Mary refused to tell Amy why she no longer seemed to want to help her family. When questioned, she would only say that she missed her job in Manchester and the friends that she had made there. She also made it plain that she had returned for Mam's funeral and had remained because it was her duty to do so, but she would be off again just as soon as Bill felt he could manage without her. 'I've been earning good money, regular money, and we can't afford to lose my wages,' she told Amy. 'Servants aren't hard to find, so if the Cottlestones replace me I may never get another job as good, let alone one where I'm valued and happy. I'm telling you, Amy, I can't wait to get out of here and back to a place where I'm appreciated.'

'But you're appreciated here,' Amy wailed, thinking how impossible life would be without her sister's help, even if that help was reluctantly given. 'I'm sure the folk in Manchester couldn't need you as much as we do, queen. Why, how could I possibly manage without you? There's baby Becky, and the fish, and the housework, to say nothing of getting the washing done, potting the shrimps . . .' The family had now agreed to call the baby Becky, because Janie was so easily confused with Amy and they were sure Isobel would have agreed.

'I know what you mean,' Mary said with a sigh. The two girls were lying in bed and talking in whispers since baby Becky was asleep in her cradle beside the bed. 'But I've got my own way to make, chuck. I'm going to tell Dad he ought to get a woman in to give you a hand. Even with the pair of us, the work's more than we can manage and it's winter now, with small catches. In the summer, when the nets are full and Dad brings in tons of shrimps to be potted, we'd simply never manage, not if we worked all day and all night, too. I never realised how much Mam did until she died, but now I *know* it's too much for a couple of girls.'

'Ye-es, but Dad doesn't have that sort of money, does he?' Amy asked. Mary opened her mouth to reply, beginning to say that her father would have to find the money somehow, when baby Becky, who had been stirring uneasily for some moments, began to scream and that was the end of that particular attempt, Amy thought, to get Mary to admit she was needed at home.

Because of the spell of mild, unseasonable weather, housekeeping became temporarily easier. Nappies hung on the washing line in the morning were brought in dry and fluffy from the gentle breeze before darkness fell and even the sad business of arranging for Isobel's funeral was conducted beneath blue skies. However, after about ten days the weather reverted to more normal winter conditions of cold and even of snow, though this last rarely laid so close to the sea. But it did mean very much smaller catches. In a way this was a relief. The girls had their work cut out to cope with the baby and what fish there was. Potting shrimps would have been impossible. Bill, who had always been an understanding and sympathetic father, had changed on losing his wife. He grew taciturn, unable to discuss the problems which beset him, because he had always relied on Isobel to arrange the shore side of the fishing. It speedily became apparent that he knew little of the preparation and potting of shrimps, save that they had to be shelled first and, truth to tell, he knew remarkably little about sales. Isobel had had her regular contacts at the fish market and Amy had realised some time earlier that her mother had different arrangements with almost every customer.

The trouble was that Amy did not know what these arrangements were and, when questioned, neither did Mary. Bill, when appealed to, merely said that it was now the girls' job to do such deals, which left his daughters in an unenviable position. To overcharge a valued customer or to undercharge one who would boast of it could do their business irreparable harm so, since Mary seemed to prefer staying at home and keeping house to dealing with the fish, Amy decided to cast herself on the mercy of Mrs O'Leary, but first she must sell the good catch of shrimps, which Bill had brought triumphantly home earlier that day.

He had gone out again, but had not taken Albert with him, so Albert had gone down to the shore to fetch driftwood and, while Amy was pulling on her only decent pair of boots, he came in with his arms full of salt-stained wood. 'I'll chop that presently,' he

95

was beginning, when Mary, at the sink, turned round and spoke sharply.

'You can do that later, Albert,' she said. 'Someone's got to sell the bleedin' shrimps and it isn't going to be me. I've put all that behind me, I have. Besides, there's a deal to do in the house, yet. I had a word with Dad earlier this morning, trying to make him see that Amy and me can't cope alone with the fish, the house and the baby, but it wasn't any manner of use. I told him he'd have to pay a grown woman to come in and give us a hand, but he just said he couldn't afford the wage and when I tried to persuade him he got downright nasty. He said he wouldn't replace our mam with some idle slut from the workhouse – as if I'd suggest such a thing! Anyway, so far as I can see, Dad's idea of us all pulling together simply means that Amy and myself do all the work. Certainly Dad never lifts a finger in the house and he's getting far too fond of visiting his pals of an evening . . . if he does visit them, that is. It's my belief he goes round to the Caradoc and drowns his sorrows, as they say.'

There was a shocked silence, then Amy spoke: 'But Dad's Temperance, Mary. He doesn't take strong drink.'

Mary turned from the sink, shaking her head sorrowfully. 'No, queen. Mam was Temperance and brought us up to think the same, but it's my belief that Dad never was. Fishing's a cruel, hard job, and Dad and the older lads deserve a pint and a bit of company at the end of a day's work. I don't *blame* Dad for taking a drink now and then, but he's got to be made to accept help. Otherwise, I'm telling you, we'll all be in the workhouse in six months' time.' She turned to point an accusing finger at Albert.

'And you will help sell the shrimps, me laddo, even if it goes against the grain.'

'What's wrong wi' Amy sellin' the perishin' shrimps?' Albert asked sulkily, turning to hold his hands out to the blaze, for it was a cold day with an icy wind blowing. 'I've bin' on that bleedin' shrimp boat since before dawn and I'm so cold it's a wonder me fingers don't snap off like icicles. Let Amy go, she's better at sellin' shrimps than any feller. Gals always is.'

Amy, who knew her chances of escaping the task were small, sighed deeply and went towards the scullery where the sack of shrimps awaited her. 'All right, all right, only you might come along as well, Albert, because I'm thinking of going to see Mrs O'Leary when I've sold the shrimps. Someone's got to have a word about the stall and prices and so on, and it might as well be me.'

'In that case Albert can push the handcart and you can carry the baby, Amy,' Mary said, brightening. 'I want to give this house a good clean through, get the messages up to date and clean down the wash-house and fish scullery – God knows it could do with it, it hasn't been done since well before me mam died. Also I want to see if I can hear of a respectable woman who can do with a few hours' work. You'd best take a bottle for the littl 'un and some carry-out for yourselves. I made scones and a meat-and-potato pie yesterday. You can have them. Now, don't start carrying on, Amy,' she added, as Amy began to protest. 'Baby Becky's a good little soul, I've heard you say so often and often. Why, folk come over to coo at the baby and end up buying shrimps, so you'll be sold out afore you know it. Now hurry up and leave, do, so I can get on.'

So it was, with Albert pushing the cart and with baby Becky in her arms, that Amy finally left the house. She was well wrapped up in a thick though ragged shawl and the baby was well muffled too. Even so, the cold wind cut like a knife and as the three of them turned into Crosby Road they gasped as it hit them, snatching the breath from their mouths. Amy instinctively curled closer round the child and Albert grabbed at the sack of shrimps.

'It's hellish cold on the boat, but at least I ain't pushin' a bleedin' great barrer over slippery cobbles,' Albert shrieked above the wind. 'Must we do the big houses today? It's them long drives and often, when you reaches the house, some snooty bitch of a maidservant says, "Not today, thanks," and slams the door on your snout. Let's try some of the streets off Knowsley Road in Bootle, shall us?'

'Good idea,' Amy shrieked back. Like Albert, she did not enjoy either the long walk up gravelled drives or the snubs that could result if an unfriendly servant came to the kitchen door. People in the poetry streets, as her mother had called them, were friendly and sympathetic towards young shrimp sellers and if they had the money would always buy. Shrimps were a treat to such people, not a garnish to already luxurious meals. In fact, the main reason that Isobel insisted on the children trying the larger houses was because such families ate more fish. Since they had no fish to sell today, common sense as well as the bitter cold dictated that they follow Albert's suggestion.

Accordingly the children, battling their way along Crosby Road with the wind off the sea hurling itself at them, dived into the temporary shelter afforded by the Rimrose Bridge and turned into Knowsley

Road. It was a real relief to enter Byron Street, out of the worst of the wind, and knock on the first door. A tall, plump woman, swathed in an enormous calico apron, smiled down at them from the doorway. 'Well, if it ain't the shrimp seller!' she said, her hand going to her apron pocket, 'and on such a wild day, too. About all I've got in the house is bread and marge, but shrimps goes well with everything, so I'll have a pint, if you please.'

Amy picked up the tin measure and filled it generously; Mam had always said it didn't do to skimp. If you were generous, your customers bought time and time again; if you were mean they would turn you from the door next time you called. 'Sixpence, please, missus,' she said, tipping the shrimps into a brown paper bag, and letting Albert screw it closed and hand it over, since she had the baby in one arm. The customer, noticing the child, leaned over and chirruped, but baby Becky never stirred. Sheltered from the wind and in her sister's familiar embrace, she was as snug as in her own cot.

'Ain't she a good little soul?' the woman said wonderingly. 'And pretty as a picture, too.' She looked searchingly at Amy. 'She don't favour you much. Your sister, is she? I suppose your mam's busy today?'

'Mam died a month back,' Amy stated briefly. It was a question she was growing used to hearing and it no longer brought tears to her eyes, though she still missed Isobel dreadfully. 'But we're a big family. My sister Mary's doing a spring clean, that's why me and Albert took baby Becky on the shrimp round.'

'Ah, that explains it.' The woman nodded. She produced a sixpence, which she handed to Albert and, after a second's hesitation, a round brown halfpenny, which she pressed into Amy's hand. 'For the littl'un,' she mumbled, and was back in the house with the door closed before Amy could thank her.

'Well, isn't that just lovely?' Amy asked as they approached the next door. 'Mary said Baby would sell shrimps for us and it looks like she was right. Come on, Albert, let's try our luck again.'

Three hours later, with the last shrimp sold and their pockets bulging with pennies, they made their way towards the nearest tram stop. By now both children were exhausted, so each took a handle of the cart and dragged it behind them with Albert taking the baby from his sister, since he was the stronger of the two. 'Are you sure you want to go to the fish market today, our Amy?' he asked as they reached the stop. 'It's gerrin' late, an' you must be tired out – I know I am. Besides, the littl'un will want feedin' again pretty soon I dare say.'

Amy, though she was sure she was every bit as tired as Albert, shook her head. She intended to see the older woman and get things sorted out today, otherwise they would go on fumbling through life, never knowing whether they might have been selling too cheap and buying too dear. 'It's all right, I'll have a nice sit-down on the tram and I've still got a bottle for Becky in my skirt pocket.' Amy let go of the barrow and took the baby from Albert's none too reluctant grasp. 'I know the barrow's heavy for you to push alone, but it won't matter how much you jostle and jounce now it's empty. Tell Mary I'll try to be back in time for tea.'

Albert snorted. 'I ain't goin' straight home,' he

said self-righteously 'Our dad's goin' to be seeing to the boat for a while yet. So I'll go an' give him a hand.'

It was Amy's turn to snort. 'In this weather our dad'll be round at old Ben Carpenter's havin' a glass of his wife's home-made wine an' a nice bit of fruit cake,' she said, just as a tram drew up alongside.

'Yeah, well ...' Albert gave a guilty grin. 'I'd sooner be wi' the Carpenters than have Mary buzzin' round me lugs, tryin' to make me scrub floors or chop wood, or even make the perishin' beds. Our Mary's good at dele-whachamacallit, but she's not so keen on workin' herself, I've noticed.'

'Delegating,' Amy said as she swung herself on to the platform and headed for an empty seat. She turned briefly to wave to Albert, but her brother was already heading back towards Trevor Street and the Carpenters'.

Amy leaned back in her seat and settled the baby more comfortably in her lap. By a piece of good fortune the tram was a number 24, which would take her all the way to her destination, for Mrs O'Leary had her stall in St John's fish market in Great Charlotte Street. Mrs O'Leary was a fat and friendly body who bought a good deal of fish, particularly shellfish, from the Logans. She was in her late sixties and because she no longer felt able to work every day in the market she had lent the use of her stall, on Mondays, to Isobel. If there was sufficient fish, Isobel would thus be able to sell at least some of their catch direct to the customers, while paying Mrs O'Leary a small sum for the privilege. Because of this sharing, convenient to both, the two women had become good friends and Isobel had impressed on Amy the importance of always leaving the stall immaculate for the real owner's return the following day.

So if there's one who'll advise me, it'll be Mrs O'Leary, Amy told herself. It might have been easier to talk to Mrs O'Leary, she reflected, had she been alone, but she was not sorry to have baby Becky with her, for the baby was company even though she could not talk and, what was more, holding her little body beneath the shawl meant they helped to keep each other warm. The wind was still bitterly cold and though the baby seemed light, Amy knew from experience that she would grow steadily heavier with each passing hour.

Amy saw several people she knew and greeted them politely, but as the tram rumbled along the Stanley Road getting ever nearer to her destination she began to feel the weight of responsibility descending on her narrow shoulders in a very unpleasant way. If Mary couldn't bring herself to do it, then Dad should have, she thought miserably. It was no good looking for help from either of her older brothers. Because the fishing was so poor at this time of year, Charlie had taken work in the brewery maltings in the Midlands and would not be returning until early May, so he could be discounted as far as help went. Gus and Albert, of course, worked with Bill on the boat and could not be spared. Even so, Amy felt increasingly put upon, especially when it crossed her mind that she was going into the city centre in the most blatant manner on a day when she should have been in school. Sagging off school was a popular pastime among the young lads, but because of Isobel's rigid principles, Amy had never feared the attendance officer before. Now, however, she knew that it would go hard with her if she were caught. The family might need her – did need her – but the authorities would not see it this way and the fact that she had been forced to go on this errand in order to keep her family solvent would not make a jot of difference.

The tram arrived at Lime Street and Amy and her burden got down without incident. She made her way round the corner into Roe Street, past the Royal Court, glancing curiously at the billboards outside the theatre as she did so. How lovely it would be to attend a performance at the theatre, she thought wistfully. Her mam had taken her and Mary to a pantomime once and she had never forgotten it. But she could not linger today to examine the photographs of the actresses nor the details of the present drama and turned into Great Charlotte Street, heading for St John's fish market.

Mrs O'Leary was sitting behind her stall but the moment she saw Amy she got to her feet and surged into the aisle between the stalls, enveloping girl and baby in a loving but odorous embrace. Gently disengaging herself, Amy remembered her mother saying that Mrs O'Leary was one of the many old shawlies in Liverpool who seldom washed the bits that didn't show. 'When they get old they get cold,' she had told her small daughter. 'Oh, they buy new clothes all right, but they just put them on over the old ones. That's why so many of 'em look fat as fivepence when they're really skinny as a sprat. So when Mrs O'Leary gives you a hug, just you take a big breath first, like someone divin' into deep water, and give her your best smile. She's a good woman, better to us than most; I wouldn't hurt her feelings for the world, nor let you girls do so.'

'Well, well, well, if it ain't little Miss Amy and the

babby,' the old woman said wheezily. 'Come round be'ind the stall, queen, and you shall have some tea from me bottle and a nice piece o' cake. There's allus a lull around now so I gorra moment to meself.'

Amy accompanied Mrs O'Leary to the back of the stall, where she perched on an empty fish box reflecting unhappily that she would pong as badly as her hostess if she stayed here long. She accepted a tin mug of cold tea, though she declined the proffered cake, producing a scone which had been left over from the carry-out she and Albert had shared earlier and biting into it. 'Me dad said I'd better bring a mouthful since I'm not likely to get home until late,' she explained thickly. 'Mrs O'Leary, we're in terrible trouble at home and I remembered my mam telling me before she died that if I ever needed advice to come to you. She said you were a good friend to us Logans and would be sure to put me on the right path, like. My dad's a grand fellow, so he is, but he's that moithered without Mam and that puzzled what to do that I can't put any more on him right now.'

Amy looked appealingly up at the old woman, feeling guilty because she knew very well that Mrs O'Leary would assume Isobel's words had been spoken just before she died; a sort of last request, if you like. Whereas, in fact, Amy had gleaned the information about her mother's old friend from chance remarks Mam had let drop over the last couple of years. Isobel had been too busy fighting for her life to give a thought to last requests, Amy knew, and felt tears rise spontaneously to her eyes.

'There, there, queen,' Mrs O'Leary said, clearly much moved. 'Don't you go starting to bawl, because your mam was right. What I can do I will, though that may be little enough, the Lord knows. So you're in a pickle at home, eh? Well, I suppose that's scarcely surprising for a better organised, more businesslike woman than your mam I've yet to meet, and folk like that take everythin' into their own hands and never consider how the people they take care of would manage without them. I'll be bound your da doesn't know how to boil an egg or wash a babby's napkin, let alone change one. But now I think back, don't you have an elder sister what's in service? Don't tell me your da hasn't sent for her? So why ain't it her askin' for me help? She'll be the fair-haired, pretty one.'

'Yes, that's Mary,' Amy agreed. 'And she's come home all right, but the fact is, Mrs O'Leary, she doesn't understand much about the fish and shrimps and that. She said she'd rather look after the house and leave the business side to me.'

Mrs O'Leary pulled a doubtful face. 'You'se awful young and small,' she said thoughtfully. 'They'll scarce see you acrost the top of the stall. Or wasn't you thinkin' about takin' your mam's day? Only I doubt you'll mek the same money sellin' wholesale as you do direct. An' if your da lets his fish go to the wholesale next door, you'll soon be scrattin' round for rent money since it ain't likely that a couple o' kids will strike the bargains your mam used to make.'

'Oh, but we want the stall, if you please, Mrs O'Leary,' Amy said eagerly. 'I'm still in school and there isn't much I can do about that, but Mary will run the stall, except at holiday times, and then I can stand on a fish box – or two, if that means folk'll take me more seriously.' She had not discussed the matter with Mary but assumed the older girl would take on the work for the sake of the family, though she knew her sister hated the thought of selling fish. 'But Mam never told us what rent she paid you, nor the prices she asked from the other stallholders for the shrimps and the crabs and that.' She lowered her voice. 'I know Mam had arrangements with folk over fish prices, but I don't know what they were, and I'm afraid of making a mess of it so folk get angry and won't buy any more.'

Mrs O'Leary smiled down at her and pulled a scruffy piece of paper and a stub of pencil from a pocket in her voluminous skirt. 'You're a sharp one,' she said approvingly. 'I'll write it all down, as much as I know that is, an' you and your sister – an' your da too, o'course – can mull over it this evening. See what's best to do. Of course, at this time o' year, with fish bein' difficult to get 'cos catches is small, us'll all pay more for what you bring in. Your da will know all about wholesale prices and seasonal variations, I'm sure of that, it's just your mam's side of the business that she kept close to her chest.'

Amy was beginning to thank her profusely when baby Becky, obviously noticing that the pleasant rocking motion of tram and walk had ceased, began to grizzle. The old woman, with a delighted chuckle, held out two fat, cushiony arms, and Amy placed the baby in them and then handed over the bottle of milk. 'Do you want to give her this, Mrs O'Leary?' she asked. 'It's time she had a feed, I guess.'

'It's cold,' Mrs O'Leary objected, folding fat fingers round the banana-shaped bottle. 'Tek it to Dorothy's Dining Rooms down the road an' ask them to warm it up for you.' She chuckled, gazing down at baby Becky's small face. 'I'll keep the littl'un quiet while you're gone. Babbies like me so don't you worry that we shan't get along.'

Since the baby had stopped crying as soon as she was handed over, Amy concluded that either Mrs O'Leary was right or the child was too stunned by the older woman's odour to utter a peep. Accordingly, she set off for the dining rooms and was soon back and watching with satisfaction as Mrs O'Leary crooned and cuddled, and the milk sank in the bottle.

When the baby was fed and changed, Amy tucked her back into the shawl once more, got Mrs O'Leary to retie the knot so that she was held securely against her and set off for the tram stop. She had all the information she would need scribbled down on the scrap of paper and felt a good deal happier. Mrs O'Leary had suggested she should tell Bill Logan to pop into the market the next time he was in the area. 'For what you young'uns need is a growed woman to keep an eye on the babby an' do the actual potting of the shrimps,' she said impressively. 'I don't deny you and young Mary is goin' to do your best but you should be in school, queen, and when times is good and catches is large, the two of you will have your work cut out to pot the shrimps, let alone sell 'em. What's more, pottin's an art an' I'll be bound your mam never let either of you tek a hand in it. That right?'

'That's right,' Amy had been forced to agree. 'But Dad reckons we'll kind of pick it up, once we start. He said he'd get a recipe . . . or at least I think that's what he said. But Mary's been in service; I'm sure she must have an idea of how to pot shrimps.'

'And by the same token, if your sister wou' rather keep house than sell fish, why have you the littl'un?' Mrs O'Leary had said suddenly. 'You'd think a gal of her age – what is she, fourteen? Fifteen? – would love a-lookin' after her little sister.'

Amy had been struck by the obvious common sense of this remark. Now that she thought about it, it seemed downright strange that Mary had chosen to burden her with the baby who would have been happier, and better off, in the cradle which the two girls lugged downstairs each morning and up again at night. What was more, Mary did seem to enjoy looking after Becky, often telling Amy how to do small jobs, such as bathing the baby in a comfortable manner, for Mary could still remember how her mother had treated Amy herself when she had been small.

But Mrs O'Leary had looked at her questioningly so Amy said inadequately, 'I don't know, I'm sure, except I suppose she'll be able to get on better without having to see to baby here. Thanks again, Mrs O'Leary.'

But right now, standing at the tram stop with the bitter wind cutting through her second-best skirt and whipping strands of hair out from under the shawl, she thought rather bitterly that Mrs O'Leary's question had been a good one. Whatever had possessed Mary to insist that she take the baby on such a freezing cold day? To be sure, Becky was sleeping contentedly enough, warm in the shelter of the shawl, but Amy could see that her little nose was like a cherry where the wind had caught it and knew that such intense cold was not good for babies. She decided that she would have a talk with Mary when she arrived home and would make it plain that she, Amy, was not a servant who would do all the work and take all the responsibility, while Mary flicked a duster around their small house.

Standing there in the cold, she grew more and more indignant with her sister, until her cheeks burned with righteous anger. She rehearsed the pithy speech she would make when she got indoors, and planned to tell her father that such behaviour was unfair and should be punished.

By the time she got off the tram at the Seaforth Sands terminus, she found she was quite looking forward to getting home. The kitchen would be warm, there would probably be a cup of tea waiting, she had got the information they needed and her courage was high. She would make Mary see that; as Gus had said the day her Mam had died, the Logan family must pull together.

She began to walk briskly in the direction of Seafield Grove, and the baby awoke and started to grizzle. 'Never mind, baby,' Amy said breathlessly. 'Soon have you home in the warm and then won't we tell our Mary some home truths!'

She reached the jigger, trotted down it and entered their yard. The men were not yet back from the fishing for there were no seaboots lined up in the wooden porch against the back door and no cart full of fish awaiting gutting. She opened it stepped into the kitchen and paused. It felt chilly, almost unlived in, and though the fire was alight it burned sullenly beneath a layer of white ash. Amy began to undo the knot of her shawl and put the baby down in the cradle, realising as she did so that she was very tired indeed.

'Mary!' she shouted sharply. 'Mary, where in heaven's name have you got to? The fire's dam near out, and me and baby is fruzz wi' cold. Sure

I've done enough today without having to remake the fire while you lie around in bed?'

But even as she spoke some instinct told her that she was wasting her breath. The house was empty. Mary might have gone to do the messages or simply round to see a neighbour but she was definitely not at home. With a most uncomfortable feeling in the pit of her stomach, Amy ran up the stairs and flung open the door of the bedroom that she and Mary shared. One glance was enough to tell her that her sister had gone. None of her clothing or personal possessions remained in the small room. A second glance revealed a pencilled note pinned to Mary's pillow. With a sinking heart, Amy unpinned the note and read it as she made her way downstairs.

Amy, don't be cross, [the note began], *I just can't live like this and our dad won't fetch anyone in to help while I'm at home. Dear Amy, I know you will think I'm being hard on you, but it's for the best. Don't let our dad try and fetch me back for I'll only run away again. This is so important to me and not just for now but for my future. I'm really sorry, but one day, you'll understand.*
Your loving Mary.

Amy put the note down and slumped into a chair. This changed everything. For a start, there was no way she herself could run Mrs O'Leary's fish stall while school was in session. Nor could she look after the baby or pot the shrimps, let alone sell from door to door without her sister's help.

But a little hard thought brought a ray of sunshine ɔ lighten what had seemed at first a real catastro-
ɹe. Mary had shown no enthusiasm at all for

staying at home, let alone coping with the multitude of tasks her mother had daily tackled. She and Mary had longed for Bill to employ a grown-up woman, someone who knew all about rearing children, and coping with the task of potting shrimps and selling fish.

However, sitting here worrying would not get the fire going again, nor sort out what the family were to have for their suppers when they came in. Amy got off her chair, went and riddled the fire, and walked into the pantry. It was odd, really, she mused as she took potatoes from the sack and dumped them in the sink, how at first Mary's defection had struck cold and chill. Now, having thought about it only a little, she realised that Mary was right. Two girls might stumble along somehow, but sooner or later they would need outside help. Whereas if Dad was forced to get a woman in . . .

Please, God, let it be someone kind, who can cook as well as my mam and who'll love baby Becky, she prayed, as she began to scrub. Someone cuddly, like that nice widder-woman from Belgrave Road, who made those lovely apple pies for the harvest festival supper last year. Or there was a kind soul on Clarendon Road who had been known to give kiddies sweets when they sang carols outside her door come Christmas. Just so long as Dad doesn't go giving us over to some slut like Suzie Keagan, who doesn't bother to do her own work, let alone anyone else's. Only Dad would have more sense, surely? He must know as well as she did that Suzie never did anything if she could get someone else to do it for her. He must know that she liked a little drink as well; that she wasn't above pinching the odd copper or two from an employer's till and that the feller

111

said she gambled on the horses and the dogs whenever she could afford it, and sometimes when she couldn't.

Thinking of these drawbacks to Suzie's character eased her mind; Bill would never allow such a woman into his home and among his children.

Satisfied on that score, she continued to scrub potatoes. Surely, with Mary gone, her dad would have no option but to employ some woman? So if Mary's flight forced his hand, it would be for the best . . .

Chapter Four

It was a bright September day, with a soft breeze
bringing the sense of the countryside into the small
end house on Seafield Grove. Suzie was hanging out
the washing, knowing that in the kitchen behind her
Gran would be making the breakfast porridge for
the three of them. Paddy had gone off long before
Suzie had got up; Gran always roused early and got
his breakfast, although Paddy tried to assure her that
he would do very well on a slice of bread and jam,
and a sup of cold tea. He was now lowest of the low,
working for the dairy on Dryden Street, off Great
Homer Street. He started at five in the morning and
he mucked out the cows, saw to their clean bedding,
their feed and their general health, and was responsible for rolling the milk churns out of the cowshed
and into the dairy itself. The work was poorly paid,
but Suzie thought her son quite enjoyed it. It was
better than being cooped up in a shop or a factory
and the staff were kind to him, giving him odds and
ends of food that were not quite up to the dairy's
usual standard.

Suzie herself had been working for the Logan
family ever since early March, when Mary had run
off back to Manchester. She rather enjoyed being
able to come and go as she pleased in someone else's
house, for the Logans were mostly absent while she
did her work. She also enjoyed running Mrs
O'Leary's fish stall on Mondays each week, becaus

it brought her into contact with other people, both customers and stallholders, and enabled her to salt away the odd bob or two, as well as taking home for the Keagans' tea any unsold fish still fresh enough to eat.

During the school holidays, of course, Amy looked after the baby and did a good deal of the housework, which was a bonus since Suzie very much disliked scrubbing floors, polishing furniture and preparing enormous meals for the family. But in term-time she was forced to do quite a lot of these things, and disliked the dullness and repetitiveness of the work.

Not that she worked very hard. She didn't mind looking after Becky who was nearly seven months old now. At first the baby had been colicky and difficult, quick to cry and slow to smile but gradually, as the weeks passed, Suzie got her into a routine and now she was easier. Housework itself, which meant cooking, cleaning and washing, was divided pretty equally between Amy, Gran and Suzie herself. Suzie had pretended to be shocked when she discovered that Bill boiled the shrimps in the Logans' copper, but it had been a good reason to take their washing back to her own house, where Gran dealt swiftly and capably with it. 'I don't know about you, queen,' her mother-in-law was fond of remarking, 'you oughter be a colonel in the army or an admiral in the navy, 'cos you're so bleedin' good at gettin' other people to do your work.' She had shaken her head sadly, only half joking. 'Us Keagans've always bin workers and your Abe was just another such, but you've got a lazy streak as wide as the tramlines runnin' down the Scottie.

You'll never do owt you can wriggle out of – ain't that so?'

Sometimes Suzie admitted that it was and sometimes she simply shrugged and laughed, but in her heart she knew that her mother-in-law was right. Without the two old ladies to give a hand, her home would soon have degenerated into a slum and without the money which she was now bringing in she would have been in deep financial trouble months ago.

The truth was, she reflected, pinning baby Becky's nappies on the line, that she had to watch her Ps and Qs in front of Bill. He did not approve of women gambling, or drinking, though he thought there was no harm in himself going out of an evening and having a bevvy or two with his pals, or with his two elder sons. The idea that she might either go drinking or gambling had not, she was sure, ever entered his head. And because it was clear that he both liked and trusted her, Suzie was determined that such ideas should remain a mystery to him. She had always liked Bill Logan but now, being around him so much, she liked him even better. He was a generous, amusing, even affectionate man for, though the loss of his wife had grieved him deeply, he was gradually coming to terms with it. She pinned the last nappy to the line and returned to the kitchen, reminding her mother briskly that she would be gone from the house now until about four that afternoon, when Amy returned from school and could safely be left in charge of both house and child.

Old Mrs Keagan gave a derisive sniff but made no other comment. However, she went to a large pile of linen standing on the draining board and shovelled it into an oilskin bag, remarking as she handed it to her daughter-in-law, 'Don't forget all them shirts *you* so neatly ironed nor all them nappies *you* boiled till they was white as snow, queen. It wouldn't do to let anyone else take the credit for *your* work, would it, eh? And if young Amy were to come round a-fetchin' of it, she might see more than you'd like, Mrs Clever Keagan.'

'Oh, young Amy's gorra head on her shoulders and a mean streak even wider than the tramlines on the Scottie,' Suzie said with a chuckle. 'I doubt she believes I do me own washin' and ironin', let alone theirs. But she don't go tale-clattin' to her dad, I'll say that for her. And though I don't like the kid, she won't try an' put a spoke in me wheel so long as the work gets done. Now that we've got the pottin' of the shrimps sorted out, she's content to sell 'em for as much as she can get. And I never get a sniff of that money,' she finished, with only the slightest trace of bitterness. She glanced around the kitchen. 'Paddy go off all right this morning?'

'Aye,' Gran said briefly. She held out the bulging bag of clean linen. 'Here you are. You'd best gerroff now, queen, 'cos young Amy can't go to school till you're there to look after the babby. Unless Albert's staying behind today?'

Suzie snorted, taking the bag of clean linen, and turned towards the door. 'Bill wouldn't let Albert stay behind on a day like this, Gran. A fine September is a grand month for the shrimps and now that Charlie's livin' away, Bill needs Albert as well as Gus. Mind, if it looks as though I'm goin' to be held up, young Amy will bring the babby down to meet me. Not that she minds bein' late in school 'cos she's a clever kid, top of her class. She's got big ideas, has Miss Amy, and her dad encourages her. Still, there you are. Men's often fools over their daughters I'm told.'

'I wouldn't know,' Gran said, as Suzie opened the door, 'havin' only had sons meself. And how come Mr Logan is suddenly Bill, eh?'

Suzie, halfway out of the door, chuckled. 'That's just between ourselves,' she said. 'Don't worry, there's a load of perks attached to this job an' I'm not goin' to risk muckin' things up by gettin' too familiar. I'll call him Mr Logan . . .' she smiled wryly at the older woman '. . . until he asks me to use his Christian name,' she finished and shut the door gently behind her.

Walking up Seafield Grove with the heavy bag of clean linen, Suzie saw Amy poised on the pavement outside her own home. As soon as the girl noticed the woman approaching she jerked her thumb at the open door behind her. 'She's asleep,' she called softly. 'Awright if I go now?'

'Aye, you bugger off,' Suzie bawled cheerfully. She would not have said such a thing had Bill been at home, but it amused her to try to shock Amy when there were no other members of the family within earshot. Not that Amy ever acted shocked, but Suzie had a shrewd suspicion that the girl was aware how Isobel would have disliked such language. 'Got your carry-out, chuck?' The question was rhetorical, since Amy always saw that the family had food of some sort for their midday meal; Bill liked his bread cut fresh in the morning and not prepared the night before. Suzie baked the bread, or rather Mr Marsh, the local baker, did the actual cooking, while Gran or even Aunt Dolly usually made and proved the round cottage loaves. Suzie could cook and at first had taken some pride in making bread for the Logans, but Bill had complained that the loaves were heavy and lay on his stomach like lead. He had suggested that Suzie should buy bread, but since Isobel had not done so, Suzie pretended that the loaves were heavy because she was trying to use Isobel's recipe and had commandeered Gran for the task. Bill, totally unaware of this, had been heard to tell friends and relatives about Suzie's delicious bread, and although Amy might purse her lips and give an exasperated sigh, she had not mentioned the facts of the case. Suzie concluded that either Amy was ignorant of the ruse or she had some other motive for keeping her own counsel. Whichever it was, it suited Suzie's book to be thought a first-rate cook, for she had a plan of her own, which she had confided to neither the Keagans nor the Logans.

Softlee, softlee, catchee monkey, Suzie thought to herself, as she moved around the Logans' house, which was twice the size of her own and infinitely more pleasant. If I play me cards right I'll be so indis ... indis ... Oh, I'll be so useful to 'em that when I say I's got to leave they'll do anything, just about, to get me to stay. Oh aye, Bill Logan has gorra rely on me so much that he won't know how to go on wi'out me. Once I gorrim to that stage, it'll be plain sailin' for Suzie Keagan, 'cos nothin' will be too good for me. Thank Gawd, our gran knew how to pot shrimps, though, or there wouldn't be the money for any extra perks lerralone the ones I get already.

She dumped the basket of linen on the kitchen table and went over to the cradle. The baby was sleeping, as Amy had said, but Suzie knew that it would not be long before the child awoke and demanded attention. In the meantime there were the breakfast dishes to wash up, the porridge saucepan to scour and a number of small jobs to be done, before she dressed the baby and took her up the road to do the messages. Amy could be persuaded, or even commanded, to do a great deal, but she stuck her heels in over such things as the porridge pan. She told Suzie frankly that she was too busy on school mornings to heat water for the dishes. 'I do more than my share,' she had said bluntly, right at the beginning, when Suzie had first started working for the Logans. 'But I'm not a skivvy to keep your hands out of water, Mrs Keagan, when my dad thinks you do the lot. And if you don't wash up and keep baby Becky nice when I'm at school, I'll tell my Dad, honest to God I will. I'll do what I can, but I won't be pushed around and nor will Albert, not if I can prevent it.'

But that had been back in March, when Albert was still in school. Now, with Albert working on the fishing boat alongside his father and his brother Gus, there was no question of Suzie having two helpers. When it came to peeling the shrimps, of course, she had both Gus and Albert to help, and often managed to rope Paddy in as well, but for the ordinary everyday running of the house she had to make do with Amy.

It often crossed Suzie's mind to wonder why Amy, who she knew had never liked her, did so much of the housework without ever complaining to her father. There must be something behind it. Perhaps she's writing lists of what I do and what she does and one of these days, when I need to have her on my side, she'll split on me to her dad and it'll b all up wi' me, Suzie thought. But she had alwa

119

lived for the moment and knew that whatever the challenge, she would face up to it when it came. She was aware that the longer she worked for Bill the less likely he would be to believe ill of her. So if young Amy was storing up grievances she would probably find, when the time came to reveal all, that she had left it too late. By then, even if he believed her, Bill Logan would not be able to envisage life without Suzie.

Smiling with satisfaction, Suzie hauled the big kettle over the fire and began to pile the dirty dishes in the low stone sink.

Amy, meanwhile, making her way to school, was also thinking about Suzie and the future. Not that she called her Suzie, of course; Bill would have been outraged at such familiarity. He always addressed her as Mrs Keagan and expected the children to do likewise. But Amy, though she did as she was bidden, always thought of Suzie by her first name and usually with contempt. She told herself that she was well aware of the game Suzie was playing but was not prepared to put a spoke in her wheel, since she knew, probably even better than her father did, how dependent they were on the older woman. Without Suzie they would not have old Gran Keagan's help, just for a start. Nor would Paddy allow himself to be roped in for the shrimp shelling and even Paddy's Great-Aunt Dolly had her uses to the Logan family, though Amy was not supposed to know this.

So, for the time being at least, as Suzie had guessed, Amy made a mental note of each and every one of Suzie's peccadilloes and having a phenom-nal memory – which stood her in good stead at school – knew she would be able to recite the ever lengthening list, should it become necessary. This gave her some comfort when she was up to her eyes in work and saw Suzie idly slopping around the kitchen with a cup of tea in one hand and a cigarette in the other. Bill did not approve of women smoking, but so far he had never caught her at it. Amy thought the smell of the Woodbines, the cigarettes which Suzie favoured, was disgusting and always knew when the older woman had been having a crafty puff, but Bill was a pipe man, so she assumed that his nose was so used to the smell of the strong shag he smoked that other smells tended to pass him by. When Amy had first started noticing how Suzie behaved she had faced Bill with some of her less pleasant tricks and had been astonished at Bill's reaction.

He had grabbed her by both shoulders, given her a good shaking and slapped her face so hard that his fingermarks had lingered for a whole day. 'You wicked, clat-bearin' little liar,' he had shouted, his eyes glittering with fury. 'We couldn't manage wi'out Mrs Keagan and well you know it! She's been a grand friend to this family, none better, and I'll thank you never to let another spiteful word pass your lips when you're speaking of someone who's saved our family from bein' split up. If it hadn't been for her, likely you an' baby Becky would've been sent to the Culler children's home by now. How d'you think I'd ha' looked after two little girls on me own, once your mam was gone, eh?'

Amy, who had been her father's favourite for so long, had been appalled by his violence towards her and shocked that he could call her a liar. As for his blindness over Suzie's faults, she could only marvel at it, but for the time being, at least, she held her tongue.

'Hey, Amy! Ain't you a-goin' to say hello to your pals, then? I hollered to you twice as you were comin' up the road and you never so much as looked up.' Ruth, with a younger sister on either hand, came panting up beside Amy and immediately all thoughts of Suzie and the Keagan family went out of Amy's head.

'Sorry, Ruth,' Amy said contritely. She took hold of the other hand of the smallest Durrant and the four of them began to walk along the pavement in the direction of the school, 'Have you got a carry-out or is it a ha'penny for a milk roll today?'

'Slice of bread and jam, but the jam's spread awful thin,' Ruth said, patting the pocket of her faded tweed jacket. It had once belonged to a man and had probably been bought second- or even fifth-hand from Paddy's Market, but Mrs Durrant was good with her needle and had cut it down to make her daughter a coat for school. 'I say, you know that Paddy Keagan, the one whose mam works for you?'

'Course I know him, worse luck,' Amy said scornfully. 'Wish I didn't know him, nor his mam neither, but I do. Why? What's he done *this* time?'

'He's been an' gone an' got hisself caught nickin' sweets from Miz O'Mara's confectionery on Whitefield Road,' Ruth said. 'He's gorra good job, too. Me mam says he don't need to nick sweets when there's two of 'em in work and they's ever so generous in the dairy. He gets milk, butter, cheese – oh, all sorts – give him to take home at the end of each week. So why nick?'

'I dunno,' Amy said doubtfully. She did not like Paddy any better for being thrust into his company when shelling shrimps, but she did acknowledge, albeit grudgingly, that he did his share without more than the usual grumbling. Furthermore, she did not envy him having a mother like Suzie, who always put herself first. 'I think he probably has to make his own carry-out and I expect his mam takes most of his money, if not all. Besides, who said he nicked the stuff? That Mrs O'Mara is a right spiteful old gal. If he so much as touched a liquorice stick, or a sherbet dab, she'd want to be paid for 'em. Did she call the scuffers?'

'No-o-o,' Ruth admitted, having thought the matter over. 'I don't know as how she'd caught him, come to think. But she told Mrs McGregor and she told my Aunt Ethel, and Aunt Ethel told me mam that young Keagan had been nickin' when the shop was busy, so I thought . . .'

'Well, of all the nerve!' Amy gasped, truly shocked that her friend could repeat such unfounded gossip as if it were fact. 'I'm not saying anything against your Aunt Ethel, but I wouldn't trust mad ole Ma McGregor as far as I could throw her, which isn't far since she's the size of an elephant. Don't you go saying that to anyone else, Ruthie, or you'll get in real trouble, so you will. Paddy's horrible, I can't stand the sight of him, but fair's fair. I mean, when we were kids, most of us nicked the odd fade off the market – what's one rotten apple to a stallholder, after all – or a handful of aniseed balls, if they were parked low on the counter. Human nature, isn't it, when your mam and dad can't afford to give you the odd ha'penny?'

'Yes, I suppose so,' Ruth admitted. 'I won't say nothin' to nobody else then, Amy. It was just . . . well, now he's got a job . . . it seemed worse somehow than a schoolkid takin' the odd sweetie. Still an' all, mad Ma McGregor is a nasty piece of work and she do hate Mrs Keagan. She reckons Mrs Keagan took her job at the pub last year and she says as how she might've fallen for the shrimp pottin', if Mrs Keagan hadn't shoved her nose in.'

'Huh!' Amy said succinctly. She did not like having Mrs Keagan around the house, but the thought of mad Ma McGregor shuffling around their kitchen, smelling like a midden and poking her long nose into everything, made her realise that things could have been worse. And she felt quite proud of having scotched the nasty story about Paddy before it had really got going. She might not like him – in fact she absolutely hated him – but she had defended him almost as though he had been a Logan.

She had looked into the shippon when doing messages for Suzie along Great Homer Street and had thought Paddy was lucky in his work. She liked horses and a dairy had a great many horses for pulling the milk carts, and she also liked cows, with their big soft eyes and, at certain times of year, their wobbly-legged calves trotting at heel. She thought it must be an amusing place to work and when she went into the dairy to buy a dewy slab of butter or a triangular cut from one of the big cheeses she quite envied the young girls in their neat white coats, who sliced the butter, weighed and wrapped it in an instant. She was only twelve, of course, but she was sure that her time remaining in school would pass like a flash and she wanted to choose a job for herself, rather than take anything that was offered. She was bright, top of her class in almost everything and her teacher, Miss Musgrove, had told her mother the previous autumn, 'Young Amy has great potential and might easily go on to higher education, if you so wished.'

Amy was well aware, however, that further education was unlikely to be an option now. While her mother was alive and Mary at home, they would have managed somehow, but as things stood at present Amy's help, and eventually her wage, were essential to the Logan family. So instead of letting her mind dwell on a future as a teacher, secretary, or bank employee, she thought about shops, the dairy or possibly even a waitress in a dining room. But she would have preferred a job that kept her out of doors; she had had enough of being cooped up in the house to last her a lifetime she had decided.

But right now, she was just a schoolgirl, making her way to school with her pals. Work – or, rather, paid work – was something for the future.

Paddy, sitting in the hayloft with his pal Tommy Chee, was eating his snap in the twenty minutes allowed by the dairy. He and Tommy often took their carry-out up there, to keep out of the way of the milk cart drivers. Tommy was Chinese and though he had been born and bred in Liverpool, some of the men made crude jokes about his father cooking rats, lizards and other disgusting things for the family meals, and pretended that Tommy could only speak pidgin English. They also thought it amusing to set the two boys tasks which prevented them from having a sit-down while they ate their carry-out. They had tried various tricks on Paddy when he first came to work there, sending him off to the hardware shop to buy three-penn'orth of square holes, or a couple of yards of scotch mist, but Paddy would have none of it. 'You must think I were born yesterday,' he had said scornfully. 'If you mess wi' me you'll find yourself deliverin' watered milk, or that old dobbin you drive will cast a shoe just when you're in a hurry to get back to the bleedin' dairy. So it's your choice, me dear old mates. Leave me alone or live to regret to it, right?'

They had not liked it, of course, and one or two of the younger men had tried to take him on at his own game, but Paddy was too streetwise to be taken in for long and very soon the jokers were regretting their actions, as he had said they would.

Tommy Chee, however, had led a far more sheltered existence. He was the youngest of seven brothers, sons of the owner of a Chinese laundry on the Smithdown Road. Because he was the youngest there was no job for him in the laundry and besides, he had been keen to work at the dairy, longing for some independence from his close-knit, almost smothering family. The Chinese were known to be hard-working, clean and tidy, and Tommy must have known that he stood a good chance of getting the job be wanted; at any rate he told Paddy he wanted to work in the dairy because he thought it quite possible that he might rise to a managerial position in a few years. Mrs Briggs, who owned the business, had no children and was already in her late sixties. Clearly, there would be an opening there for a bright lad and Tommy was very bright indeed.

However, he had not reckoned with having to start on the very lowest rung of the ladder, actually in the shippon. He was not fond of animals and hated the work of mucking out morning and night, though he had grown accustomed to the chores of feeding, changing bedding and other such tasks.

Neither had he reckoned with the drivers' coarse sense of humour and, until Paddy had come to work there, had spent a good deal of his time running fruitless errands and being mocked and derided by men who should have known better. He had tried to take all such teasing in good part, but Paddy's championship had come just in time to stop him throwing in the sponge, sick and tired of the constant barracking. So when Paddy made it clear that he would not allow his pal to be bullied he was only too delighted to have found such a friend and, although he was the older by more than a year, he hero-worshipped Paddy and would have done anything in his power for the younger boy.

So when, sitting in the hayloft, Paddy remarked that later on he would be forced into helping to shell shrimps for the Logan family instead of having his evening to himself, Tommy volunteered at once to give a hand. 'I've shelled shrimps at home, for me mam and dad,' he assured his friend. 'I'm quick at things like that – we all are, all us boys – so mebbe wi' the two of us we could get through it in half the time. Then we could walk on the beach, or see if we can find someone playin' pitch and toss.'

Like most of his race, Tommy was a gambler, though not an obsessive one. He would put money on a horse, or on the dogs, and he would bet on which of two snails would crawl up a wall first, but he never went too far. He never gambled with money he could not afford to lose for a start and in Paddy's book that meant merely that he liked a flutter, not that he was a true gambler. Unlike me mam, Paddy thought now, remembering the times that his mother had left the house with money in her pocket intending to buy food and had come home penniless, without so much as a slice of bread to show for her shopping trip. Still, she had improved no end since she had taken the job with the Logans.

But right now they were talking about peeling shrimps, not pitch and toss. Paddy was thankful that he himself was not a gambler, was not even interested in such things, so pitch and toss was not his favourite way of spending an evening. He took a big bite of food and considered Tommy's offer. It was a good one. Picking over the shrimps would be a good deal more fun with a pal beside you, someone to grin at and have a laugh with. 'That 'ud be grand, though you'll have to put up with horrible Amy, the youngest Logan gal,' Paddy said through a mouthful of bread and jam. 'She's a mean one if you like. Always on at me, criticisin', findin' fault, sayin' I've left the legs on half the perishin' shrimps when I done no such thing. Nasty little red-haired beast; I dunno how me mam puts up wi' the gal, honest to God I don't. Now her sister Mary was different . . . oh, different as shrimps and sparrers. Pretty as a picture, wi' lovely golden hair and the bluest eyes . . . I were sweet on her, truth to tell.'

'Will she be there?' Tommy asked hopefully. 'She sounds more fun than her sister, that I will grant you.'

'No, Mary went into service in Manchester, as a parlour maid or some such thing, and she hardly ever comes home no more. Don't know as I blame her, though it seems a rum thing not to visit your parents save once in a twelve-month. But goin' back to the shrimps, Tommy, many hands make light work, so no doubt we'll finish miles quicker wi' you as well as me a-pickin'. In fact, we should have some time to ourselves when the shrimps is done, so what about a bit of night fishin' afore you goes home?'

Tommy took a swig of milk from the tin mug at his side and considered. He was a good-looking boy, with the soot-black, straight hair of his race, brilliant black eyes and skin that was a smooth, very pale golden-brown. Despite his name and parentage, Paddy thought he looked only slightly oriental and of course, as soon as he opened his mouth one forgot his antecedents entirely, for his voice, expression and mannerisms were pure Liverpool. Right now, he was clearly tempted by the thought of a night's fishing on the beach, for the weather was still very good for September and, judging by the clear blue sky, the night was likely to be fine and moonlit. What was more, September was an excellent month for fishing and the Chees, Paddy knew, were extremely fond of fresh fish.

'Well?' Paddy said, when Tommy went on staring into space and chewing thoughtfully. 'Are you game for a bit o' night fishin'? It 'ud be a rare old lark, Tommy boy, and it seems ages since I had a lark. The trouble is, once you leave school there ain't much time for larkin' about. So what do you say?'

Tommy swallowed the last of his bread and jam, folded up the piece of greaseproof paper in which his food had been wrapped and pushed it into his pocket. Then he dusted his hands together and smiled apologetically at his friend. 'I'll come and shell shrimps wi' you, but I can't come night fishin,' he said. 'Me mam's a born worrier, bless her, and me dad's almost as bad. They won't fret if I'm home by nine, even though it'll be dark, but they'd have the scuffers out searchin' for a missin' lad if I were much later. If there was some way of lettin' them know . . .'

But there was not and both boys knew it. If the drivers had been friendlier or more reliable, they could have sent a message by Joe Coutts who lived in Thornycroft Road and had to pass the Chee laundry on his way home. Old Joe wasn't a bad sort and very likely would have popped a letter or a note through the letter box in the front door, if Tommy had asked him to do so, but you never knew. Joe was rather simple and if he had been persuaded by one of the other drivers that it would be more amusing to chuck the letter into the nearest bin, then Tommy would be in real trouble at home and neither boy wanted that.

'Oh, well, it was a thought,' Paddy said, getting to his feet and heading for the ladder which led down into the stables below. 'But you'll still come and shell shrimps? Me mam will give you tea, a'course, and it'll be a good one.' He grinned sideways at his friend. 'Only the best for me pal, I'll tell me mam. A nice slice o' fried rat, garnished wi' beetles . . .'

Tommy tried to grab him; Paddy dodged and flew for the ladder. Swearing and scuffling, the two boys made their way back to the offices where they would be told what their next job was to be.

Mary was having an afternoon off and spending it with her friend Josie in the park. They meant to have their tea out and then to visit the theatre, which was showing a tragedy, *La Dame aux Camélias*, that both girls were keen to see. In their opinion there was nothing like a good cry to set one up for a happy day out. But now, having bought and eaten a cream-ice each, they were killing time and enjoying both their leisure and the lovely sunshine, until such time as they were hungry enough to make their way to the

Kardomah Café for the high tea they had planned before the visit to the theatre.

Mary was lying on her stomach, searching for four-leaf clovers and watching an ant busily making its way through what must seem to it to be a great forest of grass blades. It was an idyllic afternoon and she was almost asleep, when Josie spoke: 'Mary, why don't you go home when you get a bit of time off? You've worked for the Cottlestones for an age, but you only seem to go home for a day or so, no longer. Don't your mam and dad ask why not? Oh, I know some girls have rotten homes and bad parents, and naturally they ain't keen to go back; you don't often talk about your dad and your mam and even your brothers and sister ... but you seem fond enough of 'em. It's only natural to wanna spend all your time with your young man.'

'I've got a stepmother,' Mary said briefly. She liked Josie but had made it a rule never to discuss her home life, except in the vaguest of terms. Even admitting to a stepmother was a concession and she was vaguely surprised that she had told Josie about her brothers and sister. Then she remembered the letters, and supposed that Josie had noticed how frequently Amy wrote and had guessed the sisters were fond of one another. Whatever her faults, Amy was a pretty good correspondent. She was still at school, of course, but Mary guessed that Suzie worked her sister pretty hard whenever she wasn't actually in class, yet Amy still found time to write to her at least once a week and now and then, perhaps every other month, Bill also dropped her a line in his large, ill-educated scrawl. Mary supposed, now, that Josie must have taken a good peek at the envelopes – she always destroyed the contents, once read – and put two and two together and rather neatly made four.

'Oh? I didn't know you had a stepmother, but wouldn't it be nice to see that sister of yourn? And ain't there a baby, too? You like babies; think what you're missin' by never goin' home.'

'My dad's a fisherman and the house always smells of fish,' Mary said without thinking. 'It makes me sick, that smell. And ... and when I'm home they'll expect me to clean the bleedin' fish and gut them, and shell the shrimps and dress crabs ... Anyway, I will go home next time they give me a week or so off. Probably.'

'Well, I don't understand you,' grumbled Josie. She was a pretty girl, with a neat figure, and long, dark hair, which waved luxuriantly away from a high, white forehead. She and Mary, one so dark, the other so fair, were perfect foils for one another and were well aware of it. Young men, they knew, were fascinated by such opposites, not that this mattered much to either of them. Josie had a 'steady', a well set-up young fellow who was gentleman's gentleman, or valet, to a rich industrialist. He and Josie were saving hard and meant to marry in a year or two so, as far as Mary was concerned, Josie was the ideal friend. They were able to go out and enjoy meeting young men without ever wanting to form relationships with them.

Mary had met a young bank clerk when she had first gone to work in Manchester. His name was Roderick Campbell and, like Mary, he was a stranger in the city, having arrived there only a few weeks before they met. He was from Scotland and was working for Scott and Burrows Bank, whose main headquarters were in Glasgow. However, the

132

branch in Spring Gardens was a big one, with plenty of opportunity for advancement if you were a young man with ambition, which Roderick certainly was.

Mary often suspected that the reason Roderick was not willing to talk much about their relationship was due to that very ambition. He thought it beneath him to be going steady with a housemaid, and Mary knew that had she not been both extremely pretty and very smart, she would not have held him for long. So instead of going home for her holidays, she usually took on some part-time paid employment, to help to keep her in the smart clothes and shoes which Roderick admired. Mary did not think that Roderick liked smart clothes for themselves, he liked the impression they made upon other people. Folk meeting him when he was out with Mary would never have guessed that she was a humble housemaid. They would have taken her, she thought proudly, for a sales assistant in one of the smart shops on King Street, or perhaps even for a fellow worker in Roderick's bank, since they were a go-ahead firm who employed some female clerks.

On two evenings a week Roderick went to night school to study for examinations which would enable him to apply for a better-paid position in the banking world. He was already doing better than most young men of his age, but often told Mary that his career was only beginning; once he had the exams he needed he would forge ahead, right to the top, if such a thing were possible.

Perhaps Mary was infected by Roderick's ambition, but it was certainly true that she very soon realised she would have to keep pace with her young man if she wanted to marry him one day and be a credit to him. So Mary, in her turn, began to go

133

to evening classes a couple of times a week. She enjoyed domestic service, but would not have hesitated to leave and get a job in a shop or an office, where her good appearance and quick intelligence would have been more appreciated than they were in the Cottlestone household. However, the Cottlestone lifestyle would have been way beyond the means of a shop girl or office worker, no matter how ambitious. Mary enjoyed having good food provided, which she did not have to cook, having her own little room in the attic, with a soft bed and a wardrobe full of uniforms, which were laundered for her along with the rest of the Cottlestones' linen. She loved the beautiful furniture, carpets and curtains by which she was surrounded, and did not fancy changing all this luxury for a shared bed-sitting room, in some sleazy back street, which would have been her lot had she not taken to domestic service.

So Mary studied English Literature, because she had always loved reading, and the French language, since she had a hazy idea that French might be useful to her, should she ever become a lady's maid, or seek employment in an office.

Fond though she was of Roderick, Mary had few illusions about him. He would have been astonished had he known how few. And because she was ambitious and also down-to-earth, she had never told Roderick that she was a fisherman's daughter. She had not told him either that she knew Philip Grimshaw, because that would have meant revealing her humble origins.

When she had first come to Manchester, Mary had been walking in the square garden enjoying the spring sunshine, when a voice had hailed her.

Turning to the sound of her name, she had seen a tall young man, in a brightly striped blazer and cricketing flannels peering at her through the railings. Hesitantly, for she knew no one in Manchester apart from the other servants in the Cottlestone house, she had walked towards the young man and had been astonished to recognise Philip Grimshaw. Indeed, at first she could scarcely believe her eyes, for the last time she had seen him must have been quite two years before on the Seaforth beach. She remembered *that* Philip clearly enough, with his hair rumpled by the breeze and his trouser legs rolled above the knee, but this Philip was a young gentleman, though his smile was as friendly and unassuming as it had been on the day of the King's coronation. In fact, so unaffected was he, so friendly and natural, that Mary had no hesitation in returning his greeting. 'Well, if it isn't Philip Grimshaw,' she said, not trying to hide her astonishment. 'Whatever are you doing here, Philip?'

'I live here,' Philip answered, grinning. 'What about you though, Mary? You really *are* a long way from home.'

'Not really; I live here as well now,' Mary had told him and proceeded to explain all about her job with the Cottlestones. Some young men, on finding that she was a housemaid in the home of a neighbouring family, might have dropped the acquaintance forthwith, but Philip clearly never considered such a thing. In fact, he went out of his way to be kind to Mary, always greeting her in a friendly fashion when their paths crossed, and something in his glance made Mary suspect that he admired as well as liked her. Had things been different ...

So in the back of Mary's mind, whenever she

thought about her future, there was the tiny almost unacknowledged hope that one day, if she and Roderick did not marry, she might get to know Philip a little better.

But this was only dreaming and Mary had never mentioned to anyone that she knew Philip Grimshaw. What was more, although Philip was perfectly polite when they met, this was seldom and, in her heart of hearts, Mary knew that she was nothing to him and never would be.

'I'm gettin' a trifle peckish,' Josie remarked suddenly, bringing Mary abruptly back to earth and out of her pleasant daydream. 'Whatever were you thinkin' about, Mary? You looked all daft and soppy for a moment.'

'Oh, just fellers and that,' Mary said vaguely. She sat up and began to brush bits of grass off her clean pink blouse. 'I could do with a snack myself, now you mention it; let's go.'

Amy was not having a good day, which was strange because the weather was lovely and Evie O'Brien had a wonderful new skipping rope, with real painted wooden handles. Of course, it could not improve one's skipping and was really no better than an orange box rope, but there was something about the sensation of the rounded wooden handles nestling in their palms which made the girls feel as efficient as any circus performer.

Evie let everyone have a go and, because it was such a lovely day and the autumn term had only just begun, Miss Musgrove allowed the girls to stay in the playground for an extra half-hour, which was a great treat. Yet even as they played, jumped rope and sang the innumerable skipping songs, which every girl knew as well as she knew her own name, Amy felt uneasy.

The day had not started well, of course. Mrs Keagan had been late arriving to take care of baby Becky, so Amy had had to run all the way to school and had arrived just as Miss Musgrove was calling the register. Amy had slid breathlessly into her seat beside Ruth, who had hissed, 'Where *was* you? I waited for ages but you never come, so I had to run meself, an' only got in 'alf a minute before you. The Muzzle won't 'arf give it to us!'

It was unfortunate that 'The Muzzle' should have looked up just as Amy was, in her turn, telling Ruth why she herself had been late. The teacher said sharply, 'What was that, Amy Logan? Kindly give the class the benefit of your explanation as to your late arrival.'

Amy, with a hot face, had mumbled that she was very sorry, but the babyminder had been late arriving. 'Baby is only seven months, so I can't very well leave her alone in the house,' she explained. 'But I ran all the way, miss, honest to God I did.'

Miss Musgrove gave Amy a hard look over the top of her little gold-framed glasses. 'Please don't take the name of the Lord in vain,' she said briskly. 'And why didn't you take the baby round to the childminder, miss? Wouldn't that have solved the problem?'

It would have, of course, but Amy knew from bitter experience what happened if the baby went to the Keagans' place. Granny Keagan promptly took over the care of the child, Suzie Keagan took herself off on any excuse and, when Amy got home, the house would be precisely as she had left it, with the breakfast things still on the table, the fire very likely dead, and no preparations for supper even begun. Naturally, however, she could not say any of this to Miss Musgrove. Instead she mumbled that in future ... and hoped that Miss Musgrove, who was in reality a very understanding person, would let it go at that.

'We was lucky not to get order marks,' Ruth remarked later that morning, as they sat companionably on the low brick wall which divided the coke tip from the playground. 'Old Muzzle must ha' bin in a good mood on account o' the sunshine. It were lucky she didn't pick on me as well, since she'd say waitin' for a pal was no excuse for lateness.'

'It was the whispering which got her goat,' Amy said wisely, 'rather than us nearly being late. After all, *nearly* doing a thing isn't wrong, it's not doing it at all which they get you for. I mean, if I were to nearly tip you into the coke pile, you wouldn't have a mark on you, whereas if I gave you a good shove ...'

The two girls wrestled half-heartedly on the wall, then they linked arms in perfect amity and began to walk round the perimeter of the playground, chatting as they went. Amy had confided her vague discontent with the day and, even as she spoke, had suddenly known the cause. She stopped short, grabbing Ruth's arm so hard that Ruth gave a squeak of dismay, which Amy ignored. 'It's the shrimps!' she said triumphantly. 'It's fine weather, Dad and the fellers were out at the crack o' dawn, so the chances are they'll be home around three, with sacks of bleedin' shrimps. Oh, Gawd, Ruthie, and we'll spend the whole evening shelling the little buggers.'

Ruth, whose main knowledge of shrimps came

from picking over a handful and eating them between two rounds of bread, giggled. 'I dunno why you hates peelin' shrimps so much,' she observed. 'You was sayin' only the other day that Suzie never pinches any of the money you get for potted shrimps. You said that no one checks what you gets for loose shrimps what you sells from door to door, so you an' Bertie can keep back a penny or two for the things your dad won't shell out for.' She giggled again. 'Did you hear that, Amy, shell out! That were a joke.'

'Oh, aye,' Amy said gloomily. 'Very funny I'm sure, particularly if it isn't you who gets to shell the bloody things. Oh, Ruthie, I do hate it. Still, if I play my cards right I'll mebbe get out of it this once. After all, I work like a perishin' dog to keep things right. Why should I shell shrimps and all?'

Ruthie, still giggling, remarked that shelling shrimps was a regular tongue twister. 'Like sister Susie shelling shrimps for sailors,' she said. 'Though why sailors should want selled shrimps . . . oh, shelled. Oh, hang it, you knows what I mean.'

This made Amy laugh and presently the bell rang and they had to go back to class, but although Amy joined with the rest of the girls in tackling the long division sums which the teacher chalked on the blackboard, her mind continued to plot how she would avoid picking the shrimps.

When school was over she and Ruthie set off briskly for home. Amy went breezily into the kitchen, where the baby was grizzling on the hearthrug and Mrs Keagan was desultorily scraping carrots, and asked if there were any messages. Suzie looked up. 'Change the baby before you does anything else,' she said at once. 'I been meaning to do it, but somehow something else always crops up. I went round to Elm Road and got some scrag end for a stew, and then I remembered your Dad said he'd likely be bringin' fish home. Still an' all, you can get mighty tired of fish when you've had a good season, and I know your dad and the boys are mortal fond of a scrag end stew.'

Amy went straight to the rag rug on the floor where the baby was struggling to sit up. At the sight of Amy she beamed broadly, showing two tiny pearly teeth, and held up her arms. Amy whisked the child off the rug, wrinkling her nose as the smell of stale urine, and worse, assailed her nostrils. There was a pile of clean nappies on the dresser and she snatched one up as she passed, then took the baby with her into the little low scullery and laid her on the shrimping table, where the shrimps were dealt with once they had been boiled. She whipped the sodden nappy off and dropped it into the wooden bucket half full of salty water kept for the purpose. Then she poured clean water into an enamel bowl, seized a worn scrap of towelling and got to work.

Ten minutes later a clean and happy baby was set down once more on the rag rug, this time with a piece of oven-dried bread in one hand. 'That seems to have shut her up,' Suzie said without turning round. 'She's bin squalling this past hour or more; enough to drive you crazy.'

'She doesn't cry when she's clean,' Amy pointed out. 'You didn't oughter leave her dirty, Mrs Keagan, she gets awfully sore and that makes her bad-tempered. I can't see why you don't change her regularly for your own sake, if not hers. She's a good kid, but you can't expect her to be happy when she's in pain.'

Suzie sniffed. 'I got all the work of this house to do,' she said. 'I did oughter have help wi' the littl'un. It's all right when it's school holidays and you can give a hand, but what'll I do when she's walkin' an' gettin' into everythin'? I'll have to speak to your dad.'

Amy, who was even now considering speaking to her dad about the state the baby was getting into, sighed. Bill was proud of his little daughter and fond of her too, but knew nothing about the care of young babies. He would not understand that clean nappies, several times a day, were necessary for the baby's comfort. I'll have to find a way of blackmailing Suzie into doing right by the kid, Amy decided. Even as the thought crossed her mind, however, she knew she was being unfair. Suzie had many faults, but neglecting the baby was not one of them. Amy knew this to be true, but nevertheless she felt angry with the older woman. Lately Suzie had left the midday nappy change for Amy to deal with, which meant that Becky's nappy area was usually in a bad state by the time Amy got back from school. She glanced at the clock above the mantel. Any minute now the men would return home, trundling the handcart laden with sacks of shrimps. If she was to escape, she would have to find an excuse to do so pretty quickly; she glanced at the baby and made up her mind.

She picked up Becky, settled her comfortably on her hip and made for the back door. 'The poor little beggar's got running sores on her little bum,' she said as she left the house. 'I'm takin' her up to the pharmacy to see what Mr Keir can give me for her.' She did not linger to give Suzie the opportunity of saddling her with other messages, but walked briskly down Seafield Grove and turned left into Crosby Road. When she reached the corner of Elm Drive she turned into it, already aware that she had been foolish to rush out in such a hurry. Becky was getting heavier and was far easier to carry in the loop of a shawl – better still, if she had thought of it, was the ancient wooden cart which the boys used when collecting driftwood. However, that was what happened when you let your temper get the better of you and had she lingered for even a moment, Suzie would undoubtedly have added to her errands.

The pharmacist had a neat shop front on Elm Road, the window decorated by two enormous glass flagons, one filled with a brilliant red liquid and the other with green. Many a time, when her mother had been alive, Amy and Albert had played around outside the shop, while Isobel went in. If you got the right distance from the window and then slowly walked towards it, you could see strange reflections of yourself, either bright red or bright green, looming and leering in the glass. When she had been very small, Amy had thought the liquid in the flagons had some sort of magic which made a small girl appear to be hugely fat, scrawnily thin, or strangely mishapen, but Isobel had briskly disabused her of this idea. 'It's only coloured water in those jars,' she had informed her children. 'Water and glass, when they get together, act like one of those mirrors at the fair, the sort that make you die laughing at your reflection.'

Despite knowing that there was nothing wonderful in the green and red jars, Amy lingered by the window a moment, moving her head from side to side and grinning as her small nose grew as long as a duck's bill one minute and shrank to a button the next. She tried to interest the baby in the reflections, but Becky merely gurgled and went on clutching at a hank of Amy's hair, wound securely and rather painfully round her small and chubby fist.

Inside the shop Mrs Keir was sitting behind the counter, knitting something in soft pink wool. She looked up and smiled when Amy entered and got to her feet. 'What can I do for you, young Amy? Baby not well?'

Presently Amy left the shop once more, with a fat tube of cream for the baby's sores and a rather dusty liquorice stick for herself. She liked Mrs Keir, but reflected that for some reason, liquorice bought – or given – at the pharmacy, always tasted a bit like medicine, whereas liquorice bought at the sweetshop on the other side of the road was unmistakably a treat.

She did her best to linger on the way home, but Becky was too heavy for her to hang around for long. She wondered whether to go round to Ruth's, but the impulse to get out of the house – and away from the task of shelling shrimps – was leaving her. What was the point, after all? If she went back now she would make a pot of tea and spread some bread with margarine and jam, and she could be comfortably fed before the task began.

She was just turning off Crosby Road when she saw, ahead of her, a couple of lads. She recognised Paddy, even from the back, and groaned inwardly; despite the fact that his mother worked for them he was still as rude and nasty to her as ever. Indeed, he had more opportunity now, since his mother made him come in and help shell shrimps or gut fish when the catch was good. Amy was glad that he seemed to dislike the task as much as she did, and also glad that her father had resisted Suzie's blatant attempts to get him to take Paddy aboard the *Mersey Maid* as another hand. 'One boy is all I can cope with for now,' Bill had said gruffly, when Suzie's suggestions that he should employ her son became perilously close to demands. 'There ain't the room for more than the three of us and that's the truth, Mrs Keagan. But if Gus ever decides to move on . . .'

The matter had rested there, but Amy guessed that Paddy himself would have preferred life aboard the boat to the dairy on Dryden Street and was meanly glad that he had been rejected. He might get nicer if he had to muck out cows and cart heavy milk churns for a few years, she thought. And then there were deliveries. He might get called in to work on the milk carts and in winter, when they went off in the dark and cold of early morning, he wouldn't be too keen on that.

She reached the jigger at the back of the house and turned into it. Moments later, she opened the back door and went into the kitchen. The small scullery was to her left, and already she could hear the boys scuffling themselves round the table. Gus helped with the shelling, despite being almost a man, so did Albert and herself, of course, and even Suzie occasionally lent a hand, but Bill held aloof. He was the skipper of the boat, after all, and did most of the gutting and cleaning of the fish, and besides, there was really only room round the table for six at the most. So Amy skipped into the kitchen and sat the baby down on the rug, surrounded by cushions; then she went over and took a slice from the plateful of bread and jam, which Suzie – miracle of miracles – must have prepared when she realised that Amy would not be back in time to do so. Only then did she go into the scullery.

Gus, Albert and Paddy were already seated at the table, with a great glistening pile of shrimps in front of them, but seated beside Paddy was a stranger. He was tall and thin with dark hair cut in a fringe across his forehead and liquid black eyes which, when he glanced at Amy, sparkled with amusement. He was shelling shrimps with amazing speed, scarcely seeming to need to glance down at his work, for his thin, strong fingers continued to pick the shrimps, even while he was looking up at Amy. A second glance at the stranger confirmed that he was not English, though Amy could not have said with any accuracy from which country he had come. His skin was a very pale golden brown and, though his eyes were almond-shaped, they were not slitted, like those of many Chinese, nor was his skin dark enough to lead her to believe him of Indian blood.

However, it was none of her business where the boy came from. She slid along the bench and settled opposite him, beside Gus, who was working away stolidly, head bent, shoulders rigid with effort, for the tiny, finicky movement necessary for peeling shrimps was harder for Gus's big, clumsy fingers than for the smaller ones of the younger members of the family.

Amy picked up a shrimp and began to peel, kicking Albert under the table as she did so. 'Who's your pal?' she enquired, low-voiced.

Paddy looked up and grinned maliciously. 'He ain't Albert's pal, he's mine,' he said. 'Tommy, that there's 'orrible Amy, what I've telled you about. This is Tommy Chee, me bezzie at the dairy.'

To Amy's amazement Tommy promptly held out

145

a thin hand, smiling at her as though, she thought, he was in the Queen's bleedin' drawing room instead of the shrimp scullery. However, they shook hands and grinned at each other, before Amy turned back to Paddy. 'If I'm 'orrible Amy, then that there's perishin' Paddy,' she said composedly, continuing to peel shrimps. 'Why are you helping us, Tommy? You're awful good at it, I could see that at a glance, but it isn't a job as many people want. If I could get out of it, I'd never peel another perishin' shrimp all my life long.'

'Oh, I don't mind it,' Tommy said easily. 'Many hands make light work, they say. Besides, Paddy an' me's going to take a walk up the Scottie, get ourselves a paper of chips, when the shrimps is done.'

'Right.' Amy told herself she was not particularly interested in Paddy's friend or in what they intended to do that evening. What mattered to her was getting the shrimps peeled, so that she could have a good wash and get to bed early for once. Suzie went home when they had had supper, which meant that a good many other chores, such as washing up and damping down the fire for the night, would fall to Amy's lot. Bill sometimes took pity on her and told her to run off to bed, saying he would finish her chores for her, and Albert did his share by drying the dishes and bringing in water for the morning. But even so, Amy usually got to bed late and worn out. But this evening it was clear that the shrimps would be finished betimes. Amy had been doing them for years now, and had never seen anyone work with the speed and efficiency which Tommy brought to the task. She began to copy him, modelling her movements on his and, in an amazingly short space of time the shrimps were finished, the empty shells disposed of and the little pink curls of shrimp flesh placed in the big black cauldron, ready for potting.

'I'll have me supper when I get back,' Gus said, eagerly jumping to his feet. He was courting a girl who lived in Rawson Road and knew that Peggy's mother would be glad to feed him if he and Peggy meant to go out for the evening. Gus turned and grinned at the younger ones. 'Thanks, kids. See you later, Dad.'

Supper tonight was the scrag end stew, with mounds of potatoes and carrots. This was followed by apple pie and Amy stared covertly at Tommy, as they sat down to eat. On hearing his name, she had guessed he was of Chinese origin and wondered whether he ate ordinary food, as well as the rats and small dogs, to say nothing of cats, which rumour and hearsay had attributed to them. It was soon obvious that Tommy was well used to ordinary British food, however. He tucked in with the rest and congratulated Mrs Keagan on the apple pie, which made Amy smirk; she knew Granny's pastry when she tasted it.

Bill walked over to the fire and stood with his back to it, warming himself. 'If young Paddy's off out with his pal, I'd better walk Mrs Keagan home when she's finished with the washing up,' he said. with studied casualness, which did not fool Amy for one moment. 'You'll keep an ear open for the littl'un, won't you, Amy?'

Amy nodded, but raised her brows at this, pulling a face. Her father never walked Suzie home – why should he? She only lived at the end of the road, no more than thirty yards further along the pavement, so she assumed that Bill had something to say to Suzie, which he did not want the rest of the family to hear. She devoutly hoped that he intended to give old Suzie a good telling off, for surely by now Bill would have realised that Suzie shirked her work and gave poor value for money? She wondered if she might sneak quietly out and hide in the back jigger to hear what Bill wanted to say, but Albert put the lid on any such plan by suggesting that he and she might accompany Tommy and Paddy up the Scottie and have a paper of chips on their own account.

'Dad won't be two minutes, takin' the old girl home,' Albert said, lowering his voice to a whisper. 'And baby Becky's asleep, so she won't bother. What do you say, Amy?'

Amy's hopes of an early night promptly disappeared. A walk in the dark up to the shops, a bag of chips and some light-hearted banter was just what she needed. But suppose her father decided to pop into the Keagans' house, or took longer than usual for some reason? She guessed that Albert would want to leave at once and she could not risk baby Becky waking to find herself alone in the house. 'Oh, but we can't leave the baby . . .' she began, only to be interrupted by Bill, emerging from the fish scullery.

'That's all right, chuck,' he said heartily, 'I dare say Mrs Keagan can see herself safe home if I go into the road and watch till she reaches her door. You go off and enjoy yourselves.' He delved into his pocket, producing some coins which he held out to them. 'Here, buy yourselves a bottle of ginger beer to drink wi' your chips.'

Amy took the coins, thanking her father profusely, and presently the four of them made their way along the road, all thinking gleefully of the bright lights ahead and the fun they could have, since they had finished early for once.

It was getting on for ten o'clock when Albert and Amy made their way back along Seafield Grove. Paddy had decided to walk part of the way home with Tommy but though Albert said he would very much like to accompany them, he felt the walk would be too much for Amy's shorter legs.

'If you think them linen poles is short,' Paddy growled, 'then you's is madder than old Ma McGregor. The gal looks as though she's on stilts. Still an' all, gals ain't got no stamina, I grant you that. Why not let her go home, whiles you come wi' us? No one ain't goin' to interfere wi' a beanpole like young Amy here.'

Amy bristled and gave as good as she got. 'I dunno how you dare say things about my legs, which you've hardly seen, when your ugly face is on view all the time and enough to turn the milk sour,' she said briskly. 'Can't you find nothing else to do than to be rude to your betters? I'm a lady, but if I weren't I'd thump you on your bloody snout.'

'Oh, very ladylike,' Paddy sneered.

But Tommy, though he was grinning, tugged at his friend's sleeve. 'You've gorra give her best, old son,' he said. 'Ta-ra Albert, Amy. Been nice meetin' you. See you again some time.'

'I hope you do see us again, 'cos you're the quickest shrimp picker I ever did meet,' Amy called over her shoulder, as she and her brother headed for home. The chips were all eaten, but there was quite half a bottle of ginger beer left and they shared the drink, turn and turn about, until Albert drained the last drop as they entered the jigger.

'It's been a grand evening, Albert,' Amy said gratefully, as they made their way across the cobbled yard. 'Thanks ever so much for taking me along.'

'That's all right.' Albert opened the back door and ushered her inside. 'It were good of Dad to keep an eye on the baby for you an' all.' He glanced round the empty kitchen. 'Think he's gone to bed?'

'Not likely, it isn't even ten yet,' Amy said, glancing at the clock above the mantel. 'Mebbe he's nipped out back for a jimmy riddle. No, he can't have done that, the lamp's still on the hook by the door.'

'I dare say Becky woke,' Albert observed, glancing towards the stairs. 'I'll pull the kettle over the fire, then we can all have a drink before we goes to bed.' He chuckled. 'It'll be a change for our dad not to have a pint to send him to sleep, but he's never been one for havin' drink in the house, so it'll have to be tea.'

Amy stared round-eyed at her brother. 'Do you mean that he goes out to the pub every night?' she enquired incredulously. 'Mary told me he wasn't Temperance and hadn't signed the pledge, but she said he wasn't a drinking man either.'

'Nor he is,' Albert said stoutly. 'But he's only human, Amy. Fishing's a hard job and he likes a bit o' company, apart from us kids, I mean, so he goes down to the pub and meets his pals and has a pint or two. What's wrong with that?'

'I dunno.' Amy's, illusions of her father's character were crumbling round her ears. 'Does he get drunk, Albert? Only I'm never up when he gets back, or not often anyway.'

'One beer don't make a feller drunk,' Albert told her. 'It's the company he goes to the pub for, not the drink. There ain't a better man livin' than our dad, queen, even Mam never grudged him the odd drink now and then just to relax, like. Now she's gone and he's got all the responsibility and that, it's a wonder he don't take more than a glass. Ah, hear that? I said he were probably givin' an eye to baby.'

Sure enough, Amy heard the sound of feet crossing the bedroom and beginning to descend the stairs, and presently her father, looking very self-conscious, entered the room. He looked across at them, and it struck Amy that there was a flush on his cheeks and a glittering brightness in his eyes, but before she had done more than notice the fact, someone else came down the stairs. It was Mrs Keagan, pink-faced and bright-eyed, with her hair, which was usually pulled back from her face, tumbling about her shoulders and her blouse done up on the wrong buttons.

Amy, never renowned for her tact, said blankly, 'Wharron earth ...? I thought you said you were seeing Mrs Keagan home when we left for our chips, Dad.'

'Oh aye.' Bill turned to stare at the woman beside him. 'But we ... that's to say ...'

'The baby woke,' Suzie said brightly. 'Anyhow, your dad's got something to say to you.' Her glance, Amy saw, was defiant and even as she looked, Suzie reached down and took Bill's hand in a possessive grasp. 'Go on, Bill,' she urged, 'tell 'em'.

Bill took a deep, steadying breath. 'I've asked Mrs Keagan to be me wife,' he said bluntly, 'and she's accepted. We'll be wed before Christmas and all one big, happy family. And now, since the two of youse is home, I'll just walk Mrs Keagan – I mean Suzie –

151

back to her place, so's we can break the news to Paddy, Gran and Aunt Dolly.'

Neither Albert nor Amy said a word. They simply stared unbelievingly, as Bill got cap and coat off the back of the door and helped Suzie to throw her shawl round her shoulders. Then the two of them left, with only a valedictory wave from Bill, and a gloating and glittering smile from Suzie.

'Well, I'm buggered!' Albert said slowly, as the sound of his father's footsteps faded. 'Who'd have thought it, our Amy? What'll happen, d'you suppose? They can't all move in here, that's for sure. Well, I suppose Paddy could share with us boys, but there's nowhere for Gran and Aunt Dolly. Your room's a squeeze for you and Becky ain't it, and Mary, when she's home? I suppose they'll keep both houses on, even though it's double the rent.'

'He can't do it! Living in the same house with *her* and having Paddy here all the time, would be hell on earth,' Amy stated vehemently. 'Do married people always live in the same house? Couldn't they be married and still stay the way they are right now?'

Albert sighed at her ignorance but shook his head decisively. 'Course not. Married folk don't just live in the same house, they sleep in the same bed. Remember what it says in the Bible about the pro . . . procreation of children? You've gorra sleep in the same bed to do the procreatin' bit,' he ended.

On the other side of the kitchen the kettle began to hop and sizzle. Amy crossed the room automatically and made a pot of tea, set out three mugs and went to the milk jug in the scullery. When she had made three cups of tea, she carried one over to the sofa and, sitting down, began gingerly to sip. Albert followed suit and for a long while the kitchen was silent as the two youngsters were lost in thought. Then Amy got to her feet, picked up the third cup of tea and tipped it into the slop bucket. When she spoke at last it was with little or none of the shock and bitterness she had shown earlier. 'Dad won't be wanting that,' she said heavily. 'This is going to change everything and not for the better, either. Oh, Albert, why couldn't things have stayed the same?'

Chapter Five

JANUARY 1908

Amy came out of the small house in Seafield Grove and gasped as the wind blew large cold flakes of snow against her warm face. She wrapped her scarf more tightly round her neck, then turned and headed along Crosby Road towards the tram terminus where she would presently catch the tram into the city centre. She was seldom unhappy to leave her home now, not since Bill's marriage, about three years previously, had given her a stepmother. It would not be fair to say that Suzie disliked Amy – but she certainly made use of her. Indeed, starting work had been, in a way, a relief.

Baby Becky had to rely on either Suzie herself or old Granny Keagan for her upbringing, because Amy was now out of the house from eight in the morning until seven in the evening. By that time, of course, Becky was safely tucked up in bed and, though Suzie left as much of the housework as she could for Amy to tackle, she had long ago realised that she must treat the younger girl reasonably, or Amy, who had a very strong will of her own, would manage to ignore any tasks set her.

But right now, hurrying towards the Rimrose Bridge with her head bent against the blizzard, Amy almost regretted leaving her home. The kitchen had been warm and cosy, the fire burning up brightly and Bill sitting before it, with a round of bread on a toasting fork held out to the flames. In weather such as this there was no point in even going down to the beach, let alone taking the boat out, so Bill would occupy himself with domestic tasks which needed doing and would then mend nets in the comfort of the kitchen.

Amy was almost at the tram stop, could actually see a tram about to depart, when a voice hailed her, shrieking above the wind: 'Hey, Amy! It *is* you, ain't it? My word, I've not clapped eyes on you for ages. How're you doin', queen?'

'Ruth!' Amy squeaked. She had not seen her old friend since Ruth had gone into service with a family in Southport. Somehow, when Ruth had been home Amy had always been at work, but she had heard rumours that her pal was sick of service and wanted a job where she could live at home. She had thought it would be grand to have Ruth back once more and now it looked as though the rumours had been true, for here she was, muffled in coat and scarf, heading for the tram terminus, as she was herself.

Trams, however, wait for no man. 'I've got to get on this tram, Ruthie,' Amy said breathlessly, raising her voice above the sound of the wind. 'It's a number 24 so it takes me all the way to Lime Street. Where are you going?'

'A number 24 will do me fine,' Ruth said, as the two of them scrambled aboard the waiting tram.

The conductor, blowing on his hands in their fingerless mittens, grinned at them. 'Hon you gets, young ladies,' he called cheerfully. 'Me driver's raring to go because, what with the slippery roads and the bleedin' snow blowin' in his face, we's almost bound to be late and the inspectors fair haunt this route in bad weather, hopin' to catch us out.' Another shrouded and bent figure, in the all-

155

enveloping shawl and draggly skirts of a street trader, came slogging towards the tram. She was struggling with a huge basket covered by a checked cloth and the conductor shouted to his driver, 'Wait onna moment, George, ole pal. This 'ere passenger needs a hand by the looks. Once the lady's aboard, you can go fast as you like.'

Amy smiled at the old woman as she was heaved on to the step and collapsed into the nearest seat. She recognised her as one of the women who sold flowers outside Lime Street Station, but could not imagine there would be much sale for such wares, even if she had managed to acquire flowers in this dreadful weather. Probably she was now selling oranges, apples and the like.

However, it was Ruthie's presence on the tram which interested her right now. She waited until they were seated and the tram had jerked into noisy motion, then turned to her old friend, who was removing her dark-blue headscarf and brushing snow off her shoulders. 'Ruthie! So you *are* home! Well, that's a piece of luck for me, I tell you straight. What with working at the fish market and doing all my stepmother's housework, keeping an eye on the kid and trying to see the boys don't go short, I've not made a friend of my own age since you left. It'll be grand to have you home again. But what are you doing on the workers' special? Don't say you've got a job already!'

Ruthie replaced her headscarf, tying it firmly under her chin, and smiled at Amy. She had not changed much in the years since she and Amy had been to school together, though her pale-brown hair was coiled into a low bun on the back of her neck and Amy suspected that a dusting of powder covered her friend's small, straight nose. 'Yes, I'm home for good. Two years of service is enough for anyone – not that they wasn't good to me in their way, but it weren't our way, Amy. It was all right while I had a young feller interested in marriage, but when he took up with the second parlour maid – oh, I dunno, I just wanted to come home and do a job of work which finished at a proper time, so's I wasn't always on call, like. And I have got another job, though it may only be temporary. But what's been happenin' to you, Amy? And the rest of the family, of course? Have you gorra feller?'

'Not so's you'd notice,' Amy said ruefully. 'As for the family, the boys and my dad are fine, and Becky's fine, and Mary seems to like service more than home life; at least she never comes back for more than a couple of days and even then she's raring to go back to Manchester just as soon as she can. She's got a feller, I believe, though she doesn't talk about him. As for me, I used to go to the dances at the Daulby Hall, but it wasn't much fun without a pal. Of course, I've been out with fellers from time to time – remember that Tommy Chee, Ruthie, the boy Paddy was friendly with? Him and me went to the theatre once or twice and last summer we went over the water a couple of times, but to tell you the truth, my dad didn't approve. It was stupid because we're just good pals, there's nothing in it really. Still he's a deal nicer than most of the fellers Paddy hangs out with. But I'm sorry about your feller, queen. Were you much upset?'

Ruth snorted. 'Upset? Over a two-timing bugger who thought if he played his cards right he could have the pair of us? No, chuck, I weren't upset so much as furious. In fact, now I've got over the shock

I pity Flo Williams – that's the gal's name – because it won't be long before he's seein' someone else on the sly. That's men all over for you. But you can put it down to experience I suppose.'

'It's experience I'm short of,' Amy said ruefully, glancing enviously at her friend's smooth prettiness. She could well imagine the sort of effect Ruth's cherubic countenance had had among the young men of Southport. 'Still, with you to go around with me, Ruthie, perhaps I'll begin to have some fun as well as working every hour God sends. Where did you say you had a job?'

'You know Dorothy's Dining Rooms on the corner of Rose and Elliot Streets? Well, I'm workin' in the kitchens there and doin' some waitin' on because they's several people away with influenza. This'll be me first day. Mrs Owen said I was to start this morning and work for at least three weeks, mebbe longer. She said it depends on me work and on whether everyone who's off ill comes back.'

'Well, I'm blowed!' Amy exclaimed, turning to beam at her friend. 'Those dining rooms are ever so popular, chuck. They're always crowded with folk from the offices, fellers poppin' in from the station when they want a quick bite before their train and, of course, with actors from the theatre – as well as one or two from the market, when they've a few pence to spare. Oh, Ruthie, it will be grand to have you so close! We'll be able to catch the same tram to and from work, and tell each other how our day has gone – so long as you don't mind the smell of fish,' she ended, sighing regretfully.

'You don't smell of fish,' Ruth said mildly. 'You never did, Amy, even when you were running the fish stall in the school holidays. But you always thought you did, I seem to recall,' she added with a reminiscent smile.

The tram, which despite the conductor's fears had done the journey in good time, swung into the terminus by the station and the girls, lifting their scarves to cover their mouths, climbed reluctantly down into the teeth of the blizzard. Amy looked across at St George's Plateau, where the snow was already lying in a thick white blanket, criss-crossed with footmarks. She was amused to see the lions wearing neat white snow caps and smiled to herself as she accompanied her friend into Elliot Street and saw her into the dining rooms, before heading towards Great Charlotte Street and St John's fish market. Normally she would have walked the other way down Roe Street because this would enable her to have a good nose at the theatre as she passed it, but in weather such as this the quickest way was best. The familiar smell surged out to meet her as she approached the enormous green-painted wooden doors. There were clouds of steam coming from the direction of Mrs O'Leary's stall, so Amy knew her employer had arrived before her, despite the fact that she herself was at least ten minutes earlier than usual. She went over to the stall to hang her shopping bag on a hook beneath the counter and greet Mrs O'Leary cheerfully. 'Morning, Mrs O! Isn't it a cold, horrible day? It's enough to freeze the wotsits off a brass monkey, as my dad says.'

'Mornin', queen,' Mrs O'Leary answered. She was cleaning down her concrete stand, red in the face from the effort. Amy promptly took the long brush, the big bar of red soap and the bucket of boiling water from her employer's hands. 'You sit yourself down, Mrs O,' she said gently. 'It's my job to clean down and yours to sort out a float for the till. It won't take me but a minute to get this done and then I'll be off to Harry Roper's for the ice. Though if you ask me, we might as well get it free in weather like this by scraping it off the pavements.'

Mrs O'Leary chuckled wheezily and sank thankfully into the creaking old basket chair in which she now spent most of her working day. 'You're a good gal, Amy.' She mopped her brow with a large checked handkerchief. 'I dunno how I ever managed wi'out you and that's God's truth. As for ice, I dunno as we're goin' to need much wi' that bleedin' blizzard a-blowin',' she added ruefully.

Amy smiled. 'Yes, it's the sort of weather to keep customers at home,' she agreed. 'What's more, the boats won't be going out while it's so bad, you can be sure of that. My dad and the boys will be mending nets, knocking up new fish crates, checking ropes and sails and doing anything else ashore that comes to mind, but they won't venture out in a blizzard, not for all the fish in the sea.'

'And the shrimps all lie low while the weather's bad,' Mrs O'Leary remarked. 'But it's a grand time selling potted shrimps, smoked and salt fish, so it is. And praise be to heaven, we don't need ice for such as them. Still an' all, we're not out of fresh fish stocks yet nor likely to be, so when you've finished scrubbin' down the floor, you'd best get off to Harry's for the ice.'

Amy sluiced the last few inches of hot and now filthy water into the channel which ran along the front of the stalls and hurried the little river along faster with her broom. Then she turned back to her employer. 'Right, I'll do that. I say Mrs O, what a piece of luck I had this morning! I was getting on the

160

tram out at Seaforth when someone called my name. It was my best pal, Ruthie Durrant, who was in school with me. She's been in service away from home but she's back now and working in Dorothy's Dining Rooms. What about that, eh? It'll be grand to have a pal to chat with on the tram going home after work. I'm that pleased, even the weather doesn't get me down.'

Mrs O'Leary surged to her feet and took broom and bucket from Amy, to stand them against the back of the stall. 'I'm real glad, queen,' she said sincerely, 'there's no one your age workin' in the fish market, or no one 'cept young lads what's too ignorant to pass the time of day, it bein' mortal hard to get young 'uns to work here on account o' the smell and the cold. Why, if you've gorra pal you might even rent a room in the neighbourhood here, so's you could do wi'out the journey to and from.'

Oddly enough, this thought had not occurred to Amy, though she had been longing to leave home ever since her father had remarried. Suzie took advantage of her, she knew that and thought that if she were not around the older woman would have no alternative but to do her own work or be shown up before Bill and the boys. What was more, it would get her away from Paddy, whose dislike became more difficult to deal with every day. He had bitterly resented her friendship with his pal Tommy and at one point had actually accused her of deliberately stealing his bezzie away from him. 'It's norreven as though Tommy could possibly be interested in a scrawny little red-headed beast what smells o' shrimps, like you,' he had shouted at her when he had first spotted the two of them sitting on the grass in the Bowersdale Park one day the

161

previous summer. 'You're not even the same colour – it's all wrong – you want to leave Tommy Chee alone!'

'We aren't thinking of getting wed, you know,' Amy had said, giggling, 'We're just pals, same as you and Tommy are.'

'There you are, then!' Paddy had yelled, red as a turkeycock with frustrated anger. 'Tommy's *my* bleedin' pal, not yours! He's me workmate and me bezzie, and I won't have you horning in and spoiling things, so just you back off, Shrimpy Logan.'

Amy had not wanted a fight so she had said nothing more, but if she had bitterly resented Bill's interference in her friendship with Tommy, how much more bitterly had she resented Paddy's attempts to force her hand and make her give up seeing his pal. She would not have changed her behaviour one iota because of Paddy's words, but her father's strictures were a different matter. Therefore, since she had no intention of forming any relationship other than friendship with Tommy Chee, she had gradually stopped seeing him altogether, though it had cost her some pangs to make excuses every time he issued a casual invitation.

Consequently Amy had begun to feel herself friendless indeed. Her school friends had scattered, many of them working away, and those who were still at home had made other friends among their new workmates. So Amy, working hard at the fish market all day, preparing and selling shrimps in the long summer evenings and working for her stepmother in the house whenever she was free to do so, was scarcely conscious of the social life she was missing and had begun to feel like a caged rat on a wheel, with escape impossible.

Now, Mrs O'Leary's suggestion danced enticingly before Amy's inner eye, presenting a delightful picture of independence, not only from Suzie Keagan but from the abominable Paddy Keagan as well. If only Ruthie would agree they could have a lovely time, just the two of them, managing for themselves. So Amy set off to fetch the ice, with an empty bucket swinging from either hand and with her mind full of exciting plans. She was forced to reflect, however, that the money she was at present paid would scarcely cover half the rent of even the tiniest room, let alone feed and clothe her. But there were other jobs; in winter her working day ended early and she supposed she could get a job from, say, six to ten, working behind a bar in one of the many public houses which surrounded St John's Market or even waiting, or skivvying for the cook in a popular dining room. Alternatively she and Ruthie could approach a third girl to share a room with them. This would make the rent cheaper and, what with odds and ends of fish which Mrs O'Leary would doubtless give her and whatever the other two could provide, surely it would be possible for three of them to find somewhere they could afford?

'Mornin', Amy,' Harry Roper said cheerfully, as Amy clanked her buckets on to his cold stone floor. 'Wharra day, queen! Have any difficulty reachin' the market today? You come in from Seaforth way, don't you? I dare say it'll be possible to get into the city for a while, but what with this blizzard and the folk all wantin' to go home at the same time, you'd best ask Mrs O'Leary to let you leave work after

163

dinner while the trams is still runnin'. It's a helluva walk out to Seaforth from here.'

'Don't I know it,' Amy agreed gloomily, as Harry began to chop at a block of ice and drop the pieces into her buckets. 'Mrs O'Leary was asking why didn't I think about moving into the city, sharing a room with a pal, so I didn't have the journey in winter. But I dare say it would cost more than me and a pal or two could afford. Rooms are pricey round here, so I've heard.'

Harry filled the second bucket and pushed both across the floor towards her, then straightened, his hand in the small of his back. 'If it were just a room you were after, I dunno as it'd break you to take a bit of a room in one of the courts, or somewhere like that.'

'The courts?' Amy said doubtfully. Ever since she had been small she had been warned by Isobel about the courts and those who inhabited them. 'Dens of iniquity, that's what they are, those courts,' she had told her small daughter, as the two of them hawked shrimps round the city streets. 'They live there, all crowded in like animals, ten to a room, they say, and if there's money missing or some old woman hit over the head for the sake of the few pennies in her purse, then it's to the courts that the scuffers go first. So we'll not hawk our shrimps round the courts, queen. We'll take 'em to honest folks.'

Bill, who was less prejudiced than his wife, informed Amy privately that the folk who lived in the courts were not all bad. 'Some of 'em's just poor, luv,' he told her when she repeated Isobel's remarks. 'You get real respectable folk livin' in the courts, folk who'd take as much care of their little houses as your mam does of ours. Proper little palaces, some of 'em. But your mam went sellin' shrimps round the courts on the Scottie when we was first married. She were expectin' and she got a mouthful of abuse and a stinkin' old boot hurled at her head by a drunken docker. Your mam ain't never forgot it and you could say it coloured her feelings about the courts. So don't condemn folk out of hand just because of where they live.'

However, it seemed that Suzie had shared Isobel's bad opinion of the courts, though possibly for a different reason. 'I get more customers for the shrimps in the pubs than in them courts,' she had told Amy, when Amy had suggested trying the narrow, crowded little alleyways. 'Besides, landlords reckon shrimps give you a thirst, so we're always welcome in the pubs.'

'There's nowt wrong wi' the courts, queen,' Harry said gently now, walking with her to the doorway. 'I only suggested it because I know a little place at the back of Skelhorne Street, off Hilbre Street, where's there a widow woman by the name of Mrs Beckham, ever so respectable, who lives at number 8 Kingfisher Court and who might let a room to a couple of nice young girls what wouldn't mess up her home.'

Amy, who had been about to cross Rose Street, stopped on the edge of the pavement. 'I'm sure a place like that would suit me and Ruth just fine,' she called over her shoulder. 'Thanks ever so much for suggesting it, Mr Roper. Me and Ruth will have a talk and I'll come back to you. Thanks again.'

The rest of the day went with amazing speed. Despite the fearful weather – for the blizzard continued to blow for most of the day – there were sufficient customers to keep Amy busy gutting and

165

filleting fish. Because of it, however, Mrs O'Leary closed the stall at four in the afternoon and advised Amy to go home while the trams continued to run. 'If they're still runnin', that is,' she added darkly, buttoning her long black cloak up to the neck and winding her black scarf round her face to the eyes, so that her voice emerged muffled. 'If the trams have stopped there's always the overhead railway, so be a sensible girl and make for it, if the trams ain't runnin. You don't want to be benighted here, do you? See you tomorrer.'

'Thanks, Mrs O'Leary,' Amy said but she did not commit herself to going home at once, since she intended to wait for Ruth, so that they might discuss the exciting proposal of renting a room between them. She went through to the sinks at the back and washed as thoroughly as she always did, rinsed her apron and hung it over a hook, took off the clumsy wooden clogs she wore for work and donned her outer clothing. Having muffled herself up, she went briskly out of the fish market into the bitter wind and headed for Dorothy's Dining Rooms. She had money in her pocket for a cup of tea and a bun, and decided that if she did not see Ruth she would send a message to the kitchens by one of the waitresses. If Ruth could tell her at what time she would finish work she could stay in the dining rooms, spinning out one cup of tea, or possibly two, until her friend was free to join her.

When she reached the dining rooms they were already crowded, with people staring anxiously out at the snow and ordering tea and crumpets or something more substantial. The bustle and busyness were a revelation to Amy, who did not frequent such places as a rule, and she realised that it would not be possible to do as she had planned and wait in a corner until Ruth was free. Instead she decided to approach the woman sitting in the little glass-fronted box at one end of the room, taking the bills and the money, and handing out change with a smile and a pleasant word to her customers.

This must be Mrs Owen, who owned the establishment, Amy supposed, so she approached her with a certain amount of caution, not wanting to get Ruth into trouble on her first day in the job. But Mrs Owen no sooner heard her say that she was Ruth's friend than, with a harassed glance at the crowded room, she said, 'Why, if you're going to wait for Miss Durrant then you might as well be useful! We're rushed off our feet, as you can see, and there's piles and piles of dishes and cutlery waiting to be washed up, so if you nip through into the kitchens and borrow a clean apron you might give Ruth a hand with 'em.'

'Well, yes . . . of course, if I can be . . .' Amy began uncertainly, to be briskly interrupted: 'Good girl. Off wi' you, then!'

In a daze, Amy followed the woman's pointing finger and pushed her way through a baize door, nearly knocking over a perspiring waitress as she did so. She tried to apologise but the woman merely said, 'Gerrout of me way, young 'un. Two beef dinners for table 6!' and continued across the dining room as though Amy did not exist.

In the kitchen Amy saw Ruth up to her elbows in hot suds, frantically working her way through a large pile of dinner plates, cups, saucers and glasses. She also saw, on a hook above the long wooden draining boards, a number of white aprons. Hesitantly, she took one down, hung up her heavy

167

coat and put on the apron. Then she approached the sink. 'Ruthie? Your boss told me to come through and give you a hand, so you'd be free sooner and we could go home. The snow's still falling, so Mrs O'Leary let me go early, but it seems your boss thinks trade's too good to turn down. Shall I wash or wipe?'

Ruth turned and grinned at her, then unhooked a red and white striped cloth from a line of them under the sink and handed it to her friend. 'Wipe,' she said briefly. 'Someone just told me this is the teatime rush and we'll go home soon's it's over. Mrs Owen – she's the boss – isn't a bad sort, but she lives in the city so she don't have to rely on trams an' such to get her home. Start on the plates, will you? It's mainly the smaller ones coming through now; they're not half so mucky as plates what've had dinners on 'em.'

So Amy, used to hard work, settled down to wipe up the mound of crockery and, because the water was very hot indeed and Ruth a thorough and conscientious worker, it was not too bad a job. The dried plates soon began to pile perilously high on the big kitchen table behind the sink, while the piles of unwashed crockery dwindled at last.

At first, Amy had simply worked as hard as she could, but gradually, as the pile of clean plates grew, along with another of cups, saucers and side plates, she began to realise that she was enjoying herself. It was warm in the kitchen and the workers seemed to be a happy crowd. They called out, chaffed one another and even teased Ruth, though she was a newcomer and this was her first day's work. It was hard not to draw comparisons between this sort of work and that of the fish market. The older people in the market were friendly with one another and were quite kind to Amy, but everyone was selling for themselves just as fast as they could and the camaraderie, which was so evident in the Dorothy kitchen, was simply not present in St John's fish market.

Despite Mrs Owen's fears that they might have to close early, business continued to be brisk. It was soon obvious to Amy, peeping into the dining room, that a good many of the customers had come in for a bite to eat because their trams or buses were either not running or running so late that they would miss their evening meal. 'It's good business for Mrs Owen, that's for sure,' she whispered to Ruth as she thumped a pile of plates on to the draining board. 'But what's it going to mean for us, queen? If our tram isn't runnin we'll have to get the overhead railway and I don 't know the times of the trains, do you?'

'No, I don't,' Ruth admitted.

'Well,' said Amy, 'I usually catch a tram. Still, if we're late our folks'll guess it's the weather what's held us up. How long will we be here, do you suppose? Only Mr Roper, who sells ice to the fish market, told me about a good sort of woman called Mrs Beckham who lets rooms cheap.' She went on to tell Ruth all about Mrs O'Leary's suggestion and Harry Roper's information, and Ruth listened, bright-eyed.

'If only we could rent the place,' she said longingly when Amy finished her tale. 'I won't deny I'm happier at home than I were in service, but I miss havin' me own space, if you know what I mean. And I shall miss not being able to relax when the day's work is done, because Mam will expect me to set to and help wi' the younger ones. You can't blame her, but if I weren't livin' at home . . .'

'Shall we go round to this court, off Skelhorne Street, when we finish here, then?' Amy asked eagerly. 'I'm game if you are, Ruthie. After all, we're going to be late whatever we do, so we might as well get some good out of it.'

This somewhat garbled reasoning seemed eminently sensible to Ruth, so the two girls continued to work hard until seven o'clock, when Mrs Owen came into the kitchens to tell them that they had done very well and might go home now. 'I'll see you tomorrow morning,' she said to Ruth and then turned to Amy: 'Thank you very much, young 'un. If you ever need a job you can come to me for a reference.' She held out a hand and dropped several coins into Amy's palm. 'You've earned every penny, my dear,' she added as Amy stared blankly at her. 'You didn't think I'd expect you to work for me wi'out so much as a penny piece in payment, did you?'

'I . . . I didn't really think, Mrs Owen,' Amy stammered. 'It was so nice and warm in the kitchen and I was helping Ruthie to get finished sooner . . . but thanks ever so much. Why, I reckon we could go home in a taxi cab if we wanted!'

Mrs Owen laughed, but shook her head. 'Gerron a tram, chuck,' she advised, turning to take down her heavy coat from its peg and beginning to struggle into it. 'There's bound to be a tram goin' your way.'

Presently the two girls, well muffled against the storm, stood on the edge of the pavement waiting to cross. Despite the lateness of the hour the street was still busy and, as they waited, a tram swept past, sending a bow wave of filthy slush towards them.

Amy jumped back with an exclamation of disgust, grabbing Ruth's arm to pull her out of danger as well and, as she did so, saw a white and malignant face leering at her from the tram window. It was Paddy, plainly delighted to see her soaked and probably imagining that she had missed the last tram into the bargain, which might well get her into trouble at home.

'Still, he'll tell Mr Logan you're goin' to be late,' Ruth observed when Amy told her who had been pulling faces at them from the tram. 'So you needn't be afraid they'll worry or owt like that.'

The roadway being temporarily clear, the two girls hurried across straight into Skelhorne Street. It was wide and well lit, but when she glanced to her right, for the bulk of Lime Street Station lay to the left, Amy saw that the streets leading off were very much narrower and far darker. 'Let me see, Mr Roper said the court was off Hilbre Street. He said number 8 Kingfisher. Can you see it, Ruthie?'

'Dunno, but this here's Hilbre Street,' Ruth said, turning briskly to her right. 'Better try the first entry we come to.'

The courts off Hilbre Street proved to be as dark and confusing as Amy had imagined. At first the two girls wandered up and down the central pavement between the tiny terraced houses, hoping to meet someone who could tell them where Mrs Beckham lived. Because of the inclement weather, however, doors were firmly closed and finally they were forced to begin to leave the courts and search for a friendly shopkeeper who might have the information they required.

The first small general store they reached was run by a weary, grey-haired old woman in a draggly purple skirt, with a grey shawl closely wrapped round her meagre frame. She did not know Mrs Beckham but suggested they try the fried fish shop a short distance away. 'They know everyone, the Dempseys, and if they don't the customers will,' she assured them, going to the doorway to point them in the right direction. 'Folk in the courts all know one another, even if they'd slit each other's throats for a farden,' she added with a toothless grin.

This was not encouraging but the two girls took her advice. 'We're only *looking*,' Amy pointed out as they made their way through the fast-falling flakes. 'We can say we've got to talk it over with our folks and if we don't like it, we just won't go back ever again.'

Ruth agreed that this seemed sensible and when they reached the fried fish shop the atmosphere was so friendly – and the smell of frying fish and potatoes so tempting – that it was easy to forget the old woman's embittered words. What was more, at the mere mention of the name Beckham the man behind the counter paused in his task of heaping a generous scoop of golden chipped potatoes into a square of newspaper to say cheerfully, 'Oh, yes. I know her well, queen. She lives at number 8 Kingfisher Court, though I dare say you won't be able to see the street names at this time o' night. It's the second entry along.' He finished serving the customer before them and raised grizzled eyebrows. 'Want two penn'orth o' chips to keep out the cold, girls? I dare say you can share a paper between you.'

Feeling that the information was worth at least tuppence, Amy and Ruth handed over a penny each and leant on the end of the counter, eating their chips and watching Mr Dempsey's deft movements, enjoying their impromptu meals. Then they set off once more, tracking down their destination without more ado.

'Though this place hasn't seen a kingfisher for a hundred years, if then,' Amy grumbled, as the two girls followed Mr Dempsey's instructions. 'Blackbird would be a deal more appropriate, wouldn't you say?'

'You may be right, but kingfisher is more cheerful,' Ruth said, as they turned into the dark and grimy court, lit by one flickering gaslight. 'Lordie, ain't it dark, though? I can't see a number on a single bleedin' door.'

Once they had established that this was where Mrs Beckham lived by the simple expedient of knocking loudly on the nearest door until their knock was answered, it was the work of a moment to walk another four doors along and knock there.

Mrs Beckham, though she had not expected visitors in such appalling weather, asked them inside and, clucking over their wet coats and shoes, sat them down in her kitchen before a cheerful fire. 'I've just put the kettle on for a nice cup o' tea and I was going to toast meself a couple o' rounds o' bread, 'cos it's no weather to be chasing down to the Dempseys for fried fish,' she observed, settling herself in a creaking basketwork chair. 'I dare say someone telled you I have a room to rent?'

Amy explained about Mr Roper. She had already decided that she liked the older woman – who, despite being in her late sixties, seemed both lively and humorous – and thought that she and Ruth could be happy in this cheerful little house.

Mrs Beckham immediately got to her feet and gestured to them to follow her. 'I'm not sayin' as it's a palace,' she said over her shoulder, as the three of them mounted the narrow stairway. 'But it's newly decorated every spring and nicely furnished, though I do say it as shouldn't'. She flung open one of the brown-painted doors on the small upper landing and stood back, so that the two girls could look into the room by the light of the lamp she held.

It was not a large room, and the beds were narrow and pushed back against the wall to give more space, but the walls were freshly whitewashed, the linoleum shone with polishing and the curtains, already drawn to shut out the night, were brightly patterned and cheerful. Amy saw two comfortable fireside chairs, a primus stove and a washstand with an enamelled jug and basin upon it. Both beds had matching pink and white counterpanes and the small fireplace had a narrow mantelpiece above it, on which were a couple of china figures, one a flower seller with a basket of blossoms at her feet, the other a shepherd boy with two lambs.

'I asks ten shillin' a week and you've use of me kitchen, since there ain't much you can cook on a primus and the fireplace is turrble small,' Mrs Beckham said. Amy was grateful that the information was unsolicited, since she would have felt shy about asking the rent of the room. She nodded and smiled, and Mrs Beckham added that she provided neither towels nor bed linen, but was happy to allow the girls to wash such items either in her kitchen or the communal wash-house in the court. 'I've gorra line what stretches from my place to Mrs Haddock's,' she explained. 'These houses is back to back, you see, so there's no jigger nor no yard, worse luck. But there's two taps at the far end of the court and two lavvies, o' course.' She turned to leave the room, ushering the girls before her and closing the door. Then she went ahead of them down the stairs, lighting the way with the lamp.

In the kitchen once more, she removed their steaming coats from the wooden kitchen chair on which she had placed them and handed them to her guests. 'You'll want to talk this over between yourselves,' she said briskly, ushering them through the doorway by which they had entered. 'But I'd be obliged if you'd give me an answer in a couple o' days. Me rooms is popular; I've got two nurses sharin' the attic room already, but I don't deny I could do with a couple more lodgers. We're conveniently situated here,' she went on, 'only a step away from St John's Market, so food's cheap and it's not far to go for your grub. Dearie me, I never asked your names, but plenty of time for that if you decide to take me room.' She flung open the front door, gave them a bright smile and exclaimed that it was a devilish cold night, so she'd not linger in the doorway. Almost before the words were out of her mouth, the door slammed briskly shut, leaving Amy and Ruth with only the slight illumination of the solitary gas lamp to guide their footsteps back to the road.

'Wasn't it a dear little room, though?' Amy said wistfully, as they trudged across the snow-covered paving. 'But five bob a week each – we wouldn't have enough money to buy food with, let alone clothes and that.'

'I might,' Ruth said thoughtfully. 'I get tips when I'm waitin' on the customers and the other girls say they mount up. But of course, the job ain't permanent, I might be out of work in a couple o' weeks. You . . . you really don't think we could

175

afford it if we got ourselves a second job, like? I'd be willin' to try ... and we'd save our tram fares.'

But delightful though the thought of being independent was, both girls knew that taking the room as things stood was impossible, so it was rather sadly that they turned their steps towards the main road.

'Tell you what, though, I'm ever so glad we saw the room,' Ruth said, as they paused in the court entrance. 'I never knew what I wanted before. Now I do. I want to live in a little house like that, with a dear little room two pals can share.'

Amy, agreeing, felt exactly the same. At least it was a goal, something to aim for. Escape from Suzie's despotic rule would have been good, but to share a room like that with her best friend would have been even better. So it was in reasonably high spirits, despite their disappointment over the rent, that the two set off on their journey back to Seaforth.

The girls had gone on their court hunt for Mrs Beckham at seven o'clock, but it was past nine before they had finally left Mrs Beckham's little house and as soon as they re-entered the roadway Amy realised that, far from easing, the storm raged harder than ever. She stopped short as they left the comparative shelter of the narrow little road and gazed at Ruth in blank dismay. 'We'll never get a tram in this,' she said, pulling down her muffling scarf so that Ruth could hear her words. 'Shall we make our way to the Pier Head and catch the overhead railway? 'Cos I don't fancy trying to walk in this weather.'

'Ye-es, only I ain't too sure which way we should be headin',' Ruth said, glancing at the confusion of whirling flakes which had already effectively hidden such aids as street names. 'Is it far, Amy?'

'Shouldn't think so,' Amy answered cheerfully. She did not intend to admit that, what with the confusion of searching the courts and the way the snow changed the aspect of the little streets, she had no more idea than Ruth in which direction the Pier Head lay. But surely when they reached the more frequented streets there would be somebody from whom they could get directions? So she pulled her scarf over her mouth once more, linked arms with her friend and set off in what she devoutly hoped was the right direction. She told herself that, no matter how ferocious the weather, the docker's umbrella would continue to function, but a nagging doubt reminded her that she did not know the time of the last train, so they had better not linger. But of course Ruthie, who had been away from Liverpool for so long and had never worked here before, would not think of such a thing. Therefore it's up to me, Amy told herself stoutly, head bent against the gale, to think for both of us. So it was with the resolution to keep Ruthie cheerful and unworried that she set off into the storm.

Bill grew anxious as the evening progressed, and Amy did not put in an appearance, and suggested to his wife that it might be as well if he walked up to the terminus to see whether the trams were still running. 'Amy's terrible late,' he said bluntly. 'It ain't like her, Suzie. I can't see Mrs O'Leary keepin' her till after dark on a night like this, but I suppose somethin' must have come up to detain her. If she catches the tram it's a fair walk against the wind, she'll do better with my arm to hang on to.'

'You spoil that kid, Bill,' Suzie grumbled. She was sitting in front of the fire, roasting chestnuts and whenever a nut blackened she would hook it out with the end of the toasting fork, shed the husk and, as soon as it was cool enough, would crunch the delicacy down. 'What's a bit of a walk through the snow when you're her age? It's a lark, that's wharrit is, but you'll go off and leave me alone wi' young Becky, just so's your precious Amy gets give an arm.'

Bill, halfway across the kitchen to fetch his coat, stopped and glanced uneasily across at his wife. He did not understand her attitude. She often accused him of favouring Amy, yet the girl worked hard, both in her job for Mrs O'Leary and at home. On the other hand, Suzie was very good with the baby. As he sighed and scratched his head over the problem of his daughter's lateness, he wondered, not for the first time, why on earth would his wife resent the kid? Making up his mind, he went over to the door and took his coat off the hook. No matter what Suzie thought, or why, he knew his duty and that meant a walk in the snow on such a night. 'There's a worse storm ragin' out there than there's been for many a year,' he said, slipping into the coat. 'She's mebbe young and healthy, as you say, but Amy's a skinny little thing; this wind could blow her down like a ninepin if she weren't careful, so I'll just walk up the road and . . .'

He was reaching for his cap and scarf when the back door opened abruptly, cutting him off in mid-sentence. Paddy entered the kitchen, looking like a snowman, with a package in his hands which he slammed down on to the table, before beginning to divest himself of his snow-laden garments. 'It's

178

bleedin' terrible out there,' he said breathlessly, stamping his feet and rubbing his hands to try to get the feeling back into them. 'Where's you goin', Uncle Bill? I wouldn't send a dog out on a night like this, honest to God I wouldn't.'

'Amy's not in,' Bill told him briefly, reaching for his muffler. 'Did you catch the last tram, Paddy, or are they still runnin' like normal?'

'I've been back in Seaforth an hour or more.' Paddy pointed to the package on the table. 'Them's chipped potatoes. I come home wi' Donny Fisher and we had to queue at the fried fish shop. I dunno about the trams, but I saw Amy crossin' Lime Street.' His tone grew sharp with malice. 'She were clutchin' some fella's arm – I reckon it were Tommy Chee – and makin' for the backstreets, so no wonder she's late.'

Bill stopped in the act of pulling on his thick wool gloves and stared unbelievingly at Paddy. 'You saw her with Tommy Chee?' he asked incredulously. 'That can't be right. I told her months back that she weren't to see no more of that young feller. She wouldn't go agin me.'

'I'm only tellin' you what I saw,' Paddy said rather belligerently. 'Theys was all muffled up but she don't know any fellas 'cept for my pal Tommy, what she's been and gone and stole off of me. Still, I suppose if you want to walk up to the terminus, there's no harm in it.'

'Yes, there is,' Suzie said aggressively, rising to her feet. 'I'm tellin' you, Bill Logan, if you go out after that spoilt brat and mek yourself ill, I shan't be nursin' you, 'cos you'll have asked for it, that's what you'll have done. Look at Paddy there, more like a pillar of ice than a human bein' and he's not half your age. Just you tek them things off and give over bein' so foolish and I'll mek you a nice hot cuppa. By the time you've got it down you, likely the gal will be back – and the young feller with her if he's got any sense.'

'I telled her not to have nothin' to do wi' Tommy Chee,' Bill said, going towards the back door and opening it into the teeth of the gale. 'I'll not have me daughter larkin' around in this sort o' weather with anyone, let alone a chap as I've forbid her to see.' And before Suzie could say another word, he was out through the door and battling his way towards the tram terminus.

It was gone midnight before two thoroughly exhausted girls reached Seaforth once more. For the overhead railway had not been able to battle all the way out to Seaforth, so they had been forced to walk from Alexandra Station. As Amy dropped Ruth off at her door, however, she remarked that the storm seemed to be lessening at last and, weary though they were, the girls agreed to meet next morning on the tram that would take them both in to work – if they were running by the following day. But the salt wind from the sea usually saw off snow and ice quite quickly, so there was a good chance that by next morning things would be at least nearly normal.

Amy let herself into the kitchen as quietly as she could, guessing that the rest of the family would be in bed. Sure enough, the kitchen was empty. When she had hung her soaking outer garments over the clothes horse to dry before the fire, put on some more fuel so that it would not go and die on her and made herself a hot drink to take up to bed, she heard a sound from the stairs. She thought that perhaps Albert might have worried over her lateness but to her astonishment it was Suzie who came out of her bedroom on to the little top landing, a scruffy shawl round her shoulders and her hair in curl papers. 'Where've you been, you wicked gal?' she hissed, as Amy began ascending the stairs. 'Oh, you deserve a good thrashing for keepin' your dad out so late in this terrible weather. What's more, I've not slept a wink for worryin' over the pair of youse. I told Bill you was old enough to manage for yourself and come in when you felt like it, but would he listen? No, off he goes into that fearful weather to wait at the tram terminus till you turned up, no doubt. Is he still below? You should ha' sent him up first, 'stead of scurrying for your own bed, like the spoilt little madam you are . . .'

'Tram terminus?' Amy exclaimed, quite bewildered by this flood of invective. 'But I didn't come by tram, I came by the docker's umbrella. The last tram was hours and hours ago, so Ruthie and me went along to the Pier Head and caught the train. Only it stopped at Alexandra and couldn't go any further, so we had to walk.'

'You didn't . . . Oh, my God! But you must have walked past the terminus. Didn't you see no sign of your dad? I'm tellin' you, he set off to walk there hours since and he's still not back.'

'There wasn't a sign of anyone waiting,' Amy said doubtfully. 'There was one tram standing in the middle of the road, all covered in snow, but no sign of my dad. He must've gone into a house nearby for shelter – Mr Benbow lives near there, on Peel Road, doesn't he? Do you suppose he's popped in there and got benighted?'

'No, of course he hasn't – wouldn't dream of doin' such a thing and worryin' the life out o' me. Oh, Gawd, wharrever's happened to my Bill, then?' Suzie spun round and hurled the door of the boys' room so wide that it crashed against the wall. Amy could hear her hollering at them, and guessed she was shouting at Gus and shaking Albert and Paddy, who slept like the dead once they had gone off. 'Oh, my Gawd, oh, my Gawd,' Suzie wailed. 'Gerrup fellers, we're in real trouble. Here's that blamed Amy come home by the docker's umbrella and she says she never saw my Bill when she passed the tram terminus. So gerrup the lot of you, you've gorra go and search for him.'

Amy took a hasty swig of her hot drink and then went towards the clothes horse where her coat still steamed. She began to struggle into it again, as sounds of stirring came from upstairs. She was still searching for a dry headscarf to replace her wet one when the boys came clattering into the kitchen, Gus in the lead. All three of them were pale-faced. Gus stared at her as though he were still dreaming. 'Amy? Is it true what Suzie just said? Is me dad out in this awful weather?'

'He must be, since she says he's not come in,' Amy said briefly. She went over to the dresser and rummaged through the cupboards for another pair of woollen gloves to replace her wet ones, then pulled them on. 'Is Suzie coming to search, too? Or is it just us three?'

'Four,' Albert said gruffly. 'Unless you'd rather stay in, our Amy? Only you're already awful wet – I reckon our dad would rather you didn't go searchin' for him in this weather and at this hour.'

'I'm coming,' Amy stated, but did not explain that

she had not expected Paddy to join them. He was not a Logan, after all, though had she been forced to give her honest opinion she would have had to admit that she thought the boy was very attached to her dad. Despite the fact that there had been no work for him on the shrimp boat, Bill took Paddy with him as a replacement for Gus or Albert when they had a day off, and said that Paddy was useful and had all the right ideas. 'But three's plenty for a boat the size of the *Mersey Maid*,' he was wont to say half apologetically. 'If Gus ever wants to go his own way, same as our Ed and Charlie have done, then I'd tek Paddy aboard like a shot. But until that day it's the just three of us.'

So now, the boys wrapped up, all four of them set out, Amy walking with Gus. They reached the tram terminus in good time and, having seen nobody waiting, were about to turn back when Albert gave a shout. 'What's that . . . in that doorway? It may be some old tramp . . .'

The four of them ran, slipping and sliding through the thick layer of snow, to where a figure lay slumped, half in a shop doorway, but more across the pavement. The reason he had been difficult to see was that he, too, was thickly covered with snow, but as soon as Gus rolled him over, Amy gave a cry. 'It's our dad!' she gasped and began to try to lift him, with the boys doing the same. 'Oh, whatever's come to him, Gus?'

Gus was a quiet young man, not given to much shows of emotion, but when Amy looked into his face, as they gradually lifted Bill up into a sitting position, she saw tears shining in his eyes. 'Reckon he had some sort o' attack,' he said. 'Or mebbe slipped and hit his head. There's a bump over his right eye . . . see?'

Amy looked, but could make out little in the dim light. 'But . . . but he's alive, isn't he, Gus?' she quavered. 'He wouldn't die from a fall, would he? Suzie says it's my fault because I was late coming home, but how could I possibly know our dad would come looking for me and have a fall? Oh, Gus, I do love our dad, I can't bear to think of him hurt bad!'

As though he had heard, Bill gave a deep, rather frightening groan, then said in a husky whisper, 'I'm awright, thanks. If you'll help me to me feet, gentlemen all, I'll be mekin' me way home for me wife will be worried that I'm so late. I must ha' fell as I got down from me fishin' boat . . . the snow's that confusin' . . .'

'We aren't gentlemen, Dad, it's me, Amy, and the boys,' Amy said, her voice breaking. 'Don't you know us?'

Bill looked vaguely up at her, then his eyes slid away and his head sagged. He was plainly barely conscious; had probably not heard what she had said.

'Don't worry him, Amy love, he's not hisself,' Gus said authoritatively. 'Albert, you're a sturdy feller, you take hold of him round the waist and we'll make him a chair atwixt us. Paddy, you take him under the knees and see he don't slide forward. Amy, you run home and get the brandy out of the little end cupboard in the fish scullery. Oh, and warm a blanket, and pull the kettle over the flame.'

Anxious to do everything she had been told, Amy fairly flew back to the house, burst into the kitchen and told Suzie, in a gabble, that they had found Bill, that he had been lying in the snow and was, she feared, ill. 'He seemed not to know us, but Gus said I was to warm a blanket and bring out the little bottle of brandy in the end cupboard.'

Suzie immediately bridled, as though Amy had somehow insulted her. 'No, that you won't.' Her tone was vicious. 'Anything that's to be done for my Bill I'll do meself, I thank you. You've done harm enough already.'

'I've done nothing wrong,' Amy said, defensively, heading for the stairs. There were blankets on her bed which she could bring down for her father. 'I didn't *know* he was going to wait up for me, did I?'

She disappeared into her room, grabbed a couple of blankets and came hurrying down the stairs once more. Suzie came over, took the blankets and spread them over a chair before the fire, then said spitefully, 'Get out of me sight. It's your fault that we're in this terrible fix, your fault . . .'

The opening of the door stopped her dead in her tracks. Gus and Albert came in, Bill's moribund form between them, with Paddy holding the door wide, then closing it quickly behind them to keep the weather out. Without another word they began to get Bill out of his wet clothes and into the warmed blankets, while Suzie made a drink from the boiling water in the kettle.

'We need a doctor,' Gus said, after they had settled Bill as comfortably as they could upon the sofa. 'Albert . . .'

Albert was out of the door on the words and Amy followed him, anxious now only to get away from Suzie's sharp tongue. Once her father was better she would explain to him why she had been late. Dad would understand, she was sure.

The matter, which had seemed grave enough in all conscience when the young people had brought Bill home, turned out, upon the doctor's arrival, to be even more serious. 'He's concussed, following a nasty bang on the head, and freezing cold from exposure,' he said briefly, having examined Bill. 'He'll be best in hospital.' He had looked rather hard at Suzie. 'Might he have taken a drink or two?' he asked. 'If he was somewhat uncertain of his footing . . .'

Suzie was silent, looking a little self-conscious, but Gus said at once, 'My father only has the occasional pint, Doctor Payne. He couldn't have had a drink tonight anyway, 'cos he went out far too late.'

'Then perhaps he slipped on the icy pavement,' the doctor said quickly. 'I don't think he should be moved, not immediately at any rate. I'll come in first thing tomorrow – only it is today already, of course – to see how he's going on. In the meantime keep him warm and quiet. There's nothing broken, only a nasty bruise on his head.'

Amy looked in on her father early next morning before the rest of the family were up and found the kitchen quite warm, despite the fact that the fire had burned very low. Of Suzie there was no sign, but while she was making up the fire with fresh logs brought in from the backyard, she came in from the scullery. She had a shawl wrapped round her shoulders and must, Amy supposed, have been out to the lavatory, for she was holding up her night-gown so that the hem would not get wet and wore on her feet the short rubber boots which she kept by the back door. She gave Amy a baleful glance, then went and sat in the old armchair, which she had drawn up close to the sofa.

Amy finished mending the fire and pulled the kettle over the flame. It was already hot and soon boiled, so she made a pot of tea and poured out two cups, carrying one across to her stepmother. 'Has he woke at all yet?' she asked, eyeing her father's pale face anxiously. The livid bruise had swollen the right-hand side of his brow, giving him a lopsided, angry appearance. 'He doesn't look too bright, poor Dad.'

Suzie appeared to give this question some thought before replying, briefly, 'He ain't stirred all night. I've not moved from his side save to go out to the lavvy just now.' She took the proffered cup of tea without a word of thanks and sipped it noisily.

'The doctor said he'd be round early; I wonder if I ought to wait until he's been?' Amy said. It worried her to see Bill lying there so pale and still.

But Suzie shook her head.

'You gerroff to work. Your dad ain't going to be fishing for a bit, so we'll need every penny the rest of you can earn.'

Amy finished her tea and began to struggle into her coat. She went over to the sofa and kissed her father lightly on the forehead. 'See you tonight, Dad,' she said in a low voice. 'Wish I could stay, but I wouldn't be welcome – I reckon you know that. The boys will be up soon, though, and they'll see to anything Suzie wants done.'

For a moment Amy thought she saw Bill's eyelids flicker, but he continued to lie absolutely still and she concluded that it was wishful thinking. He was still far away, in a land of his own, where none of them could follow him. So she wrapped herself as warmly as she could and left the house, closing the door behind her.

The previous day's storm had given way to a brisk, salt-laden breeze and a clear sky. The snow still lay piled up beside the road, but Amy guessed that it would probably not linger long. She did not know whether the trams would be running, but thought it would be better to walk in to work, rather than return to the house to face Suzie's anger and resentment. She did not know why her stepmother was blaming her so cruelly and unreasonably for what was most certainly not her fault, but she already knew that Suzie's bouts of ill temper were best avoided.

She reached Ruth's house just as her friend emerged from the jigger and hurried eagerly to meet her. 'Oh, Ruthie, we're in awful trouble at home, just wait until I tell you . . .'

Chapter Six

The day of the storm, which was to remain vivid in the minds of the Logan children for many years, was almost equally bad for others. When Amy arrived at the fish market the stall was not manned. Mrs O'Leary, it transpired, had gone to the home of her married daughter but had insisted on setting out for her own house as soon as tea was over, on the grounds that if she did not leave soon she would miss the last tram. She had caught it all right, but had also caught, along with it, a severe chill through hanging around in the snow and wind. She was now in bed and would be for some time. The man on the next stall informed Amy, with a certain amount of relish, that he had had a visit from Mrs O'Leary's sister Bridget, who ran the flat they shared nearby. She had told him that Mrs O'Leary was in bed, with a fire lit in her room, a hot toddy by her bedside, with Bridget waiting on her hand and foot and telling her at frequent intervals that she had been a fool to rush round to young Maria's place in such weather instead of coming straight home.

'I wonder what I ought to do?' Amy mused, more to herself than to Mr Mosscrop, but he answered her anyway, being a man fond of both the sound of his own voice and the airing of his own opinions.

'Do? Why, gal, there's no point in you hangin' around here, for no craft will set out in weather such as this, so there'll be no fresh fish bein' brung in.

Why, your da is a fisherman. I doubt he's took the boat out today, has he?'

'He's ill,' Amy said briefly. Mr Mosscrop could be pleasant enough, but being the stall next to Mrs O'Leary, he was also their chief competition. Amy knew very well that if there was any business going Mr Mosscrop would do his very best to see that it came to him and not to herself. If that meant encouraging her to go home and leave the stall unattended, he would not think twice about it. Accordingly she said, 'I'll hang on, thanks all the same, Mr M. We've still got a bit of fish left in the icebox and you never know. Customers do turn up when you least expect 'em.'

Mr Mosscrop, his advice clearly flouted, grunted and turned away, and Amy began to scrub down and then set out the stall. As she worked she thought once more of her father, then of the possibility of her moving out of the house in Seafield Grove. She had always been a favourite with Bill and she adored him, but since Suzie – and Paddy, of course – had entered their lives, things had not been so simple. She knew that Suzie was jealous of the affection between herself and her father; knew that Paddy, in his own way, was equally jealous of the friendship between herself and Albert and probably, for all she knew, of the good feeling which existed between Gus and herself. But she did not see why Suzie should resent so bitterly a relationship which was no threat to herself, that of father and daughter.

But whether she understood it or not, Suzie's antagonism had, of late, made life in the little house in Seafield Grove very difficult. Paddy never missed an opportunity to let Bill see his daughter in a bad light and Suzie not only criticised everything she did, but grumbled to Bill that his daughter thought more of her job in the fish market than she did of the 'little tasks' she was asked to perform at home. And though she took five of the seven shillings and sixpence which Amy earned each week, she was always saying it was not enough to feed such a greedy great girl, though admitting sourly that the fish Amy brought home from the stall at the end of each day's work was a bit of a help towards her keep.

Yet Amy knew it was not simply the fact that she was not happy at home which made her want to move out. Ruthie was very happy at home, but she felt she wanted a bit more independence. They might tell each other it was because they needed to be nearer their work that made the move attractive, but Amy knew this was not so. They were growing up, growing away from the family background, the brothers and sisters sharing beds; for the bed which she and Mary had shared was now occupied by herself and baby Becky. 'Little birds want to leave the nest and spread their wings,' a particularly annoying teacher had been wont to say to the class, when talking about what jobs they would wish to do. At least, Amy had thought her a particularly annoying woman, but she had merely been putting into words what all the class should have been thinking – that growing up meant getting away, leaving home, finding a place of one's own.

Despite early fears that she was wasting her time by setting out the stall, Amy soon realised that she had done the right thing, which was comforting. Mr Mosscrop and herself did good business, for folk who had not shopped the day before because of the inclement weather were doing so now in earnest. By four o'clock, when dusk was falling fast, Amy was able to clean down and change out of her fishy apron and her stained wooden clogs, knowing that there was a nice little sum of money in the black japanned box to take round to Mrs O'Leary, now that work was finished for the day.

Mrs O'Leary lived with her sister Bridget in a two-bedroomed flat over a millinery shop on Mount Pleasant. Amy had visited the place before and had thought it very snug, and this evening, with a bright fire burning in the bedroom grate and Miss Bridget Flynn toasting slices of bread before it, it seemed an idyllic place to live, particularly when compared with her own home.

The young girl who had let Amy into the flat and accompanied her to Mrs O'Leary's bedroom said, 'Here's someone to see you Miz O'Leary,' ushering Amy into the room and closing the door behind her.

Bridget turned away from the fire and smiled at Amy, while slipping a slice of toast off her fork and beginning to butter it. When it was done she held it out to Amy with the words, 'You'll be fair clemmed, workin' all day in the fish market wi'out me sister's help. Eat this whiles I pour me sister a cuppa. Then you can tell her how it's gone today.'

Amy crunched the toast and watched, as Bridget set about pouring the tea and waking her sister, who had clearly fallen into an uneasy slumber. Presently, with Mrs O'Leary supping the tea, Amy was able to ask Bridget in a quiet voice how her employer was going on. The younger sister was a skinny, self-reliant woman in her fifties. Amy knew she worked as a supervisor at a big clothing factory and was much valued by her employers, for Mrs O'Leary was proud as well as fond of her sister and frequently talked about Bridget's 'career', a word she would never have used about her own work. Amy guessed that the little girl who had let her in was the maid the sisters employed to keep house while they were at work, so there would be no necessity for Miss Flynn to be away from the factory while her sister was ill.

'She's got a bad chill, there's no denyin' it,' Bridget told her. 'And it's gone on her chest, like her chills nearly always does. But I've known her a good deal worse than this and we've caught it early, so mebbe, in a week or ten days, she'll be back in the fish market.' She eyed Amy keenly. 'Can you manage till then, chuck? I know you're only young, but me sister sets great store by you, so she does. There'll be a few bob extra in your hand at the end of that time, 'cos I know it ain't everyone who'd stand by Mrs O'Leary the way you will. I s'pose there's no chance of your dad or one of your brothers givin' a hand? You won't need help while the weather stays severe, but if we have a mild day or two, when the fleet can get out, then folk'll fancy fresh fish again and you'll mebbe need some help.'

Mrs O'Leary, who had been sipping her tea, suddenly seemed to realise that Amy was in the room. 'It's good of you to come, queen,' she said huskily. Amy could hear the breath wheezing in her chest as she spoke. 'Done much today?'

Amy went over to the bed and opened the japanned box. 'Look, we've done quite well,' she said proudly. 'And we're clear out of fresh fish to sell. But it's been a fair day today, so maybe the fleet will have sailed and there'll be more to sell tomorrow.'

'You're a good gal,' Mrs O'Leary wheezed. 'Has

193

your dad sailed today? If so, I'll warrant he'll bring his catch straight to us.'

'My dad's ill with concussion,' Amy said dolefully. 'But maybe Gus and Albert will have taken the boat out. I'll find out when I get home.'

'Your dad's ill!' Mrs O'Leary exclaimed, real sympathy in her thickened voice. 'You shouldn't ha' bothered to bring the money round, queen, when you must be anxious to gerroff home and see how he's a doin'. Tomorrer, I'll send young Alfie – he's me grandson – to collect the money, so's you don't have to trail round here. Off you go then, Amy, and give your dad me best wishes for a quick recovery.'

'Thanks, Mrs O'Leary.' Amy headed for the door. 'But I reckon I'd rather come round myself, if it's all the same to you. It wouldn't be fair to put all that on a little lad. Good night, both.'

Freed from the responsibility of her employer's money, Amy fairly flew along the pavement towards the tram terminus at Lime Street. Her luck was in and the tram waiting was a number 23, which would take her all the way to Seaforth Sands.

During the journey on the tram her thoughts had been divided between a half-apprehensive fear of the responsibility of looking after the fish stall while Mrs O'Leary was ill and pride that her employer was willing to trust her. Once she was on Seafield Grove, however, worry over her father simply took over, and it was with quickened step and fast-beating heart that she hurried down the jigger, across the yard and in at the back door.

Suzie was standing by the fire, staring down into the flames. Her face was bloated and blotched by the heat, Amy thought, but on hearing the door open Suzie swung round and Amy realised that the older woman's face was wet with tears. Her heart jumped into her mouth. 'Is ... is Dad ...?' she faltered, staring at Suzie. 'Oh, Suzie, is me dad worse?'

'They've took him to the hospital.' Suzie's voice was thick with tears. 'He were real bad, delirious, the doctor said. I stayed with him until it were time for the boys to come in; then they said I should come home and they would spell me for a bit while I got meself some food. He were still unconscious and he sounded mortal bad.'

'Which hospital?' Amy asked baldly. She had unbuttoned her coat and now she buttoned it up again. 'Which ward, come to that?'

'They've took him to the Stanley,' Suzie said dolefully. She sniffed, dabbing at her face with a filthy rag of a handkerchief, then she seemed to remember that she disliked Amy and looked up, her mouth twisting spitefully. 'But don't you go there worriting the nurses, Amy Logan, for I won't have my Bill made any worse than you've made him already.'

Amy, who had been pulling on her gloves and turning towards the back door, stared at Suzie. 'What on earth do you mean?' she asked, genuine puzzlement in her voice. 'It wasn't my fault that I worked late and came home by the docker's umbrella instead of the tram, though you keep saying it was. There's no sense in casting blame anyroad. It doesn't do anyone any good, it might even make my dad worse if he knew what you were saying.'

'Knew what I were sayin'?' Suzie tipped back her head and laughed without amusement. 'Why, your dad knows all about it. He were that distressed when my Paddy told what he knew that nothing

195

would do but for him to go out into the storm to make sure you didn't get into no more trouble. Bad enough that you ignored my Bill's wishes and did what he 'spressly telled you not to do . . .'

'Suzie, I haven't got the foggiest idea what you're talking about,' Amy said helplessly, but she was beginning to be very angry. 'I never did what my dad told me not to do, though he wasn't one for laying down the law, not in general, he wasn't. So just what did your Paddy tell him about me? Because I'd take money it wasn't true, whatever it was.'

Suzie ruffled up indignantly, her cheeks reddening at the implied insult. 'Why, Paddy telled your father that he saw you junketing around the Liverpool streets wi' that chinky feller what my Bill telled you never to see no more,' she said triumphantly. 'He were on the tram, but he said you weren't even tryin' to catch it, the two of you went giggling off into one of the side streets – up to no good I'll swear, what with you comin' home after midnight, brazen-faced as any streetwalker. Oh, yes, me lady, your father knew what you were up to and . . .'

'If your son told my dad that I were with anyone but my pal Ruthie, then he's a worse liar than all the rest of your bloody family put together,' Amy screamed, crossing the room in a couple of bounds and ending up almost nose to nose with Suzie. 'I told you I was with Ruthie and *I'm* not in the habit of telling lies, unlike some! As for Tommy Chee, I stopped seeing him when my dad told me to, though I thought it were a pack of nonsense, and if Paddy told him different then it's him who's responsible for

196

my dad being in hospital 'stead of home with the rest of us. So what've you got to say to that?'

Suzie had stepped back a pace but now she said, 'Paddy had no reason to lie. He just told my Bill what he saw and . . .'

'You make me sick,' Amy spat, turning to the door. 'I'm going to see my dad and you may be sure I'll tell him that your precious son filled his head with a pack of lies. And don't you try to stop me,' she added, as Suzie grabbed at her sleeve, 'because you've done enough harm, you and your precious Paddy!'

Amy arrived at the hospital just as Albert and Paddy came down the stairs and crossed the foyer towards her. Albert put an arm round her shoulders and gave her a squeeze. 'Dad's still unconscious, Amy, but there's a bit of colour in his cheeks and the nurses seem a little more hopeful. He was awful grey when we first arrived and he's breathing kind of funny, but he doesn't seem so bad, somehow, as he did at first. Gus has gone to the telegraph office to let Edmund, Charlie and Mary know what has happened,' Albert said gently, and Amy saw that both boys were pale and anxious-looking.

She had known for some time that Paddy was very fond of her father; thought of him as though he were a much-loved uncle, but she found she could not even look at him after one quick, initial glance. He had told lies about her to her father and she had been unable to repudiate them. She thought desperately that Bill's recovery might be held back by what Paddy had said. She had never liked Paddy, but now she hated and despised him, and would do so, she told herself, for the rest of her days. 'Do you

197

mean Dad's still very ill, Albert?' she asked and her voice only had a tiny shake in it. 'But Suzie said they'd sent her home to get a meal and a change of clothing – I thought he must have improved, must be holding his own.'

'The doctor thought the same and likely he's right; but he's with Dad now. They told us to come down and get a breath of air while he's examined,' Albert replied. 'Seems they're worried about the possibility of pneumonia, what with him lying out in the snow for so long.' Albert's voice broke and he hugged her shoulders convulsively.

'Pneumonia!' Amy thought of her father, his loving ways, his gentleness. People died from pneumonia, she knew. As soon as she possibly could she must tell Dad that Paddy had mistaken Ruth for Tommy, which would clear up the whole horrible misunderstanding. If only Albert was wrong and it wasn't pneumonia. It would break her heart if Bill were to die, particularly thinking ill of her. She felt tears rise to her eyes and closed them, praying with all her might that her father would recover, would not leave them, as her mother had done. Amy felt another hand on her arm and realised that both boys were steering her across the foyer towards the stairs; the wards, she knew, were all on the first floor. She opened tear-drowned eyes and saw Paddy's face, only inches from hers. She glared at him and tried to drag her arm away, but he held on.

'I told him, Amy,' Paddy said in a constricted voice. 'I told Uncle Bill I'd been mistook, that it weren't Tommy you was with. I ... I'm sure he heard ... I'm real sorry, Amy, I never meant ...'

'Get your bleedin' hands off me, Paddy Keagan,' Amy said and now her voice was rock steady and cold as ice, and even the tears seemed to have dried on her cheeks. 'You're a liar and a troublemaker and I don't want anything to do with you, now or never. Bugger off! It's my dad lying ill in this place, mine and Gus's and Albert's, not yours. Go back to your mammy – she believed your lies and tried to make things worse . . . why, she did her best to stop me coming to the hospital.'

Albert jerked his head at Paddy. 'She's right, Paddy . . . oh, I know you love Dad near on as much as we do, but for now . . .'

'I'll wait here, then,' Paddy said in a low voice. 'Amy, I swear to God I didn't mean no harm . . .'

'Shut up!' Amy said, but still coldly, not with the heat that the phrase implied. 'Go back to Seafield Grove, to your gran's house mind, not ours. Because I never want to set eyes on you again.'

To her secret surprise, Paddy turned and went down the stairs with dragging steps.

The two Logans made their way towards the ward where Bill lay. Albert turned to his sister. 'You were a bit hard on him, queen,' he said gently. 'I know you think he were tryin' to make mischief – likely he was – but you could have accepted that he were sorry. He did try to tell our dad that he'd been wrong, it hadn't been Tommy Chee you were with, but . . . to tell you the truth, I don't think Dad believed what Paddy had told him in the first place, honest to God I don't. I think he wanted to go out to meet you, and Paddy saying what he did was a good excuse for ignorin' Suzie and getting out of the house anyway.'

There was a commotion up the corridor, and a group of people came through the swing doors on the left and walked towards them. 'It's the doc,'

Albert whispered, drawing Amy to a halt. 'We'll have a word.'

The doctor was a tall, elderly man, with tiny gold spectacles perched on a long, thin nose. He was almost bald and he looked weary and preoccupied, but when his eyes fell on the two youngsters he smiled kindly and patted Albert's shoulder. 'You'll be young Logan, William Logan's boy, and this must be your sister,' he said in a thin, educated voice. 'Well, I'm afraid your father does have a touch of pneumonia, but he's a strong man with plenty of staying power and I see no reason why he shouldn't pull round – with good nursing, that is.' He glanced at the two young women who flanked him, one on each side. The ward sister and a staff nurse, Amy guessed. 'These ladies will see to that, you may be sure. I've had a word with your father . . .'

'Oh, sir, is he conscious?' the words broke from Amy and Albert simultaneously. 'I thought my brother said he hadn't come round,' Amy added.

'Yes, he's conscious, and presently we hope he'll take a mouthful or two of nourishing broth,' the doctor told her. 'You may go and see him to calm your fears, but you may only stay two minutes. He's still very weak and needs all the rest we can give him.'

'Won't we be allowed to sit with him?' Albert asked with a strange mixture of timidity and belligerence. 'Me stepmother and me big brother was spelling each other by the bed, and we were going to take over until one of them comes back.'

The doctor smiled at them very kindly, but shook his head. 'No need, now, to keep a constant watch on him,' he said. 'He'll rest a deal easier without eyes on him for, as I've said, it's sleep and nourishing food which will restore his strength. You tell the rest of your family they may come in for ten minutes only tomorrow morning and then we'll see.'

'I don't like the sound of that,' Albert muttered, as the doctor strode away from them. 'What if Dad needs something? I'd sooner one of us is by, even if it's Suzie.'

But the staff nurse, who had stayed with them, smiled and shook her head. 'No, lad, your dad's on a general ward now he's come round and norrin the end cubicle by hisself. The nursing staff will keep an eye on him, of course, but the other patients will fetch someone if your father needs anything. Why, if we had relatives at every bedside twenty-four hours a day, we wouldn't be able to get inside the ward, let alone nurse the patients.'

As she spoke she had guided them into a long ward with at least twenty beds, in the nearest of which Amy immediately recognised her father. He was propped up in the narrow iron bedstead, with a number of pillows and another nurse was bending over him, helping him to drink out of an object which looked like a small white teapot. Bill took a long swallow; Amy could see his throat convulsing, then he shook his head and the nurse stood the teapot down on his bedside locker. 'Well done, Mr Logan,' she said softly, 'you'll feel all the better for that I'm sure. And now you've got visitors, so I'll leave you for a while.'

Albert slid a wooden bench out from under the bed and pulled it close, so that Amy could take her father's hand in hers. 'Oh, Dad, you're looking much better,' she said eagerly. 'We've been so worried – especially me. I felt it was my fault that you'd had to go out in the snow because if you'd not gone to meet me, none of this would have happened.' She gestured vaguely towards the bed.

Bill looked puzzled. He put a hand up to his head and winced as his fingers encountered the enormous lump on his brow. 'I slipped on the ice when I were comin' to meet you off your tram,' he said in a small voice, totally unlike his usual firm tones. 'Only you never come. Where was you, queen?'

Amy hesitated. She did not really want to tell her father what she and Ruth had been doing, but she reflected that lies and evasions never did anyone any good in the long run. 'Do you remember my pal, Ruthie?' she enquired. 'Well, she's come back to Seaforth to live. She's got a job quite near the market so, after work, her and me went looking for a room to share, so's we'd be nearer our work, like. We found a place . . .'

Bill had been listening, with his eyes fixed on her face, but suddenly his hand shot out and gripped hers. 'Amy, you mustn't leave home, queen,' he said urgently. 'Suzie's a good wife to me, but she's not a manager like your mam was. I know she hasn't always treated you like she should, but I'll change all that if only you'll promise me you won't leave us in the lurch.'

Amy was touched by the entreaty in her father's blue eyes and worried by the trembling grip of his hot, damp hand. 'It's all right, Dad,' she said soothingly, 'we couldn't afford the room we saw, but if you truly want me at home then we shan't go looking for anything else. Honest to God we won't.'

Bill's fingers slipped from hers and he heaved a satisfied sigh. 'You're a good girl, queen,' he said huskily. 'I dunno what we'd do wi'out you and that's the truth. Promise me . . .'

The staff nurse who had brought them up to the ward appeared by the bedside and tapped Amy on the shoulder. 'Your two minutes is up, dear,' she said briskly. 'You run along home now and come back to see your dad again tomorrow. By then he'll be much more the thing – and don't forget to tell Mrs Logan that Mr Logan is on the general ward now and she can come in for just ten minutes tomorrow morning, no longer.' She turned to Bill. 'Nurse tells me you had a couple of sips of beef tea for her, so how about having another couple of sips for me?'

All the way home on the tram, Amy sat beside Albert in thoughtful silence, murmuring replies to his remarks, but never making any contribution of her own to the conversation. She had promised her father that she would go home, would not leave either the family or Suzie in the lurch, but she was beginning to realise that if life in the Logan household were to be bearable she would have to have a serious talk with Suzie. What was more, she would have to sort things out with Paddy, because no matter how you looked at it, if she kept her threat and never spoke to Paddy again it would make for a very uncomfortable atmosphere.

The tram was an old and noisy one, however, and very soon Albert fell silent, defeated as much by the effort of shouting to Amy above the rattle and roar of the vehicle as by Amy's long silences. But when they reached the Rimrose Bridge and climbed stiffly down, Albert asked her outright what she intended to do. 'I didn't know you were so unhappy, queen,' he said gently, giving her shoulders a brotherly squeeze. 'But I heared you tell Dad you'd been after a room share wi' young Ruthie Durrant and, now I think about it, it can't have been much fun for you livin' in the same house as Paddy. I dunno what's the matter wi' him,' he added broodingly. 'When you was kids he were always rude and nasty to you, but I thought that was on account o' Mary – him havin' a crush on her, I mean. I thought he were nasty to you to ... to kind of contrast with how he danced attendance on our Mary. I thought it'd stop once Mary left, but it didn't, did it? He's still gorrit in for you, though he don't call you "Shrimpy" so much, nor shout at you in the street.'

'Well, I don't like him much,' Amy admitted honestly. 'Looking back, I can't for the life of me remember how it started, or who started it for that matter. It should be different now we're older, but somehow Paddy always seems to want to get me into trouble and once he moved in ...'

'Yes, I know, it's just gone from bad to worse,' Albert cut in. 'But it'll be different now, Amy. He's rare ashamed of what he told our dad and if you play your cards right he'll be your pal from now on, I'm thinkin'. All you've gorra do is accept his apology. Then you can start afresh, like.'

'But I said I'd never speak to him again and I meant it,' Amy pointed out. 'He told a deliberate lie to put me in Dad's bad books and look what has happened as a result, Albert. Our dad's ever so ill. He could easily die and it was all Paddy's fault.'

'No it weren't, queen,' Albert said reprovingly. 'You've gorra take some of the blame, you know. You went gaddin' off to look at rooms and missed the last tram, off your own bat, in a bleedin' blizzard, you know you did. Why, our dad would've gone chasin' off after you, Paddy or no Paddy, once it got to ten o'clock in that weather an' no sign of you. Be fair, our Amy.'

Since this uncomfortable thought had already crossed Amy's mind, she felt her cheeks grow hot and nodded grudgingly. 'Yes, you've got a point, Albert. It's no use trying to blame Paddy for everything – what is it Dad says? It takes two to make a quarrel. But Albert, you should have heard the way Suzie lit into me. She called me every bad name she could lay her tongue to, screaming like a fishwife and saying it was all my fault her Bill was took bad.' She snorted derisively. '*Her Bill*, indeed! He's our dad, isn't he, and he's been our dad a lot longer than he's been *her Bill*!'

'Yes, I know what you mean,' Albert admitted. 'When they was first wed I thought Suzie had hooked him like you hook a big sea bass, and hauled him aboard her boat an' all, but since then I've watched 'em a fair bit an' that Suzie's rare fond of our dad, queen. He's older than her and he don't take her about much, but she fair worships the ground he walks on. The reason she's nasty to you is jealousy, pure an' simple. You're our dad's favourite and always have been, so she resents it o' course. Now, be honest, our Amy. Ain't that the truth?'

'Ye–es, but there's nothing pure or simple about jealousy,' Amy pointed out. 'I can't help being Dad's favourite – if I am, that is. Why, I'm a kid and Suzie's a woman grown. She ought to know better than pick on me the way she does. I often want to tell her to do her own work when I come in from the market to find cleaning and housework waiting to be done, but I never do. Sometimes she's not too bad, but Paddy

205

sets her agin me whenever he can. He's tried tale-clatting to Dad, too, in the past, but he knows his mam wants to believe bad of me, so he does better telling his tales to her. So what'll I do, Albert? I can't move out now I've promised Dad I'll stay, but things are bound to be awkward.'

They had walked down Crosby Road, so busy discussing their problem that Amy had scarcely glanced at the big houses which lay between them and the sea. Turning into Seafield Grove, she tugged at Albert's arm, drawing him to a halt. 'What'll I do?' she asked plaintively. 'I know I promised Dad and I'll stick to my word but it isn't going to be much of a life for any of us if Suzie goes on picking on me, and Paddy and I don't speak.'

Albert laughed. 'Talk to them,' he advised. 'Tell Suzie you're doing your best and don't need the constant nagging she hands out. Tell Paddy you'll be civil if he will. If that don't do the trick you'll have to talk to Dad again – when he's well, I mean. But Paddy's awright really, you know. He's been a good pal to me in the past and maybe, once things are sorted out, he'll be a good pal to you as well.'

Amy sniffed, but began to walk towards their home once more. 'I'll do it for Dad's sake,' she said decisively. 'Oh, Gawd, I think I'd rather face a man-eating tiger than that Suzie when she's got a cob on and she isn't going to be happy when we tell her she can't see Dad except for ten minutes tomorrow morning. Still an' all, I'm doing this for Dad. Come on, Albert.' And with head held high and bumping heart, she headed for home, with Albert close on her heels.

Amy hurried along Crosby Road, taking deep

breaths of the mild spring air. She was excited because Dad was coming out of hospital today after almost two months of illness, for he had indeed contracted pneumonia and, despite good nursing, there had been times when even the doctor had doubted Bill's ability to pull through.

But Bill had fought the disease and conquered it. Some four weeks ago the medical staff had known they were going to win the fight, and Sister had told Amy that Bill's lungs were clear and it was just a matter of building up his strength. Since then, Amy had been able to chart his improvement on her daily visits, and she and Suzie had watched with delight as Bill began to fret against his imprisonment. He wanted to be out and about for, though he trusted Gus, Charlie and Albert so far as it went, he could not believe that the lads could possibly bring in catches such as he habitually did when spring arrived.

What was more, although Charlie had been willing to help in the boat while Bill was in hospital, he was eager to return to the maltings, where he had not only a good job but a young lady, whom he missed badly. 'They're keepin' me job for me and Lottie's not the sort of girl to let a feller down,' he had told Amy. 'But I'm doing well down there, queen, and though I know Dad's happy with Suzie, I can't say I care for her much meself. I'll stay whiles I'm needed, but as soon as Dad's well enough to work again I'll be off.'

However, it had not been necessary for Charlie to remain, once Dad had turned the corner. Bill's old friend Ben Carpenter, who had been a fisherman in his time but was now mostly retired, had agreed to help the boys work the boat and Charlie had gone back to the Midlands, knowing he had not let his family down.

Walking briskly towards the tram terminus, Amy reflected that she had done a great deal of growing up over the past couple of months. It had started, she supposed, the night after Bill had been taken into hospital when she and Suzie had finally got down to brass tacks and talked plainly, because they had realised that night that they shared a common fear – that Bill might be taken from them.

'I love me dad better than anyone else in the whole world,' Amy had said earnestly, staring at Suzie's pale and woebegone face across the table which had separated them. 'The way the two of us are behaving, Suzie, isn't likely to help his recovery, because he loves us both, you know, though in different ways. I'm willing to stay here and do everything I can to help you bring up baby Becky and to look after the boys, but I can't do it if you're set agin me. I told Dad this evening that I meant to move out, take a place of my own, even if it took my last penny, but he begged me to stay. I dare say you'd rather I went, but it'd put Dad in a rare worry to know you were trying to manage alone, so if we can come to some agreement . . .'

'We must agree,' Suzie had said, looking Amy squarely in the eye. 'I don't deny I've been hard on you, queen, but I knew right from the start that you didn't want me takin' Isobel's place. You didn't want Bill marryin' anyone, least of all meself. I knew you were watchin' me and thinkin' your dad could have done a deal better, an' it made me mean towards you. Then Paddy weren't no help, were he? I reckon he knew how you felt about me – I am his mam, after all – so he made things hard for you, same as I did. And he lied about Tommy Chee, didn't he. Well, he told me himself not an hour since that he couldn't tell who the feller was, he were so muffled up. He said it were Tommy because he thought Bill would lose his rag wi' you and leave you to gerron with it. But it had the opposite effect. An' now Bill's in hospital and ... and we've gorra pull together, queen, for his sake and for our own. Paddy's gone to sleep at Gran's tonight, 'cos he said you'd not stay if he were in the house ...'

'It's true I said I'd never speak to him again, but that was in the heat of the moment,' Amy had said quickly. 'Mind you, it'll be for the best if he stays with Gran for a bit, seeing as how Gus telegraphed Edmund, Charlie and Mary to come home. There won't be room to swing a cat once they arrive, so Paddy will be best at Gran's.'

That night, Amy thought now, heading for Ruthie's house, had been the beginning of a completely different relationship between her and her stepmother. It was as though Amy's eyes had been opened to the very real love which Suzie had for Bill. She had never looked past Suzie's shiftless and lazy ways to the depth of affection that she showed in every action she performed for Bill. Suzie had made her way to the hospital two or three times a day with small comforts for her sick husband. She had bought the *Echo* each evening and stumblingly read him news of local events, though reading had never come easily to her. Little Becky had not been allowed on the ward, but Suzie knew how Bill adored his little daughter and had recounted all Becky's exploits with as much interest and affection as though the child had been her own. What was more, on several occasions she had taken Becky to the hospital and lifted her up to the window nearest to Bill's bed, so that he could see for himself how well and happy the child was. It had meant a lot to Bill, Amy knew, but it had been just one more task for Suzie, who suddenly found herself with more work than she had ever had to cope with in her life before.

For within a couple of weeks of Bill's being taken ill, Gran, too, had fallen sick. She had contracted influenza and had been very ill indeed for three weeks, with the doctor calling daily and Aunt Dolly almost out of her mind with worry. The older woman had nursed her sister devotedly and had done her best to bring her back to health, but though she was now pottering around and doing her own housework once more, Amy acknowledged that Gran would never again be able to carry Suzie, as she had in the past.

So, though at the time she had felt some pangs of conscience over her insistence that Paddy should live with his grandmother, Amy soon realised that it was a blessing in disguise. She might dislike Paddy – well, she did – but she had always known that he was neither workshy nor lazy. When Gran had taken to her bed, all the messages, cleaning and a good deal of the cooking had fallen to Paddy's lot, for Aunt Dolly was too old and frail to do much besides nurse her sister. Paddy had risen to the occasion and, though he had come round to the Logan house for advice from time to time, he had never asked them for help in his own predicament. Though she could not like him, Amy was forced, reluctantly, to admire the way he had coped. He was a young man, after all, not used to housework or cooking, let alone taking care of two old ladies, but somehow he had managed to keep the household going, though he must have been heartily glad when Gran had been able to leave her sick bed once more, albeit falteringly.

Ahead of her the front door of the Durrants' house opened and Ruthie shot out on to the pavement. She was carrying a round of toast, folded over, and spoke rather thickly between bites. 'Awright, chuck? It's your big day today, in't it? Did they say it was still all right for your dad to come out today, eh? I bet you're excited, ain't you? But how will you stop him tryin' to help wi' the fishin', now the weather is so fine?'

Amy laughed and tucked her arm through her friend's. 'Dad's not a fool, chuck,' she said, answering the last question first. 'He knows as well as the rest of us do that tomorrow or the day after the weather will probably break and turn windy and rough. He's been in hospital so long that he won't risk putting himself back by taking foolish chances with his health. As for being excited, of course I am, same as the rest of the family. Edmund wrote and said he'd come home and see Dad again, once he's settled in, and Mary's going to do the same. As for Charlie, he's been home most weekends, as you know, so he'll probably leave it a bit before he visits. But the rest of us are so excited ... Little Becky's made him a picture to hang on his wall and Suzie's been cooking all the stuff he likes best since yesterday morning. Gus and Albert have clubbed together to buy him a new muffler and even Paddy came round with a bag of bull's-eyes for him to suck while he's mending nets. The doctor reckons he must take it easy until the weather's truly warm.'

As they had been speaking, the two girls were hurrying towards the terminus and now they climbed aboard a tram and took their seats just behind the driver. 'My mum's bakin' some currant buns for your dad's tea,' Ruth said presently, as the tram began to rattle along Knowsley Road. 'And I've bought him a bag of seed potatoes for his allotment. It ain't much, I know, but I talked to Albert when he were bringing the catch ashore last week, and he told me he and Paddy had dug over your dad's allotment as a bit of a surprise, like, so I thought mebbe they would put the seed potatoes in for him as well.'

'That was kind. Dad'll be just thrilled,' Amy said appreciatively. Bill had put his name down for an allotment five years previously, but had not managed to get one until the last year, and it was his pride and joy. Despite the hardness of a fisherman's life, he had told Amy that he found digging, planting, weeding and above all, harvesting his crops thoroughly relaxing and enjoyable. In summer he went there every night, making his way along Sandy Road until he reached the bridge over the railway, from where it was only a step. And Bill swore that the combination of soot from the engines and salt from the sea improved the soil and was partly responsible for the excellence of his crops. Once he had got well enough to worry, he had fretted over his beloved allotment and, though the family assured him that lying fallow until the spring came could do it nothing but good, he was unconvinced. Amy guessed that Albert and Paddy had dug the allotment chiefly so that Bill would have no excuse to do so himself before he was fit for the work, and was grateful, though she was sure it had been Albert's idea, rather than Paddy's.

'I bet it'll be like a party tonight when your da

comes home,' Ruth said enviously. 'I'll bring me seed potatoes and me mam's buns, but I won't stay. Mr Logan will want his home and his family to hisself after so long away.'

'It won't hurt to pop in for a moment.' Amy smiled at her friend. 'I wouldn't be surprised if Dad went to bed pretty early tonight. It's an exciting day for him, but though he's much stronger, he won't be his own self for a while yet. The doctor said not to work until the summer, but I can't see my dad sitting there idle. He'll be mending nets and doing the accounts before many days have passed, if I know him.'

'Well, I'll pop in for a moment,' Ruth conceded when the tram came to a halt beside a long queue of would-be passengers. As they began to scramble aboard, she turned to her friend. 'I haven't liked to ask, chuck, but does your dad know Paddy is living with Gran? Has anyone told him?'

Amy heaved a sigh. Despite the fact that there was now an uneasy truce between Paddy and herself, she had insisted that he continued to live with the two old ladies rather than in the Logan house. She had told Suzie that Paddy was needed more by Gran and Aunt Dolly than he was by themselves. It eased the congestion in the boys' room, especially when Charlie came home to see his dad, and it also gave Paddy freedom to have his friends in and to come and go as he pleased, for Gran and Aunt Dolly did not attempt to restrain him.

However, she had a nasty feeling that Bill would not approve of this arrangement, so satisfactory to herself but so galling both for Paddy and his mother. She wondered how long it would be before Bill realised that his stepson was no longer living under his roof and thought apprehensively that it could not be many days before he twigged. Paddy had most of his meals with the two old ladies but occasionally, when he had been helping with the boat, he had his tea with the Logans. Bill was sure to notice his absence at mealtimes, particularly at weekends, and would doubtless comment on it.

Suzie and Amy had been getting on very well ever since they had come to terms with one another and Amy was able to see Suzie's point of view better than she had ever done before. Despite her step-mother's casual-seeming attitude towards her only child, she was very fond of Paddy and, though her life was busier than ever with Bill in hospital, she made a point of seeing him at least once every day. She agreed with Amy that the old ladies needed Paddy, particularly since Gran's illness, but Amy knew Suzie missed her son and imagined that, at times, she must feel quite beleaguered by Logans, especially with Bill not there to protect her. But she had never even suggested that Paddy should come back to live with her, so Amy supposed they would all have to wait and see how Bill reacted to the change.

The tram jerked to a stop, the conductor bawled down the length of the vehicle, 'Lime Street Station! We doesn't go no further, ladies and gents all,' and Amy and Ruth joined the exodus. Ruth was still working at Dorothy's and was very happy there, so Amy usually walked her as far as the kitchen entrance, then continued round the corner into Great Charlotte Street and along to the fish market. Mrs O'Leary and Amy reached the stall simultaneously and smiled at each other as they automatically began their morning preparations.

214

'Mornin', chuck,' Mrs O'Leary said breezily, struggling out of her thick winter coat and changing her button boots for wooden clogs. 'So, today's the great day, eh? I reckon your stepma is all of a twitter with her man comin' home after so long. And I dare say you and your brothers is pretty excited.'

'That's right, Mrs O,' Amy agreed, hanging up her coat and shedding her boots. 'Gus and Albert will be along later, because they had a right good catch yesterday and they'll be wanting to set sail as soon as they can today, since the weather's clement at the moment. Gus said they ran into a regular shoal of whiting yesterday afternoon, though they were a bit small. And when he pulled up the crab pots he got at least a dozen decent-sized ones, and crabs always go well.'

'Crabs!' Mrs O'Leary exclaimed, her face lightening. 'Now crabs is something that we can always sell and seein' as they're alive, alive-oh it wouldn't matter if they did hang about for a day or so, 'cos no one could say they wasn't fresh. What time do you think the lads will be along?'

Amy was about to reply when a rumbling made her look up. Gus and Albert, pushing a handcart between them, came skidding across the slippery cobbles and stopped, panting and grinning, alongside the stall. 'Your fish delivery, ma'am,' Gus said, bowing mockingly in Amy's direction. 'All fresh as a daisy, especially them perishin' crabs. I got a nice tweak from the big 'un in the right-hand corner, 'cos he started trying to make his way out. You'll want me to leave the basket, I 'spect?'

'Yes,' Amy said, coming round the stall to help the boys to unload the catch, while Mrs O'Leary briskly weighed the fish and wrote down price per pound in the shabby little ledger she kept for the purpose. None of the Logan family ever haggled with Mrs O'Leary over the price, because it had long ago been agreed between herself and Isobel that she would pay according to scarcity value, demand and quality, and they knew that Mrs O'Leary would never cheat them.

Mr Mosscrop, on the stall next door, was a different proposition, though. When he cast envious eyes at the heavy basket of clacking and furious crabs, and asked if he might buy some to boil and dress, Gus promptly named a price which made Mr Mosscrop stagger back in pretended horror. 'I bet you didn't pay that for 'em, Mrs O,' he grumbled, eyeing his neighbour. 'Still an' all, I dare say I'll get a bit extry for dressin' them and no one else seems to be bringing crabs in today, so I'd best pay up wi' a good grace.'

Accordingly Mrs O'Leary, who was a fair woman, picked out the two largest crabs and handed them to her neighbour. The boys, pocketing the sheet of prices and the money she gave them, reminded Amy to bring something good back for tea since it was Dad's first day home and rattled off, pushing the cart before them.

'Suzie's already got a steak and kidney pud ready to put on to boil when the time's right,' Amy shrieked after them. 'And Gran's made a nice apple pie for afters, so don't you be late, fellers.' She turned to Mrs O'Leary as the boys disappeared. 'If Dad's being in hospital has done one good thing it has made me and Suzie get on much better; you could say we were friends even. She's worked like a right one these past weeks and never a cross word between us. Dad'll be right pleased when he realises we're pals.'

Mrs O'Leary, who had set about cleaning some of the whiting for display on the front of the stall, looked up quickly. 'Aye, it's true you've been much easier wi' one another whiles your Dad was out of the way,' she said slowly, 'but human nature is human nature, queen, and jealousy is one of them emotions you can't just stifle – or not for long, any road. I don't want to seem to look on the black side, but it wouldn't surprise me if your stepma don't revert to her old ways once your dad comes home.'

'Oh, I don't see why she should do that,' Amy said. Surely the good understanding which had grown up between herself and Suzie could not simply disappear just because Bill was home? 'I'll keep on being friendly and helping her as much as I can without giving her dirty looks, so Dad will be able to love the pair of us and not have to choose.' She turned back to the stall and picked up the two big wooden buckets which stood behind it. 'Shall I go for the ice, now, Mrs O? Looks like we'll need it with all those lovely whiting to sell.'

It seemed strange to Bill to leave the white, echoing cleanliness of the Stanley Hospital and to breathe the cold March air into lungs that were used to the mixed smells of disinfectant, carbolic soap and boiled cabbage, which seemed to make up the air in his ward. What was even stranger was the chill which touched his cheeks and hands, and the sudden realisation that his legs were no longer to be relied upon. Instinctively he clutched at Suzie's arm and felt the reassuring strength of it, even as Charlie, on his other side, grasped him firmly by the elbow.

'Feelin' kind o' shaky, Dad?' Charlie asked gently. 'Never you mind, I dare say anyone would feel the same if they have been flat on their backs for gerrin' on two months. But don't worry, we ain't goin' to ask you to walk all the way to Seaforth, there's a cab waitin' in the road, so you'll travel home like the King of England.'

Suzie, on Bill's other side, gave his hand a comforting squeeze. 'Tek it slow,' she advised, helping him across the pavement. 'The cab's no more than three yards away and Charlie and me's strong, so lean on us.'

'I'm awright,' Bill said a trifle breathlessly, as he climbed the creaking steps into the cab. He lowered himself gingerly on to the warm leather seat, while Suzie settled herself beside him and Charlie jumped aboard, carrying a small carpet bag which contained Bill's few possessions. 'My, but don't it take it out of you? I've always been a chap as could tackle any physical work and I thought I were doin' well in hospital, but right now I feel as weak as any kitten.'

'Never mind, Dad.' Charlie gave him a reassuring grin. 'They tell me when a woman has a babby she feels uncommon shaky when she first leaves her bed. Just you pretend you're a nursin' mother and . . .'

'Stop your clack, you wicked young devil,' Bill said, giving a reluctant grin. 'I don't need to pretend nothin'; it's not many fellers as recover from con . . . concussion *and* the nastiest attack of pneumonia the doctor said he's seen for a long while. Anyroad, once I'm in me own home and had a good night's sleep in me own bed, I'll be beatin' you at your own game, young Charlie. Why, I'll be fishin' in a week or so!'

Suzie and Charlie exchanged quick, guilty glances

and Bill, settling back against the seat with a sigh of relief, grinned to himself. He knew well enough that it would be impossible for him to stroll down to the beach, let alone go out in the boat, for many weeks to come, but it would do no harm to pretend to be fitter than he really was. He had no intention of risking his future health by being foolish, for though he knew the boys had done well – or well enough – in his absence, he also knew that neither Charlie nor Gus had yet gained that special knowledge of the waters they fished, which it had taken him almost fifty years to acquire. Besides, Charlie's heart was in the Midlands. The boy enjoyed the work and the independence and, of course, the company of his young lady and would, Bill knew, be reluctant to exchange his new life for the terrible harshness of fishing. Charlie worked under a roof during the severest months of the winter, whereas a fisherman would be out in all weathers, risking his life for his catch, which sometimes rewarded him well and at other times seemed scarcely worth the effort.

Edmund, working on distant water trawlers, had an even worse and harder existence, but trawlermen did at least get amply rewarded for their work – they were not known as 'three-day millionaires' for nothing. Bill sometimes thought that if something should happen to him, Gus might follow Edmund up to Fleetwood; perhaps the two boys might end up sharing a trawler between them, for fishing off the Great Burbo Bank was becoming harder, as fish stocks shrank and more boats came in to search for what fish there were. Now that he came to think of it, if Gus did go, Albert, Paddy and himself could manage the *Mersey Maid* and still make a living. Paddy was not experienced, but he was a hard worker and was already a useful member of the crew when one or other of the boys was unable to work; he would do very well once he had built up some experience.

The cab lurched as the horse left the smooth surface of Crosby Road South and entered Seafield Grove. It jolted on for a short way, then the driver's face appeared in the trapdoor. He was grinning encouragingly. 'We's arrived, lady and gents,' he said, then withdrew and descended. He opened the door, seized Bill's bag, stood it on the pavement and offered Suzie his hand. 'Out wit' you, queen,' he said breezily. 'You go ahead and open the front door, so's I can give your man me arm.'

And presently Bill, with a sigh of contentment, found himself sitting in his own chair, beside his own fire, with the kettle hopping on the range and Suzie bustling around making the tea. Despite himself Bill felt a slow smile spread across his face. They had been kind in hospital, the food hadn't been bad, the other patients were friendly and the staff nursed the inmates devotedly. But it was not home. Bill, looking around him, felt confident that his true cure had begun.

Paddy came along Crosby Road and turned into Seafield Grove, then hesitated. It was Bill's first day home and he knew he ought to go into the Logans' house to have his tea and say hello to his stepfather. The nicer side of his nature wanted to do just that, for he was extremely fond of the older man and thought of him as the father he had never known. Bill had been kind to him from the very beginning – not just when he became his stepfather – but ever since he and Albert had become bezzies. Paddy often told himself that he no longer hated Amy, who had stood by his mother when she had needed help most. However, old habits die hard. Try though he might, Paddy could not forget the stuck-up, know-all Amy, who had so often made him look a fool by twisting his words, so that a sneer meant to make her look small ended up by making him appear spiteful and ignorant.

So now, standing undecidedly on the pavement, he reminded himself that if he went in for his tea, Bill would not realise that he had been forbidden the house by Amy Cleverclogs Logan. It was not that he wanted to get Amy into trouble, exactly. It was not even that he wanted to live under the Logan roof once more. He rather enjoyed staying with Gran and being the man of the house, though he missed Albert's constant companionship. It was more that he felt he had been cheated of his rights as a stepson. Amy, when all was said and done, was only a girl with no right to boss him around. Dammit, she was two years younger than him and, though he admitted he had been in the wrong when he told Bill Amy had deliberately flouted his wishes, that had been two months ago. He had apologised, hadn't he? Surely by now the unpleasantness should have been forgotten? He could not imagine Bill bearing a grudge and thought that if he played his cards right he might yet see Amy humbled and himself brought back into favour.

So if he went into tea now, Bill would think everything was normal and would not discover that his stepson only came into the Logan kitchen on sufferance. On the other hand if Bill was still in the kitchen when tea was over and Paddy about to depart, surely he would ask where the boy was bound?

While Paddy hesitated, a hand smote him between the shoulder blades and a voice bellowed cheerfully, 'Hey up, Paddy! Wharrer you doin' standin' in the middle of the road, gaping like a cod? Ain't you comin' in for tea? It's Dad's first night home and your mam's made a steak an' kidney pud.'

'Albert! You damn near knocked me teeth down me bleedin' throat,' Paddy said aggrievedly. 'Well, I dunno. It's your sister; she . . . she may rather I went back to Gran's.'

'Well that's something new, you worrying what our Amy thinks,' Albert observed, linking his arm with Paddy's. 'Amy never says a word when you come in for tea, you know she don't.'

'Ye-es, but today's kind o' special,' Paddy pointed out, but he allowed himself to be pulled down the jigger and into the Logans' small backyard. Presently he found himself in the warm kitchen, with his mother about to dish up a large steak and kidney pudding and Amy bustling about, setting the table and making a big pot of tea. Baby Becky, who was scarcely four, had had her tea and been put to bed earlier, and Bill was sitting in his usual chair, looking tired but happy, and Paddy forgot his doubts and the desire to see Amy in trouble, melting away under the warmth of Bill's greeting. He handed over the bag of bull's-eyes and Bill stuck one in his cheek at once, promising the rest of the family that they might have one later, once tea was finished, but adding that most of the bull's-eyes would follow the one at present in his mouth, for they were easily his favourite sweets.

Paddy was still grinning over the success of his small gift when Gus came in from the backyard, carrying more driftwood for the fire and Charlie followed close on his heels with a net slung over one arm. They both greeted Paddy pleasantly and very soon the family were settled at the table, with the best meal they had had for weeks before them, though Bill remained in his fireside chair with a tin tray on his lap. And somehow, Paddy did not quite know how, he realised that clever Amy had managed to slip into the conversation the fact that he, Paddy, was no longer living squashed up in the boys' room above stairs, but was staying down the road with Gran and Aunt Dolly.

'Since Gran's been ill, Paddy's been the man of the house, doing all their messages and keeping an eye on the old ladies,' she observed, smiling with saccharine sweetness into Paddy's enraged face. She had done it again, he thought bitterly. If he told Bill now that Amy had slung him out of the house on the night Bill had been taken into hospital it would merely make him look bad. What was more, everyone round the table, and possibly even Bill himself, would realise that he was trying to get Amy into trouble. All his old animosity against Amy flared for a moment, then died into sulky mutterings. It was no use; he would have to accept what Amy had said with a good grace and see how things panned out.

'If you've finished your tea, Paddy, you might take a tray round to Gran and Aunt Dolly. I promised them their tea tonight, seein' as it was somethin' special,' his mother said when Paddy's plate was empty. 'And your gran's got an apple pie cookin' in her oven, so you can bring that back with you. If she hasn't cut it, you can take off a couple of slices for them and bring the rest back here.'

Paddy got to his feet but Amy was before him. 'No need for that,' she said sweetly. 'Paddy can take the pudding helpings round – they'd be a bit heavy for me – but I'll go with him and bring back the apple pie. He can eat his piece with Gran and Aunt Dolly so there won't be any need for him to go out in the cold again.'

Paddy opened his mouth to protest but Bill said, rather wearily from his place by the fire, 'I don't think I'll be having apple pie, thanks, queen. I dunno how it is but I feel as if I've run a mile today. I'll be makin' me way up to me bed and maybe, Amy love, you'd fetch me up a cup o' tea next time you put the kettle on.'

So Paddy took the tray with the two helpings of steak and kidney pudding and floury boiled pota- toes, without demur and set off, with Amy tagging at his heels. He put the food down on Gran's kitchen table and the two old ladies settled themselves eagerly before it. Then he went to the oven, drew out the apple pie and plonked it rather crossly on the draining board. He got out three battered tin plates, while Amy poured cups of tea for the old ladies, then addressed her in a hissing whisper: 'Well you've done it again, young Amy. You've seen me off on Uncle Bill's first night home without anyone but me seein' what you're up to. But just you wait. One of these days I'll be workin' on the boat wi' the other fellows, and you'll still be selling shrimps door to door and slaving for old Ma O'Leary in St John's fish market. And when I've a share in the boat . . .'

But Amy was not staying to listen. She gave him her sweetest smile, snatched up the apple pie, called her farewells over her shoulder and disappeared through the kitchen doorway.

Paddy, sitting down to his own share of the apple pie, wondered why he bothered to try to needle Amy. He always got the worst of it in the end. And what did it matter, when all was said and done? They were no longer a couple of kids, vying for Albert's or Bill's affection; they were young people in work with their own lives to lead. He determined, not for the first time, that he would stop irritating Amy. After all, she was Mary's sister and Mary was an angel.

Pouring custard over his apple pie, he decided the best thing to do would be to ignore the girl completely. After all, he longed to join the crew of the fishing boat, hoping in his heart of hearts that one day he and Albert would own it between them, with a young lad as the third member of the crew. Once that happened he would have the position in life that he wanted and the hateful Amy, though ugly as a can of worms, would doubtless find some poor sucker to marry her and would go away from the little house in Seafield Grove.

Smiling to himself, Paddy ate the last of his apple pie and collected the empty dishes. 'You goin' to wash up, Gran?' he enquired cheerfully. 'If so, I'll give you a hand with the wiping before I fetches in water for the morning. Then I'll make up the fire and be off to bed, for I've an early start tomorrer.'

It was a brilliantly sunny day in July, and Amy had got off the tram at the St Martin's Market stop (usually known as Paddy's Market). She needed a lightweight jacket for the warmer weather, which she should be able to pick up in the market and, since she ran the stall on a Monday and business was usually slack after the weekend, she had decided not to open until eleven o'clock that day. What was more, because there was no fishing done on a Sunday she sold mainly salt fish, smoked fish and potted shrimps, which meant that takings were usually down. Now that Mrs O'Leary had given her a second day on the stall, most of her money was made on a Thursday, so opening late on Monday was acceptable both to Amy and her customers. Accordingly, she decided to walk the rest of the way, enjoying the sunshine. She also wanted time to think and the walk would enable her to do so without interruption.

Once again, after a gap of several months, she was seriously considering moving out of the little house in Seafield Grove. For within a month of Bill coming home, Amy knew that Mrs O'Leary had been right. Gradually, over the course of those weeks, Suzie's attitude had begun subtly to change. At first she only found fault with Amy's work or attitude when Bill was out of the way, but because Amy did not fight back and simply accepted the criticism with what good grace she could muster, Suzie began to return to her old ways.

Bill was back on the fishing boat, but he was far from his old self; after so long in hospital it would have been strange indeed had he not found an ordinary job exhausting, let alone the extraordinarily taxing job of catching fish. Amy worried about him and knew Gus and Albert did as well, but she hesitated to mention the matter to Bill himself. His pride in his ability both to find and to catch the fish was understandable and Amy thought that to take this pride from him – to insinuate that he was no longer capable of such work – would be cruel indeed. However, she wished fervently that there were some tactful way he could be persuaded to find himself an easier job.

Apart from the fishing, Bill seemed to be coping admirably with the rest of his life. His allotment was flourishing – although any heavy digging was still being done by either Albert or Paddy – with new potatoes, peas, tender young carrots and even a row of onions, as well as the thick hedge of pinks and sweet-williams, which Bill grew for the house. Because of the allotment and because of Bill's deep knowledge of the fish they searched for, the Logan family were doing well and pulling back from the lean days of the winter in excellent style. Amy knew they would miss her dreadfully if she were to leave, but she did not know for how long she could continue to put up with the atmosphere in their small house.

Baby Becky was now at a dame school and although this would seem to lessen Suzie's responsibilities, it soon became apparent that taking Becky to school each morning and fetching her in the afternoon was an excellent reason, or perhaps excuse would be a more appropriate word, for Suzie to leave a good many tasks to be done by her stepdaughter. This usually consisted of large piles of ironing, for although Suzie sold shrimps from door to door when the catch was good, taking little Becky with her during the school holidays, she no longer did any other work inside the home. Instead, she had managed to find herself a job laundering the linen from one of the big houses along the front. She used Gran's copper to boil the whites because the shrimps were boiled in the Logan copper, but the ironing, great mounds of it, were piled up in the kitchen waiting for Amy's attention. Amy had to concede that the flat irons were always stood ready for her in the hearth, the nearest one to the fire being the first employed, but this did not help much when she came home tired from a day in the fish market to find the back-breaking work of pressing the dry linen awaiting her.

Suzie left her other jobs, of course. She had never been able to make good bread and had relied on Gran to do so for her. But since her illness Gran had not baked her own bread, let alone Suzie's. So on a Sunday, before church, Amy would get up early and go down to the kitchen to begin the task of making bread. She would leave the loaves to prove beside the fire while she went to church with the rest of the family and then, upon her return, would pop them into the small bake oven beside the fire. Amy quite enjoyed making bread – she certainly enjoyed the result – but she resented being no longer able to call her Sundays her own. Bill was strict about the family going to church, Amy thought more in memory of his dead wife than from any profound conviction, but he had always been happy for his children to make themselves scarce once the service was over. Even on Sunday the main meal of the day was eaten in the evening, which should have given her several hours in which to meet her friends, walk along the beach and visit the Bowersdale Park. But because Suzie could not be relied upon to check the loaves and stand them to cool on the kitchen table when they were done, Amy was denied even this freedom.

At first she had not realised why Suzie either took the bread out too soon or left it in until the crust was black as coal, but it was soon borne in upon her that this was yet another skirmish in the war which she had declared on her stepdaughter. She told Bill that Amy couldn't even make bread without spoiling it, said the loaves were heavy when they were merely undercooked, complained that Amy had weighed the ingredients wrongly when the crust was burnt to a crisp. So Amy decided she must stay with the bread until she had it safely out of the oven, and since the family was a large one and she was baking bread for Gran's household as well as her own, the task usually lasted her until early evening.

Now, with a sigh, Amy turned into Paddy's Market and immediately forgot her troubles in searching the many and various stalls for the garment of her choice. Ruth had recently bought a nice one in a dark-grey gabardine and Amy wanted something similar. After some good-natured haggling, she managed to buy a brown linen jacket, which seemed ideal. Having completed her purchase, she slipped the jacket across her shoulders, for it was easier to carry it thus on such a warm day, and set out once more for the fish market. She was passing the free library when she remembered glancing at the clock over the jeweller's on Byron Street and realised that it had shown only half past ten; she had another half-hour before she needed to go to work. Accordingly she headed for St John's Gardens, wishing she had had the foresight to purchase a bag of buns. She had passed a confectioner's window displaying mouth-watering cakes and could easily have spared a copper or two. It would have been nice to sit on the benches beneath the cherry trees and have a little picnic; a sit-down would be infinitely preferable to arriving at work half an hour early.

Crossing William Brown Street, she headed for the gardens and was on the further pavement when she heard a considerable commotion coming from her left. She glanced towards St George's Hall and realised, with a shock of surprise, that the plateau before it, the long rows of steps and even the roadway itself were crowded with figures, most of whom were shouting, gesticulating or singing what sounded, at this distance, like ribald songs. For a moment she simply stood where she was, staring, and then decided to take a closer look. The pavement upon which she stood was relatively empty but as soon as she got nearer the hall and the stone lions which guarded its frontage, she realised that this must be a political meeting of some description. The police were out in force, apparently trying to control the crowd, who were taking absolutely no notice of the long arms of the law. The people surged to and fro, and roared applause whenever the small figure perched at the very top of the long line of steps stopped speaking for an instant.

Amy had watched for several moments before she realised that, with one or two exceptions, the crowd consisted entirely of women. Old ones, young ones, fat ones, thin ones; women shabbily dressed in calico aprons and clogs, women in smart town clothing, country women in gingham gowns and stout boots, and young women in straw hats, leg-o'-mutton blouses and straight, pale-coloured skirts.

Quite near Amy, a man began to shout abuse at the speaker and immediately the women nearest him turned on him, telling him to shut up in no uncertain terms. 'Shut your bleedin' face, you hairy little nothing,' a hugely fat woman, wearing a straw hat richly furbished with curled ostrich plumes, screamed at him, her face inches from his own. 'If you don't shurrup I'll . . . I'll flatten you and believe me, if I were to roll on you, you wouldn't be eatin' no dinner, nor shoutin' at your betters for a week or more.'

The man began to reply, his words clearly couched in offensive terms, when two policemen approached. Amy thought hopefully that this would end the fracas but, to her astonishment, the policemen walked straight by the offending man and grabbed the fat woman by both arms. 'You just keep your evil mouth shut, you great boiled puddin',' the larger of the two policemen said. 'Gawd, you bleedin' suffragettes make more work and more trouble than a couple of hundred protesters – the male sort, that is. Now, are you goin' to shut up or shall we take you in charge?'

Amy stepped forward, full of indignation; this was prejudice the like of which she had never encountered before. The poor were always discriminated against, she knew that, but in her experience the scuffers were more inclined to stand up for the poor and indigent than to persecute them and had always seemed well-disposed towards women. Before she could interfere, however, a tall, stately woman in her mid-fifties, carrying a small parasol and wearing an extremely smart walking dress, had acted. With one swift poke of her parasol, the first policeman's helmet was sent spinning into the crowd and, turning as if to apologise, a neatly judged blow from her elbow had the second policeman releasing his prisoner to straighten his helmet and tenderly caress one tingling scarlet ear.

'So sorry, officer,' the woman said in a cultured, self-confident accent. 'These little . . . accidents . . .

happen when too many people are squeezed into too small a place, don't you know?'

The first policeman was chasing after his helmet and paid no heed to her words, but the second one growled ungraciously, 'Ho, I dare say, but a decent woman wouldn't be seen dead among all these trouble-makin' bitches, I'm telling you.'

Amy, open-mouthed, watched this drama, trembling for the fate of the tall woman but then the crowd surged forward again and the policeman, muttering beneath his breath, lost sight of both combatants and went grudgingly off to find his companion, still rubbing his inflamed ear.

The woman standing at the top of the hall steps had a megaphone and, as she spoke, whole phrases suddenly began to make sense in Amy's mind. She was talking about women's rights and Amy remembered that the policeman had called them suffragettes. Instantly she knew what this was all about – getting women the right to vote for members of parliament, a right which had been denied them for so long. But listening as hard as she could, Amy realised that the speaker was addressing other issues, issues which affected her far more than the parliamentary vote. The woman was talking about the right to work, to earn a decent wage, to be regarded equally with men in the workplace, ideas so revolutionary that Amy gasped and began to wriggle through the crowd in order to get closer to the speaker.

She had got within perhaps ten feet of the bottom step when someone addressed her. It was a girl of about her own age, dressed in a striped toilinette blouse and a dark-blue skirt, her small waist clipped into a neat black leather belt with a silver clasp. Her light-brown hair was piled on top of her head and held in place by a silver and tortoiseshell comb, and she held a straw hat, with a chequered ribbon round the crown, in one hand. She looked neat, smart and collected, but the smile she gave Amy was warm and natural, and when she spoke her voice was low-pitched and pleasant, with no trace of a local accent. 'Hello! Is this your first suffragette meeting? I was quite frightened initially, because the police seem so aggressive. It's almost as if they hate us, wouldn't you say? Mrs Blenkinsop is such a wonderful speaker, though, that I've stopped minding about the crowds and the police. In fact, I'm really enjoying myself.'

Amy smiled at the other girl. 'I wouldn't say it was my first meeting, because I'm not here really at all,' she explained. 'I was on my way to work, only I'm half an hour too early, so I thought I'd sit down in the gardens for a bit, seeing as how it's a lovely day, but then I heard the rumpus and I came over to take a look. I saw the scuffer grab hold of ever such a nice lady, who'd done nothing wrong, and I was moving forward to tell him what I thought, when another lady knocked him for six and sent him running after his helmet. Then I heard what Mrs ... Mrs Blenkinsop was saying and it caught my fancy. Only it's hard to hear, because the women keep shouting and cheering, and the fellers at the back keep hollering to drown out her voice.'

'She's talking a great deal of sense,' the other girl said. 'We could try and get a bit nearer, though. Put your arm round my waist and I'll put mine round yours and we'll shove our way through somehow. She's been talking about education for women, saying that ordinary girls, girls like us, ought to have equal opportunities with young men, so we could take degrees and go to college like they do. My employer would be mad as fire if he knew where I was, but it's my day off and I told everyone I was going shopping in Blackler's to choose a nice new hat for my cousin Lucy's wedding. I bet half the girls here had to tell untruths to someone, just to get away for a few hours. It isn't right that we should have to descend to such expedients, but . . . Oh, look, there's a gap! Let's see if we can squeeze through. If we could reach one of those pillars . . .'

But at this point it was as though all hell had broken loose. A phalanx of policemen had forced their way through the crowd, mounted the stone steps and completely surrounded the speaker. One moment the crowd was quiet and orderly, the next a policeman had seized her megaphone, another twisted her arms behind her back and, while the crowd was still gaping, unable to believe what was happening, they found more policemen were among them, swinging their truncheons, cursing and kicking, and doing their best to break up the meeting.

Amy and her new friend had been forced apart by the sudden pressure of women tumbling down the steps to avoid the police, but now the other girl grabbed Amy's hand and together they began to fight their way out of the mêlée. It was not easy. Men who had no connection with the police force had joined enthusiastically in the rout, hitting and punching indiscriminately at the women and, it must be confessed, frequently being hit back. Amy saw sturdy shawlies dealing mortal blows with their shopping bags, smart women using their parasols to good effect and even girls like her and her new friend, kicking and punching with all the strength they could muster. Indeed, Amy herself punched a whooping boy on the nose when he tried to grab her friend's hat from her hand and was delighted to see she had drawn blood. Though by the time they had escaped from the crowd and were sitting innocently in the Lyons Café in Lime Street nearby, she found she was trembling with a mixture of fright and excitement, and saw in the window glass that she had managed to get considerably rumpled by her recent activities. Her hair, which had been pulled back from her face in a severe bun, straggled in witch locks round her shoulders. Her neat white blouse was torn and had two buttons missing, and though she had been unaware of it at the time, she now realised that her feet had been trampled and kicked in the scrum and were extremely sore.

But it had been an adventure and one she would not have missed for the world. She accepted the cup of tea which the waitress handed to her and turned to her new friend. 'Phew! I feel as if I've been run over by a tram, but it's the most exciting thing that's ever happened to me. Oh, my name's Amy Logan, by the way, and I work in St John's fish market. Who are you?'

'I'm Ella Morton,' the girl said, taking a sip from her own cup of tea. 'I work in the Bon Marché on Church Street. And I share a room with another girl who works in Bunney's on the corner of Whitechapel. Where do you live, Amy? In the city?'

'No, I live out at Seaforth with my dad, my brothers and my little sister Becky. Oh, and with my stepmother. But to tell you the truth, Ella, I've been thinking for a long while that it was time I moved out – came into the city to be nearer my work. I've got a pal called Ruthie and last winter we began looking for a room to rent, but the prices were more than we could afford on the sort of money we earn. Then my dad was taken ill and spent nigh on eight weeks in hospital, and I realised I couldn't walk out on them, not with my dad so poorly. Only now that he's better I'm beginning to think about a room share again.'

And presently, with Ella's gentle encouragement, she found herself telling her new friend everything, beginning with Isobel's death and Mary's defection, and continuing to the present day with Suzie's jealous attacks and the amount of work through which she, Amy, was supposed to wade unaided.

Ella had listened with interest and sympathy to Amy's story, and her friendly attitude allowed Amy to utter the thoughts which she had been unwilling, at first, to voice. 'Excuse me asking, but is your room very pricey? Only I guess you earn a deal more than I can, seeing as how the Bon Marché is a posh shop and you speak nicely and look so smart.'

'I don't know what you earn, but I don't get paid anything like they would pay a young man in the gents' department,' Ella said. 'The rent of the room does seem to swallow up a good deal of my wages and, of course, one must dress respectably if one is selling clothing to women with a great deal of money. They're fussy, you see, which is why the managerial staff tend to pick girls with unaccented voices and a good appearance. But Amy, you must have been in work a year or so, since you look to be about my own age. I don't imagine selling fish is either much fun or well paid, so why not try for something different? There are jobs for women to be had in big offices and banks. In fact, I am attending evening classes at the YWCA in order to better myself. Have you ever thought of doing that? It is one of the things Mrs Blenkinsop believes in and she is an example to us all.'

Amy felt quite dazed, as though one moment she had been trudging along in her own dull old world and the next had been dragged, without her own volition, into somewhere quite different. She looked carefully at her companion, noting the smooth young face with its big brown eyes and merry mouth and then, at a second glance, seeing there was sadness in the eyes and the wariness of experience behind what she was sure was usually a sunny and trusting gaze. 'How is it that you don't have any trace of an accent though, Ella?' she asked. 'And why aren't you living at home? If you're my age – and you look about sixteen, same as me ...'

'Oh, it's a common story,' Ella said with a tiny sigh. 'I was born and brought up in my parents' home in Southport. We were what you might call well to do ...'

'That means rich,' Amy said, grinning, 'you can't pull the wool over my eyes, old Ella!' She half thought that this was a test; if her new friend secretly regarded herself as superior to Amy then she would dislike the familiarity of the remark.

But Ella grinned back at her, clearly not at all offended. 'Oh, well, I didn't mean to boast or anything like that, I just wanted to tell you the truth. Now, are you going to let me get on with it, or are you going to keep putting your spoke in?'

'I'm going to have to teach you to speak Scouse,' Amy said, smiling more broadly. 'We say "Gerron with it" in these parts, so you do just that. Gerron with it and I won't put any spoke in any wheel; in fact, I'll hold my clack till you reach the end.'

'Gosh, she's giving me a carte blanche,' Ella said in an exaggeratedly posh voice. Then, returning to her normal tones, she added, 'Right then, Amy, I'd better tell you from the start.'

The story, as Amy heard it, was both a dramatic and a sad one, for Ella Morton had had the privileged life of an only child of rich and loving parents until a year previously. Mr Morton had decided to take his wife on a tour of Europe, visiting places of which they had both heard but had never seen. His business partner was prepared to take full responsibility for the firm in his friend's absence and had urged the Mortons to go ahead with the trip. The tour was to have taken them three to four months, but Ella was away at a boarding school in the south of England for most of this time and, when she came home, there would be a house full of servants who had loved her since she had been small and would, she knew, take great care of her. Ella herself had had no qualms over her parents' extended absence, but had quite looked forward to having friends to stay.

Mr Morton had been in partnership with a Mr Fortescue in the running of a large finance company. Since the relationship was purely a business one, Ella had scarcely known her father's partner, but what she had known of him she disliked. Her father had often remarked ruefully, 'Jim can be a bit too sharp at times; one of these days he'll cut himself and I hope to God I'll be able to staunch the blood before he ruins both of us.' Since this had been said half laughingly, however, Ella had been totally unprepared for what followed. One day her father's chief clerk had come to the house with a worried expression on his usually cheerful face. 'Oh, miss, I've got to get in touch with your father. Can you give me his direction? I shall have to send a telegram – it is of the utmost importance that I contact him without delay.'

Ella had been unable to help him since her parents had merely told her the extent of their tour and not precisely where they would be situated at any one time. She had received letters and postcards, but usually these were headed with the name of the town in which they were staying and gave little or no indication of where they would be next.

However, Mr Jones, the chief clerk, was a man of considerable persistence and as soon as he realised that Ella was unable to help him he set about finding his employer via the telegraph office, even consulting such persons as the mayors of small towns who might be able to help trace the Mortons.

'Sometimes I ask myself if it might not have been better had he not managed to find them,' Ella said ruefully, now. 'For he did find them, you know. They were in a tiny principality in the Pyrenees called Andorra, famous for its wild scenic beauty, I believe. Mr Jones's telegraph message had reached them there and the news that Mr Fortescue had absconded and the business was ruined brought my parents chasing home. Much alarmed, my father hired a coach and they set off for Toulouse, where they could have caught a train for Paris and then on to Calais.'

She gazed ahead of her, as though she were seeing pictures of the past. 'If they hadn't been in such a hurry they might not have had the accident which killed them.' She turned her large eyes on

Amy and a tear slid slowly down one cheek. 'I sometimes fancy that the driver of their conveyance must have been the worse for drink because he managed to overturn the vehicle, God knows how, on a narrow mountain track, high above a steep ravine. Mr Jones told me later that death would have been instantaneous, for they must have fallen a good three hundred feet, ending up half submerged in one of the raging torrents which abound in those parts. The driver was killed as well, however, so no one will ever know the truth of it.'

Amy could only stare at her companion as her own eyes filled with tears. 'Oh, Ella, what a terrible thing to happen,' she said, her voice trembling. 'You poor creature – how did you bear it?'

'I bore it very badly at first,' Ella admitted. 'I raged against Mr Fortescue and railed against the fate which had taken my parents from me. When they said there was no money, that the house would have to be sold to satisfy the company's creditors, I was so sad that I barely took it in – scarcely realised what it would do to me. I told myself that they were welcome to have every penny of the money, to take the house, my pony, everything I owned, if only it could all have been a mistake. All I wanted was my parents back. But it wasn't a mistake. They had gone and the house, our possessions, every penny that we had in the bank had gone too. Mr Jones thought I should appeal to my papa's relatives, but I did not intend to do that. They had not approved of his marrying my mother and had never attempted to get in touch with us, not even a letter of condolence when the tragedy was reported in the newspapers. So I left my boarding school for, at seventeen, I felt I had been educated enough and in any event there was no possibility of paying the fees once my parents were dead. Mr Jones managed to get me a position in a small shop on the Scotland Road, owned by a relative of his. I was grateful, of course, but she was a slave-driving old creature, who let me sleep on a mattress under the counter in her shop, underpaid me dreadfully and used me pretty much like a slave. Still, it kept the wolf from the door until I managed to get a better place and moved out to share a room with Minnie Miniver – her real name's Ethel Miniver, but everybody calls her Minnie and she's a good laugh.'

At the end of the story there was a long silence while Amy gazed, awestruck, at her new friend. It astonished her that a girl who had clearly been raised in cotton, as the expression goes, should have been able to earn her own living, dress herself well and become independent in the way that Ella had. In fact, it made Amy feel ashamed. She had her father, brothers and even Mary, to say nothing of Mrs O'Leary, all of whom would have supported her had she got herself into some sort of financial trouble. But Ella had had no one and had been strong enough to turn inwards and to use resources which she had probably been unaware she possessed.

She said as much to Ella, who leaned across the table and clasped her hand. 'We women are stronger than we realise ourselves,' she observed. 'You aren't happy at home, Amy, but if something terrible happened, if your father and stepmother were no longer able to support you, I'm certain you would do just as I did. Why, I thought from the moment I saw you that you looked the sort of girl I could be friends with and I'm a pretty good judge of character, let me tell you. If you want to take Mrs

Blenkinsop's advice and better yourself, then come along to the YWCA with me this evening when you finish work and see what's on offer. Don't ever sit down under the weight of your troubles; push them aside and start changing things, as Mrs Blenkinsop advises. For a start, you can spend a night sleeping in a blanket on the floor of our room, so you don't have to go all the way back to Seaforth after classes. Well? What about it? Are you game?'

'I certainly am,' Amy said, her voice still revealing her astonished surprise. 'When do they hold these classes, queen? Can I start at once? Only I'll have to go home first and tell my dad I'll be staying away for – what? A couple of times a week?'

'That's right, only it's Mondays, Wednesdays and Fridays,' Ella told her. 'We won't charge you to sleep on our floor so long as the landlady doesn't find out, but I do think you might provide us with a bit of supper on those evenings, just bread and marge and some jam, perhaps, or half a pound of broken biscuits and a pint of milk.'

'How about a nice piece of smoked haddock, or a pair of kippers?' Amy suggested, giggling. 'I dare say your landlady might not like the pong, mind.'

'Kippers!' Ella said longingly. 'It seems a lifetime ago that I had kippers for breakfast and, if you fit in and can afford it, perhaps we might manage to turn our two bedder into a three bedder, particularly once your family can manage without you. Why, we might even rent a larger room between the three of us.'

'Or the four of us, if Ruthie came in,' Amy said eagerly. 'Oh, Ella, you don't know what this means to me. You're a sport and the nicest girl I've ever

242

met. What's more, you've made me see that even a
working girl like me can better herself. You're a pal,
so you are!'

Chapter Seven

JUNE 1911

The train was crowded. Amy and the others had known it would be, which was why they had arrived at Lime Street Station early. The four of them – Amy herself, Ella, Ruth and Minnie – had thought long and hard before deciding to take their week's holiday from work and spend it in London, attending a big suffragette rally in the Albert Hall, then staying on to see the coronation of King George V five days later. Unfortunately others had also decided to arrive early in order to get seats on the train, so though the four girls had done their best to stick together, they had speedily realised it was to be every woman for herself. Amy and Ella had managed to get into the same compartment, but were separated at each end of it and could scarcely exchange more than smiles.

However, a train journey of such length was a delightful novelty for Amy. She had been lucky enough to get a corner seat, and now she settled down to gaze out of the window and reflect how her life had changed since she had met her friend.

It had all begun with the evening classes, of course. Miss Maple, who taught shorthand, type-writing and bookkeeping, was startled and impressed by the speed with which Amy assimilated knowledge. After barely two terms in her class she had suggested that Amy might like to try for a position as an office junior, which had just become vacant in the Adelphi Hotel. She pointed out that Amy would have to continue with her classes in the evening for some considerable while, but that working in an office all day, instead of in the fish market, would greatly increase her chances of passing the necessary examinations.

If it had not been for Ella, Amy reflected now, she might never even have applied for the post, but Ella had taken her in hand as soon as Amy had explained about the job.

'I don't want to hurt your feelings, Amy, but the very first thing an interviewer will notice is your clothing and general appearance,' Ella had said. 'You really should do something about your hair and complexion, you know. I realise it's difficult for you with a large family crammed into a little house, but you've got really pretty hair. If it were washed regularly and well cut to get rid of split ends, then it would do a great deal for your appearance. And though your complexion is good, just a touch of pencil on those fair eyebrows would give your face more . . . more character. I hope you don't think I'm being critical, love, but jobs for women are scarce and if you really want to get one . . .'

'I know you're right.' Amy had sighed, looking despairingly at her reflection in the small mirror which stood on the dressing table in the girls' room. 'The truth is, Ella, that when my mother was alive she used to wash my hair every week, regular as clockwork, and we had a bath every week, too. But now I'm working on the fish stall, it doesn't seem to matter what I look like, and Suzie's so mean with hot water that I'm lucky to get a bath once a month. As for clothes . . .'

'I'll lend you something suitable,' Ella said

eagerly. She looked critically at her friend. 'Yes, I've got a lavender blouse with a high neck and long, full sleeves and a navy skirt with a frilled hem which will suit you very well and impress the interviewer, whoever he or she may be. Tell you what, Amy, you come and stay with us the night before the interview and we'll send you off the next morning, neat as a pin and smart as paint, and if you don't get the job I'll eat my new chapeau.'

Amy had been delighted to fall in with this suggestion and, despite Suzie's grumbles, had insisted on a lengthy hot bath in the scullery the previous day. Back in the girls' room, Ella had scrubbed Amy's hair until the water ran clear, while Amy cleaned her nails with an orange stick. When Amy's abundant auburn locks were dry, Ella piled the red-gold tresses on top of Amy's head, holding them in place with three curved tortoiseshell combs. Only then did Amy don the clothes which Ella had set out and presently, looking at her reflection in the mirror, she had seen a young woman she scarcely recognised as the Amy Logan who served each day behind Mrs O'Leary's fish stall. The blouse clung tightly to her slender figure, the well-tailored skirt emphasised her tiny waist and the face which smiled back at her was pink and white from vigorous washing, the large, hazel-green eyes bright with excitement. 'Oh, Ella,' Amy had breathed rapturously, 'I never knew I could look like this – why, you could take me for a real lady.'

'You *are* a real lady, goose,' Ella said, laughing, 'and once you're away from that wretched fish market and working in an office or a shop or something similar you'll know I'm right. Of course I hope you'll get the job at the Adelphi, but there's bound to be stiff competition, so we mustn't despair if you don't get offered the very first position you apply for. And having seen how nice you can look, dear Amy, I'm sure you'll want to keep it up. Now, it's time you were off. Good luck!'

Amy had duly gone for the interview, along with a great many other young ladies of her own age, and had been waiting to hear whether she had got the job when Mrs O'Leary had her fall. Sluicing down cobbles when they finished work one evening, she had stepped back on to her empty bucket and had fallen heavily. She had made light of the accident at first, though it was clear she was in great pain, but the next day her sister had come to the fish stall to tell Amy that Mrs O'Leary's leg was broken. Two days after that Mrs O'Leary had asked Bill and Amy to call on her and had told father and daughter that the doctor who had set her leg had said that she would be unable to walk on it for three months. 'For as you know, I'm past seventy and I've an uncommon heavy frame,' she said frankly. 'What's more, I don't fancy employing someone to help Amy out just for three months, so it seemed to me and Bridget that the best thing would be for me to retire and sell the business.

'As you know, I rent the stall from the council,' she told them, sitting in a fireside chair, with her injured leg resting on a stool drawn up before her. 'But I've a good little business and the money I'll get for it will give me a bit of a nest egg for the years to come, though me and me sister have always put a bit by, like.' She looked from Bill to Amy and back. 'But your girl's worked hard for me, Mr Logan, with never a moan or complaint, and you've let me have the pick o' your catch even when you might have sold it better elsewhere, so I's offering you first refusal, like.'

She named a sum and Amy waited for Bill to consult her or to say that they could not afford it, but instead he leaned forward in his chair, rested his elbows on his knees and said earnestly, 'To tell you the truth, Mrs O'Leary, I've known ever since me illness the winter before last that I'd have to give up the fishing, lerrit go to a younger man. Gus is capable and finds the fish, and Albert's near on as good. I reckon if they takes on young Paddy Keagan the three of them will do just about as well as we did when I were aboard. But I've no mind to retire yet, so I've been looking about me for a nice little business. And what could be better than the stall? It'd keep it in the family, like, and now young Becky's in school I'd mebbe get me wife to give a hand.' He turned to Amy, sitting on a stool at his feet, and patted her shoulder. 'If you wanted to run the stall wi' me, queen, that'd be just grand, so don't think I'm trying to ease you out. But ever since you started them evening classes at the YWCA last September I've knowed you had your eye on an office job of some sort.' He turned back to the older woman. 'So the answer's yes, Mrs O'Leary. I'll buy the business with the greatest of pleasure and take over as soon as it's all signed and sealed.'

Amy had gone to her evening classes that night with a light heart. Although she had longed for the opportunity to work in an office and use her newly acquired skills, she had felt that by so doing she would be letting both Mrs O'Leary and the family down. But her father's buying of the fish stall changed things completely and her heart swelled with love for Bill, who had understood her yearning

248

to be something other than a fish seller, and was now happy for her both to move out of her home and to take up different employment.

For Bill had made it plain, as the two of them had made their way to the tram stop, that living in a room share in the city with friends of her own age was the natural thing to do. He told her that with himself on the fish stall, the boys running the boat and Suzie selling the shrimps, they should be able to manage very nicely without Amy's money coming in. Secretly Amy doubted that Suzie would agree with him, but she cared nothing for that. At first she would have her work cut out to feed and clothe herself, and pay her share of the rent, for office juniors got very little more than she had earned on the fish stall. She did not, however, intend to remain an office junior for ever. She had been overawed by the appointments of the great hotel, though the offices, when she reached them, were far from plush. She was to work in a small room with five other girls, sitting at plain deal desks with their typewriting machines before them.

'We have a policy of promoting from within,' the office manager told her. 'So the successful candidate might rise to giddy heights if she stays with us, Miss Logan.' And with this in mind, Amy had been glad to take the job when it was offered. Ella and Minnie immediately said she must move in with them and Amy did so, quite content with a mattress on the floor and with a diet which consisted largely of porridge, bread and margarine, and the oddments of fish which her father saved her from the stall, though while on duty the staff were given their meals at the hotel.

She had been a little in awe of Minnie at first; the

other girl was five years older than she and worked as chief assistant in Bunney's china department, earning a good deal more than either of the others. She and her widowed mother had originally lived in the lower half of a house in Huskisson Street, opposite St Bride's church, but after Mrs Miniver's death, Minnie had retained the largest room for her own use. Some months later, however, loneliness had impelled her to put a notice in a newsagent's window, asking for a room sharer, and Ella had applied.

The two girls had got on famously, but had found the rent of such a large room in such a pleasant neighbourhood difficult to find; hence Ella's invitation to Amy and subsequently Amy's own suggestion that they should ask Ruth to join them.

It had been, Amy thought now, gazing out at the flat fields of Cheshire as they passed the window, a good move for everyone. She visited the house in Seafield Grove at least once a month, sometimes oftener, and though Suzie had been strange and stiff with her at first she had managed to hide her animosity under a pretence, at least, of friendliness. Bill and the boys were always glad to see her, though Paddy was apt to mutter some excuse and leave the house as she entered it. He was living with the Logans once more, since Aunt Dolly had died soon after Amy had moved into the city and, though Gran had always behaved as if Aunt Dolly was nothing but a burden, she had not survived her sister by many weeks. So the house had been let to someone else and Paddy had moved back into the boys' room.

The train, which had been puffing along slower and slower, drew to a halt. Amy peered out and saw that they had reached Crewe. Every seat in the carriage had been taken and a great many men were standing in the corridor outside. There was a great deal of bustle and movement as people began to rise from their seats and push their way out on to the platform, while others reached up to the luggage racks for their possessions, heedless of those still seated. In the ensuing scramble Ella managed to get a place beside Amy and the two of them smiled at each other as the train began to fill up again. 'That's a bit of luck,' Ella observed, settling herself into her new seat. 'I wonder how many people on this train are bound for Hyde Park, like us? Did you notice there are a great many women aboard? I saw one woman on the platform with a purple, green and white riband under her jacket, but I couldn't read what it said. I'll be bound she was one of us, though.'

'I expect lots of them are heading for the rally,' Amy agreed. She and the other girls had their sashes beneath their jackets and did not intend to reveal them until they reached the rallying point in Hyde Park, where they were to march on the Albert Hall to hear the speakers. Amy was secretly fairly indifferent to getting the vote, which she thought was of little or no importance, but she understood Mrs Pankhurst's point that in order to get equal opportunities with men, women must first have a say in who ran the country and how they did it. She had supported the suffragette movement ever since that first memorable rally before St George's Hall, but neither she nor the other girls were active members.

'We're too young and too poor to be able to risk a term of imprisonment and bad marks against us,' Ella had said long ago, when the matter came up for discussion. 'We aren't going to chain ourselves to railings or throw ourselves under steam locomotives, but we'll do what we can to show our support for the movement.' So when the girls heard of the rally in London, and realised that it was to take place just five days before the coronation of King George and Queen Mary, they had decided, recklessly, to blow their week's holiday and the money they had saved up on a week in the capital. They had managed to get lodgings quite near Euston Station, where they would cheerfully sleep two to a bed, and planned to attend the rally, to see the sights of London and, on the day before the coronation, to take up good positions somewhere along the route. They had brought with them umbrellas, a warm coat and a blanket each, and intended to spend the night on the pavement rather than miss the wonderful spectacle of the royal procession.

'I think we ought to go straight to our lodgings and leave our suitcases,' Ella said, as the train began to pick up speed once more. 'Euston Station is a huge place so we'll have our work cut out to find the other two. The train is so crowded we can't possibly search for them until we reach London. Is Ruth wearing her poppy hat? That should be easy to spot.'

Amy chuckled. 'Yes, I think she is, and Minnie's got that carpet bag with the red fringe. Anyway, they'll be looking for us too, remember.'

'True,' Ella said. 'I suppose the thing to do is just to stand still. Then when everyone else is gone we'll be able to spot each other easily. Oh, Amy, I haven't enjoyed myself so much for years. Dear old London, I'm longing to see it again.'

'What a glorious day!' Amy lay on her back on the

cool green grass, gazing up into the blue sky above her. 'And isn't this the most beautiful place you ever saw, Ella? Aren't I glad we decided to have a day off from sightseeing before the coronation tomorrow. Mind you, when you suggested Hampton Court, I remembered old Cardinal Wolsey and Henry VIII and all that history stuff, and thought that we were in for another boring old museum. But this is prime!'

Ella, lying beside her on the grass, smiled and rolled on to her tummy. Propping herself on her elbows, she reached for the bag of buns they had bought earlier, selected one and proffered it to Minnie and Ruth sitting beside her. 'Yes, I know what you mean,' she admitted, taking a large bite out of the bun in her hand, 'but to tell the truth, Hampton Court is one of the few places around London I've never visited before myself. So coming here was a bit of a gamble.'

'Well, it was a gamble that paid off,' Minnie observed, chosing a bun covered in virulent pink icing. 'The rose garden is really beautiful, the scent of those big, dark-red ones made me feel as drunk as the bees. And the palace is most impressive, from the outside, that is. Our tickets allow us to go inside, only it's such a glorious day ... but I suppose we ought, don't you think?'

'I think we oughter have another go at the maze,' Ruth observed, taking a bite out of her own bun. 'We very nearly got to the centre last time, you know, and I'd rather do that than go inside a palace, no matter how impressive.'

'It's too hot,' Amy moaned. She picked up her straw hat which she had laid down beside her on the grass and fanned her face vigorously with it. 'Only fancy if the weather is like this tomorrow! But at least we shan't spend the night huddled under our umbrellas. That wouldn't have been much fun, would it?'

'Oh, I don't know,' Ella remarked, finishing her bun and rolling on to her back once more. 'It seems to me we have fun whatever we do, us four. Don't you agree, girls?'

It was true, Amy thought, remembering life in their large but crowded room in Huskisson Street. Having spent the first years of her life in a male-dominated household where women were expected to do all the jobs, save for such things as the bringing in of fuel and water, she appreciated more than the others how good it was to share household and domestic chores. Everyone did their own washing and ironing – sometimes the lines of washing criss-crossing the yard seemed to belong solely to the girls in the large front room – and took turns at practically everything else. Shopping and cooking were arranged on a rota basis, but it was a free and easy rota. If you were down to cook the Sunday roast and wanted to go out with a young man, or visit a relative on that particular day, you simply swapped with someone who was not so engaged. If doing the messages meant a visit to the dairy and another of your room-mates was going in that direction, then a simple request would be enough.

'If we're going to try and solve the puzzle of the maze again, then we really should be moving,' Minnie observed, standing up and beginning to dust crumbs off her long grey skirt. With varying degrees of reluctance the others joined her and, passing a bench where trippers had been picnicking, Amy spotted a copy of the *Evening Standard* and pounced on it.

'A free paper! And it's last night's, too,' she announced. She began to flick idly through the pages as they made their way towards the maze and presently, her eyes caught by the word Liverpool, she stopped short, a hand flying to her mouth. 'Hang on a minute, girls. You'll never guess what it says here! There's been trouble at the docks, a strike or some such thing, because they wanted a ten bob a month rise and the bosses turned it down. Good lord, aren't we the lucky ones? There's bound to be more fuss and we're out of it. It says here that there's been unrest in the streets, whatever that may mean.'

'Ooh, perhaps they'll stop the trams running, then I shan't have to go and tell me family all about the coronation,' Ruth said, grinning at Amy. 'Mind you, I'd walk to Seaforth sooner than miss telling Mam and the kids all about London and the King and Queen and everything. What's more, there's the souvenirs. The kids will be that eager to get their hands on what I've bought them, they'd probably walk into the city centre theirselves.'

'Good thing they aren't striking in London, that's what I say,' Ella remarked, as they stopped outside the maze. 'Still, as you say, it will all be over by the time we get back. Now, shall we tackle the maze separately or in pairs?'

It was still fine that evening when the girls made camp on the pavement along the procession route. They were by no means the only people so disposing themselves and, by the time they began to eat their sandwiches and drink tea from the bottles with which they had provided themselves, they were already on friendly terms with the people camping on either side of them. Both parties were Londoners, large family groups with what seemed, at first, like a dozen children apiece, all of whom raced up and down the road carrying news and gossip from one group to another, and being rewarded with sweets and fruit.

'This'll be the fourth night this century as I've spent on the pavement,' the mother of the family on their left informed Amy. 'Fust there were Queen Victoria's funeral, then King Eddie's crowning, then poor old Eddie's funeral and now young George's coronation.'

Amy would not have described King George as young, but she was intrigued to learn that her new friend – Mrs Potter – was such a connoisseur of royal events. As the night drew on, she encouraged Mrs Potter to talk about her previous experience of royal processions and was very moved to hear how, at King Edward's funeral, his charger was led behind the coffin with King Edward's riding boots reversed in the stirrups, and all the girls wept over the fate of the King's little dog, Caesar, who followed the coffin, searching constantly for his master.

'He were only a little mongrel,' Mrs Potter informed them, 'but on his collar it said "Caesar: I belong to the King". Oh aye, there's no doubt Teddy adored that dog; Caesar went with him everywhere – he'll be lost wi'out Teddy, poor little chap.'

It was after midnight before the excited, chattering crowd began to settle. Amy wrapped herself in her blanket and, using her bag as a pillow, managed to snatch a few hours' sleep. She guessed that the other girls had done the same, but woke slowly and grudgingly as a grey dawn crept across the sky, with a nasty taste in her mouth and her elbows and hips as stiff as boards. She sat, knuckling her eyes and looking around her. Presently someone further up the line lit a primus stove and boiled a kettle of hot water. She served her companions first, then came along the pavement edge, offering hot water to anyone who, as she put it, was 'dyin' to wet their whistle'. The girls eagerly proffered their enamel mugs and made themselves milkless tea, which greatly refreshed them and, as Ella put it, 'woke them up with a vengeance'.

Behind the pavement on which the girls had camped lay a park and on the previous evening they had noticed a drinking fountain on a small circle of gravel. Accordingly they went to it in pairs and had as good a wash as was possible in a public place. They combed their hair, pinned on their hats, shook out their jackets and brushed down their skirts, then made their way back to their camping site where they ate bread and margarine and apples for an early breakfast.

They recognised several of the women camping on the opposite pavement as members of the suffragette movement whom they had seen in the Albert Hall, and exchanged waves and smiles, but it really did look as though they were the only Liverpudlians, in this part of the crowd at any rate.

As soon as it was light enough, various enter-tainers began to stroll along the sides of the road. There were men with mouth organs, concertinas and penny whistles; there were tumblers who performed amazing acts, climbing upon each other's shoulders to form a huge pyramid, tightrope walkers who brought their stand and rope with them and danced as merrily along it, six feet above the roadway, as though they were performing on a stage. They got a great reception from the waiting crowds and were doing quite well when the police began to clear the roadway – obviously something was about to happen.

'We've got an excellent place here. We shan't miss much,' Ella remarked to Amy, as the first of the carriages containing the dignitaries began to arrive. The upper ten thousand, as Amy remembered Isobel calling them, would take their places in Westminster Abbey long before the royals arrived and Amy wondered what would happen should one of them wish to use the privy. There were public lavatories in the park and the girls had made use of them in the early hours, realising how crowded they would become later. But a lord or a lady, dressed in heavy ermine-trimmed robes of state, would be in no position to make a dash for the outside world, no matter how urgent his or her need.

By the time the young princes had driven past Amy felt quite hoarse from cheering, but when the King and Queen arrived, in an open carriage drawn by six cream-coloured ponies, she managed yet another cheer and waved her little Union Jack with as much enthusiasm as, five days earlier, she had waved her 'Votes for Women' banner.

'Oh, ain't I glad we came,' Ruthie said rapturously when the last of the colourful companies of soldiers had marched past. 'I won't ever forget today, our Amy. Are we goin' to wait until they come out? Only if we're goin' to catch our train . . .'

'I think we ought to be getting back to our lodgings,' Amy said regretfully. 'Judging by the newspaper report, we may find Liverpool in a bit of a state when we reach Lime Street, even though the strike will probably be over by now. What's more, I could do with a proper wash and a good meal. What do you say, Ella, Minnie?'

The girls all agreed that they had best begin to think about their journey home and turned, rather regretfully, back towards the environs of Euston Station.

The station was crowded, as they had guessed it would be, but not, Amy thought, as crowded as it would probably become later in the day, when the procession had returned to Buckingham Palace, shouted and cheered every foot of the way. She and her friends settled down with their baggage on one of the green wooden seats provided by the railway company, but as soon as their train came in they made a dash for it, hoping this time to be able to sit together.

They found a carriage in which two young men were piling their cases on to the luggage rack and settled themselves in a row. The young men finished with their luggage and one of them turned courteously towards them and offered to help them heave their belongings on to the string rack above their heads. For a moment Amy stared at the young man, wondering where she had previously seen him. But before she could say a word he suddenly beamed at her and, seizing her hand, shook it vigorously. 'It's Amy Logan, by all that's wonderful! Well, I'm darned, I've not seen you since you were a scrubby little kid with your skirts hiked up to your knees, helping to haul a fish ashore on Seaforth Sands. Don't you remember me? I'm sure you've changed a great deal more than I have.'

'Philip!' Amy said, considerably astonished. She thought he had changed greatly, despite his words.

He was wearing a boater tilted at a rakish angle, which he raised momentarily to reveal his light-brown hair, and he had a moustache which, in Amy's view, completely changed his appearance, making him look years older.

'Yes, it's me,' Philip agreed, grinning. 'My goodness, Amy, how you've grown! You're quite the young lady – but what in heaven's name are you doing in London? Don't say you've left home?'

'Yes, I have left home,' Amy admitted, 'but I don't live in London, we just came up for ... for the coronation, me and my pals here.' She indicated her friends with a wave of her hand. 'Come to that, what are you doing in London yourself, Philip? Or do fellers watch coronations as well as girls? And what are you doing on this train? You live in Manchester, near where my sister Mary used to work; she said so in her letters. Oh, I suppose you're getting off at Crewe and catching another train, is that it?'

Philip laughed. 'You aren't the only one who can leave home,' he observed, sitting down opposite Amy and leaning forward. 'I've been living and working in Liverpool for almost a year now. My father's firm has its head office in Manchester, I know, but two years ago we decided to expand and started up a branch in Liverpool. You could say I was in charge of it.' He suddenly struck his forehead, looking abashed. 'But whatever am I thinking of? Amy, this is Mr Maynard, one of my colleagues and a very good friend. Dick, this is Amy Logan, the sister of my pal Albert. Not that I've seen either of them for years. After my grandfather died the family sold the house in Seaforth, which meant Laura and I didn't visit there any more. A pity, because I loved the place, but life's like that.'

'I should have introduced you to my friends,' Amy said, conscience-stricken. 'This is Miss Morton, sitting next to me, Miss Miniver on her other side and Miss Durrant in the corner. Girls, this is Mr Philip Grimshaw and Mr Maynard.'

The girls murmured polite greetings just as the train jerked violently, causing Ella, who was sitting on the edge of her seat, to fall forward, landing almost in Philip's lap. This broke the ice in a way which nothing else could have done and presently the six of them were chattering away as if they had known one another all their lives. Amy took advantage of the situation and leaned forward to tap Philip on the knee. 'Philip, do you see much of our Mary? She's done well for herself and risen in the world. She used to work for a family who lived near your parents so I dare say you saw her now and again, but she's working in a departmental store on Deansgate now. She's in ladies' hats and doing ever so well, only she hardly ever comes home and we've never met her young man.'

'I do remember seeing Mary two or three years back,' Philip said slowly, after giving the matter some thought. 'Yes, now you mention it I did see her with a young man more recently. Well, not young exactly. In his mid-twenties I would say, but then she may have had several young men since then.'

'No, I think she's been going steady with Roderick ever since she moved to Manchester,' Amy said. 'He's in a bank and doing most awfully well, Mary says. She often mentions him in her letters but, reading between the lines, I don't think they mean to marry until they're in a really good financial position.'

'Marry? But she can't be more than twenty-two or

three?' Philip asked. 'They'll want to be able to afford a decent place of their own and also be able to do without Mary's wages before they wed. At least,' he added hastily, 'I imagine they will, because once they're married and the little ones come along . . .'

Amy giggled. It seemed strange to think of Mary marrying some unknown young man, let alone having children. Without fully understanding why, she realised that Mary had never talked about a home and children, only about marriage. Her sister was ambitious and the young man with whom she was going steady had his whole mind fixed on advancement. Perhaps, she thought now, they would never marry but would continue to keep company for years, until each attained the height of their ambition.

But Philip was talking now, telling her about the service flat which he shared with Mr Maynard and asking her about Albert, her parents and, of course, the Keagans and Paddy. Taking a deep breath, Amy told him rapidly all that had happened since that day on the beach. The birth of baby Becky, her mother's death, Bill's remarriage and her own move into the city. She said as little as possible about Suzie's attitude to herself and nothing about her job in the fish market, but she did tell Philip of her father's illness. She also told him that Bill now had a stall in St John's Market selling his own fish and was, consequently, better off than he had been since her mother's death. 'My stepmother's not a worker like my mam was,' she said. 'But she really loves my dad and she's good to the boys and little Becky, and since I'm not living there any more it's the most I can hope for.'

'What about Paddy?' Philip asked after a moment.

'I seem to remember you and he weren't exactly pally when we were kids.'

Amy laughed. 'We were sworn enemies from the first time he called me "Liverpool Shrimpy" and said I smelled of fish,' she admitted frankly. 'It was really difficult living under the same roof, once Bill and Suzie married, because he didn't like me any better for sharing our home and of course I simply hated him. But now he's working the boat with Gus and Albert, and when I go home he usually slopes off so I don't have much to do with him at all. A good job, I reckon.'

'I don't think he disliked you for yourself,' Philip told her, after a thoughtful pause. 'He was that fond of Albert that he was jealous of you. And he had a terrific crush on Mary, you know. He thought you were against him there and might set Mary against him too. I remember him going on about it one afternoon when the three of us went digging for cockles. Albert kept telling him he was talking nonsense and afterwards your brother told me privately that Paddy might as well forget all about Mary, because she would be after better game as soon as she was able. Anyway, don't tell me Paddy still dislikes you? You're a young woman and he's a young man now, not a couple of kids. Feelings change as you get older, the person you disliked may be quite different now that . . .'

At this point they were interrupted. 'If you two have stopped swapping family histories, how about a bite to eat?' Minnie said plaintively. 'We've got ham sandwiches wi' mustard, cheese-and-tomato rolls and a bag of sticky buns. They'll go round six easy, if you'd like to share 'em with us.' The young men agreed eagerly and Philip said that when the train stopped at the next station he would get out and buy six paper cups of tea from one of the platform vendors. Very soon a pleasant picnic was taking place and the conversation had become general.

Ella, always a lively and vivacious talker, told the two young men all about their room in Huskisson Street and made everyone laugh with a description of getting up in the early hours of a winter's morning, while it was still dark, and becoming horribly entangled with a pair of wet stockings which someone had strung on a line across the room. 'I thought it was either a web spun by the biggest and most horrible spider in the world, or a desperate robber, trying to tie me up,' she admitted. 'I shrieked so loudly that poor Minnie nearly had a heart attack. When I managed to find the candle and light it, she was sitting up in bed clutching a boot in one hand and the front of her nightgown in the other, with eyes as big as saucers and her mouth open to shout for help.'

'Why a boot, queen?' Ruth asked, giggling. The incident had happened, it appeared, before either she or Amy had come to live in Huskisson Street. 'Was you thinkin' of gettin' dressed and runnin' out on your pal?'

'No, indeed,' Minnie said with dignity. 'I thought it was a burglar, too, so I was going to brain him with me boot.'

'You make sharing a room sound great fun – much more fun than living in a hostel as a lot of girls do,' Philip said presently, his voice almost wistful. 'Dick and myself have a good time, of course, but we're sober citizens compared with the four of you. We go to the theatre, eat out most nights in the dining room below the flats, go dancing sometimes . . . do you ever go dancing?'

'Course we do, when we can afford it and there's a decent dance on,' Amy said at once. 'But even with four of us sharing, money's a bit tight. Why, we saved up for a whole year so that we could go to London for the . . . the coronation.'

'Tell the truth and shame the devil, Amy,' Ella said, smirking. 'We went to the suffragette rally first, fellows. We don't chain ourselves to railings or throw ourselves under steam trains or racehorses, but we do support the movement. We think we should have as much of a chance to earn a decent living as any young man. Don't you agree?'

'I do, up to a point,' Philip said cautiously. 'But I'm not sure I approve of the suffragette movement. It . . . it's unwomanly, don't you think? Surely there must be a better, *gentler* way of making your point and getting your own way? I mean, fighting the police, going to prison, chaining yourselves to railings . . .'

'The *gentle* way, as you put it, has been proving itself useless since the dawn of time, Mr Grimshaw,' Ella pointed out. 'No one wanted to have to use violence, or go to prison, or be force-fed in order to get what should be ours by right. Nor, for that matter, do any women I know want to give men carte blanche to bully and ill-treat the weaker sex as we are called, because that is how a good many members of the police force behave. Nothing gives them greater pleasure than to be allowed – nay, encouraged – to attack and beat distinguished and intelligent women who are merely asking that they be taken seriously. Such women, the average police-man knows, are intellectually and morally their

265

infinite superiors. So they are taking a sort of revenge on every suffragette whom they ill-treat and arrest.'

'Gosh!' Amy said, very much struck by this speech. 'Well, Philip, I hope that's given you something to think about. And there's no need to be *ashamed* to support the suffragettes, you know, for a great many gentlemen do. Even members of parliament,' she added.

Philip, who had been bending forward and listening to Ella with great attention, leaned back in his seat and expelled his breath in a long whistle. 'Phew! Well, thank you, Miss – er – Morton for the lecture, which I'm sure I richly deserved. I can't say you've changed my opinion, exactly, but you've certainly made me think.' He turned to his friend. 'You haven't said much, Dick. Are you a secret supporter of the suffragette movement? If so, you've kept it very quiet until now.'

Dick looked uncomfortable. Amy had often observed that among gentlemen who had not yet taken a stand, discomfort seemed to be their chief emotion. But finding himself the object of everyone's attention he cleared his throat and spoke: 'I don't know what I felt before, Miss Morton, but like my friend here, you've certainly given me something to think about. I must admit I've seen the police behaving in a very brutal and uncouth fashion during demonstrations ... but then, what choice have they? I suppose they have to use rioters roughly, whether they be male or female.'

Amy was about to reply wrathfully that violence against women who were for the most part incapable of using equal force, could never be right or fair when Minnie, ever the peacemaker, spoke up.

266

'Let's not argue,' she said placatingly. 'After all, there's been a seamen's strike in Liverpool while we were away, and I don't suppose anyone of us girls intends to go on to the streets and join the dockers' protest, even if we believe their cause to be just. So why should we expect these gentlemen to interest themselves in our cause? Let's change the subject, girls, and ask Mr Grimshaw and Mr Maynard to tell us a bit about their work.'

From then on conversation became general. The six of them discussed plays they had seen, actors and actresses they admired and the new kinema-color shows which had appeared for the first time at the Argyle Theatre in Birkenhead.

'Have you seen Vesta Tilley at the Empire? We went a week ago and we all thought she was superb – she looked more like a man than some men do,' Ella said.

'Do you go often to the theatre?' Philip asked eagerly. 'We might meet you there some time and perhaps go for a meal afterwards. Then we could tell each other what we thought of the show while we ate. Why, if four young women and two gentlemen seems wrong, we could get a couple of the fellows from the office to come along – just to make up the numbers you know,' he added hastily.

Amy was about to agree enthusiastically that this would be a great idea when Ella spoke. 'It might be fun, but you know we're all in work and fully employed until seven or eight in the evening,' she pointed out. 'Apart from this, our holiday, we don't get much time we can call our own. Mind you, we can go to the last house on a Saturday, because then we can lie in on Sunday, but other than that . . .'

'We do get half-days,' Amy put in. She sighed.

'But they aren't usually the same, unfortunately. Working at the Adelphi as I do, I often work shifts, which cuts down my social life, you might say. Ella and Minnie aren't too badly off because Bunney's and the Bon Marché close at a reasonable hour, but poor Ruth works in Dorothy's Dining Rooms and she can be kept really late some nights.'

'Dorothy's Dining Rooms!' Philip exclaimed, his eyes brightening, 'I *thought* I'd seen you somewhere before, I just couldn't think where. Dick and I often pop along to Dorothy's for a quick snack when we are working late and sometimes we take business clients along there for luncheon. It's very handy for Lime Street Station and most of them come and go between Manchester and Liverpool on the train.'

Ruth, who must have felt a little out of it, Amy considered, was delighted to find herself recognised and, after staring very hard at Dick and Philip for several moments, said she believed she remembered them as well. 'You're the young gentlemen who came in last week with a huge feller, old-fashioned looking, with a shiny top hat and a dickie bow,' she said triumphantly. 'He weren't with you,' she added hastily. 'I think he was in the Music Hall Show at the Royal Court Theatre. He's a magician or something, and ever so kind and jolly to us girls. He tips well and all,' she finished reflectively.

Philip's brow cleared and he grinned delightedly. 'What a memory you've got,' he marvelled. 'Yes, I remember now, old Marvo, the magician – he was in front of us last Tuesday and bagged the window table we'd got our eye on so we went and sat with young Stebbings and Mr Alcock.' He turned back to Ruth. 'Well, fancy you remembering that! Every time

I come into Dorothy's Dining Rooms in future I shall demand to be served by Miss ... Miss ...

'I'm Miss Durrant,' Ruth said, smiling shyly. 'Well, isn't that a coincidence? Are you sure you haven't met Miss Morton when you've been shopping in the Bon Marché? Or Miss Miniver when you go after sports equipment in Bunney's?'

The two young men laughed, but shook their heads. 'We don't frequent the department stores much,' Philip said, 'but now we know where to find you, perhaps we'll do so.' He turned to Ella. 'Why, you might even give me a discount, Miss Morton.'

With much similar chatter and a great deal of laughter, the journey passed in a flash and soon they found themselves on Lime Street Station once more. The young gentlemen offered to help pile their bags into a taxi cab but the girls refused, having every intention of getting a tram back to Huskisson Street. They walked along to Renshaw Street and very soon they were scrambling on to a number 15 and heading for home, tired but happy after their holiday in London and delighted to think that they had made two new friends.

A week later the girls were sitting round the open window of their room, eating supper from plates on their knees, for the day had been oppressively warm and they felt they would sleep better for some fresh air. Amy finished her brawn sandwich and set the plate on the floor, then picked up a letter from Mary, which had been delivered earlier in the day, and slit the envelope open. 'I wrote to Mary the day after we got home from the coronation, but I didn't expect a reply for a couple of weeks,' she observed, pulling out the thin lined sheets of paper. 'But here she is, writing to me a matter of days later. I wonder what's up? Perhaps she's coming home. Well, if she is, I'll have to see her weekends or evenings, because I've used all my holiday and I don't intend to take unpaid leave just because Mary's coming home.'

Ella finished her sandwich and put her own plate on top of Amy's, then shook her head sadly. 'What a one you are for leaping to conclusions,' she remarked. 'Poor Mary probably only wants to tell you what she did on the King's Coronation Day. Why don't you read it instead of making nasty remarks?'

Amy giggled. 'All right, all right, I'm just going to, no need to bully me,' she said and smoothed out the first sheet. She read the letter right through once, turned back to the beginning and read it again. Then she raised round eyes to her friends' faces. 'Mary *is* coming home,' she said in a dazed voice. 'I must be psychic, Ella, because she hardly ever comes home and I didn't really believe she meant to do so this time either. That's right at the end of the letter, mind. She begins by telling me that she and Roderick had the day off for the coronation and went out into the countryside on their bicycles with a picnic. Then she goes on about the street party which she and Roderick attended in the evening and the fun they had, and how people danced on the cobbles, and someone turned her ankle, and she and another girl took her to hospital . . . and after that she just sort of mentions that she's coming home and says she's looking forward to seeing me.'

'I wonder what's bringing her back all of a rush like that?' Ella mused. She stood up and began to collect the girls' used plates. 'I suppose she's going to stay with your parents, Amy? I mean, there isn't

270

room for a visitor here, no matter how tiny. Well, I suppose she could share your bed . . .'

'No, she couldn't,' Amy said firmly, going over to put the kettle on the gas ring. 'My dad would be terribly upset if Mary came to us instead of to Seaforth and besides, Mary's got a bit . . . a bit high and mighty you could say, these past years. One of the reasons she doesn't come home often is because she's ashamed of being a fisherman's daughter and living in crowded conditions. No, if she's coming home – and from her letter it looks as though she's planning to stay a week – then it's for some definite reason. If I didn't know about her bank clerk I'd wonder . . .'

'You'd wonder what?' Ella asked after a moment when Amy said no more, but Amy only shook her head. This did not mean, however, that she had not had what amounted to a revelation. She had written to Mary and had not omitted to tell her how they had met Philip and his friend on the train and what a jolly journey they had. Was it possible that Mary's early fancy for Philip was actually causing her to come back to Liverpool? Now that she thought about it seriously, she realised that it was highly unlikely Mary would have known that Philip no longer lived in Manchester until she had received Amy's letter. But the more Amy thought about it, the less she believed it possible. She did not know much about Mary's young man but surely her sister would be well aware that a bird in the hand was worth two in the bush? To come flying back to Liverpool just because Philip, whom she hardly knew, had returned to that city seemed an act of madness and Mary had always been level-headed, with an eye to the main chance.

I'm letting my imagination run away with me, Amy decided, taking the kettle off the gas ring and pouring hot water into the basin which they used for washing up. But having allowed the thought to take possession of her mind, she knew she would have to go to Seaforth that very Sunday and find out just why her sister had decided to come home.

Amy had planned to catch the early tram on Sunday, so that she might arrive in Seaforth in time to go to church with the rest of her family, but she had reckoned without the number of people who would want to travel from the city centre to Seaforth Sands on a fine Sunday in June. Three trams sailed past her, crammed to the eyebrows, with at least fifty people perilously strap-hanging, before she was able to climb aboard the fourth. So it was well past noon before she eventually got off the tram at the Rimrose Bridge.

It had been several weeks since she had last visited her family and she had not told them that she intended to do so today, so she was delighted, as she turned into Crosby Road, to find a small figure hurrying towards her along the pavement. It was Becky, pigtails flying, one ribbon already missing, but with a broad beam on her small face. 'Amy!' Becky squeaked, hurling herself into her older sister's arms. 'I come down the road 'cos our mam said our Mary were goin' to be on the next tram and there's you!' She gazed anxiously up into Amy's face. '*Was* Mary on your tram, our Amy? She writ to our dad sayin' she were gettin' a train today, 'cos her young man were takin' her to the pictures, Sat'day, only Sunday trains ain't good, our dad says. She weren't on your tram, were she, Amy?'

'No, she wasn't. And she may not be on a tram for some time, queen, because it's a lovely day and everyone wants to get to the seaside, so the queues for the trams are miles long – I had difficulty myself in getting aboard.'

'What'll I do then, our Amy?' the small girl enquired. Amy smiled down at her sister; she was a pretty thing, with her blonde hair cut into a fringe across her forehead and the rest plaited into two fat little pigtails. She had a rosy, cherubic face and large, light-blue eyes, and Amy had to admit that Suzie dressed the child beautifully now that she had the money to do so, and always saw to it that she was spotlessly clean. Today Becky wore a blue and white gingham smock dress, covered by a frilled white pinafore with white cotton stockings and neat brown shoes. Amy remembered how she and the others, including Paddy, had always gone barefoot in the summer, and thought there were advantages in being the spoilt youngest of the family, when the older children had all grown up. But she did not grudge Becky her boots or pretty clothes and was just glad, for the child's sake, that both Bill and Suzie clearly adored the little girl.

'Amy!' Becky shook the hand she was clasping impatiently. 'Shall I wait for the next tram or can we go home? I didn't really want to come up to meet Mary all that much 'cos I don't know her very well, not nearly as well as I know you. Besides, she's stayin' for a week this time an' I dare say you've only popped in to have tea with us. So shall us go home, Amy? The boys are home, of course, though Gus usually goes out of a Sunday. Oh, Amy, did you know Gus has fallen out wi' Peggy Higgins? And they've been goin' steady for three years – longer!'

'Well I never,' Amy said, as the two of them, hand in hand, began to walk up Crosby Road. 'Mind you, people do fall out from time to time, you know; it's probably what they call a lover's tiff and in a few days they'll be going steady again.'

'They won't, though,' Becky said positively, swinging vigorously on Amy's hand. 'Peggy's gorra little sister what's only two years older than me and she says Peggy don't care for Gus no more; she's gorra feller who ships aboard the *Devanha* what goes regular to India and the Far East. Elly, that's Peggy's sister, says he brung back a china tea set for Peg wi' little cups like eggshells, all painted wi' pagodas and such. She says Gus never give Peggy nowt but the odd bag o' shrimps.'

'Well!' Amy said, considerably shocked to hear her small sister passing on such gossip. 'I tell you what though, queen, if all Peggy thinks about are what presents a feller can hand out, Gus is better off without her. Although it seems a shame he wasted all those years courting her.'

'Oh, Gus don't mind,' Becky said cheerfully. 'He says women just hold a feller back and he's goin' to take a berth aboard a trawler like our Edmund done and make his fortune that way. Then Peg will be sorry, he says.'

'I dare say she'll be sorry long before that,' Amy said, as they turned into Seafield Grove. 'You know the strike everyone's been talking about, queen? Well, it means there's a great many sailors hanging about the city, bored with having nothing to do. Probably Peggy's new young man is one of them and when the strike's over and his ship sails he won't give Peg another thought. And serve her right,' she ended, as the pair of them crossed the yard and entered the Logan kitchen. She could not help reflecting, however, as she glanced round the room, that things had changed greatly in the years since she had lived at home. The kitchen had been freshly painted and the worn and shabby furniture she remembered had been replaced by a new upholstered sofa and two easy chairs. The old stoneware sink, with its slippery wooden draining boards, had gone and there was a modern sink unit where it had once stood. Instead of the rickety sideboard, which Isobel had told her had been left in the house by the previous tenants, a smart mahogany one now leaned against the wall. Also, bright damask curtains hung at the windows and, when Becky sat down, it was on a sateen-covered pouffe instead of the three-legged wooden stool which had usually accommodated the youngest Logan child.

The changes had come gradually, of course, and Amy had long realised that the ownership of the fish stall had done wonders for the family's economy. As Bill said, they had cut out the middle man completely, selling virtually from the boat to the public so that the fish was always the freshest available and customers' recommendations meant that there was scarcely any waste.

What was more, now that they only paid the rent on this one house, Bill had taken on an extra allotment and he, Gus and Albert – and probably Paddy, too, for all she knew – grew vegetables there, for when Suzie took her shrimps from door to door, she had begun to sell fresh vegetables, and found they were as popular as the fish and sold every bit as well.

With a little more money available, things had

become easier all round. Suzie no longer took in washing and the family ate shop-baked bread, though Suzie's cooking had improved considerably. Gran had left an old exercise book in which she had noted down her favourite recipes and Suzie, carefully conning it, began to present her family with cakes, pies and puddings, and was delighted with their enthusiastic response.

Now Bill, who had been sitting reading an old copy of the *Echo*, puffing away at his pipe, turned at Amy's entrance and stood up. 'Well, blow me down!' he exclaimed, crossing the room towards her and taking both her hands in his. 'Here was I expectin' one daughter and who should turn up but t'other! I'm delighted to see you, queen, but where's you sprung from, eh? We were expectin' Mary. She wrote and said she were comin' home today so Suzie sent our Becky down to the tram to meet her. Though I'm powerful glad to see you, Mary or no Mary,' he ended, giving her a kiss and a hug.

'There's a deal of fuss going on in the city because of this here strike,' Amy said, carefully unpinning her hat and hanging it on the back of the kitchen door, 'and on a fine day, everyone wants to get away from trouble and down to the beach. So the trams were chock-a-block. Still, I got here in the end. The truth is, Dad, that Mary wrote to me as well and I thought, since I was off today, I'd pop over and see her – and the rest of you, of course – so we could have a good old jangle. But it looks as though, if I want to see Mary, I'll have to make some other arrangement.'

Bill had returned to his newspaper, but now he looked up. 'Suzie, Gus and Albert have gone up to the allotment. They won't be long but Suzie fancied

276

cookin' a mess of peas for our supper, so they've gone to pick any that's ripe. You know we sell 'em now. We do well with 'em in summer and in winter the root vegetables go down a treat, so one way and another we ain't doin' bad.'

'I know and I think it's grand,' Amy said, taking the chair opposite her father's. 'The kitchen looks lovely, too, Dad. Isn't Mary going to have a surprise when she gets here? It must be months since she was last home.'

Becky, having come in with Amy, asked brightly, 'Can I go to the 'lotment, Dad? I can help carry the veggies home.'

'Yes, but don't you go eatin' all the peas afore we've had a chance to shell them,' Bill said, grinning. As the back door slammed behind Becky, he turned to his older daughter. 'Did our Becky tell you about Gus?'

'Yes, she couldn't wait to tell me,' Amy said, smiling. 'It's a pity, but these things do happen.'

Bill was beginning to reply when the back door opened and the rest of the family surged into the room, with Becky dancing ahead. Suzie came over and kissed her stepdaughter with a warmth that Amy appreciated, since when she had lived at home such warmth had been notable only by its absence. Albert came over and punched her in the shoulder, the way brothers do, and Gus ruffled her hair, saying jovially, 'Where's you sprung from, our Amy? We were expectin' Mary, but not yourself. Have you heard about ...'

'If you mean that you and Peggy have split up, you can't enter Seaforth without someone giving the news,' Amy laughed up at her big brother. 'I'm not going to offer you my condolences, though, because the general opinion seems to be you're well out of it. Met anyone else yet?'

Gus snorted. 'No, nor I don't want to,' he said gruffly. 'I wasted the best years of me life on Peggy Higgins; now I'm goin' to have me some fun before I'm too old to appreciate it. Wharr I want is a fast woman – do you know any, young Amy?'

Amy spluttered and rose to her feet to give Gus a slap, but he had carried the heavy basket of vegetables through into the scullery, so she sat down again. Albert, who held a string bag full of pea pods, came over to her, tipped a quantity into her lap and stood a heavy saucepan down by her side. 'Shell 'em for our tea, there's a good little sister,' he said, going over to the door to kick off his muddy boots. Over his shoulder he went on, 'No one said as how you were comin' home today, Amy, you could've let us know. That young Durrant girl comes home most Sundays, don't she?'

'I don't really know,' Amy said, surprised, 'just lately I've been doing a lot of shift work, so I haven't had many Sundays off myself. Still, I couldn't have told Ruthie I was coming home because I only made up my mind yesterday, when the boss said he wouldn't be needing me in today. Hotels aren't like shops and such, we have to have a full staff in seven days a week.'

'Well, it doesn't matter; you're here now,' Albert said lazily, sitting down beside her and beginning to ping peas into the saucepan. He followed Amy's example and dropped the empty pods in a neat pile by the fast-emptying string bag. 'Wharrabout young Peggy Higgins, then, did Gus tell you . . .'

'Everyone's telled her,' roared Gus from the scullery. 'Honest to God, there's no need of a town crier in Seaforth; every perishin' person knows your business almost before you know it yourself.'

'Well, it's the most excitin' thing to happen in Seaforth for half a century,' Albert said, grinning. 'I wonder when our Mary will arrive, though? Paddy said he were goin' to come home via the Rimrose Bridge to see if he could meet her, so mebbe the two of them will turn up in time to eat supper, if not help prepare it.'

Amy was making a joking reply when the back door burst open and a tall, broad-shouldered young man entered the room, closely followed by a girl, dressed in the height of fashion and wearing a hat so large and flower-bedecked that it was all she could do to get it through the doorway. Amy stared hard at the young man, scarcely able to believe that this was Paddy, but when Becky jumped up from her pouffe, squeaking 'Ooh, ooh, our Mary, ain't you grand!' she was almost betrayed into a gasp of astonishment.

Apart from the hat, which completely hid Mary's abundant curls, her sister was wearing a plum-coloured silk two-piece suit, with a lace jabot at the neck and a nipped-in waist. The skirt was full and brushed the ground. It must, Amy thought, have been uncomfortable for such a hot day, but her sister did look very smart and she supposed that her appearance mattered more to Mary than her comfort.

There was a concerted shout from the assembled family and, while Paddy crossed the kitchen quietly carrying Mary's bags, Amy managed another covert glance at him. She had not seen him for several months, since if she came on a Sunday and he was pre-warned, he always absented himself from the house and on a weekday, of course, he was out with her brothers in the fishing boat. Now, reluctantly almost, she saw that Paddy had grown into a sturdy and self-reliant young man. He was not handsome but he had a pleasantly tanned face and his dark hair curled attractively across a broad forehead.

He saw her looking at him and shot her a quick glance, accompanied by a smile which revealed even white teeth. 'Hello, Shrimpy,' he said as he passed her chair, his eyes twinkling wickedly, and Amy, who had intended to be coolly friendly, found that at the mere mention of the old nickname her hackles had risen and her brows had drawn into a frown. She would have liked to ignore the remark – and Paddy – altogether, but remembering how she had promised herself not to be nasty, said coldly, 'Hello, Paddy.'

She expected him to pass on, but instead he lingered. 'You've changed, queen,' he said, sounding almost surprised, as though he had expected her to remain a child for ever. 'You were such an ugly, gingery kid, but now you're quite a looker! Gerrin' away from this household – and me, of course – seems to ha' done you a power of good.'

'How nice of you to say so,' Amy said sarcastically. 'I wish I could say the same of you, but honesty forbids it. Though you're a lot larger, naturally.'

He grinned, a flash of white teeth in his tanned face. To Amy's fury he looked amused rather than outraged. 'Well, now, isn't that just typical? I never knew you to say a nice word if you could think of a nasty one. And despite your looks, you're still not half as nice as your sister Mary.'

Amy opened her mouth to say that she knew very

well Mary was beautiful and she was not, but he had continued on his way past her and was mounting the stairs. When he came down again, having left Mary's bags in her room she assumed, he went over to where Albert and Gus were sorting out vegetables and fell into conversation, leaving the two girls and Becky to chat among themselves. And presently, when Amy stood up to carry the peas and their pods into the scullery, she saw Paddy disappearing, without a word of farewell, through the back doorway.

Paddy had been genuinely impressed by the change in Amy. As he walked along, heading for the beach, he marvelled at how the ugly duckling of a few years back had changed into a beautiful swan. Not that she resembled a swan in the slightest. With her flaming red hair, and eyes green as sea water, she was far more exotic than any swan. What was more, though she had changed so much, she still had the sharp tongue and quick wits which he had once hated but now rather admired.

Pity they had never got on, because in different circumstances he would have liked to take her out, enjoy her company, instead of feeling bound to remain her enemy.

But there you were; she disliked him, so no chance there of a reconciliation. Shrugging philosophically, Paddy continued to walk and whistle, and to try to forget Miss Amy Logan and her fascinating but prickly personality.

Amy saw no more of Paddy until supper was actually on the table, though the rest of the family remained at home, making much of herself and

Mary. When she asked Albert, on the quiet, where Paddy had gone, he gave her a hard stare and said, 'He'll have gone to the allotment. Why do you want to know, queen? Paddy always clears out when you're around, you know that.'

'Yes, but he's that keen on Mary, I should have thought he'd have stayed indoors,' Amy said rather feebly. She told herself she did not care whether Paddy stayed or went, but she did wonder if his old feelings for Mary had survived their years apart. She could not say this to Albert, however, and allowed the subject to drop.

The tête-à-tête which she had wanted with Mary did not occur until late in the evening, when supper had been eaten. Becky had been put to bed and the family had spent a pleasant hour exchanging news. Bill told them all about life in the Great Charlotte Street fish market, Albert prattled on about the fishing, as did Gus, and Suzie spoke in a sprightly and affectionate manner of Becky's progress at school and of the pleasure she herself took in home-making, now that there was a little more money available.

But Mary, rather to Amy's disappointment, did not do much talking at all. On previous occasions when the two girls had met, Mary's tongue had run on wheels; the other girls in her department, her neighbours in Young Street, friends of both sexes whom she had made in Manchester and the grand entertainments available in that city, had come pouring out. But now, although she answered questions readily enough, she was strangely reticent about her own life. She commented, rather sourly, upon the bedlam that had been caused on all forms of public transport during the recent unrest and how bad it been for sales in her department. Amy, who had thought the strikes had been confined to Liverpool alone, was surprised, but did not say so. It would not do to antagonise Mary by making light of the troubles in Manchester compared with those of Liverpool, so she decided to hold her tongue. Under cover of the general conversation, Amy looked long and hard at her sister and realised, with a pang of mixed astonishment and dismay, that Mary was looking almost haggard. Her cheeks, which had always been round and pink, were hollow and the white skin in which she had taken such pride looked weary and almost sallow beneath the layer of fine powder that disguised it. Amy thought her sister had lost weight and she had certainly lost the air of confidence which Amy remembered.

Rather to Amy's surprise, Paddy had not put in an appearance until the family were halfway through their meal, but then he had come in and taken the place beside Mary. He had spoken little, simply eating his food as rapidly as good manners permitted and gulping down three cups of strong tea. Then he had scraped back his chair, muttered to Mary that he would see her later, raised a hand to the rest of the company and left the house. Albert, noticing Amy's surprised glance after his friend, told her that Paddy meant to fetch up the nets which needed mending, so that they might work on them before the light failed, but since Paddy did not reappear, Amy guessed that this was just an excuse. No matter what anyone might say, Paddy could not bear to be in the same room with her. Not that it mattered; she was happier with his absence than his presence and with the rest of her family around her he was quickly forgotten.

Presently Amy glanced at the clock over the mantel and realised that, unless she wanted to miss the last tram, she had best begin to say her goodbyes. She stood up. 'Bless me, look at the time,' she said gaily. 'I've got to be going just in case the tram's on time, though with this bleedin' strike there's no saying what will happen. Thanks for a grand supper, Suzie – my day off's Wednesday this week, so maybe I'll come over again . . .' She turned to Mary. 'Unless you'd rather come into the city, queen? We could have a day out together and I could introduce you to the girls I live with.'

'I'd enjoy that,' Mary said quietly, 'it seems an age since I walked down Church Street and visited the big shops. Yes, a day out together would be fun.'

Amy walked to the back door and, reaching her hat down, pinned it on, then turned to find Mary standing beside her and donning her own magnificent headpiece. 'I'll walk down to the Rimrose Bridge with you, our Amy,' Mary said with almost studied casualness. 'It's a warm night and I could do with a breath of fresh air.'

Amy waited for Albert or Gus to offer to accompany them, which would have spoilt everything, for she guessed that Mary wanted to talk, but neither of her brothers moved from their places around the table. Albert was carving a piece of driftwood into a little horse, which he intended to give to Becky, and Gus was deep in his father's cast-off newspaper. Hastily, before either boy looked up, Amy called her goodbyes and the two girls slipped out into the cool of the night.

Until they reached Crosby Road they walked in silence, apart from Amy murmuring that it was good to smell the salt breeze again, but once they turned the corner Mary began to speak: 'Amy, I've got to tell someone and I'd rather it were you than anyone else. You know Roderick, my feller?'

'You've mentioned him once or twice in your letters,' Amy said cautiously, 'but you never *said* much about him, if you understand what I mean. I don't know if he's tall or short, dark or fair, fat or thin. In fact, to be honest, Mary, I don't even know if he was the sort of feller I'd like above half. Tell me about him.'

Mary sighed and stared ahead for a moment without speaking and, when she did, it was in a low tone, almost as though she were speaking to herself. 'There's no point in talking about Roderick,' she said, 'because he isn't my feller any more. Just about the time your letter came, telling me about your trip to London, I found he was two-timing me with a young piece who worked in Buss and Sons, the ironmongers on Deansgate, just next door to William Wright's, where I worked. So that's five years of my life down the drain, queen.'

'Oh, Mary,' Amy gasped, 'I'm so sorry, but you must think of it same as Gus thinks about losing Peggy. He says better to find out now than later and I'm sure he's right. How could anyone do that to you, Mary? He must be a real swine.'

'He was ambitious,' Mary admitted. 'But so was I, come to that. He was doing well in his bank, looking to be head clerk one of these days and I've moved up from just being a counter hand to being second-in-command of hats and gloves. We've been putting money away and in a couple of years we'd have had enough to buy a decent little house in the suburbs . . .'

'Buy?' Amy squeaked, quite stunned by this

remark. People in their situation simply did not buy property, it was far too expensive. Everyone she knew rented their own homes, so why should Mary and this Roderick have been different? But perhaps renting property was not so easy in Manchester; her experience of such matters only encompassed Liverpool and its environs.

'Yes, we meant to buy,' Mary confirmed. 'Roderick said that owning property was an investment for the future and he was keen on the future, was Roderick. What was more, he always liked me to look nice and dress well, because appearances are so important. He said he was proud of me – but then he goes gadding off with some horrible little tart what's no more than sixteen. I ask you, Amy, what would you do?'

'I'd do what you've done,' Amy said immediately. 'I'd come home for a bit of a holiday and maybe look around me for a job in Liverpool, where I wouldn't have to see horrible Roderick or his tart. Is that what you mean to do, Mary?'

'Well, I'm definitely thinking about it,' Mary told her. 'Fancy you guessing, Amy! The truth is, I've applied for a job as senior sales lady in Blackler's department store and if I get it . . . Why, I've even sorted out accommodation. A friend of mine from Manchester moved to Liverpool six months back and she's offered to let me share her rooms – she's a bit out of the city but on a good tram route, so I shall be able to get in to work easily enough. If I take the job, that is. It's a big move, but I'd be nearer home and nearer my family . . . Do you think I'd be doing the right thing, though? I mean, I've been in Manchester a long time now and I know the city a good deal better than I do Liverpool.'

The two girls had reached the tram stop but the driver was not in his seat, so Amy leaned against the vehicle for a final word before climbing aboard. 'I don't know whether I'm the right person to give you advice, since I've spent all my life in Liverpool and never so much as seen Manchester,' she said after a moment's thought. 'But I've heard Blackler's are a good firm to work for, and if you really don't think there's any chance of you and Roderick getting back together . . . well, it seems sensible to come home and . . . and sort of start a new life. You are sure you won't want to . . . to start things up again with Roderick? I don't know much about young men, you know, because I've never had one and neither have any of my friends, not the ones I room with, I mean. We're all fancy free, you might say.'

There was a short, somehow startled silence, then Mary gripped her arm and spoke. 'But what about Philip?' she asked. 'You told me in your letter you had met up with Philip and were going to see him again. Don't tell me you're not interested in him, because I shan't believe you. He liked you when we were just kids. He told me so and to tell the truth, Amy, I think he liked me as well. Whenever we met in the square or down Deansgate he was always most polite, raising his hat and giving me the friendliest smile.'

Amy stared at her; so her first wild guess had been right; Mary had come back to Liverpool in the hope of getting to know Philip once more. However, she knew better than to let Mary realise she had guessed and was on the point of saying that her sister should not read too much into smiles exchanged in the street, when the driver and conductor abandoned the cigarettes they had been smoking and climbed aboard the tram. 'Come along, ladies both,' the conductor shouted jovially. 'No time to lose, we'll have folks all along the route cursing us if we don't gerra move on, 'cos this is the last tram tonight.'

Hastily Amy scrambled aboard. She turned in the doorway and called back to Mary, 'See you on Wednesday. Come to Huskisson Street around ten o'clock – don't be late – and we'll talk then.'

Within a month of the visit to Seafield Grove, Mary had accepted the job in Blackler's and settled in to her friend's rooms in a small house in Mather Avenue, out Allerton way. It was a suburb of the city which Amy did not know at all, but she had called for Mary after work one evening and gone home with her, and had been pleasantly surprised, almost envious, at the two airy rooms the girls shared, with the use of a kitchen and – wonder of wonders! – a real bathroom. It was not cheap and Mary had to get up early in order to catch the number 8 tram which would carry her in to the city centre, but she and Faith, her friend, were clearly very satisfied with their little home. In fact, Amy thought as she sat on the last tram back into the city centre later that night, Mary had really fallen on her feet and seemed happier – and better tempered – than she had been for a very long time.

All those ambitions to be something she wasn't hadn't done much to make her happy, Amy told herself, as the tram rattled and creaked onward. Nor did trying to live up to that Roderick feller. But being a person in her own right, earning her own living, meeting up with her relatives now and then . . . well, it had turned Mary back into the gentle, thoughtful young person who had adored her mother and loved her little sister, and Amy was happy that it was so.

Presently the tram stopped in Renshaw Street and Amy stepped down, thankfully climbing on to a number 15 almost immediately, which would take her the rest of her way home. She turned into Huskisson Street, thinking that it was nice to have a sister close enough to visit for an evening and hoping that Mary, too, would come visiting in the not too distant future.

Chapter Eight

It was a burning hot day in August, and Amy and Ella were walking in to work, not because they felt they needed the exercise but because, due to the railwaymen's strike, which was now established, and the consequent riots that had been rocking the city, the trams were running a restricted service. The tram drivers had gallantly refused to go on strike too, but because of the ugly mood of the rioters they had insisted upon some form of protection. Every tram now carried an armed soldier on board, but despite the fact that the troops came from the barracks in Seaforth, the girls felt uneasy in their presence. Many strange soldiers had been drafted in to help control the crowds and Amy felt that such men might fire first and regret it later, unlike the men who usually manned the Seaforth barracks. So rather than face the few trams that were running, the girls had decided they would walk in to work that morning.

'I never knew a strike of railway workers could lead to such complete chaos,' Ella grumbled as the heat rose off the paving stones, making their feet feel like live coals. 'There's hardly any food in the shops and someone told me that last night the crowds pelted the police with fruit, which seemed a great shame. I could just do with a nice basket of raspberries right now and I wouldn't throw them at anyone; I'd eat the lot. When you think of all the fuss the authorities made over the suffragette rallies – and now look at this crew! There are scarcely any public service vehicles running, most of those who want to work have to walk into the city, the rioters have been giving the police as good as they get, looting shops, chucking bricks, and you can walk a mile and not find a loaf of bread or a pound of sausages for sale.'

'Yes, I know what you mean. But better not say it too loud,' Amy advised, tucking her arm into Ella's. The two girls had always been good friends, but since Ella had got a job in the offices of the Adelphi Hotel and worked side by side with Amy, they had become almost inseparable. Not that they were doing the same work; Ella's good education had won her an unusual sort of job, for as well as taking shorthand notes and typing them up on her machine, she was called for regularly when French or German guests arrived and had difficulty in making themselves understood, whereupon she would interpret for the management.

'There's a lot of folk about,' Amy said rather uneasily, as they continued to make their way towards the hotel along crowded pavements. 'Oh, look, that window's been smashed, and there's fellers all in among the display ... they're helping themselves ... oh, Ella, look out!'

A group of men were charging along the pavement towards them, all dressed in working clothes, and behind them, in hot pursuit, came a number of policemen, batons in hand, clearly intent upon catching the miscreants, if miscreants they were. Amy and Ella ducked into the nearest shop doorway, their light shoes crunching on broken glass, but even the doorway was no refuge for long, for behind the policemen came an excited crowd of men, many of whom brandished various objects with which they clearly intended to do violence. The shop doorway they had chosen – or rather had been forced to choose – belonged to an ironmonger and, as soon as he realised this, a large, disreputable-looking man from the crowd swung the brick he was carrying at the window. It shattered and long, wicked-looking shards of glass showered every-where, some of them descending like daggers into the flooring where they stayed upright, quivering every time anyone moved.

Clinging together with their hands up to their faces to save them from flying splinters, the two girls crouched against the shop door. Amy put up a hand and tried the brass doorknob, but the door remained obstinately closed; clearly the owner had been too wary to open his premises while the unrest continued. Without taking her hands from her face, Amy thought she could tell very well what was happening by the sights and shouts alone. Booted feet trampled on broken glass, heavy objects fell with a thud and men's voices exclaimed as they picked over the contents of the window. Amy guessed that for the most part they were looking for weapons rather than simply looting, for beyond the policemen she had seen the flash of military uniforms and the light reflecting off gun barrels. So they had called the army in. But during the many weeks that the strike had been in force she had begun to understand the desperation which drove the strikers. If need be, she thought now, they would fight the army as well as the police, using any weapon that came to hand.

As the footsteps began to leave the ironmonger's window once more, she risked a peek from between her hands and saw men armed with garden spades, forks, rakes and weighty-looking carpentry tools, brandishing them as they abandoned the premises. To Amy's amusement, one of the strikers had protected himself by placing a coal scuttle on his head and another followed suit with a large white chamber pot, which fitted snugly round his outstanding ears. She could not help reflecting, however, that one good blow from a policeman's baton would shatter the chamber pot, probably causing the wearer more trouble than it had saved him. She also noticed that most of the men streaming past looked as though they had not had a square meal for a week and her heart bled for them when she saw the stout, well-fed policemen who followed close on their heels.

Beside her, Ella dropped her hands from her face and gave vent to a long, whistling sigh. 'Cripes!' she said inelegantly. 'What have we got ourselves into this time? This isn't just a protest meeting, nor a gathering of strikers, this is a full-blown riot. Should we go home, do you think, or will it be safe to press on to the Adelphi?'

Amy, picking pieces of glass out of her cotton skirt, looked at the crowd pressing close against the doorway as they passed. 'I don't think we're going to have much choice,' she said doubtfully. 'I think the moment we poke our noses out on to the pavement we'll simply get carried along with the crowd. It isn't that they won't let us go in the opposite direction, it's a bit like throwing yourself into the Mersey when the tide's coming in. You don't get any choice and nor does the river; it'll carry you inland, willy-nilly, until the tide starts to ebb again.'

'Oh, very poetic,' Ella said, shaking her own skirt free of splinters. 'Well, we can't stand here for ever, we'll have to make a move sooner or later, so how about now?' And without giving herself time to think, she grabbed Amy's hand and the two of them plunged into the maelstrom of people who they could now see filled the roadway as well as the pavement.

'Put your arm round my waist, Ella!' Amy screamed at the top of her voice. The one thing suffragette rallies had taught her was to hold on physically to anyone from whom you did not wish to be parted. 'The first chance either of us gets, we'll turn aside, pulling the other one with her.' She turned to a burly, cloth-capped man in the coat and gaiters of a carter, who was being borne alongside her. 'Where's the crowd heading?' she shouted. 'And when did the troops arrive?'

The carter shrugged massive shoulders, or at least Amy guessed that he had, for it was difficult to see small movements when being urged forward by people behind. 'I don't know as we're goin' any-where,' he bawled back. 'I guess we're running away from the scuffers and the soldiers. There ain't much unarmed chaps like us can do against a bleedin' brigade wi' fixed bayonets and loaded rifles.' He glanced curiously down at them from his great height. 'Whot's a couple of young ladies like yerselves doin' in this 'ere scrum, anyway?' he enquired. 'This is no place for the likes of you. Come to that, I ain't seen a female all mornin', 'cept for you two.'

'We were on our way to work at the Adelphi Hotel when we got caught up and carried along with the crowd,' Amy shouted back. 'Where are we, do you know? I can't see anything, save for people all crushed together and moving like a river.'

'Dunno,' the man roared back. He opened his mouth to say something else but in the strange way which happens in a crowd he suddenly dropped behind them, while Amy and Ella, quite without their own volition, surged forward. The last Amy saw of her friend the carter was his hand reaching for his cloth cap as it was knocked from his head by an advertisement sign.

Half an hour later, still trapped by the many people around them, Amy at last managed to recognise their whereabouts. Towering to the right of her were the well-known cream-coloured stones of the free library, where she and Ella spent a good deal of time searching for the books they needed. And on the other side of William Brown Street, as she well knew, were the shaded lawns and pleasant pathways of St John's Gardens. If they could only push their way through the crowd and reach that haven, surely they would be safe?

She shrieked the information into Ella's ear and the two of them began, for the first time, actively to attempt to push their way through the crowd, though they both realised that this was a dangerous move, for one stumble would mean you could be thrown to the ground and trampled to death beneath heedless feet, the owners of which were not even aware of your presence.

Nevertheless, Ella must have thought it was worth a try for she nodded, indicating that she understood and the two girls began to try to make their way through the close-packed crowd.

They had actually succeeded, though not in time

to enter the gardens, for the forward movement of the crowd had not stopped, so it was close against the St George's Plateau that they finally got more or less free. Amy was just drawing in her first unhampered breath of relief, when she saw, on her left, a number of men in military uniform. They appeared to be kneeling and pointing something across the heads of the crowd, but before she had taken in what was happening there was a shout of command and a ragged volley of shots rang out. Amy gave a violent start and turned to her friend, as Ella, with a face as white as a sheet, dropped like a stone to the ground.

Philip and Dick Maynard had decided the previous day not to open their offices since, with the riots becoming worse with every hour that passed, there would be little or no business transacted in the city. But it was a hot and sunny day, not at all the sort of weather to remain within doors, so Philip had suggested that the two of them might make their way down to the Pier Head to see whether the ferries were running. There were no trams or buses, of course, but surely there would be someone willing to take passengers across the great width of the Mersey? If not, Philip thought they might hire a fishing boat, so at least they could gain the further shore and spend a few hours away from the city, which had become more like a battlefield than a busy commercial centre.

They had scarcely begun the walk to the Pier Head, however, when the crowd had come roaring along the roadway and simply engulfed them. They were both strong and determined young men, but wasted a good deal of time in searching for one another since, lacking the experience of suffragette rallies, they had not held on to one another when they plunged into the crowd.

Philip was a tall young man but even so he had difficulty in spotting his friend in the sea of heads that surrounded him. There was a good deal of noise as members of the crowd shouted to one another, whistled and cat-called, and adjured their neighbours to 'Get your bleedin' elbow out of my mouth', or, 'Doncher know whose perishin' feet you're stampin' on, sonny?' But even so, Philip raised his voice in a shout: 'Dick? Dick? Give us a wave, old fellow.'

To his relief, Philip heard a voice answering him almost immediately and saw a hand raised. Dick was no more than twelve feet away and by dint of shoving and pushing against the tide, he managed at last to reach him.

'Link arms,' Philip commanded as soon as they were together once more. 'Where are we, do you know? We could be treading on acres of grass in some park for all I can tell. Hang on a mo', though – that's St George's Hall – you can't mistake that.'

As Philip spoke, Dick pointed to the line of figures above and ahead of them on the St George's Hall steps. 'Soldiers, with rifles at the ready,' he said. 'We'd better get out of this in case there's real trouble.' Almost before the words were out of his mouth, firing broke out and at the same moment Philip heard a scream and saw a slim, girlish figure, topped by a cluster of red-gold curls, fall from his sight. He knew her instantly and immediately began to fight his way towards her. 'Did you see,' he gasped, dragging Dick with him through the crowd, which was now fighting as desperately to get back as they had tried before to go forward. 'It was Amy

Logan, the girl we met on the train on the day of the coronation. She's been hit. I saw her fall. Come on!'

The two young men had been only yards away from where the girls stood and in a remarkably short space of time, for they were the only ones going towards the hall, they reached Amy's side. She was kneeling on the ground, trying to lift her companion in her arms, but the other girl's head flopped back, her face a deathly white, save for a scarlet furrow, sluggishly bleeding, across her left temple.

'Amy! Good God, we thought you'd been hit – who's your friend?' Philip said breathlessly. 'How come she's . . . My God, it's the little suffragette, the one who lectured me on women's rights – Miss Morton, isn't it? Let me take her from you and carry her out of this. The soldiers fired over the heads of the crowd but I suppose a bullet must have ricocheted and hit her. Here, Amy, have you got something to staunch the blood? I'll make my handkerchief into a pad and hold it over the wound if you can find something to secure it.'

Amy, without a second's hesitation, bent down and ripped the frill off her petticoat, offering it mutely to Philip who took it and bound it swiftly round the padded handkerchief he had placed over Ella's wound, which was already soaked with blood. He hoisted the girl into his arms and Dick helped Amy to her feet. Then the three of them, with Philip carrying the unconscious girl, began to make their way across the road towards the North Western Hotel.

'Is . . . is she dead?' Amy asked fearfully as they entered the imposing portals. 'I didn't think she was because she stirred and moaned just before you

298

arrived, but now she looks so white and lies so still . . .'

'I don't think she's dead, because bleeding stops when the heart does and she's still losing blood,' Dick commented, giving Amy's hand a reassuring squeeze. 'I'd say the bullet ploughed along her skull, causing a very nasty wound, which needs attention urgently, but there's bound to be a doctor, or a nurse perhaps, who can be summoned by the clerk on reception.' He glanced around the empty foyer. 'Why is it so dark in here? The place is usually ablaze with lights and full of people.'

Philip looked too. 'For the same reason that the trams aren't running – no electricity,' he said briefly, then pointed to a sofa against a wall. 'I'll lay her on that couch, Dick. You go and get help, and make it snappy.'

While Philip and Amy made Ella as comfortable as they could on the shiny, gold, satin-covered chaise longue, making a pad of Philip's jacket beneath her head in the hope of not staining the sofa with Ella's blood, Dick went over to the desk and could be heard shouting for attention. Meanwhile Philip sent Amy scurrying to fetch a bowl and some water, so that they might bathe Ella's face and wrists, for even in the cooler darkness of the hotel it was still very hot.

Amy flew across the foyer, her experience of hotels telling her not to waste time searching for someone in authority but to go straight through the green baize doors which would lead, she guessed, to the kitchen quarters. She ran along the dark corridor, heedless of the clatter her shoes made on the tiles, and burst through some swing doors and into the first of a series of kitchens. Startled faces turned towards her, but she ignored them all, making for the big stone sinks she could see ranged along the wall in the next room. A man in a tall chef's hat and the white jacket and checked trousers of his calling stood up as she ran past and tried to grab her, but Amy was too quick for him. 'There's a girl been shot,' she said over her shoulder, grabbing a large white pudding basin from the sideboard and whipping down a pudding cloth from where it hung on the overhead rack. She turned the cold tap full on, half filled the basin, then turned back to retrace her steps, going very much more slowly so that she would not lose the water she was carrying.

'Did you say someone's been shot, chuck?' a fat woman in a frilled cap and apron asked incredulously. 'Well, if that's so, it's a doctor you'll be needin' – and some antiseptic – I've got a bottle of Listerine in me room; where's the young woman at?'

'She's in the foyer, on one of the sofas, with two of my friends taking care of her,' Amy said briefly, not pausing in her steady onward progress. 'If you could bring the Listerine along there . . .'

She reached the foyer without further incident, the housekeeper close on her heels, to find the little tableau very much as she had left it, save that Dick now stood by the sofa as well as Philip. Both men were wearing the distraught yet helpless look worn by young males the world over when a woman they regard highly is sick or in trouble.

Philip swung round at Amy's approach and said briefly: 'There's a doctor coming. Dick rang and explained. He said ten minutes and five have passed already.'

'Let me through, young gents,' the housekeeper said, briskly pushing both men to one side and dropping to her knees by the patient. 'We'll loosen her clothing – it's what you do when they faint, as I well know, for if there's one thing housemaids excel at it's faintin' fits.' With careful fingers she undid the tiny buttons, slippery with blood, at the high neck of Ella's blouse, then at the cuffs and finally, at the waist of her skirt. Amy took the Listerine from her and tipped some of it into her basin. Then she began to stroke her friend's brow, cheeks and neck with the water and antiseptic mixture.

She was wondering whether to move the handkerchief in order to clean the wound, when Philip's hand shot out and caught her wrist. 'Don't!' he said urgently and Amy could feel his strong fingers trembling. 'She's unconscious at present and feeling no pain, but if you put antiseptic on to raw flesh . . .'

Amy shuddered at the thought and was about to assure him that she would do no such thing, when the street doors opened and a short, sandy-haired man in a frock coat and high collar came briskly across the foyer towards them. 'I'm Doctor McKay, is this my patient?' he asked in a strong Scottish accent. 'Someone said she'd been shot.'

He sounded so incredulous that Amy's hands moved instinctively to show him the wound, but once again Philip stopped her. 'Yes, doctor, it was probably only a ricochet but she's been shot, nevertheless,' he said quietly. 'I don't think the bullet entered her body, I think it has merely ploughed a furrow along the side of her skull, but as you can see, she's bleeding heavily. Ought she not to be in hospital?'

'Ah, a flesh wound,' the doctor mused. He had been carrying a small black bag, which he now stood down and opened. He brought out a pair of scissors with which he snipped through the strip of petticoat holding the handkerchief in place. He stared for a moment at the mess of blood and hair which had formed beneath the impromptu dressing and then, to Amy's horror, began with practised ease to snip away her friend's long, blood-drenched tresses. When the wound was revealed, Amy had to turn away for a moment, a hand flying to her mouth. The wound must have been at least six inches long, and narrow, and the bullet – if it had been a bullet – had carried away the top inch of Ella's ear. Amy imagined that most of the blood had probably come from the shattered ear, for the head wound, though still bleeding, did not seem as bad as she had feared from the amount of the blood that had soaked through the dressings.

The doctor, however, continued to clip busily until a good half of Ella's beautiful hair lay on the floor. 'This will need cleaning and probably stitching,' he said at last, 'now I can see it properly without all that damned hair in the way. I would have liked to get her to a hospital, but we'd never do it, not with the crowds, the police, the troops and no possibility of finding a vehicle which could carry her.' He turned to the housekeeper. 'Prepare a room on the ground floor, Mrs Ellis. I'll want a great deal of hot water, bandages and someone with a steady hand to assist me. Normally I'd send for my nurse, but if this young lady is to recover quickly we must act at once.' He turned to look consideringly at Amy. 'How about you? It seems you don't faint at the sight of blood.'

'I'd help you willingly,' Philip said, before Amy could reply. 'I have had some experience, since I joined a first-aid class in my last year at school.'

The doctor gave a snort, which he tried to turn into a cough, but shook his head. 'Thank you, but I'd prefer the young lady, since I shall have to examine my patient to make sure there are no other wounds; a ricocheting bullet can cause more than one, you know.'

So Philip and Dick carried Ella, with great care and gentleness, through to the room which Mrs Ellis had prepared and laid her tenderly on the bed. She had still not recovered consciousness, which Dr McKay seemed to think a good thing, but as he left the room, Philip turned to take one more look at her. The still whiteness of her face went to his heart. She must get better, she must, he told himself, as he and his friend crossed the foyer and began to clear away the blood-draggled hair and all other signs that the wounded girl had lain there. Philip then took advantage of the gentlemen's cloakroom to wash off the blood that had soaked into his jacket and had even penetrated as far as his white shirt. Then they sat on the shiny little sofa and waited, Philip suddenly conscious of a dreadful sense of fore-boding. Dammit, I liked the girl from the first, he told himself, staring towards the door of the room they had just left. She's brave and outspoken and . . . and a real little darling; I can't bear the thought of her suffering, let alone . . .

But even to himself he could not admit that Ella might die of her wounds, so he sat and waited, with Dick beside him, and said a silent prayer for the girl lying so pale and still beneath the doctor's hands.

Ever afterwards, Amy could not remember the time she spent assisting Dr McKay without giving a strong shudder. It was not too bad while Ella remained unconscious, but when she suddenly came to herself and uttered a long, whimpering scream, it was all Amy could do not to run out of the room, running and running until she no longer had to hear, or even think about, her friend's agony.

The doctor, who had been inserting stitches in the wound, merely stopped work long enough to say gruffly to Amy, 'You'll find a small bottle of chloroform in the side pocket of my bag and a soft pad of gauze close beside it. The chloroform bottle has a dripper fixed in the neck; allow two or three drops, no more, to fall on the pad, then hold it firmly over Miss Morton's nose and mouth.' He looked up at Amy over the small pince-nez glasses, which he had perched on his nose as soon as he began the operation, and gave her a penetrating but friendly glance. 'You've done your friend proud so far, lassie; don't go letting her down now. Keep a steady hand and a brave heart and Miss Morton will be unconscious again in moments.'

With fumbling hands Amy got the necessary items out of the doctor's bag, dripped the chloroform – which smelled perfectly beastly – on to the muslin pad and shrinkingly held it to her friend's face. Ella had been breathing jerkily and uttering moans and little cries, her eyes opening and rolling desperately from side to side, even though the doctor had momentarily paused in his work, but within seconds of the pad being applied her breathing slowed and deepened, and the half-moons of her dark lashes sank on to her cheeks. With a sigh of pure relief Amy continued to assist Dr McKay until at last he stood back, laid down his needle and reached out a hand to grip Amy's shoulder reassuringly. 'You've done well, Miss Logan, and greatly assisted both myself and your poor friend,' he said gruffly. 'I'm no' in the habit of complimenting the young women who assist me, but they are trained nurses, which I take it you are not?'

'No indeed,' Amy said faintly. 'I've often wondered if I might like to be a nurse, but today has changed my mind. I work in the offices of the Adelphi Hotel as a shorthand writer and receptionist, so perhaps I'd better stick to what I know.'

The doctor, busily cleaning his instruments in a kettle full of boiling water, laughed shortly and once again gave her a penetrating glance. 'It's a very different thing assisting at an operation with none of the facilities of a hospital theatre,' he observed. 'And what's more, you know the patient – she is, I gather, a close friend of yours. Even I, Miss Logan, would hesitate to perform an operation without benefit of proper anaesthesia upon a loved one, so accept my congratulations.'

Amy glanced towards the bed, where her friend now lay peacefully upon her back, her head and neck swathed in bandages and her eyes closed. 'Thank you, Doctor McKay,' she said humbly. 'But what must I do now? I don't suppose the hotel will allow her to remain here until she is fit to be moved and God alone knows how long this strike will last. Liverpool people are not easily cowed; sometimes it is worse to try to outface them when they feel themselves to be in the right. Unless the government is prepared to give *something*, the strike could still be going strong at Christmas.'

The doctor, packing away his instruments and clearing up the debris from the operation, tutted and shook his head gently. 'The hotel will keep Miss Morton until I can find a conveyance to carry her to a hospital,' he said firmly. 'As soon as I am able I shall send a nurse round to look after your friend.'

'But the cost . . .' Amy breathed. 'We none of us have much money, doctor, although there are four of us sharing our room. I don't know how we shall ever repay you, let alone the hotel and a nurse . . .!'

'Don't try to meet trouble halfway,' the doctor said briefly. 'This wound was caused by a stray bullet, presumably fired by a member of the army. They may well be responsible for the cost of putting right what they did.'

With that he left the room, and Amy was sitting by her friend's bed and wondering what was to become of them, when there was a tap on the door and Philip's head appeared round it. 'The doctor says she's come through it pretty well,' Philip whispered, tiptoeing in. 'He said you were worrying about the cost – don't. I'll see to everything, not that I think we'll end up with a huge bill. Now stop fretting and as soon as the nurse arrives I'll take you home. The crowd outside seems to have dispersed, so I'll get you there easily enough.'

'I can't leave Ella, not with the best nurse in the world,' Amy whispered back. 'I'll stay. But Philip, could you go round to Huskisson Street and tell the others what's happened?'

'I'll go right away.' But Philip lingered, looking down at Ella's pale face and mangled cropped head. 'Poor little devil, I'd give anything . . . but the doctor seemed to think she'd be all right in a day or so. Is there anything else you want, though, Amy? I don't like to think of you sitting here alone without so much as a book to read or a drink. I could nip out and bring something back at once, before I make for Huskisson Street. How about if I fetch you in a newspaper and some . . . some biscuits, or peppermint humbugs? Come to that, you may need proper food later on. And how about a book to read while you wait for Miss Morton to wake up? And toiletries? A change of clothing?'

Amy laughed softly, but shook her head. 'Thanks, Philip, but Mrs Ellis said the hotel would feed us, and I'd rather you went straight to Huskisson Street and didn't waste time fetching me stuff I can do without. But when you do come back it would be nice if you could bring in some beef tea, if such a thing is available, because the doctor said Ella would want fortifying drinks at first rather than food. Oh, and some lemon barley water, if you would be so good.'

'I'll bring whatever I can find,' Philip promised. He grinned ruefully across the bed at Amy. 'I'll be as quick as I can, I promise, but because of the looting it may not be easy to find everything you want. Still, I'll do my best. Goodbye for now.'

When he had gone, closing the door softly behind him, Amy leaned back in her seat with a tiny sigh. He was a nice chap, was Philip, she had always known it but now she knew he was a good friend in a crisis as well. After all, he scarcely knew Ella but was prepared to stand by her for his old friend Amy's sake. Presently, worn out by the rigours and excitements of the day, she snoozed in her chair, though she never allowed herself to fall asleep completely. She was too anxious about Ella to risk missing her friend's slightest move.

Amy could not have slept for more than ten minutes when the doctor himself came in, telling her that he had arranged for Ella to have a bed in the Royal

Infirmary nearby. 'I met Mr Grimshaw in the foyer,' he told Amy. 'He had managed to get hold of a hansom cab, so I told him to keep hold of it . . .' he smiled grimly at his own joke '. . . so that my patient might ride to the Infirmary in relative comfort. If you will wrap her in a blanket I will fetch Mr Grimshaw. He has volunteered to carry the wee lass out to the cab and since he tells me it was he who brought her in after the shooting, I'm sure he is quite capable of doing so.'

When Amy, Philip and Ella arrived at the hospital they were shown directly to a long ward and as soon as the stretcher bearers had gently rolled the still unconscious Ella on to a high white bed, Amy and Philip were told to wait in the corridor, while the patient was examined by a hospital doctor.

'Doctor McKay told us the history of the case when he booked Miss Morton in,' a middle-aged sister, in a navy blue dress with white celluloid collar and cuffs, told them. 'But even so Mr Rivers, the consultant, will want to make his own examination. A blow to the head can seem straightforward but it can also lead to complications.'

Left to themselves, Philip and Amy sat down on the long benches provided and looked anxiously at one another.

'Complications? Could that mean damage to her skull? Or can a blow on the head affect the brain?' Amy asked in a worried undertone.

'I'm sure if there had been any question of brain damage, Doctor McKay would not have let her travel between the hotel and the hospital in a hansom cab,' Philip said reassuringly. He took Amy's hand between both of his own and looked earnestly into her round, worried eyes. 'Your friend is young and strong, and has had a blow on the head, which she might have got during a game of hockey. She was seen very quickly by an excellent doctor, but naturally, the surgeon in charge of this ward wishes to reassure himself as well as his staff that the damage is only superficial. So stop *worrying*, you little goose. In five or ten minutes we'll know what Mr Rivers thinks and you can be easy.'

'It's only that Ella's my best friend, Philip,' Amy said apologetically. 'We understand one another as though we were sisters – better than sisters, because I never have understood Mary. Although we are so different, Ella and I could scarcely have been closer. Ella is an only child and her parents were wealthy . . .'

Sitting there in the corridor, waiting to be allowed back on the ward, Amy related to Philip Ella's sad story, emphasising how brave she had been in the face of such appalling adversity. 'She had had so much, yet at the age of seventeen she found herself with nothing,' she told him. 'For the first time in her life she was forced to earn her own living, working in a miserable little clothing shop on the Scotland Road and sleeping at night on a mattress behind the counter. A lot of girls would have forgotten their ambitions, gone on struggling just to keep alive, but Ella has the courage of a lion, honest she has, Philip. She worked hard to learn what sort of staff the big departmental stores wanted and very quickly got her herself a job in one of them, and answered an advertisement for a room share. She was only a junior assistant, filling the shelves when stocks ran low, running up and down from the basement to the top floor, carrying heavy boxes of goods. But she soon rose to be a counter hand, then a sales assistant and now, as you know, she works with me at the Adelphi. Only she's more important than I am, because she translates French and German for the management and is already indispensable, although she has been with them less than six months.'

At this point the doors to the ward in which Ella lay opened, and the surgeon and his team came out. They walked up the corridor towards Amy and Philip, who both rose to their feet. Mr Rivers was a tall, skinny man, probably no more than forty years old, with a calm and confident manner, which instantly put both young people at their ease. 'Your friend has an admirable constitution and an extremely strong skull,' he informed them, smiling genially as he did so. 'She has not yet regained consciousness – I fancy she may have a touch of concussion – but I am sure she will come to herself over the course of the next few hours. I would strongly advise you both to go home now, leaving Miss Morton in the capable hands of the nursing staff. You may return this afternoon with such small necessities as the patient needs – her own nightgown perhaps – and by then your friend will have regained consciousness.'

Amy's relief was so great that she found she could only stare at the surgeon while her eyes filled with tears, but Philip said at once, 'Thank you, sir, I know you have relieved both our minds and we will feel happier as a result.' He turned to Amy as the surgeon and his team moved off down the corridor. 'Well? Has that satisfied you? I think we ought to take Mr Rivers's advice and go home now, and come back this afternoon.'

Paddy, Albert and Gus brought the boat up into the

estuary alongside Seaforth Sands and lowered the brick-coloured sail, each one performing his task without a word spoken, so familiar were they with this daily routine. They had sailed at dawn, realising that the heat would become oppressive as the day progressed, and had filled their dragnet before the shrimps had sought shelter in deeper waters. Thus they were now heading for home after only a few hours' fishing. This meant that the shrimps could be boiled and piled on the handcart in plenty of time to be sold straight to the public that same day. And fresh shrimps, especially at this time of year, always commanded top prices.

As soon as they were in shallow water Paddy and Albert jumped out and began to pull the boat ashore. In winter, when they performed this task, they would have been clad in great fishermen's thigh waders but now, because of the heat, they were barefoot, with trousers rolled up as high as they would go and Paddy, splashing in first, thought the cool water against his hot and sunburned legs was a delightful experience.

Like most of the lads in Seaforth he could swim like a fish, though the older men still insisted that it was bad luck for a fisherman to be able to swim. 'Askin' for trouble, thass worrit is,' the old salts, sitting outside the Caradoc would tell each other. 'A fisherman's place is atop the water not innit. My da always told me that fishes were the only ones what needed to swim and since I'm still here to tell the tale, I reckon he were right.'

But right now, with Gus joining them to pull the boat up the beach, Paddy thought longingly that a quick swim would be just what the doctor ordered. He was so hot and carrying the shrimps back to

Seafield Grove would be hot work as well, to say nothing of boiling them in the crowded little wash-house and then shovelling them, still hot, into the large, loose-weave sacks.

Of course, in the usual way his mam would take over at this point, setting off with the handcart to sell the shrimps round the houses and pubs, but because they had such a large quantity of shrimps he, Gus and Albert would probably take the remainder of the catch into St John's fish market for Bill to sell on his stall. They had bought a second handcart a while back and though Bill had often talked of investing in a donkey to bring the fish from Seaforth to the city centre more rapidly, nothing so far had come of it.

Normally the two younger boys would have pushed the handcart into the market by themselves, but because of the strike, and the looting and rioting that had followed, they felt a good deal safer with Gus along to help, in the event of trouble. By and large, the rioters did not interfere with the poor, but attacked the city centre shops and stores, though on one occasion a group of rowdy, undisciplined youths had overturned the handcart, thinking it a great joke to see Albert and Paddy scrabbling on the cobbles to retrieve what shrimps they could.

The boat being satisfactorily beached, Albert and Paddy checked the sails, sheets and oars, and then began to fasten the necks of the sacks. Gus, mean-while, had strode up the beach and was returning, dragging the handcart behind him. He did not come too far, because the sand was soft and the cart, when laden, could easily get bogged down, so presently he abandoned it and came and joined them. Each of them hefted a sack on to his back and began the hard slog up the beach. Paddy, with sweat trickling down his brow and stinging his eyes, looked sideways at Gus. 'Any chance of a swim, Gus?' he asked plaintively. 'I'm as hot as fire and we'll be red as lobsters afore we're much older, what wi' boiling the shrimps and carting them to St John's Market. And it won't take nobbut a few minutes, just to set ourselves up, like, wi' a dip in the briny.'

'Tell you what,' Gus said, as they reached the handcart and began to unload their sacks on to it, 'I'll take a couple of sacks along to the house, so that Suzie can get on wi' cooking them, and you two can have your dip. I won't bother with the handcart, you can bring that when you've had your swim.'

Paddy and Albert agreed with this suggestion and very soon, clad only in their working trousers, they were washing the sweat and the heat away in the cool waves. When they reached the house in Seafield Grove half an hour later Paddy announced breezily, as they hefted the remaining sacks of shrimps into the wash-house, that he felt a different feller. 'If you want to go down to the shore now, Gus, and have your dip while we boil the remaining shrimps, I'm sure Albert and me are willin',' he said.

Gus, however, shook his head and said that he meant to go indoors and have a strip-down wash and put on clean kecks and shirt. 'For when we've delivered the shrimps to Dad I've a mind to stroll round to the Crown and have a beer or two,' he said with assumed casualness. 'That is, if you think the two of you will be able to get the handcart back to Seaforth wi'out the aid of me bulgin' muscles?' he added with a grin.

Paddy and Albert exchanged meaningful looks, but said nothing. They were both well aware that Gus had taken a fancy to the little blonde barmaid who worked at the Crown public house, and was plucking up his courage to ask her out. Rather to Paddy's surprise, the girl was not unlike Peggy Higgins to look at, but there was no accounting for tastes. If I'd been dumped by a blonde, the way Peggy dumped our Gus, then I reckon I'd go for a brunette next time around, Paddy told himself, as they began to empty the sacks of uncooked shrimps into the boiling, salty water. But there you are, everyone's different and no doubt Gus will take out several girls before he starts getting serious again.

Aloud Paddy said, in answer to Gus's question; 'Oh aye, we'll get the handcart home all right, don't you worry about us, old feller. But seeing as we're early today, I think I'll go round to the dairy and have a word wi' me old pals. It's ages since Tommy and I met – we might make an evening of it.'

'Well, if we're going to make an evening of it, then we'd best all change our kecks and shirts,' Albert said hopefully. 'What's on at the Palais de Luxe in Lime Street, Paddy? I wouldn't mind seeing a film ... Mind you, there's dances and all sorts in the city centre. Anyway, we can decide what we want to do later. We'll leave the handcart wi' our dad and get him to pay a kid a few coppers to wheel it back to Seaforth.'

Accordingly, as soon as the shrimps were boiled, Paddy and Albert hurried into the kitchen. Suzie was sitting by the open window darning a pair of Bill's socks, and Becky and her small friend Etty were playing at shop with a number of empty packets arrayed on top of a wooden box, which served both as counter and stall room. Paddy tugged one of Becky's blonde pigtails as he passed and she turned to smile up at him. 'Hello, Paddy! Me an'

Etty's playin' shop,' she said unnecessarily. 'Amy told me, the last time she was home, that she an' Mary played shop when they were small. So Mammy's been savin' empty packets and jars, an' now I'm the shop lady and Etty's me customer.'

'That's grand, queen,' Paddy said absently, but the mention of Amy's name made him remember when he and she had been forced to share a roof. How they had argued and even fought one another when there was no one about to keep them apart! He had called her nastier and nastier names but somehow she had always got back at him. Life was much quieter now she had moved out but, he reflected ruefully, it was much duller too. She had been – was – a sparky little thing, with plenty to say for herself, always full of tales of her work or her friends' doings. Looking back, he knew that both he and his mother had been jealous of Bill's affection for his younger daughter, so it was better for all of them to live separately, as they did now.

He skirted the chair in which Amy had sat and exchanged tart remarks with him the last time she had come home, and found himself remembering every detail of her appearance on that day. The small, pointy chinned face, with its large, greenish eyes, the pink lips which could fold so tightly in disapproval and the long auburn hair, piled on top of her small head and held in place by tortoiseshell combs. He had called her a looker, not intending to compliment her, but simply speaking the truth. And what had she done? Snubbed him as usual. So she was best forgotten, he decided, mounting the stairs at a run. Heaven knew, their paths did not cross often and when she came home he usually kept well clear. Last time they had met he had hoped to bury the hatchet, but Amy's attitude clearly made this impossible, so he would think of her no more.

Having washed, slicked down their hair with brilliantine and donned clean shirts, kecks and shoes, the boys thundered down the stairs again and it was not long before the sacks of cooked shrimps were piled on the handcart and being pushed along Crosby Road by three neatly attired young gentlemen, eager for a bit of fun.

Neither Gus nor the younger boys had been into the city centre for several days and they were shocked to find the streets buzzing with policemen and with obvious signs, such as smashed shop windows and litter everywhere, that a crowd had recently rioted there. Now, however, apart from the obvious police presence, the streets were almost empty and the boys and their catch proceeded without interference right up to Bill's stall in the fish market. There were few customers and even fewer stallholders, but Bill thanked them for the shrimps and sent Kenny, the little lad who helped him when he was busy, round to Roper's for more ice.

'We had a rare do here this morning,' Bill told his sons as they unloaded the shrimps. 'The strikers came in a body to hear some feller address them from St George's Plateau. It seems things got out of hand, though, and there was no end of damage done. They called the troops in, I've heard, and someone was shot. We heard the burst of gunfire from here, but Jack Gibson, who were doin' a delivery along Lime Street, said the troops fired over the heads of the crowd. Bullets go astray, though,' he added wisely, 'and sometimes it ain't only the troops what get themselves armed – there's fellers here what fought in the Boer War an' never handed in their weapons, so I've heard.'

'It's quiet enough out there now,' Gus observed. 'The place is crawling wi' scuffers, mind, so I suppose it would be. I were goin' round to the Crown for a beer, but will they be open? I noticed several shops closed as we came along.'

Bill shrugged. 'Who knows? I reckon the pubs closed at the height of the trouble but they may well be open again by now. Publicans have got a living to make, same as the rest of us. No harm in going along there to check, anyroad.'

So presently, having arranged with Kenny to push the handcart home in exchange for a threepenny joe, the boys split up. Gus made determinedly, for the Crown; Albert went off towards Lime Street Station and Paddy headed for his old workplace.

Paddy walked into the dairy and grinned across the counter at Tommy who was serving a customer with milk, dipping a ladle into a tall churn and filling the woman's enamel jug. He greeted his friend cheerfully, but continued to serve the small queue of waiting women until the last one had paid for her order and left. Only then did he turn to Paddy. 'Hello, stranger,' he said affably. 'On the run from the scuffers, are you? Or haven't you heard about the riots yet?'

'On the run from the scuffers yourself,' Paddy said indignantly. 'We were a mile off shore draggin' for shrimps when the trouble broke out. We had a jolly good haul, too, which is why we've come into the city early, so's Uncle Bill could start sellin' before all the housewives go home. Where were you, anyroad? In here, I s'pose, like a good little lad, sellin' jugs of milk and pats of butter to nice old women who wouldn't know a riot from a ... a ... prayer meeting.'

'Yes, you're right as it happens, ' Tommy admitted. He sighed regretfully. 'I missed all the fun and games by a whisker, though. Joe Coutts broke his arm last winter and from time to time he has a check-up at the infirmary. He was supposed to go today and I were goin' to do his round, but he went to his doctor at the surgery last night and the old feller signed him off, so he come in as usual this morning and did his own round.' He grinned at Paddy. 'Never mind, eh. Better luck next time. Why've you come a visitin', anyroad?'

Paddy explained his errand and Tommy agreed it would be just grand to have an evening out together. He was beginning to expand on this theme when a group of housewives entered the shop. Tommy promptly waved Paddy away, saying in a hissing whisper, 'See you outside the Palais de Luxe at six,' before turning to his customers with a courteous enquiry as to their wants.

Having made his arrangements with Tommy, Paddy decided to go to the shippon and stables, and see who was working there. The shippon was empty but he found Joe Coutts in the stable, whistling tunelessly between his teeth as he cleaned down his horse, a large chestnut gelding called Conker. He grinned at Paddy. 'Well, so you've come a visitin', young Paddy. I tek it you wasn't a part of that there riot this mornin'? I did wonder, seeing as how you're a fisherman now and fishermen is seamen?'

'Oh, no, they ain't,' Paddy retorted, 'and besides, it isn't the seamen strikin' now, you oaf, it's railway workers. What about you, Joe?'

'Oh, I were in the thick of it, I were. I were knocked off me milk cart and bowled head over heels into the gutter right outside Lime Street Station. The station were barricaded and folk were screaming and shoutin' ... oh aye, it were a nasty moment. I could see clear across to St George's Hall – that's how I come to see everything. I seed the troops, watched 'em fire over the 'eads of the crowds ... I even see the girl go down.'

'What girl?' Paddy asked lazily. He knew Joe was simple, but he also knew the man was honest. 'Was a girl knocked over, then?'

'Aye, she were shot an' what's more, I knew 'er,' Joe said triumphantly. 'Come to think of it, you'll know her an' all, Paddy. It were young Amy Logan, what used to work in the fish market. I allus buy my fish there on a Friday to take home to the wife, though it's young Amy's dad what runs the stall now. Oh aye, it were young Amy all right – I see the troops fire and she went down like a ton o' bricks, an' were took up for dead.'

Paddy stared. For one awful moment he actually thought he might faint, as a terrible coldness swept over his entire body in spite of the heat of the afternoon. Then anger stiffened his spine and he felt a wave of scarlet heat invade his face. He grabbed Joe by both shoulders and shook him vigorously. 'What the devil do you mean, you silly old fool,' he shouted right into the man's startled face. 'Are you tryin' to say me stepsister's dead? I don't believe it. I were in the fish market no more than an hour ago and Uncle Bill said nothin' about it.'

Joe tugged himself free from Paddy's vicious grip and flapped a hand in the younger man's face. 'Don't gerrin such a takin', la',' he said soothingly. 'I

319

said took up for dead, which is what folk were sayin', but later I heard she'd been took to the Infirmary, so maybe she's just badly injured. There was a deal of blood,' he went on ghoulishly. 'When the crowd had cleared, me an' old Conker 'ere went over to take a look and the paving stones were scarlet where she'd lain.'

But he was talking to empty air. Paddy had whipped round and rushed out of the yard with one thought only uppermost in his mind. Amy was injured and from what Joe had said she might be at death's door. She had snubbed him and cold-shouldered him, and tried to make trouble for him, but he realised now that he regarded her as a part of the family. He had known on that day when both sisters had returned to Seaforth that he no longer idolised Mary. The older girl had become hard-faced and selfish, with little resemblance to the sweet, mild-mannered young woman he had believed himself to love. Amy, with her sharp tongue and sharper wit, was far more his sort of girl – and now she was sick unto death and he might never get the chance to tell her how sorry he was for the way he had treated her in the past.

It was a long way from Dryden Street to the Infirmary. Reaching Scotland Road, he was about to continue running along the pavement when it occurred to him that he might catch a number 3 tram, which would drop him on London Road, well over half his way to his destination. However, he had no idea when the next tram would come along. In his urge to hurry he cursed the strike, which had made life in the city centre so difficult.

By the time he reached the Infirmary he was so out of breath that he realised he would be unable to ask sensible questions regarding Amy's where-abouts, and stopped for a moment to lean against a pillar and get his breath back. After a few moments he walked towards the glass doors which lead into the hospital foyer and saw, reflected therein, a wild figure. His hair, which had been neatly slicked back, was standing up like a gorse bush with the wind of his going and his sweat-streaked face bore the marks of many smuts. His tie was askew and his unbuttoned jacket rucked up on one side. Hastily he flattened his hair with both hands, tugged his tie straight, buttoned his jacket and rubbed his face as clean as he could get it on his pocket handkerchief. Only then did he go into the hospital foyer and move towards the clerk behind the reception desk.

He was about to ask in which ward Amy lay when two things occurred to him. The first was that it had been his duty to go immediately to Bill and tell him what Joe had said. The second that he might be denied admittance here, simply because he was not a relative in the strictest sense of the word, but that last, he decided, could soon be remedied. He would announce himself as her brother and, even if she were conscious, he doubted she would be well enough to refute the claim.

The foyer was crowded and for a moment Paddy hesitated, unsure of which way to go; then, amid the bustling throng he spotted a porter in uniform and made a beeline for him, hailing him as soon as he reached him. 'Excuse me, mate, I'm lookin' for me sister. A pal told me she'd got herself mixed up wi' some riot or other and been shot. Can you tell me . . .?'

The porter swung round and pointed towards one of the long corridors leading off the foyer. 'She's just been taken to Nightingale Ward,' he said in a strong Irish brogue. 'Sure an' isn't it a terrible thing, a pretty young critter like that. Third bed from the end, you'll find her.'

Almost before the words were out of his mouth, Paddy was running across the foyer, muttering beneath his breath, 'Nightingale Ward, Nightingale Ward, third bed along.' He found that his knees were actually shaking and deemed it sensible to stop for a moment outside Nightingale Ward to get his breath and collect his wits. It was probably as well that he did so, since a middle-aged nurse in a stiffly starched uniform swept out of Nightingale Ward, giving him a suspicious glance as she passed him. Hastily Paddy composed himself and walked past the ward doors with the air of one who knows exactly where he is going and is in no hurry to get there. As soon as the nurse disappeared, however, he turned back and entered the ward, his eyes going straight to the third bed from the end.

A figure lay in the high white bed, bandaged and still – so still that for a moment his heart missed a beat – but almost as he began to approach the bed the figure turned her head slightly on the pillow, to smile up at someone standing beside her and he realised that this was not Amy. For a moment he stopped, frozen in his tracks, staring unbelievingly at the two figures beside the bed. The girl who was holding the patient's hand and smiling down at her was Amy, looking neither injured nor unhappy. In fact, in her green cotton dress and straw hat, with her abundant hair curling around her face, she looked as composed and at ease as though nothing unusual had happened. And beside her, in a grey flannel suit with a straw boater in one hand and the other resting lightly on her shoulder, was Philip Grimshaw – it was unmistakably he, though Paddy had not set eyes on him for years.

Bewilderment kept Paddy rooted to the spot for several seconds – several seconds too long – before he began instinctively to turn away. In that moment Philip recognised him. He turned Amy so that she, too, was looking down the ward, and came towards Paddy, a pleasant smile on his handsome face. 'Paddy!' he exclaimed. 'What on earth are you doing here? Of all the odd coincidences ... or are you visiting Miss Morton too? I didn't imagine you knew her, but being part of the family now ... I suppose ...'

Feeling trapped, Paddy searched his mind desperately for a good reason to be standing on the ward and came up with the truth, though as soon as the words were out he cursed himself for having said them. 'I were told it were Amy,' he blurted out. 'A feller I used to know when I worked in Dryden Street told me he saw Bill's girl shot by the troops on St George's Plain. I ... I thought I'd better make sure it were true before fetching Bill over.'

He could not resist a quick glance at Amy's face and saw the big, green-grey eyes widen for a second before she said thoughtfully, 'Yes, I can understand how such a mistake could come about. When Ella fell – Miss Morton that is – I dropped to my knees to try to help her. Well, there was so much blood ... for an awful moment I thought – I thought ...'

Philip put his arm around Amy's slender shoulders and gave her a little shake. 'Stop it now,' he said warningly. 'Miss Morton is going to be just fine. I know she's got a head wound, a good deal of bruising and a suspected fractured rib, but the nurses say she'll be out by the end of the week, all being well.'

'Philip and I brought her in here this morning and we've just taken in an overnight bag for her,' Amy explained. 'But I can't help wondering whether I did the right thing . . .'

'The doctor said you acted with good sense and promptitude,' Philip interrupted. 'And since we don't want you going into a decline, stop wondering what else you could have done and start thinking about what you're going to eat when we nip over to Lyons Corner House for a sustaining meal.' He and Amy turned back towards Ella, clearly intent on bidding farewell to their friend, but the girl in the bed was sound asleep. 'Best not to wake her,' he whispered, 'we'll be in again later, anyway.' He turned to Paddy, the familiar quirky grin lighting up his face. 'Paddy, old pal, would you like to join us? Amy's had nothing to eat since breakfast – nor have I for that matter and there's no point in either of us starving ourselves.'

Paddy found himself staring at the arm which still circled Amy's shoulders. His sudden realisation that Amy meant something to him, despite their history of childhood squabbles, made him resent Philip's familiarity. For two pins, he told himself savagely, he would have asked Philip to stop mauling the girl, yet for all he knew, Philip might be Amy's latest beau – probably was, since she had clearly called on him in her hour of need. Not that she would have called on me, he reflected bitterly, not if I'd been the last feller on earth. Why, I might as well face it, no matter how I feel about her – and that's something I haven't really worked out yet – she hates my perishin' guts.

'Well, Paddy Keagan, are you coming with us or not, because we haven't got all day and I'm starving hungry.' It was Amy, her tone tart as ever.

Paddy pulled himself together with an effort. 'No, thanks,' he muttered. 'Two's company, they say, and three's a crowd. Besides, me mam wouldn't want me to spoil my appetite for supper.'

'Oh, come on, Paddy,' Philip said, his tone almost wheedling. 'It's been years since we met; I want to hear all the local gossip. Why, I've no idea what you're doing now – nor where you're living – and we were good pals once, when we were kids.'

'Oh, let him go, if that's what he wants,' Amy said, slipping her hand into the crook of Philip's elbow. 'Any gossip you want, I can tell you . . .' The two of them moved down the ward towards the swing doors at the end and Paddy followed, deliberately hanging back so that the others might get well ahead. Bloody Amy, he thought furiously, she had a real knack of ruining everything. Well, if Philip wanted a girl with a tongue like an adder then he was welcome to her. And with that thought Paddy slipped out of a side entrance, hoping, but not expecting, that the other two would feel concerned and come back into the hospital, only to find him disappeared.

That evening, after she and Philip had revisited the hospital and seen Ella sitting up in bed and chattering, quite like her usual self, Amy returned to Huskisson Street in a very much happier frame of mind. She explained what had happened to the other girls, trying to play down the drama so that they were not too worried, and managed to convince them that though Ella had had a horrible experience, the medical staff were sure she would recover completely, given time. After this, totally exhausted by the day's events, she took herself off to bed.

Cuddling down beneath the blankets, she expected to fall asleep immediately, but instead found herself wondering, for the first time since they had left him, just exactly what had brought Paddy to the hospital in such haste. Recalling the moment when Philip had drawn her attention to the tall, dark-haired figure, standing stock still in the centre of the ward, she also remembered how white his face had been until it suddenly flooded with scarlet and how his dark eyes had burned as his glance fell on her. He had been shocked to find her uninjured, she was sure of that, but she could not recall any look of pleasure when he had realised she was unhurt.

The old Amy would have assumed Paddy was disappointed to find her whole, but Amy knew that this was nonsense. Paddy might not like her – did not like her – but she did not really suppose for one moment that he actually wished her harm. After all, she did not like him, but she would have been truly distressed had he been injured when working on the boat. Indeed, when she thought of the sort of conditions the fishermen faced whenever they went to sea in bad weather a chill of dread crept over her. He could easily be knocked overboard by a wildly swinging boom and tossed ashore by the great, white-tipped waves which accompanied such conditions. And there were a thousand and one smaller, less fatal accidents, which were almost everyday occurrences among the fishing fleet.

Now that she had begun on this train of thought, she had hard work to dismiss it from her mind but she knew she must do so, reminding herself that her beloved brothers, Albert and Gus, were also fishermen and faced the same horrendous dangers daily. She was just thinking that the old animosity between herself and Paddy must be beginning to fade, just drifting into sleep, when she distinctly heard his voice, taunting and shrill, the boy Paddy, screaming after her as he had so often done, 'Shrimpy, Shrimpy! Who stinks of bleedin' fish, then? Keep to windward of her, fellers, else the pong will knock you out.'

Instantly Amy found herself sitting bolt upright in bed, all her gentle thoughts of Paddy forgotten. He had been a horrible little boy and was probably now a horrible young man. The fact that she did not see much of him must therefore be considered a huge advantage and she would most certainly not worry about his possible fate aboard the fishing boat, nor continue to exercise her mind with fruitless wonderings concerning his hospital visit.

Resolutely she turned her face into the pillow and presently slept. But even the best of resolutions cannot always be kept and, as she dreamed, she smiled. And the Paddy who accompanied her into dreamland was not the irritating little boy but an extraordinarily attractive young man.

At the time that Paddy was leaving the hospital, Albert was taking his place at a small corner table in Dorothy's Dining Rooms. When the waitress approached him he grinned up at her, and ordered a pot of tea and some buttered toast and then, with seeming casualness, he asked her if Ruth Durrant was on the premises.

The girl looked at him closely, then smiled. 'I seen

you before,' she said almost accusingly, 'you come in a week ago, dincher? Did Ruthie serve you then? She must ha' made an impression for you to come back so soon!'

Albert felt rather offended but did not intend to show it. The girl made him sound like one of those – what did they call them? – Yes, stage-door johnnies who hung around outside theatres trying to scrape acquaintance with a member of the chorus. He felt like telling her that he and Ruth were old friends, but instead said loftily, 'Ruth's a neighbour of mine; we both live out at Seaforth. Is she around? I'd like a word.'

The girl grinned but vouchsafed no answer, merely moving to another table to take a customer's order and presently went through the swing doors into the kitchen. Albert hoped that his message would reach Ruth and that she would not think he had a nerve to come visiting her workplace. But nothing ventured, nothing gained, his dad had often remarked and this was definitely a case in point. He had known Ruth since their early schooldays; known her better than he knew most girls, because of her friendship with his sister. He liked Ruth very much but had somehow lacked the courage to ask her out. Now, with an afternoon and evening free, he intended to do it. If she agreed to go with him he meant to take her to the Rotunda on the Scottie, since it was on their way home and would not, he thought, be likely to attract either Gus or Paddy, who would go for a theatre in the city centre.

'Hello, Albert. Lily said you was asking for me.' Ruth stood by the table, looking interrogatively down at him. She was a small, pale girl with light-brown hair and honey-coloured eyes and, though she was not pretty, there was a good deal of appeal in her neat, quick movements and ready smile. She smiled at Albert now and began to arrange a teapot, cup and saucer and milk jug on the table before him. 'Your buttered toast won't be a minute – the kitchen hand is makin' it now.'

Albert took a deep breath. 'What time do you finish, Ruthie? Only we gorroff early today on account of the strike an' that. I thought you might like to see the show at the Rotunda; we might have a bite to eat an' all.'

Ruth smiled down at him with an unaccustomed twinkle in her sparkling eyes. 'I can't leave work till after eight o'clock and the last house starts at half past seven,' she said demurely, 'but it's a lovely evening; a walk down to the Pier Head and along the waterfront might be nice, and there's bound to be somewhere open where we could get tea and a buttie, despite the strike.'

Albert beamed at her. 'It's a date,' he said exultantly. 'I'll be outside the kitchen door waitin' for you at eight o'clock on the dot.'

Ella was in hospital for a week and during that time, though she had a number of visitors, no one was as regular in their attendance as Philip Grimshaw. At first he came whenever Amy did and the two of them sat, one on either side of Ella's bed. They told Ella what they had been doing, chaffed one another over small incidents which had happened on their way to the hospital and generally behaved in a manner which, at first, led Ella to suppose that they were more than friends. This surprised her, since

329

Amy had seldom mentioned Philip after that meeting in the train and then usually only in connection with her sister Mary.

I suppose it was my accident which drew them together, Ella told herself – until, that was, Philip began to visit her on his own. He popped in at odd times of the day, charming the nursing staff, deferring to the doctors and usually bringing small gifts for Ella herself. Ella, pondering his attentiveness, did not for one moment imagine that he was courting her; his manner was in no way loverlike. What was more, she knew herself to look a positive scarecrow with her hair shaved away on the right-hand side of her head and, because she was not allowed to get the wound wet, the rest of her locks greasy and dishevelled. Furthermore, for the first few days of her stay in hospital she had been pale and listless, reluctant to move in the bed because of her fractured rib and hating the sight of her face, disfigured as it was by an enormous purple and yellow bruise. No one, she thought ruefully, could enjoy looking at a visage so battered. However, she could not believe that he was trying to ingratiate himself with her friend either – how could it be so?

Amy never even knew about the visits beforehand and, when Ella told her, took them for granted. 'He's ever so nice, Ella,' she said earnestly. 'A really kind young man who is always thinking of others and putting himself second. Why, you've even converted him to approving the suffragette movement! He told me the other evening, when he was walking me home, that he has the greatest respect for the way women are trying to claim their rights and wishes them every success.'

So when the doctor told Ella that she was well

enough to leave hospital, she was in two minds over it. Naturally, a part of her was delighted that she was escaping from hospital food and hospital routine – while another part of her thought wistfully that she would really miss Philip's company. She had begun to realise that the two of them had much in common. They had both received an excellent education and had read many of the same books. They had both visited France and Italy and, though Philip had studied mathematics and the sciences, he could also speak passable French and knew the rudiments of German. Ella loved her room-mates and appreciated their good points, but acknowledged ruefully that they had not had the opportunities which she and Philip had enjoyed and were therefore unable to share her feelings on certain issues.

However, when she told Philip that she would be leaving hospital later that day his face brightened. 'I'll fetch a hansom cab to the door and see you back to Huskisson Street,' he said at once. 'And having found you, Miss Morton, I don't intend to lose you again. Nor your friends,' he added hastily. 'Has the doctor told you when you may return to work? Until you do so, I'm sure outings to the seaside or the country would do you a great deal of good. And if this is so, I'll happily take you anywhere you want to go.' After this formal speech he cocked his head on one side and gave her a grin of such pure delight that Ella burst out laughing. It was grand to have a friend like Philip, she told herself exultantly – and even grander to know that he intended to stay her friend, whether in hospital or out of it.

Fortunately it was a simple matter to get a message

to Amy that Ella would be leaving hospital that afternoon, forestalling Amy's daily visit, which usually took place as soon as she had finished work for the day. Ella wrote a note and Philip delivered it to the front desk at the Adelphi. When the cab arrived, all Ella had to do was to get into it and be driven back to Huskisson Street in comfort. Philip took the seat opposite her, asking every few minutes if the cabby should be told to slow down, whether she found the breeze from the open window too cool and, almost in the same breath, enquiring as to how she was enjoying being outside once more after so long in the ward.

They reached Huskisson Street and Philip carried Ella's bag for her, standing it down in the front hall. The front door was seldom locked, but the door to the girls' room always was, since there was usually a new tenant somewhere in the building who might, or might not, prove to be dishonest. Ella fumbled her key into the lock, suddenly realising with considerable dismay that there would be no one at home at this hour. She could scarcely turn Philip away without asking him inside, yet she knew that her parents would have been horrified to learn that she was entertaining a young man alone.

The problem, however, was solved by Philip. He went ahead of her into the room, holding the door open for her and standing her bag down on a small table just inside the door. Then he gave her his sweetest smile and turned towards the front door once more. 'This has been a big day,' he said over his shoulder. 'The change from an institutionalised way of life to your ordinary, everyday one is always tiring, especially when you've been as ill as you have. I'm going back to the office now, and I think

332

you should lie down on your bed and have a sleep. When you wake up, you might make yourself a cup of tea and sit in the window until your friends get back from their work. Honestly, Miss – oh, this is ridiculous since I feel we've known one another for ever – may I call you Ella?'

'Yes, of course, if I can call you Philip,' Ella said gaily. She could feel the heat rising to her cheeks and pressed the palms of her hands against them. 'I'm sure you're right, because although I've done nothing except sit in a very comfortable cab, I feel absolutely exhausted. So I'll take your advice and have a rest on my bed, but before I do so Mr Gr – I mean Philip – I'd like to thank you very much indeed for bringing me home in such luxury. You've been most awfully kind.'

'It was a pleasure,' Philip said briefly, turning in the doorway to smile at her. Ella saw that, in his turn, Philip's colour had brightened. 'I wonder if you will feel fit for a short outing tomorrow? If so, I could take the afternoon off from work easily enough.'

'That would be very nice,' Ella said demurely. 'Shall you call for me here or shall we meet at some mutually convenient spot? Perhaps that would be better. I should be able to get into the city centre quite easily.'

Philip, however, did not think much of that idea. 'No such thing; I shall call for you here at two o'clock,' he said firmly. 'Mind you're ready for me!' And with a valedictory wave he was gone, leaving Ella to close and lock her door, to take off her long cotton skirt and the crisp white blouse, which Amy had brought to the hospital the previous day, and to lie down on her bed. She did not immediately go to sleep, however, but stared at the ceiling and thought, with pleasure, about Philip. He was all that Amy had claimed him to be and more, and she, Ella, was becoming remarkably fond of him. And, she told herself as her lids began to droop, I do believe he is becoming fond of me.

Chapter Nine

It was October before Ella finally returned to work and by the time she did so she and Philip were going steady in earnest. He had taken her on so many pleasant expeditions, both to the country and to the seaside, that returning to work had been hard indeed, but since she either met Philip for a hasty lunch soon after noon, or in the evening, she was able to pass her working days pleasantly enough.

After the first few weeks Philip had suggested that Amy might like to join them. He was feeling a trifle guilty at leaving his flatmate, Dick Maynard, alone most evenings, so a foursome with Ella's friend seemed the ideal solution.

Ella enjoyed the outings and knew that Amy did too, though she did not think that Amy thought of Dick as anything but a friend. He was a pleasant, intelligent person but Amy, it seemed, did not wish to get involved with any young man; or so it appeared to Ella. Ella found it impossible to guess why her friend seemed almost indifferent to Dick; it was not that Amy was secretive, merely that long experience of the treatment she had received from her stepmother had made her keep her own counsel, so though she clearly enjoyed both the outings and Dick's company, by the time Christmas was drawing near Ella was still no wiser as to the extent of her friend's feelings. What was more, Amy had heard with equanimity that Dick was to return to his home for two weeks over Christmas and was planning her own holiday with obvious enjoyment, clearly unaffected by Dick's proposed absence.

Since her parents' death, Ella had rather dreaded Christmas. It was such a family time and even the sight of carol singers in the street or a bedecked tree would bring tears to her eyes as she thought, with loving nostalgia, of Christmases past.

Once she was sharing the room with the other girls, of course, things became easier. The room was Minnie's home and had been ever since Mrs Miniver's death, and the two girls had made as merry as circumstances allowed, even endeavouring to cook a small chicken over the open fire, which caused much hilarity, as well as a strong smell of burning when the skin of the bird became enveloped in flames. With Amy's and Ruth's arrival, the run-up to Christmas was no longer something to be dreaded, but on the day itself, when the two younger girls returned to their families, Ella knew that she and Minnie both had to work hard not to let themselves fall into gloom. Amy would have liked to take Ella home with her, and Minnie too, but because of the size of the Logan family – and the size of their tiny house – this was clearly impossible. Ruthie, too, lived in a small, overcrowded house, so could do little entertaining.

It seemed, however, that this year was to be different again. Philip had actually asked Ella if she would like to accompany him back to his parents' home in Manchester to share their family Christmas. For the first time in their relationship Ella was in a quandary. It was such a commitment and, although she was extremely fond of Philip, she did not yet feel sure enough of her own feelings – or his – to want to

336

put them to the test. Inevitably, if she went home with him everyone, probably including Philip, would assume that marriage was a likely event in the not too distant future. Although Ella was an enthusiastic suffragette, she believed that a happy marriage was the best thing which could happen to a woman. She also believed in the old saying 'Marry in haste, repent at leisure' and thought fearfully that if Philip were to see her under his parents' roof he might realise that she was not, after all, the sort of girl they would wish him to marry. She chided herself for this fear, for was this not 1911? If it was generally accepted that many young women had, of necessity, to earn a living in order to keep themselves, then it followed that the Grimshaws must know such young women existed, might even admire them. It was common knowledge that, in order to get a decent position in any walk of life, a woman had to be ten times more intelligent and determined as any man. Philip himself acknowledged it, but would his parents? He had a sister, Laura, of whom he was very fond; suppose Laura did not take to her?

Ella tried, rather timidly, to put these questions to Amy, who simply stared at her round-eyed. 'You think *you* are going to feel uncomfortable among the Grimshaws?' she asked incredulously. 'You think they'll look down on you? Well, if they do so, all I can say is they aren't worth knowing. Besides, don't you think that Philip probably takes after one or other of his parents? If that's so, then they'll be lovely people who will accept you for what you are, a brave and resourceful woman, making her own way in the world.'

'But I don't want to be thought of as a brave and

resourceful woman,' Ella wailed, running her hands through her short, curly hair, for she had had to cut the left side to match the right as soon as her hair had reached a respectable length. 'I want to be thought of as pretty, eligible and . . . and charming.'

Amy laughed at this honest declaration. 'Votes for women, indeed,' she scoffed. 'You're just like the rest of us women, queen. In our heart of hearts we all want to be cherished and protected, and thought of as helpless little darlings. Well, Ella, just you go ahead and visit Philip's folks, because you're pretty as a picture and smart as paint, and worth a whole flock of empty-headed society beauties.'

'Do you know, I believe I will?' Ella said slowly. She looked around their room, which was already decorated with brightly coloured paper chains, a miniature Christmas tree and sprigs of holly tacked on to the picture rail. 'You and Ruthie will go home, of course – but what about Minnie? I can't and won't leave her here to celebrate Christmas alone.'

'Why, she must come home with me, of course,' Amy said at once, without appearing to give the matter so much as a moment's thought. 'We'll go to Seafield Grove for Christmas Day and Boxing Day, but come home to Huskisson Street at night. Then there won't be any question of who's to sleep where – though come to think of it, Mary probably won't be coming home for Christmas, so Minnie and I could share with Becky just for one or two nights. I meant to tell you, I went into Blackler's yesterday in my dinner hour and had a chat with Mary. She's thinking of staying with a pal over the holiday and not coming back to Seaforth. She took a leaf out of our book, you know, when she came back to Liverpool, and began to go about more with friends from the store. So unless she comes over for the New Year, we shan't be seeing her in Seaforth for a while. And you'll never believe it, Ella, but she's actually found a feller, someone she really seems to like for himself. I don't say she's serious, probably he's just a friend, but nevertheless, she does like him and he's only a tram driver and plain as a plum pudding, apparently. And you know our Mary, she's always put looks, money and position high on her list of requirements, so the fact that she's looked twice at a tram driver, and an ugly one at that, must mean she's head over heels.'

Both girls laughed at the thought of Mary actually falling in love with anyone, let alone with a young man whom she would plainly think her social inferior. So having decided what to do with Minnie, they continued with their plans for Christmas.

Mary had enjoyed her meeting with Amy, for the two girls did not see each other very often. She had told Amy briefly that she had met someone called Haydn Lloyd, who had made a great impression on her. She had not, however, gone into any more detail because, even to herself, the friendship had seemed a strange one. At least, it would have seemed a strange one to the old Mary, the Mary who had gone steady with Roderick Campbell for five years, during which time she had grown more and more similar to Mr Campbell and less and less like the girl who had set out to conquer Manchester with such high hopes.

At the time, Mary had scarcely been aware that she was changing, hardening. She had not realised, until Roderick had left her, that she had been slowly but surely becoming like him, embracing his attitudes, ambitions and values, and allowing her own to become almost completely submerged.

At first, when he had taken up with his little tart, as Mary had called her, she had felt bitter shame and rage for her lost years, along with the feeling that she could not hold a man, not even one as thoroughly unworthy as Roderick had proved to be. But gradually, as the weeks passed, she had begun to feel a lightness of spirit and a burgeoning of hope. It was this, at last, which gradually made her realise how bad Roderick had been for her and how infinitely better off she was without him.

She had gone back to Seaforth, however, when her bitter shame and rage over Roderick's defection had been at its height. Then she had agreed to meet up with Amy for a day out, and that day had determined her on the move back to the city of her birth. For they had met Ella, Minnie and Ruth after work and had walked back to Huskisson Street together, staring into shop windows, covertly eyeing the young men they passed and light-heartedly announcing their preference for dark men, fair ones, tall ones or cheeky ones. Then they had purchased fried fish and chipped potatoes for their supper and had eaten their meal out of newspaper wrappings, and had spent the jolliest evening imaginable in the girls' big room, chatting, laughing and exchanging frank comments about life in general and married life in particular, until Mary had truly envied Amy her room share and had begun to see that young men were really not as important as she had once thought.

She had remembered afterwards how she had

arrived in Seaforth in a white heat of rage, determined to find Philip Grimshaw so that she might somehow become his young lady, which would have shown Roderick that Mary was not to be trifled with. She knew that Roderick had been jealous of Philip, whose superior looks and intelligence had made him popular with young men and girls alike, so to flourish Philip in Roderick's face would have been a triumph indeed. She had speedily realised the futility of this plan when Amy had explained how brief their meeting had been and had added that they had not seen Philip since, nor did they expect to do so. But by then it no longer mattered. Mary had realised the fun which could be had with a group of girlfriends and had returned to Manchester no longer interested in spiting Roderick but determining, instead, to make a new life for herself in Liverpool which would not, in the early stages at any rate, include the capturing of a young man.

Deciding on this course, she had taken the job at Blackler's and accepted Faith's offer of the room share. Bearing in mind the enjoyable evening she had spent with Amy and her room-mates, once she had settled in, she had invited three girls, from the departmental store in which they all worked, back to her room one evening for a light supper and a cosy chat. This had proved so successful that later the four of them had gone off to the Empire Theatre on Lime Street to see Cecilia Loftus and Albert Whelan. This had led naturally to the suggestion that they should go dancing together at the dance academy on Renshaw Street and it was here that Mary had met Haydn Lloyd for the first time. He had asked her to dance with him within half an hour of her arrival at the hall and Mary, who was seldom without a partner, had slid gracefully into his arms and had barely noticed him as a person, save for the realisation that he was no more than an inch taller than she. Very soon she realised that he was a marvellous dancer, with a degree of expertise considerably superior to Roderick's. He was an interesting companion, too, talking in a lively fashion and, what was even nicer, his hands did not continually stray, so she was able to enjoy his company without worrying that he would presently begin to take advantage of having his arm about her, the way so many men did. In fact, she found dancing with him such a pleasure that for the rest of the evening he became her chosen partner, even taking her out during the interval and buying her a small sherry at the nearest public house.

Haydn Lloyd was as Welsh as he sounded and Mary had always rather looked down on the Welsh, considering them country bumpkins not worthy of the attention of a sophisticated city girl like herself. And now, here she was, the beautiful Miss Logan of Blackler's, who had had so many offers in her time, actually contemplating spending her Christmas holiday somewhere in the wilds of Wales with a man who was neither wealthy nor influential – a man, furthermore, who was a widower with two small children.

He had told her about his kids at their very first meeting, had admitted that he missed them most dreadfully and that they lived in Mold, in the county of Flintshire, with his mother. When he had worked down the coal mine at Llay, they had lived in a miner's cottage quite near the pit. However, his wife had died shortly after the birth of his second child and he had moved his family to Mold to live with his mother. There, he had taken work on the land but had speedily found that he could not keep his family on the wages of an unskilled farmworker. Having worked in the open air for a few months, he had no desire to return to the pit. So, with his mother taking care of the children, he had left North Wales to try his luck in the great city of Liverpool. He had speedily found work driving the trams and had hoped, at first, to bring his family to the city so that they could all be together. However, he soon realised he could not cope both with the children and with his job on the trams, and his mother, though a most amenable woman, had utterly refused to leave her neat little terraced house at her time of life. She hated cities, besides which, lodgings in Liverpool were not cheap. Accordingly, Haydn continued with his job, sending money home and retaining only enough to keep himself.

Any sensible girl would have drawn back immediately at this point, because it was as plain as the nose on his face – and that *was* plain! – that Mr Lloyd was looking for a wife to take the place of the one he had lost and Mary, like all girls of her age, wanted romance, a good life and, eventually, children of her own; she did not want to be made use of as a mam for a fellow's motherless kids. Yet despite knowing all this, Mary had not drawn back. She had liked Haydn for his ready grin, his strength of character and for the sheer *goodness* of him, which was a delight after Roderick's self-seeking, humourless attitude to life.

And now Mary was sitting in her comfortable little armchair in her rooms on Mather Avenue, wondering whether she had gone slightly but definitely mad. It was one thing to like a fellow, to want

343

to continue seeing him, but she was actually contemplating going away for Christmas with a man she had met a bare two weeks before, and not a rich or an influential man either, but a tram driver in his forties, with a thick thatch of greying dark hair, a pair of sparkling black eyes and a rather large nose.

She was still telling herself that she must be mad to consider Haydn Lloyd's proposal, when a small voice spoke in her head. *What's wrong with a tram driver – or a miner, come to that*? the little voice said. *Who are you when you're at home? Why, you're nothing but the daughter of a humble fisherman, like the girl in the fairy story, the one they told you in infant school! Oh, I know you may tell yourself that you're a senior sales lady, doing well for yourself, but what does that matter, after all? Even if you rise to be head buyer in Gowns, you'll still be nothing but a fisherman's daughter, when all's said and done.*

The little voice was right, Mary knew it, and not only did she know it, she also acknowledged it as no more than the truth. She had never taken Roderick home because she knew he would despise her background, her father and brothers, even the smell of fish that hung around the house in which she had been born and bred. But Haydn was a different person altogether. He would *like* her father and feel completely at home with her brothers. He would probably consider the little house in Seafield Grove a palace compared with the pit cottage in which he had grown up. She could imagine him helping the boys to heave the boat ashore, gathering up arms full of dripping net, carting boxes laden with flapping fish up the beach and on to the roadway. In short, Mary thought joyfully, Hadyn would be one of them; he would not think for one moment that a tram driver was either superior or inferior to a fisherman. That was not his way. He would simply think them likeable folk and would settle down to become a part of the family.

Mary jumped to her feet. She ran across the small room, dragging her coat off the hook of the back of the door and casting a light shawl over her hair. She knew where Haydn lived, though she had not previously visited him there, but she would do so now. She would tell him joyfully that she would love to go home with him at Christmas and that she very much hoped he would come home with her for the New Year. In other words, Mary told herself, as she descended the stairs and went out into the cold night air, I am about to burn my boats for the very first time in my life and I don't feel worried, or guilty, or anything like that. I feel . . . I feel as though I'm at the very start of a real adventure.

It was a very cold day. Paddy, who had just boiled a supply of shrimps in the wash-house, crossed the courtyard, opened the back door and entered the kitchen, the basket of steaming shrimps in his arms. 'It's norra good day for the fishin',' he observed, going through into the scullery to dump his burden. 'It's bleedin' cold out an' all, Mam, so if you like I'll sell these few shrimps house-to-house, while you gerron with the cookin'.'

Suzie was baking in the kitchen, humming a tune beneath her breath as she worked. She glanced up as her son passed her, nodding thankfully at his suggestion. 'That'd be grand, Paddy,' she said, pushing a wisp of hair off her damp forehead. 'You'll soon get rid of them. It's not many people will bring shrimps in on a day like this.'

Paddy continued on his way to the scullery, glancing down at Becky as he passed her. She was fiddling around with a small grey ball of pastry of her very own, imitating her stepmother, using the miniature rolling pin which Gus had made for her, flattening the pastry into a large, round circle. Then she rolled it into a ball again, wondering aloud why it was such a funny colour, whereas Mam's pastry was a nice, cool, creamy shade.

'You've worked your bit rather hard, our Becky,' Suzie told her, but she good-naturedly broke a ball off the pastry she was rolling out to fit a pie dish, and handed it to her stepdaughter. 'Don't keep rollin' it back into a ball again. If you flatten it quite lightly, just the one time, I'll give you a dab o' mincemeat and you can mek yourself a mince pie.'

Paddy, listening from the scullery, smiled to himself. His mam had really taken to Becky, loved her like her own and would go to any lengths to see the child well-clothed, well-fed and happy. Indeed, looking back to his own childhood, Paddy had to conclude that his mam had mellowed with the years. In those far-off days she had been impatient, quick with a kiss, true, but also with a slap. It had been Gran who had played games with him, taught him his letters, made arithmetic interesting as she set him to counting a bag full of dried peas, using them both as playthings and as a means to teach him simple addition, subtraction and multiplication. Gran had been a marvellous cook, he still remembered the puddings and pies she had made when circumstances permitted, but there had never been enough spare pastry over, he supposed, for her to let him play with it. Instead, he and Albert had made sand pies from the wet and muddy sand which was reachable only at low tide. They carted it up the beach in a leaky wooden bucket, crouching down amid the dunes and decorating the pies with bits of broken shell, pebbles and stems of marram grass.

Paddy sighed; thinking about his childhood always brought Amy to mind and the truth was that Amy had been on his mind for some weeks, ever since he had thought her injured in the riots. He could never forget the awful sinking feeling and the rush of cold dread which had invaded him at that time. Because of his feelings he had made a couple of honest attempts to get on a better footing with her, but these had failed pretty dismally, he thought now. She was polite, she smiled coolly at him, she had even allowed him on one occasion to carry her heavy basket back from the Rimrose Bridge to Seafield Grove. But throughout the course of the walk home she had scarcely spoken, replying in monosyllables to anything that Paddy said and making it clear as crystal that even if his antagonism had disappeared, hers had not.

After that walk, Paddy had vowed that he would stop thinking about her, but the truth was she had become an obsession with him. When she visited the house in Seafield Grove he found himself covertly watching her. He had never thought her pretty, not even passable, but now he discovered that there was a charm in her small vivacious face and tilted smile, which was missing in many prettier young women. He had watched her as she went about the kitchen noticing, without wishing to do so, the neat economy of her movements. She could heft a great basket of fish and carry it across the room without so much as growing breathless, yet she did not appear to be strong. She was slim and slightly built and, although she dressed plainly, there was something elegant, Paddy thought, in the way she wore her simple clothes. Why couldn't she like him? Or if not like, at least not actively dislike, for he knew that at present his own warmer feelings had absolutely no chance of being returned. She might no longer hate him but she certainly never thought of him as anything but a young man who had once been an unpleasant part of her childhood.

Paddy had finished cleaning himself up, so he picked up the basket of shrimps and headed to the back door once more. 'Shan't be long, our mam,' he said cheerfully. 'I'll take this lot to Bootle – any messages?'

Suzie looked up from her baking. 'You might fetch me back another couple of pounds of sultanas and some apples; I'll need to make some more mincemeat since it seems we're entertaining extra over Christmas,' she said.

Paddy pricked up his ears. 'Extra?' he said interrogatively. He glanced across at his mother, still working placidly away at her pastry. 'Oh, I suppose you mean Charlie and his young lady?'

'Oh, them. No, I weren't thinkin' about them,' Suzie said almost absently. She picked up a slice of apple and ate it. 'It's that Amy – she's bringin' a friend home for Christmas and Boxing Day. Not that I mind, particular,' she added, flushing a little under Paddy's hard stare. 'I mean, I know it's her home when all's said and done, but it's not a big house, and with all you fellers, and Becky . . .' Her voice trailed off.

'A friend?' Paddy asked rather blankly. 'Oh, yes, I did know . . .' He turned once more for the door. So I were right, he told himself savagely, as he crossed the little yard. She and that Philip were more than just friends – I should ha' knowed it. I dare say she's been meetin' him every day and gettin' friendlier and friendlier . . . well, it's no skin off *my* nose, 'cos she's never pretended to like me even a little bit. Her having Philip courtin' her won't make any difference to *me*.

But as he trudged round the wintry streets, knocking on doors and selling his shrimps, he was aware of a deep sense of disappointment, almost of loss. Despite all the facts, he had hoped that over Christmas a better understanding might happen between himself and Amy. Now it was clear that even if it did, it would not help his cause.

His cause? Now what exactly do you mean by that, Paddy Keagan? he asked himself, as he knocked on yet another door. You aren't tryin' to tell me that you thought you'd ever get anywhere with Amy Logan? I thought you just wanted to be friends, nothin' more?

But in his heart of hearts he was beginning to realise that, if he lost Amy to Philip, or indeed any other, he would be a very unhappy young man.

Ella and Philip travelled to Manchester by an early train, then took a taxi to Philip's home. Manchester seemed to have had quite a heavy snowfall during the night, for though the sun shone now, it shone on a city gleaming and glittering with snow. The streets, however, were churned-up and filthy, and Ella noticed that most of the women shoppers were lifting their skirts to avoid the slush, even on the pavements. Ella had realised, as the train drew nearer the city, that she was extremely nervous, which seemed odd considering how she had looked forward to this visit. She was very fond of Philip, knew that he was fond of her, even accepted that his intentions were honourable. He had talked of marriage, though she had never let him think that marriage was her ultimate aim. She was a working woman, earning a respectable salary, who had a career she enjoyed. The fact that she would have thrown it up willingly to marry Philip was something that she kept to herself, almost ashamed of how her high principles and desire to be a woman of independent means had crumbled beneath the warmth of his affection and his obvious and increasing desire to shelter her from the harsh realities of life.

In the cab, threading its way through the busy pre-Christmas streets, Philip took her hand in a comforting grasp. 'Nervous?' he asked, giving it a little shake. 'Well, if you aren't, I am. I've got butterflies the size of elephants lashing around in my stomach. It isn't that I'm worried my parents won't like you – they'll love you as I do – it's just ... oh, I don't know, it's just that they're bound to think we're a bit young ...'

'Just because I'm staying with your parents for Christmas doesn't mean we're anything but good friends,' Ella said rather feebly. She knew as well as Philip did that a young man did not ask a young woman to stay with his parents unless he had serious intentions. Of course, a whole week spent in one another's company might cause either party to change their minds, but she knew for her own part that this was unlikely to happen. The trouble was that Philip was not yet twenty-four and a good many parents would consider him young to be thinking seriously of marriage. On the other hand he was living away from home, managing a busy office and coping with the usual requirements of daily living. His life would be very much easier if he shared it with a wife, or so Ella thought now, as the cab drew up before a tall, red-brick house, with a flight of whitened stone steps leading to an impressive front door, upon which hung a wreath of Christmas greenery. The steps, which must have been covered with snow, were now in full sunshine but, like the pavement below, were puddled with melted snow and would have to be ascended with caution. The last thing Ella wanted to do was to make a fool of herself by slipping in the icy water and ending up on hands and knees in front of the door.

Philip gave her hand another reassuring squeeze, climbed from the cab and helped her down on to the pavement. The cab driver picked up their bags, carried them up the steps and heaved at the bell pull, and almost immediately the front door was opened by an imposing figure who beamed a welcome. 'Master Philip! It's good to see you after so long. Miss Laura's out shopping but your mama is in the drawing room.'

'Thanks, Richards,' Philip said. 'This way, Ella!'

Twenty minutes later Ella sat before the dressing table in the large and airy bedroom to which her hostess had led her, unpinning her hat, glad to be rid of its weight and beginning to brush out her crumpled locks. To her great relief she had found Mrs Grimshaw a delightful person, who looked far too young to be Philip's mama. When she entered the drawing room, which was bright with evergreens and Christmas decorations, Mrs Grimshaw had welcomed Ella with warmth and gaiety, apologising for her daughter's absence but explaining that Laura was buying Christmas gifts and would be home in good time for luncheon. 'We've planned all sorts of entertainment for you, my dear,' she said in her pleasant voice. 'We've booked seats at the theatre and there will be a great many private parties to which we have all been invited. Laura wanted to take you shopping today, but I think it would be better, personally, if you spent this afternoon settling in and this evening, when Mr Grimshaw returns home, perhaps we might introduce you to some members of the family who live nearby. Nothing formal, just Philip's grandmother and some cousins who will come in for a glass of wine before dinner.'

So now, as Ella combed out her short curls, she found herself wondering what she should wear that night. Her evening dresses, she knew, were several years out of date, but the material was good and, where it was possible, she had made changes so that she would not look frumpish or old-fashioned. She was looking forward to meeting Laura because Philip was clearly very fond of his younger sister. She sounded great fun, but in any event Ella was determined to like her for Philip's sake.

Having tidied her hair and changed her cotton voile blouse for an uncreased one, Ella was debating whether to go straight downstairs again to find her hostess when there was a tap at the door, which opened to reveal a maid in a blue print dress and white apron. 'Madam sent me to ask if I may unpack for you and iron out any creases in your clothes, Miss Morton,' the girl said in a small, shy voice, with a strong Mancunian accent. 'Is there anything else I can do for you – I dare say your shoes might need cleaning?'

Ella looked down at her neat black shoes adorned with a small velvet bow. They were new, having been bought only days earlier at Thierry's in Bold Street. They were also still both clean and dry since she had only taken a few steps between the cab and the front door on arrival in Manchester, and in Liverpool there had been no sign of snow. 'No, these are fine, thank you,' she said, hoping she was striking just the right note between mistress and maid.

She turned her foot to glance at the heel and the girl said admiringly, 'Them's the new Cuban heels, ain't they, miss? Oh, I do think they're smart!'

'Well, thank you,' Ella said, touched by the friendliness in the girl's tone. 'Oh, I never asked you your name.'

'I'm Myrtle, Miss Morton,' the girl said, 'and Mrs Grimshaw has told me to wait on you, so if there's anything you want, all you've got to do is pull that there bell and I'll come running.'

'Very well, Myrtle, I shan't forget,' Ella said bravely. 'And now if you wouldn't mind coming with me to the head of the stairs and pointing out the drawing room – if that's where I shall find Mrs Grimshaw – then I'll leave you to get on with your work.'

Myrtle, who could not have been many years younger than Ella herself, obligingly came halfway down the stairs with her, saying that Mrs Grimshaw would be in the morning room, where she had ordered coffee to be served. 'Young Mr Grimshaw is in there as well,' she said breathlessly, as she turned to retrace her steps. 'I've only worked for the family for eight weeks, so I've not met him before. Oh, miss, isn't he . . .?' She clapped a hand to her mouth, a pink flush invading her face, but her eyes sparkled at Ella over her spread fingers.

Ella smiled, but had no opportunity to comment one way or the other since the door of the morning room flew open, revealing Philip, who glanced up at her, smiling. 'Ah, Ella, you're just in time for coffee and bourbon biscuits,' he said, crossing the hall to meet her as she descended the last stairs. 'And Laura will be joining us in a few minutes; she's run upstairs to change out of her street clothes.' He held out both hands and took Ella's in a warm grasp, and immediately the worry, which must have shown on Ella's face at the thought of meeting his beloved sister, faded from her mind. 'You're going to love one another, like two sisters,' he whispered as they entered the room together.

When Myrtle had helped her to get ready for bed that night and left her, at last, in her brightly lit room, with the fire blazing and a drink of hot milk on her bedside table, Ella was able to reflect on all that had passed. It had been a wonderful day, from the moment that Philip had picked her up in Huskisson Street to the present, sitting warm and comfortable in her beautiful bedroom and anticipating with real excitement the days still to come.

She had, as she had hoped, loved Laura almost as soon as she met her, partly because she was so very like Philip, with the same taffy-brown hair and matching eyes, although in Laura's case the hair had been elaborately curled and was tied back from her face with ribbon. She was about Ella's own height and had a good deal of self-confidence, although she was not at all assertive. What was more, she was clearly determined to like Ella and had speedily dispensed with the title 'Miss Morton', and had begged Ella not to keep calling her Miss Grimshaw, either. 'For we are going to be great friends,' she had said gaily, slipping her arm round Ella's waist, as the two of them went to their rooms after luncheon to get ready for a shopping expedition.

After some earlier discussion, Laura had persuaded Ella that their shopping, if it was to be successful, had best be done that day. 'For tomorrow is Christmas Eve,' she had said, 'and the shops will be crowded with people searching for last-minute gifts. If we go immediately after luncheon, we should be home for tea. That will give you plenty of time to prepare for the family party this evening.' As they continued up the stairs, Laura turned to Ella once more and gave her a teasing glance, from her large, long-lashed eyes. 'And though I know we shall be friends, from what Philip tells me, I may yet be able to call you sister.' She smiled at Ella's astonished expression and gave the other girl a little shake. 'Silly! You must be as aware as I, that Philip would scarcely bring you home and introduce you to his family unless he was ... was serious about you. I do hope you are serious about him as well,' she added naively, 'because he's the nicest young man I know, even though I *am* prejudiced, he being my brother.'

'I like your brother very much,' Ella said rather stiffly, 'but this visit is by way of being a ... a sort of test. I'm working very hard to become an independent woman, someone who can look after herself and earn sufficient money to be comfortable, no matter what may happen to me. I haven't seriously considered marriage . . .' She met Laura's quizzical eye and felt her cheeks grow hot. 'Well, I suppose everyone considers marriage but . . . but we aren't engaged or anything of that nature.'

They had reached Ella's bedroom door by this time. She opened it and would have gone into the room but Laura detained her, a hand on her arm. 'Philip told me that this was a sort of test as well,' she admitted. 'Oh, but Ella, I do so want it to be a success!' And with that she flitted down the corridor and disappeared into her own room.

Despite the slight feeling of embarrassment which Laura's assumption had caused her, Ella had still enjoyed the shopping expedition immensely. She had asked Laura which of her evening dresses she should wear that night and Laura had unhesitatingly picked out Ella's favourite, a lavender silk gown with a low-cut neck, a dark-purple velvet sash round the high waist and tiny, embroidered, laced sleeves. With this gown, Ella had intended to wear her white lace elbow-length gloves, but Laura had shaken her head.

'Lavender kid gloves,' she had said decisively. 'And I know where just such a pair may be purchased for a reasonable price. Bradshaw and Blackmore's are having a pre-Christmas sale. We can catch a tram and be there in ten minutes, and while we're there I'd like to look at some of the oriental trousers that the magazines have been raving about. Not that I would dream of wearing them,' she added. 'Particularly not this evening, since Grandma Grimshaw would probably have a heart attack if I wore anything so daring.'

The shopping expedition had gone off well. Ella

had purchased not only the gloves, but a pair of elegant high-heeled shoes, decorated with beading and embroidery, in a lovely shade of deep violet, which contrasted beautifully with the lavender gown. Laura, having examined with close interest the outrageous harem trousers and turbans on display, bought a boa made of white swansdown which would, she assured her new friend, go with everything she possessed. The two girls returned home and spent a great deal of time dressing for the evening. Although Mrs Grimshaw had said it was scarcely a party, Ella thought that she had been afraid of frightening her young guest; according to Laura it was to be a dinner party and the cousins would all be dressed in their best.

'And Emmeline Griffith is bound to come, since her parents live next door and are great friends of papa's,' Laura remarked.

She glanced sideways at Ella, clearly wondering whether to continue with what she had been about to say. Ella, who had bound a lavender chiffon scarf around her curls, and was rather doubtfully regarding the effect in her dressing-table mirror, raised her brows. 'Emmeline Griffith?'

'She ... she likes Philip,' Laura blurted, then looked conscience-stricken. 'He doesn't like her,' she added hastily. 'Oh, he thinks she's frightfully smart and terribly amusing, but he doesn't like her, not one bit.'

Now, taking a sip of her hot milk, Ella reflected that Miss Griffith most certainly *did* like Philip and had spared no pains to show him that she was available. She had also shown that as far as she was concerned Ella was a provincial nobody who had somehow managed to enter the Grimshaws'

357

charmed circle by a method she herself would never have needed to employ.

The dinner had gone well; Ella had been seated between Philip on her left and a young man called Davidson on her right, and had managed to conduct a reasonable conversation with both of them, despite Miss Griffith's constant calls on their attention, for she was seated on the opposite side of the table and had made eyes at Philip throughout the meal.

The part of the evening which had filled Ella with lively dismay in advance, however, proved to be far less of an ordeal than she had anticipated. Old Mrs Grimshaw was a tall, straight-backed octogenarian, with white hair piled up on her head in the Queen Alexandra style. She had glittering blue eyes, which Ella found focused upon herself disconcertingly often, and a clear, commanding voice that she used to good effect. After dinner Philip took Ella to the sofa upon which his grandmother was seated and, rather basely Ella felt, sat her down beside the old lady and went off to get them both a cup of coffee.

Mrs Grimshaw promptly began to reminisce about her own girlhood, which had been spent in Southport. 'For I was a Seymour before I married Mr Grimshaw,' she explained. 'We lived in a very fine house on Lord Street and had a great many friends among the neighbouring families and Southport was a whirl of gaiety in Victorian times. Not that we were allowed the licence you young people enjoy today,' she added, fixing Ella with her glittering eyes. 'Balls were private affairs, unless one went to a subscription ball, of course – they were a little more informal. Yet though we could not go out without a chaperone, we still managed to enjoy ourselves. And naturally we met the right people, not the wrong ones,' she finished, which Ella felt to be a remark directed at her.

'My own grandmother was born and bred in Southport, and married a Southport gentleman,' Ella said quietly. 'I imagine she must have had the same restrictions that you speak of, though she died when I was only two, so I never really knew her.'

'Oh, so you're a Southport gel,' Mrs Grimshaw said at once, her interest clearly aroused. 'What was the name again?'

'My mother was Henrietta Morton, but ...'

'Mortons? Never heard of them,' the old lady said decisively. 'Can't have moved in my circle.'

'No, that was my mother's married name,' Ella said, patiently. 'She married my father, Oswald Morton, when she was only nineteen. But before her marriage she was a Hillerman.'

The old lady, who had been eyeing the young people talking in a small group by the long dining table, abruptly turned towards Ella, seeming to lose interest in the conversation going on ahead of her. 'Not Rebecca Hillerman?' she said incredulously. 'She was my greatest friend. Why, even after we both married we remained on the very best of terms – I was godmother to her eldest daughter, Matilda.' She stared hard at Ella, the bright blue eyes unblinking. 'Now that I look at you closely, I declare I can see a resemblance to your dear grandmother. She had just those big, dark eyes and always with such a quizzical gleam when something amused her. Yes, there is a *marked* resemblance – and your grandmother was a great beauty in her time.'

The incident had set the seal on the evening and not only on the evening, Ella thought now, finishing her hot milk and climbing between the sheets, but on her whole visit. From the moment that old Mrs Grimshaw had begun to tell people how she and Ella's grandmother had been great friends, Ella felt herself accepted not only by the Grimshaws themselves, but by their numerous friends and relations. The fact that Ella was now a working girl, sharing a room with three others, no longer mattered; she was a Hillerman, the child of important and wealthy people, and in future would be accepted as such without question.

I'm not a snob, Ella told herself as she settled down to sleep. Everyone wants to be accepted for themselves, but I can't deny it's very comfortable to feel that my birth does mean something. Amy says she's proud of being a fisherman's daughter and so she should be, which means I can be proud of my connections, too.

There had only been one dissident voice when her connections in Southport had been discussed and unfortunately, perhaps, Ella had overheard it. Indeed, thinking back, she found herself torn between a desire to giggle and another to slap Emmeline Griffith's face.

Ella had been sitting with a group of Philip's cousins, half listening to their animated conversation, when her own name caught her ears. Without turning her head she promptly switched her attention to the young woman who had spoken, realising immediately that the soft, affected tones, belonged to Miss Griffith.

'Ella Morton?' the voice drawled, with an edge of dislike to it which was unmistakable, 'and the old lady recognised her you say? I think it likelier that she recognised the dress.'

For a moment Ella's cheeks had burned with

mortification, but then the funny side brought a smile to her lips. It was true that her dress had been remodelled from an old one belonging to her mother, but glancing towards Miss Griffith's rear view she reflected that anyone with a bottom which could be compared unfavourably with that of a carthorse was bound to make catty remarks about someone as slim as herself. What was more the bottom in question, being upholstered in red velvet, drew attention to its size; black would have been more sensible, Ella found herself thinking. Or even a nice dark green, but not, definitely not, scarlet velvet.

On that thought she fell happily asleep.

Ella spent the following day almost exclusively in Philip's company, though they returned to the house for tea at four. Laura had suggested accompanying them when Philip had said he meant to show Ella Manchester, but he had vetoed her suggestion on the grounds that she would want to go in and out of the department stores. There were a great many things besides shops that were worth visiting, he told his sister grandly: museums, art galleries and fine architecture for a start.

But in the event, Ella realised later, the day had been spent in getting to know one another and to appreciate each other's tastes. They visited the museums and found they both enjoyed browsing among the exhibits, and in the art gallery they both admired landscapes rather than portraits. They had lunch at Lyons Café on Victoria Street and then, rather to Ella's surprise, they did a good deal of window shopping, walking down a narrow little street in which there were a number of jewellery shops. Philip invented a game which consisted of his trying to guess which of the wonderful sparkling emerald, sapphire and diamond rings she would prefer. What was more, he scored high on her preferences, making her feel they had similar tastes in other matters than museums and galleries. Indeed, when she asked him why he did not consider rubies, he said at once that he thought them too flamboyant for her own particular style of beauty and had guessed that she would prefer sapphires or emeralds.

When they reached home it was to find the whole family, including Grandmama Grimshaw, seated around a roaring log fire in the drawing room, eating muffins and buttered toast, and drinking tea from delicate china cups.

The two of them sat down and enjoyed a hearty meal, for dinner would not be served until eight o'clock and so much walking had made Ella hungry as any hunter. Presently Philip excused himself on the grounds that he had some wrapping of presents to do in his room. Ella accepted this but suggested to Laura that they themselves might follow his example, since she had bought a few small presents that morning, which she had not yet wrapped or labelled. Standing up to leave the room, her eye was caught by a movement on the other side of the window glass and, to her surprise, she saw that it was Philip, coated and hatted, making his way down the steps and along the pavement. He had hunched his shoulders and sunk his head as low into his collar as he could, and Ella thought, with a pang of dismay, that he looked somehow furtive. She was forced to wonder whether he was off to visit an old friend and thought bitterly that if it was the horrible Emmeline Griffith, then he was welcome to her. She just hoped that Miss Griffith would show her true character by making some catty remark which would send Philip home disgusted with her. She half wished that she had told Philip what the older girl had said about her ball gown, then dismissed the idea. She was being as petty as Emmeline Griffith when she allowed herself to harbour such thoughts and anyway, it was far likelier that Philip had merely run out of paper or string and was going out to renew his supplies.

Being only human, however, Ella could not help thinking wistfully how nice it would have been to have Amy near at hand; for the past couple of years the two of them had discussed every aspect of their life and thoughts – and, indeed, their loves – with a frankness that would have astonished most of the people they knew. Now, in a strange house in a strange city, surrounded by people she had met for the first time the previous day, Ella knew once again the sharp pangs of loneliness which had assailed her when she had first come to Liverpool.

But Philip was her friend; he had brought her here and would make sure that she had a good Christmas, even if their relationship never became any closer than it was now.

Vaguely comforted by this thought, Ella continued to make her way up to her room.

It was a small house with a dusty track running along the front of it, dividing it from the river, which at this time of year was in full spate and noisy enough to keep Mary awake at night, although after the first day she was so tired that she could, she thought, have slept on a clothes line.

But hard though the work was, it was done with

such happiness and delighted anticipation that Mary would not have missed it for the world. What was more, she had been impressed by the small town of Mold, set in a cup in the hills which reared around it like inverted green pudding basins; these were not the mountains of Wales but the gentle foothills, grazed by placid sheep and bedecked on their lower slopes by mixed woodland. Mary, who had only known the Liverpool area and the great city of Manchester, thought she had never seen country so beautiful.

She and Haydn had returned to the small market town on the day before Christmas Eve and had spent the intervening time preparing for the Christmas holiday. The children were wildly excited and welcomed Mary with simple delight because she was their father's friend. They clearly wanted this beautiful golden girl to be their friend also and hung around her, asking questions, telling her of their lives, their school, their friends. Old Mrs Lloyd was equally delighted with her, particularly when she found that Mary meant to take full part in all the work of Christmas, as well as the festivities. Indeed, while they were washing up the dishes on that first evening, she had told Mary that much though she loved her grandsons, she was 'beginning to be too old to handle them, good though they were'.

When Haydn and Mary had arrived in Mold, the children and old Mrs Lloyd had been settled round the kitchen table with pots of flour-and-water paste, and strips of previously painted newspaper. Under their grandmother's tuition and with Mary's help, the strips had been made into garlands, which Haydn pinned to the picture rails, festooning the room. The boys, Emrys and Geraint, were five and six, attractive, rosy-faced children with identical round, dark-brown eyes, straight fringes of equally dark hair falling across their foreheads and sturdy young bodies. Because Emrys was tall for his age and Geraint rather shorter, Mary could scarcely tell them apart, but she realised that this was only because she did not yet know them very well. They both spoke Welsh as their first language – as, indeed, did Haydn and his mother – but they spoke English at school and courteously tried to speak it whenever they were in Mary's company. Geraint was fluent, Emrys slightly less so, but Haydn said that the English of both boys would improve over Christmas and since they must speak English in school this was a good thing.

The two small boys had been out in the woods the previous day, and had cut festive greenery and a good clump of mistletoe to decorate the house. Now, the brilliant holly and ivy were wreathed around pictures and door frames, while the mistletoe was tacked to the kitchen ceiling. Haydn kissed all his family beneath it and, when the children were in bed and his mother snoozing before the fire, he kissed Mary, too, with a gentleness which touched her heart.

Preparations for the Christmas feast were already well advanced by Christmas Eve. Mrs Lloyd had baked mince pies, sugar cakes and an apple tart. The Christmas pudding, ceremoniously stirred by one and all and wrapped in its white linen cloth, had been boiled for hours, so that on the following day only a further hour's cooking would see it ready for the table. The cockerel, which was to be the focus of the meal, had spent a year in a smallish run in the back garden, being fattened on grain gleaned from the fields, dandelion leaves from the hedgerows which the boys collected on their way home from school, and any leftover scraps from the Lloyds' table. Mary was grateful that the bird had been slain before her arrival, for she gathered that every year the little boys grew fond of their forthcoming meal and shed bitter tears over his demise.

'It was not as if it was a friendly bird,' Mrs Lloyd had grumbled to Mary in her stilted English. 'Take your finger off soon as look at you, if you poked it through the wire netting. But the boys dug worms for it and thought of it as a pet, so I got Mr Evans from up the road to wring its neck while they was in school; that way, the loss wasn't so personal, like.'

Mrs Lloyd had confided this news to Mary on her first night in Mold, when the two of them were sharing Mrs Lloyd's bed in the tiny room under the eaves. Haydn and the boys slept in the slightly larger room, but Mary, who had made such a fuss about sleeping with her own sisters, was happy to share with Haydn's mother. She would have been happy, she reflected, to sleep on the living room floor if it meant that she could become a part of this poor but happy family.

That night, before they went off to bed, the children had hung their stockings from the mantelpiece and had urged their father anxiously to make sure the fire was truly dead so that Father Christmas, in his descent down the chimney, did not set his boots or beard on fire. Mary did not think that either child truly expected the stockings to be bulging with presents next day, for they admitted that such a thing had never happened at Christmas before. There had been an orange one year and a tin whistle each, but not a great many gifts. This year, however, she and Haydn had worked hard either to make or to buy small gifts for the boys, and Mary found herself eagerly anticipating their pleasure on the morrow. There would be nothing expensive, of course, but she had got Albert to whittle her a couple of toy railway engines and had herself painted one green and one scarlet, so that each child would know his own. She had made toffee and coconut ice in the kitchen of a friend and had wrapped them enticingly, and she knew Haydn had visited the penny bazaar whenever he had money to spare. One way and another, therefore, this should be a good Christmas.

When planning for the holiday she had taken Haydn's advice and had bought Mrs Lloyd several skeins of wool; his mother, Haydn told her, was a great knitter and made all her own shawls, stockings and gloves. For Haydn himself Mary had bought two ounces of pipe tobacco and a clay pipe with a curly stem. She knew he liked to smoke occasionally, but seldom did so since tobacco was so expensive.

The fire was now beginning to die down and Haydn was carefully spreading the ash, so that it would be completely out by morning. The boys' stockings hung on either side of the fireplace, satisfyingly bulky, and in one corner of the large living kitchen a small Christmas tree stood in its pot, its branches hung with paper ornaments, tinsel and a few home-made crackers. The boys, who had made the crackers in school and therefore must know the contents, were still as excited as though they were a complete novelty and were already arguing over who should have first pick when the great day arrived.

'I think everything's ready,' Haydn said at last,

looking round the kitchen. Every surface gleamed and the lamplight reflected off the newly white-washed walls, and cast into strong relief the bunches of holly and ivy, and the mistletoe on the ceiling.

Mrs Lloyd had gone to bed an hour previously, so that she and Mary were not trying to undress at the same time in such cramped conditions, and after a last glance around her Mary stood up. 'Well, I'd best be off to bed myself, because tomorrow's going to be pretty busy,' she observed. 'If we take the bird down to the baker for cooking and then go to church, do you think it will be ready by the time the service is over?' She did not add, as she had been half tempted to do, that it might seem better if she were to stay at home and keep an eye on things, for the service would be in Welsh and would mean perhaps an hour, but probably longer, of extreme boredom, while the parson rabbited on and the congregation eyed this stranger among them with curiosity, if not antagonism. But she had realised that staying away from the service would lead to awkward questions, and for Haydn's sake she wanted the day to be one of complete pleasure, so she had agreed to attend.

Haydn put his head on one side and grinned at her. 'Cooked it will be in that time and probably overcooked,' he said wryly. 'You can't stop a Welshman from preaching, cariad, especially on Christmas Day. But never fear, Roasty Jones knows all about Christmas services and all about sermons as well. He'll put everyone's bird in at the same time – and there'll be a good few of 'em, so I tell you. That way they cooks slower . . .' he smacked his lips. '. . . but taste better,' he finished.

'Right you are, then,' Mary said.

She was turning towards the stairs when Haydn

caught hold of her arms and swung her to face him. 'You're a good girl, Mary,' he said. 'This Christmas would have been nothing but hard work and sad thoughts of past Christmases if it hadn't been for you. But I want you to know, my lovely girl, that it isn't of my dear Rhiannon that I've been thinking these past couple of days. I loved her very much, but she died soon after Emrys's birth, and now I've done with grieving and can turn back to making a life for myself and the boys. And ... well, and ...' He glanced up at the ceiling and Mary followed his eyes. They were standing directly beneath the bunch of mistletoe. 'Mary, fach, you're the sweetest person, the best thing that's happened in my life for several years,' he said softly, then turned slightly to look towards the clock on the mantel; it was a few minutes past midnight. 'Happy Christmas, cariad, and I pray to God we'll share more of 'em.'

This time the kiss was neither soft nor gentle, but held all the hunger and longing a passionate man feels for the woman of his choice. All in a moment Mary knew that he loved her and that she loved him, too. She returned the embrace with a fervour which astonished her, and as his strong arms closed round her the strangest thought entered her head. I need never be alone again, the thought ran – yet Mary had never thought of herself as lonely until this moment of wonderful shared warmth and affection.

'Mary? Do you ...? Can you ... ? I know I'm a pretty ordinary sort of feller and you're a real little beauty, but I swear to you, you'll want for nothing I can provide, if only ... if only ...'

Mary moved back from him a little and then, taking his face between her hands, she studied it for several breathless seconds. He was right, he was a pretty ordinary sort of fellow and the only life he could offer her was likely to be a hard one, with a family to provide for before the banns were even called and an old mother dependent on him. Was she really considering marriage with him? Why, he was . . .

Slowly, with half-shut eyes, her mouth went to meet his and Haydn prolonged the kiss, stroking her back in comforting circles as though she had been a child. By the time she opened her eyes again and broke free of him, she knew that she would never see him as plain, let alone ordinary, again. He was her man, the one person in the world she thought she could never live without, and the fact that he came complete with responsibilities . . . well, what did that matter? What mattered most was that they loved one another.

'Mary? Oh, cariad, I want you . . . but properly, in marriage, not . . .'

'Dear Haydn,' Mary whispered, clinging. 'Oh, darling Haydn! Of course I'll marry you and as soon as you like.'

Haydn began to smile. He put both arms round her and lifted her off her feet, giving a subdued cheer as he did so. 'Oh, my lovely girl! What a Christmas this will be!'

'Amy! It's morning and you said when morning came . . . oh, Amy, *do* wake up!'

Amy struggled out of a deep and satisfying sleep to find something – or someone – sitting on her stomach while a voice, all the more imperative because it was whispering, bade her to 'wake up . . . you *promised*, so you did! As soon as it's morning, you said . . .'

Amy heaved up her middle to form a bridge and Becky, for it was undoubtedly she, rolled off her sister and landed with a plop on the cold linoleum. She also giggled, but then repeated obstinately, 'But you did promise, Amy, you know you did! As soon as it's day, you said, and there's light out there, I can see clouds . . . oh, dear Amy, *do* wake up!'

From the far side of the bed, against the wall, another voice added itself to the monologue. 'For God's sweet sake tell that kid to shurrup and go back to sleep. It's the middle of the bleedin' night,' Minnie said in a sleep-blurred voice. 'Becky, if you want my present when it's really daytime then you'll shurrup now, like I said, and let honest folk sleep. Remember, your sister and meself didn't get home till gone ten, what wi' one thing and another.'

'Oh! But Minnie, there's day on t'other side o' the curtains, honest to God there is! Wait, I'll go and pull 'em back so's you can see.'

There was a brief struggle, then thin grey light invaded the room. Amy groaned and sat up. 'Look, Becky, any fool could tell you that it isn't daylight at all, it's just . . . just that an overcast sky . . . if I let you open one present now, will you go back to sleep until it really is morning? It gets properly light at about eight o'clock I suppose, so . . .'

'Eight o'clock! But how can I open a present now, Amy? Me stockin' is downstairs, hung by the fire so's Father Christmas would find it as soon as he slid down the chimbley. I suppose I could go down on tiptoes, but like as not . . .'

'If you go over to the washstand you'll see my spongebag on the window side. Open that and you'll find a little parcel . . . wait, best light the candle or you won't know what you've got. Oh, what a pest you are, Becky Logan!' Amy sat up in bed and reaching for the matches, lit the candle. By its light Becky ran across to the washstand, fumbled in her sister's spongebag, and presently returned to the bedside with a small parcel in one hand and an expression of great delight written large on her small fair face.

She struggled a moment with paper and string, then let out a squeak. 'Oh, Amy, you are kind to me! What a pretty, fat little dolly; I have never seen one like it! And it's so brightly painted . . . I must not call you "it", though, my pretty darling. You shall be called Mabel, which is quite my favourite name at present.'

'If you unscrew Mabel, you may get a surprise,' Amy said, as her small sister squiggled back into bed and began to admire her present. 'Look!'

And presently she revealed that the fat little wooden doll contained another one, which in its turn contained yet another, until a whole line of fat little wooden dolls were ranged on the counterpane, while Becky squeaked with delight and excitement, and tried to name each doll as it emerged.

'Where on earth did you get them?' Minnie asked presently, thoroughly roused by the unfolding drama of the Russian dolls. 'I can't recall ever seeing anything like that – how pretty they are. It's enough to make you wish you was a kid again yourself!'

'A guest at the hotel showed me one . . . oh, several months ago,' Amy told her friend. 'I asked him if he could possibly get me one for my little sister if I gave him the money and a few weeks ago he came back, complete with the Russian doll. Well, chuck,' she added, addressing her sister, 'I'm glad you like your present, but Minnie and me's still worn out, so you can just do as you promised and go back to sleep until daylight.'

'I don't mind at all ... I'll just fit the dolls back together again first, though,' Becky said, suiting action to words. 'Thank you *ever* so much, Amy – I do love you!'

Paddy was down before the rest of the family, helping Suzie to prepare breakfast. Because it was Christmas Day and the main meal would be eaten after they returned from morning service, Suzie usually did a simple breakfast – buttered toast for the females of the family and bacon sandwiches for the men, and today was no exception. Paddy sat before a blazing fire with a slice of bread on the end of a toasting fork held out to the flames, and as each slice cooked it was added to the pile on the plate which stood to one side of the fireplace.

Despite the dullness of the job, Paddy was secretly very excited, more excited than he had been over Christmas for many a long year. About a week earlier Amy had brought her friend, who was to spend Christmas with them, home for tea to meet the rest of the family. Paddy had braced himself to greet Philip with a warmth that he was far from feeling and was delighted to meet Minnie, especially when the girls, in conversation, revealed that Ella Morton was spending Christmas in Manchester with Philip Grimshaw.

At the time, Paddy had continued stolidly eating his tea and had not even looked up from his plate, though he had felt a little rush of excitement at the news. Later, however, when the girls had gone back to the city centre, he had questioned Suzie closely and had learned that Philip and Ella had been going about together ever since Ella's emergence from hospital. So I was wrong, Paddy told himself gleefully; Amy's still fancy free – or at least, if she's got a feller she's keeping him pretty dark. He remembered vaguely that there had been talk at one time of Amy going about with a friend of Philip's, but it had clearly come to nothing. And Christmas is a romantic time, Paddy had told himself, as he slogged up from the beach with his share of the latest catch. Surely I can do something over Christmas to make her think of me as a friend, if nothing warmer?

After much thought in a similar vein, Paddy decided that he would buy her a present and it would be one which would show in some way that he admired her and wanted, once and for all, to forget their past differences. He began to haunt the shops, department stores and markets around Bold Street, Church Street and Renshaw Street, looking for something – anything – which Amy would really like. He was beginning to despair, to think that there was no such gift in the world, when he happened upon a tiny, narrow shop, squeezed between two very much larger ones, in Upper Parliament Street. The word 'Curios' had been painted in wobbly white letters at the top of the small window, which was crammed with a wide variety of strange objects all, at first glance, of an oriental nature. Paddy stood before the display, totally fascinated. Richly caparisoned ebony elephants jostled with striped and snarling tigers, ivory warriors and tiny, delicate porcelain cups and saucers, eggshell thin. As Paddy stared a thin, yellow hand, with long, curved nails came into the window space and sought out a tiny porcelain half eggshell, in which lay a beautifully carved naked baby, complete to the last detail. Paddy took a deep breath, squared his shoulders and pushed the creaking door wide. Inside an ancient Chinese, with his hair in the traditional pigtail, was showing a young seaman the child in the egg and extolling its virtues in a cracked but musical voice. His English, to Paddy's secret amusement, was the English of the Liverpool docks, but he supposed that if the old fellow had been living here for many years a Liverpool accent would have come more naturally to him than standard English, or even the pidgin English spoken by so many of the Chinese seamen.

While the two at the counter argued amicably over the worth of the tiny object cupped in the China-man's hand, Paddy took a thorough look around. There were so many beautiful things here. He guessed they must all be expensive and also that a good many of them were old, and he also thought that any woman would be enchanted by the majority of the objects on display. He was contemplating a tray upon which lay quantities of ivory carvings, when his eye was caught by a flash of green in a display cabinet, just behind the old man's silk-clad shoulder. Paddy moved a little further along the counter, the better to see what had caught his eye and was immediately enchanted. The cabinet was filled with jade carvings; a tiny frog, jewel-bright, perched on a jade lily pad, an imposing stork, every feather delicately carved, stared malevolently down at the frog and lizards, fish and even tiny figurines, were displayed on the shelves. He was about to turn back to the counter once more, where the seaman had clearly completed his transaction, when he noticed that above the figurines hung a slender gold chain, upon which there were suspended, at regular intervals, droplets of jade. The droplets were minute by the clasp of the necklace, but grew in size until the one at the apex was the size of a little fingernail, and the whole thing was so delicately beautiful that he longed to hold it in his hand, if only for a moment. What was more, he knew without a shadow of doubt that the necklace would look wonderful round Amy's slender white throat. The jade would match the colour of those strange but brilliant eyes and the gold would echo the red-gold of her piled-up hair.

Even as Paddy turned towards the old Chinaman to ask the price of the necklace, the man had forestalled him. He produced a little key from a bunch which jangled at his waist and unlocked the cabinet door, throwing it wide and saying, in his high, cracked old voice, 'The gentleman wishes to admire my jade? What has caught your honour's fancy?'

'Oh! Oh ... er ... the necklace,' Paddy said, almost gasping in his eagerness. 'Can I just take a look at it?'

The Chinaman took the necklace reverently from its place and draped it across Paddy's hand. Seen close to, it was even lovelier than it had been in the showcase – and even more expensive, Paddy thought despairingly. Nevertheless, he knew that it was the very thing for Amy and he had been saving up, after all. 'How much?' he asked boldly. He knew that haggling was a way of life for the Chinese but suspected that he would be no good at it, still ...

'The chain is pure gold and the jade is old, very old,' the man said, naming a figure which made Paddy gasp. It was not that it was so expensive;

indeed, he thought it was probably quite reasonable, but it was more than he had ever spent on a present for anyone, even his mother. If he bought it at the asking price it would reduce his savings considerably. Quickly, before he lost courage, he suggested tentatively that the man might like to accept half the figure named, and after a good deal of wrangling they settled on a sum which Paddy felt he could just about afford. He fished out his money, carefully counted out the required amount and took the small white box which the Chinaman handed to him. Turning to leave the shop, he thought ruefully that the rest of the family would have to make do with inferior offerings this year. But there was no denying it, he had found the perfect present for difficult, disagreeable, adorable Amy Logan.

Paddy was brought abruptly back to the present when the slice of bread on his toasting fork burst into flame. The heat of it travelled along the fork, causing him to fling both toast and implement down on the floor, where he trampled it into Suzie's rag rug, causing his mother to give an indignant shriek.

'There now, Paddy Keagan, look what you've done to me lovely rag rug, let alone that piece of toast,' Suzie said, bringing a brush and dustpan across to sweep up the embers of both toast and rug. 'That's what comes of dreamin' when you should be concentratin'. And what's more, you've toasted enough bread for an army, so leave off and start butterin'.' Paddy, considerably chastened, did so and presently the family began to gather round the kitchen table, wishing each other the compliments of the season and eyeing the small pile of presents beneath the Christmas tree, which would be opened when they got back from church. Becky had come down for her stocking as soon as it was light, but the rest of them had to wait until later in the morning. It was a ritual with the Logan family to open their presents then, so Paddy, who was desperate to see Amy's reaction to his own gift, would have to wait, as everyone else did.

'It was a nice service, wasn't it?' Amy said to Minnie, as the two girls followed the rest of the family out of St Thomas's. 'But listening to the sermon and singing all those carols has given me a good appetite. Dad bought a goose from one of the stalls in St John's Market and Suzie took it down to the baker's early, so as to have it ready for one o'clock; that'll just give us time to open the presents before we eat.'

No one ever spent much on Christmas presents for adults, though they tried to make sure that children had as good a time as they could afford. Minnie had bought token presents for Bill and Suzie – pipe tobacco and chocolates – but had not attempted to buy for the boys, or for Charlie's new wife, a pleasant girl called Lottie, who was already six months gone with child. Amy herself had bought mufflers for her brothers, a pair of silk stockings for Suzie and a pile of little gifts for Becky, and she and Minnie had agreed not to exchange presents this year. Amy knew that Suzie and Bill were going to give Minnie two handkerchiefs and a bag of pepper-mints and guessed she herself would receive something similar from her father and stepmother. So it was without any particular excitement that she joined the family around the tree to open her presents.

Charlie and his wife opened their gifts first, as did

Gus, and then the three of them went off to the baker's to fetch back the goose while the rest unwrapped their packets and parcels. Amy, seeing the small white box with her name written neatly on the lid, picked it up and glanced thoughtfully around her; surely she had opened all the presents from her family? Who could this be from? There was only her own name upon the lid, but then it was a small box with little room for anything else.

The box was fastened with string and red sealing wax. Amy undid it and lifted the lid, then gave a gasp of pure delight. Reverently, she lifted the jade and gold necklace out of its bed of cotton wool and held it up so that it sparkled in the thin sunlight slanting through the window. 'Look!' she said, her voice clear and yet hushed. 'Oh, look at this! Isn't it just the most beautiful thing you've ever seen? But who ... ?'

For a moment there was total silence. Everyone stared at the delicate necklace swinging from Amy's forefinger and nobody spoke. Then Paddy cleared his throat. 'I gorrit in a curio shop on Upper Parly,' he said gruffly. 'I thought ... I thought it 'ud suit you.' Amy's eyes travelled doubtfully from the necklace to Paddy's face and then back to the necklace. For once in her life, perhaps for the first time, she found herself completely bereft of words. From anyone else, from any one of her brothers or friends, she would have greeted the gift with the pleasure it deserved, but coming from Paddy, who had always hated her ... or had he? For the first time it occurred to her that on several occasions lately, when he could have been rude or dismissive, he had been polite, almost friendly. She seemed to remember that at some point over the past few months he had more or less said they ought to forget the old antagonism and try, at least on the surface, to behave like civilised, rational people. He had not used those very words, of course, they were probably not part of Paddy's vocabulary, but that was what he had meant.

She looked up at Paddy through her lashes, realising abruptly that the silence had stretched for too long; if she did not speak soon ... 'You really shouldn't have, Paddy,' she said stiffly, trying to meet his eye, but he would not look at her, watching the necklace as it hung from her fingers with an intensity which she found more embarrassing than a glance exchange between them. 'It's the most beautiful thing I've ever seen, but it must have cost a great deal and ... I ... I shouldn't accept it from you.'

Paddy looked up at her; it was difficult to read the expression in his dark eyes, but at least he met her own as she made an attempt at a friendly smile. 'Are you sayin' you won't take it?' Paddy asked baldly. 'Are you sayin' I ain't even good enough to give you something pretty, as a Christmas present?'

Amy was still searching for a reply which would enable her to give back the gift without appearing downright hateful, when Bill spoke. 'Of course she ain't sayin' any such thing,' he said gruffly, 'no daughter of mine would be so bleedin' rude, let alone ungrateful.' He turned to Amy. 'Why, queen, next thing we know you'll be askin' young Becky for the money for them Russian dolls you give her this morning. Or offerin' to pay me so much a pound for the spuds what I grew for Christmas dinner.'

The rebuke, though thoroughly deserved, brought the hot colour flooding to Amy's cheeks. She clutched the necklace, crumpling it into the palm of her hand, suddenly wanting to hurl it in Paddy's face and walk out of the cottage for ever, never to return. It was all his fault! He had made her look a mean, ungracious beast, which was no doubt what he had intended. She had been right to hate him, he had always been against her and now he meant to turn the rest of the family against her, too. However, unless she kept her thoughts to herself she would ruin Christmas Day for everyone and she did not intend to do that. Slowly she released the necklace from a grip so tight that the gold chain had scored deep into the palm of her left hand. She glanced around the ring of faces; everyone except Paddy was staring at her with an expression of mixed shock and disappointment. Poor Minnie, who knew nothing of Amy's past suffering at Paddy's hands, was clearly horrified by her friend's strange and ungracious behaviour. It occurred suddenly to Amy that Minnie might not know that she and Paddy were stepbrother and stepsister; certainly, she would be completely ignorant of their childhood antagonism.

Slowly and fumblingly, Amy put the necklace round her throat and tried to fasten the little gold clasp, but it was tiny and she could not quite manage it. For a moment she continued to struggle then looked across at Paddy. He was staring straight at her, round dark eyes eager, his mouth opening to form words. 'Can I . . . shall I . . . ?'

'Yes, please, Paddy, if you would be so kind,' Amy said, trying to make her voice sound friendly. 'I'm sorry I was so rude . . . I didn't think . . . I didn't realise . . . it's just that it's so beautiful and must have been such a price . . . would you do it up for me, please.'

She bent her head forward meekly and felt

Paddy's fingers against the nape of her neck. She was aware, as his fingers touched her skin, of a strange sensation in the pit of her stomach and knew, irritatingly, that she was blushing. Looking round beneath her long lashes, she saw the relief which swept like a tide across the faces, watched smiles come back as people turned towards one another and began to talk. The tension, which had been almost visible, had drained away and everyone was at ease once more. Except for me, Amy thought bitterly. I'm the only one who knows, bleedin' Paddy never does anything, except for his own ends. Well, I'll have to wear the necklace for today, but first thing tomorrow . . . no, the next day, we'll still be here tomorrow . . . I'll hand it to the first beggar I see.

The rest of the day passed very pleasantly. Amy and Minnie made an excuse in the afternoon to go out, and because Amy was well aware that no shops would be open for miles around she took Minnie round to Ruthie's house. Her friend was delighted to see them and asked them in, but went into a fit of the giggles when Amy explained her errand. 'Paddy Keagan gave you that beautiful necklace?' she gasped. 'And you come round here so as I can hand back the bag of bull's-eyes you give me for me little brothers and sisters? You've gorra be mad, chuck, they were ate afore breakfast. Still an' all, you're welcome to a box of chocolates what were give me – there's only two been took out.'

Despite herself, Amy giggled. 'No, but there must be *something* I can give him,' she said desperately, glancing around the room as though she expected a row of gift-wrapped parcels on every surface. 'Did anyone give your dad pipe tobacco? Or . . . or thick woollen socks?'

Ruthie's dad, a large, red-faced man with a shock of grey hair, was sitting by the fire, toasting a round of bread, but he turned at Amy's words, grinning broadly. 'Why not give him a lock of your 'air, chuck?' he said. 'Or what about a pair of your frilly drawers? Reckon he'd value them!'

'Don't be so vulgar, our dad,' Ruthie said reprovingly, though she was still smiling. 'Don't you think it looks kind o' worse to give him a last-minute gift, like? He's bound to guess you didn't buy him nothin' – and why should you? He's never given you anything but hard words, as I recall.'

This downright partisanship made Amy feel a good deal better, though she voiced her earlier thought to the assembled company that, once back in Liverpool, she would give the bleedin' necklace to the first beggar she saw.

She also agreed with both girls – for Minnie had backed Ruthie up – that perhaps it was best to accept Paddy's gift gracefully for the time being and not try to return it. 'But I'll knit him a perishin' muffler, so's he can wrap it round his perishin' gob or tie it round his perishin' throttle,' she said crossly as she and Minnie made their way back to the house in Seafield Grove. 'If it's around his gob, p'raps he won't speak to me, and if he ties it tight enough . . .'

'You are a horrible person, Amy Logan,' Minnie said, but she was smiling. 'Can't you see the feller likes you?'

Amy snorted. 'Like fun he does!' she said scornfully. 'He just wanted to show me up and he certainly did that.'

During the walk home, however, Minnie made

her point a little more forcibly. 'You want to use your eyes, queen,' she said earnestly. 'You should have seen the look on Paddy's face while you were unwrapping his present. He looked like little kids look on Christmas Day – all lit-up and excited, as though they expect something wonderful to happen. He bought that necklace to please you – it must have cost him a deal of money – and instead of throwing your arms round his neck and givin' him a big kiss, you looked like someone who's bit into a cream bun and found the cream's gone sour on you.'

'I didn't,' Amy said, half laughing, half horrified. 'I thought I'd put on a jolly good act . . . but Minnie, he's never liked me I tell you. I can't understand why he bought the necklace in the first place, unless he meant it for some other girl who's been and gone and let him down.'

'Amy Logan, you're an ungrateful girl and don't deserve to have any beaux at all,' Minnie said roundly. 'Why do you think he bought jade, eh? It's 'cos you've got green eyes, that's why! Now how many girls around here do you know with green eyes?'

'I don't know any, but Paddy may know a dozen for all I know,' Amy pointed out. 'Oh, do leave off, Minnie, because even if Paddy can change his feelings overnight, I don't know that I can. Now, let's talk about something else if you please.'

But though Minnie's efforts at matchmaking appeared to be unsuccessful, they had made Amy think and by the time they reached Seafield Grove she was beginning to admit to herself that she could have been wrong. Paddy could have bought the necklace especially for her and it could be the first sign of a thaw in their previously frosty relationship.

Feeling strangely light-hearted at the thought, Amy ushered her friend into the warmth and brightness of the kitchen, and began to help Suzie to prepare the meal.

When they had finished tea and washed up, the furniture was pushed back and the kitchen table was carried into the scullery to give more room. The house had been converted, at Bill's request, by their landlord many years earlier. They had knocked down a wall, losing the parlour but gaining a double-sized kitchen, which the family much preferred. Albert had gone up to Ruth's to spend the evening with the Durrants but neighbours from the surrounding houses came in and a great many games were played in the Logans' large kitchen. Blind Man's Buff, charades, and Oranges and Lemons all proved great favourites, and when they were exhausted and seated themselves around the room on chairs, cushions and even upturned fishboxes, Paddy produced his mouth organ and played carols and popular songs – 'I'm Twenty-one Today' and various other hits. When he struck up 'Has Anybody Here Seen Kelly', Minnie jumped to her feet, grabbed Amy's hands and, whirling into the centre of the room, began a spirited polka. They were speedily followed on to the floor by other couples; Bill leading Becky round with great verve, while Gus danced with Suzie. In fact, they might have danced all night, had it not been for Paddy running out of breath and insisting that someone else should take over. Gus, who was quite good on the penny whistle, started to try to play the mouth organ, but threw it back to Paddy complaining that it was full of spit, which made everyone laugh.

Jim Price, from next door but one, nipped home

for a moment and came back, carrying a fiddle. He began to play *'Shine on Harvest Moon'* and Lottie melted into Charlie's arms and immediately began to dance, speedily followed by most of the younger members of the assembled company. Amy was about to suggest that she and Minnie should take to the floor when Gus unceremoniously seized both Minnie's hands and pulled her into the dance. Minnie was a tall girl, of Junoesque build, and now it occurred to Amy what a nice couple she and Gus made, with Gus's fair hair only overtopping Minnie's gleaming dark locks by a couple of inches.

She was still standing on the sidelines, laughing and clapping in time to the music, when someone caught her hands. 'Dance?' Paddy asked gruffly.

For a moment Amy felt all the old familiar irritation rising up in her; then she remembered the necklace. Damn, damn, damn, she thought furiously, allowing him to lead her on to the floor. I can't very well refuse to dance with him, having accepted his present. Oh, why did it have to happen? Why didn't I buy him something really small and mean, then I wouldn't have to feel beholden?

Jim Price was revealing a rare talent with the fiddle, playing the beautiful music so softly and seductively that Amy, who had intended to dance as stiffly as any poker, found herself relaxing into Paddy's embrace, following his lead as though they had danced with one another all their lives and almost – only almost – she found she was enjoying herself. When Jim Price slid into another tune, which she recognised, though could not immediately put a name to, she made no effort to free herself from Paddy's arms but continued to dance. Paddy held her lightly but firmly, his head a little bent, and though she kept her eyes averted from his she knew that he was looking at her face. Presently, almost absent-mindedly, he began to sing along to the music, in a soft, but rather pleasant tenor voice. '*I wonder who's kissing her now?*' he sang, '*I wonder who's teaching her how? I wonder who's looking into her eyes, sighing sighs, telling lies? I wonder if she has a boy? That girl who once filled me with joy. I wonder if she ever tells him of me? I wonder who's kissing her now.*'

As the tune ended, Amy tried to pull herself away from Paddy, suddenly aware of a rush of the strangest feelings; sensations so strange that they made her want to stay where she was within the circle of his arm. It's just the music, she told herself wildly, and the fact that he's a feller and dances better than anyone else I know. I still hate him, I do, I do! Only it's Christmas and the necklace is beautiful, and he's got a lovely singing voice and ... and ...

Jimmy Price was beginning to play again; this time Amy recognised it at once as '*Alexander's Ragtime Band*'. Paddy tried to continue holding her, one arm firmly round her waist, his left hand grasping Amy's right, but she pulled away, saying half jokingly, 'I mustn't be selfish, Paddy; give someone else a chance – why not have a whirl with Jimmy's sister Hettie for a change?'

Paddy said nothing, but he released Amy, who scuttled across the floor and into the scullery, where Suzie was setting out cups and plates, and putting round mince pies and slices of cold pudding. 'Let me give you a hand,' Amy said rather breathlessly, going over to the draining board where a number of cups stood ready for filling. She pressed her hands to her hot face, pushing damp locks of hair off her brow. 'Gracious, it's warm in here! We ought to open the back door, let some air in.'

'Oh, folk will be goin' home soon,' Suzie said easily. She hefted an enormous tin teapot, which one of the guests had lent them, and began to pour tea into the waiting cups. 'Your pal Minnie is gerrin' on awful well with our Gus. It's about time that young feller found hisself another girl, though he's been shy of trying his hand ever since that horrible Peggy Higgins behaved so badly last summer.' She turned to refill the teapot and gave Amy a shrewd glance. 'Saw you dancin' with our Paddy just now,' she observed, her eyes flicking all over Amy's flushed face. 'Enjoy it, didja? He's a good dancer, is our Paddy, got natural rhythm like his mam. You made a fine couple, danced as if you'd knowed each other all your lives.' She guffawed, clapping a hand to her mouth. 'Wharra fool I am – you *have* known each other all your lives, of course. You could ha' been brother and sister – you certainly fought like cat and dog when you was younger.' Eyes suddenly sly, she glanced across at Amy under her lashes. 'There weren't never no love lost atwixt the pair of you, so it seems strange to see you dancin' together.'

Amy, putting the filled cups and saucers on to a battered tin tray, ignored the remark. Indeed, her own feelings were far too complex and confused for her to want to discuss Paddy with anyone, let alone his mother. And presently, when the guests had eaten their cold supper and were beginning to depart, Amy picked Becky up from the chair in which she was slumbering and set off for the stairs, observing to Minnie that it was high time they were all in bed.

She had only reached the second stair, however,

when Paddy caught her arm. 'Aren't you going to say goodnight to your dancin' partner?' he said, his voice teasing but his eyes serious. 'I can't offer to walk you home like I would after an ordinary dance, but I'll carry Becky for you if you like.'

'It's all right, thanks,' Amy said rather breathlessly. She told herself it was the weight of the child which was affecting her breathing, but had a shrewd suspicion that Paddy's nearness and the hand on her wrist also had something to do with it. 'If you take her she'll wake and start grizzling, but thanks all the same, Paddy.'

Paddy grinned at her and rumpled her curls with one large hand, then slid the hand down under her chin, tilting her face up to his. Amy's heart began to pound as his face got nearer, but then a voice spoke from behind them. 'Gerrup them stairs, you daft girl, 'cos if I doesn't get to bed soon I'll sleep the clock round. If you're goin' up, Paddy, then pass the girl. Carting that great Becky, she'll be slow as a snail and I want me bed.'

It was Albert, grinning all over his face and beginning to push his way past Paddy. Not knowing whether to be glad or sorry Amy, with her heavy burden, hurried up the stairs and joined Minnie in their room. *Had* Paddy been going to kiss her? It was probably as well that Albert had come upon them before she had been forced to snub Paddy yet again. Whether or not she would actually have done so she did not honestly know, but was glad – or told herself she was glad – not to have been put to the test.

She began to get Becky ready for bed as Minnie said, sighing blissfully, 'It's been a grand day. I do like your brother Gus, Amy, he were ever so kind to me, got me supper, danced wi' me ... he even suggested we might take a walk in the moonlight on the beach aways, only when I peeked out through the door it were rainin'. Still, there's always tomorrow.'

Amy was pleased, she told herself, that Minnie was so taken up with Gus she did not so much as mention Paddy, nor the fact that he and Amy had danced together. Yet a part of her very much wanted to discuss what had happened that evening so that she could convince herself that the strong physical attraction she had felt for Paddy while they danced was a feeling she would have felt for any man in similar circumstances. The scene at the bottom of the stairs, she told herself, was probably not romantic at all; Paddy had merely offered to carry the child, after all, and whether he had meant to kiss her or not was something she would never know.

Since there was no apparent interest in her problem from Minnie, however, she had to content herself with thinking it over in her own mind and, since she was worn out, such thoughts speedily gave way to dreams.

Chapter Ten

Boxing Day dawned bright but cold, though few in the Logan household saw the dawn; they had played, sung and danced into the early hours and consequently slept late. Becky, Minnie and Amy did not so much as stir until they were awoken by Bill banging on their bedroom door. 'Gerrup you lazy lot,' he shouted cheerfully. 'I've been down and pulled the kettle over the flame and your mam's makin' porridge for everyone, so you'd best gerra move on.'

Amy groaned and sat up, stretched and yawned, then glanced towards the window. The curtains were thin cotton and had not been properly pulled across the night before, and through the gap she could see frost flowers obscuring the bottom half of the window, though the sun had melted the top half, showing the frosted rooftops of the houses opposite. A seagull perched on the roof must have seen the movement, for it cocked its head and looked hopefully across as though it expected the window to open and a shower of bread to come forth. Beside Amy, Becky gave a mutter of protest and tried to cuddle further down under the covers, but Amy, now properly awake, would have none of it. 'Wake up, our kid,' she said in a tone of resolute cheerfulness. 'Christmas Day is over, but we're on holiday still and it's a lovely day; the sun's shining fit to crack the paving stones, so what say we go for an early swim?'

Becky, still burrowing back into bed, gave a stifled giggle but Minnie, who had appeared to be sound asleep, groaned loudly. 'Even the thought of getting out of this warm bed makes me shudder,' she said plaintively. 'As for goin' outside ... Oh, I suppose you're right an' we'd best gerrup before the perishin' boys eat all your mam's porridge.'

'What about that swim, then?' Amy said mischievously, throwing back the cover. 'Some folk do swim at Christmas, I read about it in the newspaper once. Only I reckon it were down south somewhere, where they're all mad anyroad.'

She jumped out of bed as she spoke and began to pour water into the round tin bowl on the washstand – or rather she would have poured it had the water in the ewer not been ice for the top half-inch. Seizing her hairbrush, she bashed at the ice, then took pity on the shivering mortals in the bed behind her. Becky, whimpering a protest, had just begun to remark that she would not wash at all in water so cold when Amy remembered that Bill had said he had pulled the kettle over the flame. 'All right, all right, you delicate creatures,' she said, throwing her old shawl round her shoulders and going out on to the upper landing. 'I'll fetch up a jug of hot water from Dad's tea kettle and then we can wash in comfort, providing you're quick, of course, and get washing before it freezes up again.'

When she returned to the bedroom Minnie and Becky leapt, shivering, from their warm nest and a good deal of horseplay ensued as all three of them tried to wash simultaneously before the water grew cold. Amy dressed as rapidly as she could, then turned to help Becky, who was tugging on a disreputable jersey with unseemly haste; clearly Becky had had a 'cat's lick and a promise' instead of a proper wash. Minnie, meanwhile, was selecting a clean blue blouse to wear with her navy-blue serge skirt. The matching jacket was not new but she had trimmed the neck and sleeves with some fur remnants which she had got cheap in the pre-Christmas sale and Amy thought that, with her dark hair tied up with a length of blue ribbon and her cheeks flushed from the chill, Minnie looked really pretty. Checking her own reflection critically in the mirror on the washstand, Amy felt that she, too, looked presentable enough in a cinnamon-brown dress with chocolate-coloured trimmings and Becky, even in her play clothes, always looked sweet. Amy, brushing out the child's hair which had been confined in half a dozen small pigtails in the night, told her little sister that her hair rippled like corn in the sun and Becky, smiling self-consciously, danced ahead of the older girls down the stairs, calling out to her mother that they were on their way and were desperate anxious for porridge.

Despite Bill's waking shouts, the girls had finished their breakfast and were discussing what they should do for the rest of the morning before Gus put in an appearance. He plonked himself down at the table, yawning hugely and, accepting a large bowl of porridge and a mug of tea, told the world at large that Albert and Paddy would be down presently. 'Albert's goin' to Ruthie's for his dinner,' he told them rather thickly, spooning porridge into his mouth. 'But Charlie and Lottie will be here soon.'

Charlie and Lottie were staying with the Carpenters who, having no children of their own at home, had willingly agreed to put the young people up for a couple of nights.

'Let's go round to the Durrants' and see what they had for Christmas,' Becky said eagerly, bouncing up and down on her chair. 'Etty's me best pal and she were hopin' for a proper skippin' rope, the sort with red wooden handles.' She glanced across at her mother, cleaning vegetables over the sink. 'I wish *I* had a skipping rope with red wooden handles,' she ended wistfully.

'You've got most things, you spoilt little madam,' Amy remarked, just as Paddy and Albert came clattering down the stairs. Albert's hair stuck up like a hedgehog's, but he was wearing a clean white shirt and a blue tie – courting clothes, Amy thought, with an inward grin. It still seemed odd to her that her brother should be taking an interest in girls at last, particularly Ruthie, whom he had known all his life. Paddy, blessed with a mop of curls, had clearly managed to find time to drag a brush through them, though he was wearing a grey working shirt and navy trousers. *Not* courting clothes, Amy thought rather ruefully, and scolded herself for the thought. Since Paddy wasn't courting anyone, why on earth should he wear his best?

In the end, by mutual consent, the young people helped Suzie in the house all the morning. Dinner was cold goose, mashed potatoes and swede from Bill's allotment, followed by mince pies and custard. Albert, of course, did not share in this feast, since he had gone round to the Durrants' house, but the rest of them were all hungry, despite the excesses of Christmas Day, and the meal disappeared in record time. Amy, seated opposite Paddy, caught him taking covert glances at her several times and realised rather guiltily that she was not wearing his necklace. She had dressed in such a hurry that she had not thought to put it on, but determined to do so as soon as she could. It would seem ungracious not to wear it, although the cinnamon dress had a high, round neck and it wouldn't have been visible anyway.

When the meal was over and the washing-up and clearing away done Gus suggested, with a sideways glance at Minnie, that a walk along the shore would help to settle their dinners. 'It'll make room for our teas, what's more,' he said. 'Suzie's making pancake batter and if there's one thing I love it's pancakes.'

Although Bill and Suzie elected to stay by the fire and to prepare the tea for the rest of the family, everyone else decided a walk would be a good idea. Amy and Minnie ran upstairs to fetch coats and stout shoes, and Amy glanced quickly around her, looking for the necklace. She knew very well that she had left it on the washstand the previous night, but now there was no sign of it. Oh, well, it'll turn up, she told herself, putting on her thick coat and tying a scarf round her head. No one with a grain of sense would wear a hat on Seaforth Sands – unless they wanted to see it flying off to New Brighton of its own accord, that was, and presently she and Minnie went downstairs and joined the others.

Despite the cold and the strong wind, it was pleasant enough on the beach, although it very soon became apparent that poor Becky was not enjoying herself in the least. Among the dunes they were partially sheltered, but as soon as they came out upon the open shore the wind whipped loose sand at their legs with devastating force. The older ones, in long skirts or trousers, were able to bear this with equanimity but Becky, whose thin stockings were little protection and whose skirt was too short to offer any help at all, begged to be allowed to return home. 'I could go round to Etty's,' she shrieked against the wind, clutching Amy's hand and pressing close to her sister. 'Etty's mam is always glad to see me and we could have a go with her skipping rope in the backyard. Maybe they'll ask me to tea – they often do.'

'All right, darling, you'll probably be a deal better off with Etty than having your legs sandpapered by this perishin' wind,' Amy said cheerfully. 'I'll walk you round there, just make sure that everyone's in and they've not got a family party going.' She shrieked an explanation to the rest of the party, then turned back towards the town, Becky clinging grimly to her hand. They had only gone a few yards, however, before a figure, coat collar turned up and trousers tucked into boots, joined them, taking hold of Becky's other hand. It was Paddy.

'Oh, Paddy, there's no need for you to lose your walk,' Amy said as they gained the shelter of the dunes. 'I can take care of Becky; if there's no one at Etty's house we'll go on to the Durrants' and if there's no one there either we'll go back to Seafield Grove. By then the others will have turned back so all I'll have to do is walk to meet them.'

'Good try,' Paddy said, grinning. 'I suppose it doesn't occur to you that I don't fancy playin' gooseberry? Anyway, once we've dropped Becky off we can both catch up with the others if we've a mind.'

By the time they returned to Seafield Grove it was

growing dusk and Amy, to her own secret astonishment, had allowed Paddy to put his arm round her as they walked back along the shore. For the first time in her whole life, she realised, she and Paddy had talked seriously about their lives without either one sniping at the other. She had learned that Paddy's ambition extended beyond the fishing boat, that he was tempted to try his luck aboard a trawler or even to start out as a seaman on one of the transatlantic lines, which plied almost daily from the Liverpool docks.

'I've never told anyone this before, but I guess I ought to see the world before I settle down, get married and that,' he had told her. 'Liverpool's a grand city, so it is, but do you realise, Amy, I'm Irish yet I've never seen Dublin, let alone the rest of the country. As for the truly foreign parts, what chance has a chap of seeing the world from a shrimping boat? Oh aye, it'd be grand to see a bit of life before I settle down. I don't know about girls, but most fellers feel like I do.' He turned Amy so that he could look into her face. 'How about you, queen? Don't tell me you want to share a room with your pals and work in a hotel for the rest of your life?'

'I mean to marry one day and settle down and have kids, I suppose,' Amy said, having given the matter some thought. 'But I love my job and sharing is great fun – when you do it with good friends, that is. As for seeing the world, I doubt I'll ever do that – I'd like to see a bit more of England, though. And Wales, come to think of it. Oh, and I'd like to go to Ireland one of these days. You can catch a ferry from the Landing Stage.'

'What do you say to us going together?' Paddy suggested. 'It'd be much more fun wi' the two of us.

There's all sorts in Dublin, shops, museums and a huge park. We could go in the summer if you'd like it.'

Amy felt that this was going too far and too fast, and made some non-committal reply, and presently Paddy changed the subject, telling her that catches aboard the shrimping boat had been pretty good, considering the time of year. He was saving up, since as a single man he had few responsibilities and could afford to put money away each week. 'I wouldn't leave your brothers and your dad in the lurch,' he assured her. 'But quite honestly, queen, provided they could get themselves a lad, Gus and Albert could manage the boat and the nets easy. So one of these days . . .'

He had not finished the sentence but it did not need a mind reader, Amy thought, to realise that despite what she had believed, Paddy was as ambitious as she, perhaps more so. And as they made their way to Seafield Grove through the deepening dusk, she realised with a little pang that if he did go she would miss him.

The last evening of the holiday was spent by the entire family, with the addition of Ruthie Durrant and two of her small sisters – and Minnie of course – in playing quiet games around the fire. The children had played Musical Chairs, with Paddy on the mouth organ, but this, being far from a quiet game, was soon rejected in favour of 'Chinese Whispers', which caused great hilarity, especially among the younger members of the party whose interpretation of the ordinary whispered sentences had everyone in stitches.

Encouraged by this, other parlour games were

embarked on. They played 'The Moon Is Round . . .', and, 'I Went to Market . . .'. The boys wanted to play 'Postman's Knock', but at this point Suzie, Amy and Minnie disappeared into the scullery to serve the supper, which they had made earlier, so the game was abandoned whilst they ate scones and short-bread and drank tea or beer.

When supper had been cleared away Ruthie, looking at the flushed faces of her little sisters, suggested that perhaps she ought to be taking them home, but Albert said hastily that they would play a quiet game first to calm the kids down a bit. A discussion ensued, at the end of which Bill went to the kitchen dresser and, opening one of the long drawers, produced some sheets of lined paper and several stubs of pencil. He explained the game of 'Consequences' to the younger members of the group, handed each person present a piece of paper and a pencil, and the game began. Although this was a quiet game it produced almost as much hilarity as 'Chinese Whispers' had done. When the papers were collected up and first one person and then another read the results on the page he held there was a good deal of laughter.

At this point, Ruthie rose to her feet, saying firmly that no matter how they tempted her she must go home now, for by the time she had put her little sisters to bed she would be almost asleep on her feet. 'And tomorrow I'm back in the dining rooms, probably rushed off me feet from early morning till late evening,' she said. 'I'm fond of me job and don't want to lose it, so I've gorra be on the early tram 'cos it's not just a couple of stops to work like it is from Huskisson Street. It's a fair old trek from the Rimrose Bridge to the city centre.'

'You aren't the only one who'll be catching that tram,' Amy said ruefully, also getting to her feet. 'Minnie and me will be up at the crack of dawn as well.' She turned to Suzie. 'But thanks for a lovely day, Suzie – two lovely days – it's been the best Christmas I've had for years. You worked really hard and I'm sure we've all had a grand time.'

'It's been the best Christmas I've had since me mam died,' Minnie said shyly, smiling at Suzie and Bill. 'You've made me feel one of the family. I'll never forget your kindness. When Ella and Ruthie said they were going away for Christmas me heart sank, but then Amy said I could come home with her and I'm sure the Queen of England couldn't have had a better time.'

The party having broken up, Albert walked Ruthie and the girls home, Charlie and his Lottie went back to the Carpenters' house, and Gus and Paddy began to bring the furniture back into the kitchen, to set out the rugs and to fetch the fuel and water for the next day, while the girls tackled the washing up and clearing away. When this was done they all trooped off upstairs to bed, for the girls were not the only ones who would have to work in the morning. The boys would take the boat out to search for what fish there was and Bill would catch a tram to St John's Market where he would clean down the stall, buy in fresh ice and prepare to gut and clean whatever fish the boys caught.

Outside the door of the girls' room Paddy put a restraining hand on Amy's arm. 'It were nice of you to thank me mam for all her hard work,' he said quietly. 'I know she didn't say much, but she were really pleased. It were kind, Amy.'

'It was no more than the truth,' Amy said equally

quietly. 'Your mam's been rare good to my dad and to young Becky, and now that I'm older she seems to like me a bit better too; we get on pretty well, your mam and me.'

Paddy opened his mouth to say something more, but at that moment Bill came clumping up the stairs behind them and Paddy touched Amy's chin lightly with his forefinger, grinned and disappeared into the boys' room, while Amy joined Minnie and Becky, and the three of them began to get ready for bed.

'Amy, I were talkin' to Etty today when we were skippin' in the backyard, and *she* said she'd been talking to Annie Durrant, Ruthie's sister, and *she* said . . .'

'Not now, chuck,' Amy said sleepily, burrowing her head into the softness of her pillow. 'Me and Minnie's got an early start tomorrow and I'm almost asleep on my feet. Tell me in the morning.'

'You aren't on your feet, so how can you be asleep on them?' Becky said plaintively. 'You're lying flat on your back in a nice soft bed and it won't take a minute to tell you what Etty said Annie said . . .'

A tiny curling snore issuing from her sister's mouth, however, convinced Becky that further conversation would be a very one-sided affair. Sighing, for there are few more annoying things than being the possessor of information which one cannot pass on, Becky settled down and was soon asleep herself.

Next morning, despite the best of intentions, everyone overslept. Amy, indeed, was the first to wake and realised with dismay that the bright light of morning was showing through the curtains. She gave a yelp, shook Minnie hard and jumped out of bed tearing her nightgown over her head and

beginning to hurl her clothes on, not daring to stop
for a wash in water which she knew would be ice-
cold, if not actually iced. Minnie, waking, echoed
Amy's yelp and jumped out of bed too, beginning to
dress with equal haste, while Becky curled protec-
tively beneath the blankets, an arm flung up to
shield her eyes from the intrusive light.

Fortunately the girls had packed their few belongings the night before, so now all they had to do was
to seize their bags and rush downstairs. A glance at
the kitchen clock confirmed Amy's worst fears. They
would have to run all the way to the Rimrose Bridge
and even then they might not succeed in catching a
tram.

'I've not had to run like this since I were a kid,'
Minnie gasped, as they raced up Crosby Road. She
reached into her pocket and produced a comb which
she dragged through her tangled locks. 'I feel a real
scarecrow and I 'spect I look like one too. Still, I
don't suppose we will have many customers in first
thing. Rich people lie in later than us on ordinary
days, so at Christmas I reckon they won't get
moving until around eleven o'clock. Oh, glory be to
God, the tram's there, oh, wave Amy, shout at him
to wait.'

Both girls shouted and waved and the tram, which
was half empty but had begun to move, slowed and
stopped, only starting up again when they were safe
on board. The girls thanked the conductor breathlessly and collapsed on to one of the slatted wooden
seats. 'Phew! But at least we shan't be late,' Amy
said, as the vehicle gathered speed. 'Oh, my God, I
meant to have another look for my necklace! I know
it can't possibly be lost but I wouldn't be at all
surprised if I had it on in bed, and it came off and

got mixed up with the blankets. Damn, damn, damn! And I won't be going home again till the New Year, because having had time off over Christmas they're going to keep me hard at it so's other people can have a break. Oh, look, there's Ruthie sitting up the front. Shall we go and join her?'

Ruthie, who had turned at their approach, tutted at their dishevelled appearance and moved up to make room for them. 'Lucky old Ella, off work for another four whole days,' she remarked, as the tram jolted onwards. 'She'll have a lot to tell us when she gets back from Manchester. I bet she's had a grand time!'

Half an hour after the girls had left, Paddy came lurching down the stairs, still rubbing the sleep from his eyes. He looked around the kitchen, ran a hand through his dark curls and addressed his mother, who was desultorily pushing back chairs and tidying away the remnants of the party. She had already removed the paper chains and a good deal of tinsel and holly, and was throwing the berried branches on the fire where they crackled and spat, causing her to jerk back hastily from the sudden heat.

'Who'd ha' thought folk could make such a mess,' she grumbled, as her son entered the room. 'That there Consequences game – well, the consequence is a deal of paper and mess, if you ask me.' She giggled at her own joke, then swept a hand along the broad mantelpiece, sending a mass of papers, apple cores, sandwich crusts and other such detritus to falling into the hearth. 'Wharra you going to have for your breakfast, chuck? I could boil you a couple of eggs, or there's kippers, if you can face fish,' she added.

She turned towards Paddy as she spoke, her eyebrows rising. Paddy, taking his place at the table, said, 'No, I'll just have bread and jam. I ate enough yesterday to keep me goin' for a week,' and added, rather plaintively, 'Where's the girls, then? Don't say they're still in bed!'

Suzie, pouring tea from the big, brown pot into an enamel mug, shook her head. 'No, it ain't them what overslept this morning, it's you fellers,' she informed him, shuffling back across the room with the mug of tea in her hand. 'Bill's gone an' all, though he weren't so quick off the mark as the girls, but he reckons there won't be many customers early today – and he'll only have potted shrimps and salted fish and a few kippers to sell until you fellers bring your catch in.'

'Oh. Right,' Paddy said, scooping jam out of the jar with a knife and spreading it on his bread and marge. He thought, rather aggrievedly, that Bill might have woken them when he got up and wondered why the girls had not at least banged on the boys' bedroom door. It would have been nice, come to that, if Amy had seen fit to shout out cheerio at the head of the stairs, but she had clearly done no such thing. His heart, which had been high and full of hope, sank a little at this thought. Amy had been so friendly yesterday, they had laughed and joked and told each other things which, he imagined, neither of them normally ever gave voice to, yet she had not seen fit to shout a goodbye before she went off to work.

Suzie, sitting down opposite him at the table, gave him a shrewd look. 'Lost a quid and found a penny?' she enquired amiably. 'You look sour as a lemon. What's up?'

'No one called us,' Paddy mumbled. 'I'd ha' thought young Amy might have given the door a knock or even called out. Why, she never even said cheerio.'

'I doubt they had the time,' Suzie said judicially. 'I weren't up meself, but I heard 'em clattering down the stairs an' out the door, without stopping for so much as a bite of bread or a drink.'

'Oh,' Paddy said. 'So that's the way of it, was it? Well, I hope they caught their tram or all the rushing in the world wouldn't get them to work on time. I wonder whether Amy will come back home for New Year? I dare say she will. When we deliver the fish to the market I reckon I just might pop into the Adelphi, ask her what her plans are.'

Suzie looked thoughtfully across at her son and Paddy felt the heat rush to his cheeks, and hastily crammed more bread and marge into his mouth. Suzie was smiling now, looking quizzically at him and he wondered uneasily whether he had given himself away by suggesting a visit to the Adelphi.

'If I remember rightly, it were you who used to twit Amy over the smell of fish,' Suzie said thoughtfully. 'I don't know as a visit to that posh hotel in your fisherman's gear wi' scales all over you is likely to impress them as works there. If I were you I'd go round to Huskisson Street of an evening – you might take Gus an' all, once you've changed your shirt and kecks for something more ... more suitable.'

'Less fishy, you mean,' Paddy said, grinning. 'I might take your advice an' all, Mam, because I do recall I used to rag young Amy now and then.'

'Well, you must do as you think fit,' Suzie said. She got to her feet. 'That young Becky don't do a hand's turn in this house if she can help it. She'll grow up a lazy little slut if I don't make her mind me more. Make up the fire before you go out, Paddy, while I go up and tear the bedclothes off of Becky. Do you think I ought to give Gus and Albert a knock? Only your dad wants fresh fish before the market closes, you know.'

'Yes, give 'em a shout,' Paddy agreed. His mother hastened up the stairs and Paddy guessed that she would help Becky to wash and dress, and would probably not be down again for some time. Becky was spoilt, he knew that, but thought it a good thing rather than a bad. He could still remember all too clearly how hard his mam had been on Amy and how it had affected her. He was glad that Becky at any rate would not grow up with the sort of chip on her shoulder Amy had had.

Paddy finished his bread, drained his mug and got up. He went over to the fire and began to riddle the ash. The coal bucket stood in the grate and he was about to select some lumps of coal, when his eye was caught by a crumpled ball of paper, lying between the coal bucket and the grate. It looked as though someone had aimed the ball of paper at either fire or coal bucket, but had missed. Paddy bent and picked it up, and was about to toss it into the fire when he realised that the paper bore his own name. Startled, he looked more closely, remembering the game of Consequences the previous evening. He did not immediately recall whether he himself had written his name on one of the sheets, or whether it had been added as an answer to one of the questions by somebody else, but he began to unwrap the paper, smiling to himself at the thought of the previous evening's fun.

As he unwrapped, something slithered out of the

paper and fell with a tiny *plink* on to the hearth stones. He glanced down at it and for a moment could only stare; it was a delicate gold necklace, interspersed with droplets of milky green jade.

For what seemed like ages Paddy could literally not have moved a muscle. His brain felt at first cold and sluggish and then pain and rage rushed over him. He clenched his hand round the necklace and drew back his fist to hurl it into the fire. How Amy must hate him. To write his name on a bit of paper, wrap it round his gift and simply chuck it down where he might never have found it seemed somehow to be the height of cruelty. But he would not throw the necklace into the fire; he thought confusedly that it had been bought and presented with love, and did not deserve such a fate. He would keep it and one day he would give it to someone special, someone who deserved it and could appreciate its fragile beauty.

He thrust the necklace into his trouser pocket and went across the kitchen rather blindly, dragging his duffle coat and muffler off the peg on the back of the door, and shoving his feet into his seamen's boots. He could hear Gus and Albert wrangling as they came out of their room and knew, suddenly, that he could not face them now. To his horror, as he shot out of the kitchen and into the cold of the December morning, he realised that there were tears in his eyes. Without pausing to wonder what he was about to do he turned up Crosby Road towards the tram terminus. He could not, would not, face Amy's brothers right now.

Pulling up the hood of his duffle-coat and pushing both hands deep into his pockets, he headed away from Seaforth towards the city and the docks.

Becky came down just after the boys did and wailed plaintively when she saw the empty bread and margarine plate, and realised that her mother had either used all the porridge or not made any that morning. 'Why didn't you wake me, fellers?' she whined, taking her place at the table. 'Oh, you are mean – as mean as Amy and Minnie. They woke me up and made me all cold when they gorrout of bed, but they never thought to tell me I were goin' to miss me breakfast.'

Gus leaned across the table and ruffled her silky blonde hair and Suzie, crossing the kitchen behind her daughter, began to cut more slices off the loaf. 'Don't worry, chuck, there's plenty for everyone,' she said breezily. 'The girls didn't have any breakfast at all, you know. They were so late they simply ran straight out the door and off to the tram stop.'

'Oh!' Becky said, clapping a hand to her mouth. 'I meant to see Amy before she went off but I dare say . . .' She jumped off her seat and went over to the mantel, peering up as if to discover what time it was. Then, with a sigh of satisfaction, she returned to her place at the table. 'It's awright,' she said rather obscurely. 'Can I have a cup of milk now, Mam?'

On 29 December Ella returned to Huskisson Street – but she was a different Ella from the one who had gone off to Manchester scarcely knowing how she would manage to spend the whole week in the company of Philip's grand family. She bounced into the room at eight o'clock that evening, to find her three friends making Welsh Rarebit and discussing what they should do for the New Year.

Ella came across the room in a series of twirls, threw her Gladstone bag on to her chair and advanced towards her friends, a hand dramatically held out to display her new possession – a sparkling diamond and sapphire ring encircling the third finger of her left hand. 'Philip and I are engaged,' she said rather needlessly, as the girls clustered round, admiring the ring. 'Oh, girls, it was ever so romantic – he asked me to marry him on Christmas morning after church, when he had taken me for a walk in the Square Gardens. There was snow on the flowerbeds and long icicles hanging from the trees overhead, but the sun was shining and the sky was blue and I was – am – the happiest, luckiest girl in the world.'

'I thought you'd probably come back engaged,' Amy said complacently, giving her friend a hug. 'When will you be getting married, queen? Where will you live, you and Philip? Don't say Manchester! I couldn't bear to lose you – oh, it will be awful at the Adelphi without me best pal.'

Ella laughed, but shook her head at her friend. 'What makes you think I'll move anywhere?' she enquired mischievously. 'Being engaged isn't the same as getting married, you know. Why, people wait two or three years sometimes, before they change their single state.'

'Yes, but you aren't going to,' Minnie observed shrewdly, eyeing her friend's flushed and excited countenance. 'It isn't as if young Philip's short of a bob or two, so there'll be no nonsense about saving up for a nice little house somewhere. I reckon you'll have a June wedding, probably from a very smart church. Can the three of us be bridesmaids?'

'She can't have me as a bridesmaid, because it isn't done to outshine the bride and I would,' Amy said grandly, gently easing the ring off Ella's finger and placing it upon her own. 'Does it suit me, girls? Because I'm thinking of getting married meself ... only I haven't told the lucky fella yet because I haven't met him.'

'Don't believe a word she says, girls,' Minnie advised them. 'Why, she were given the most beautiful gift by one of the fellers! You could see he were keen on her and all over Christmas they were carrying on with ...'

'*I* was?' Amy squeaked, diving at Minnie and clapping a hand across the older girl's mouth. 'Why, my brother Gus took such a fancy to our Min that he's been round here most evenings, pestering the life out of her to go to the theatre or to a dance, or just to go back to Seaforth for supper with him. If that isn't a sign of serious intentions I don't know what is.'

The rest of that evening passed, as Amy had guessed it would, with the girls hearing all about Ella's wonderful Christmas holiday and the other three recounting their own far less glamorous adventures. What Amy did not say – could not say – was how puzzled and upset she had been when Gus had arrived on their doorstep, either alone or accompanied only by Albert. She had been certain that Paddy would come to see her as soon as he was able to do so, but this had not happened. She had not liked to question Gus or Albert too closely about the third member of the fishing boat's crew and they had clearly not felt it incumbent upon them to comment on Paddy's absence. But I'll find out just what is happening when I go home for New Year, Amy told herself. I've never thought of Paddy as shy, but perhaps he is when it comes to girls. Maybe

410

the thought of visiting the four of us, after how things have been in the past, simply scared him off.

But in her heart she did not believe it. Paddy had never been shy, so there must be some other reason for his not visiting her and, when New Year arrived and it was possible for her to catch a tram and go home, she discovered the reason almost as soon as she walked into the house.

The family were eating their supper around the kitchen table. Charlie and his wife had returned to the Midlands long since, but Gus, Albert, Bill, Suzie and Becky were all eating fish and fried potatoes, and greeted her cheerfully as she entered the room.

'Nice to see you, queen,' Bill said breezily. He turned to his wife. 'Is there any fish left, love? You can soon fry a few more spuds, 'cos there were a big bowl of cold 'uns in the fish scullery.'

There was a bustle as Suzie went over to the fire and Amy took off her outdoor things and hung them on the back of the door noticing, almost without realising it, that Paddy's duffle, muffler and seaboots were missing. 'Paddy's late,' she remarked, taking a seat at the table. 'Where's he gone?'

There was moment of embarrassed silence and then Bill said uneasily, 'Well, he's on his way to South America, I think he said. Didn't you know, queen? The day after Boxing Day he come in here and said he'd got a yearning for foreign parts and meant to be off as soon as he could find a lad to take his place on the shrimping boat, which I'm bound to say he did and young Ben is as likely a lad as you'll find in all Seaforth. Still, that's beside the point. Paddy's berthed as an ordinary seaman aboard the SS *Frederica*; he left us a letter tellin' us so. I thought he'd told you. The *Frederica* is one of them coasters what go up and down the Americas for six months at a time, buying and selling, you might say. I reckon he'll see a deal of strange places afore we set eyes on him again.'

On New Year's Day, Amy sat in the office of the big hotel, typing away at her machine, but though she seemed to be concentrating on her work her mind was far from the task in hand. The previous evening, once she had got over the first shock of Paddy's abrupt departure, she had gone up to her room, stripped the bed and searched every inch of it. Suzie had not changed the bedding so there was no fear that the necklace might have got into the washing process and by the look of it, Amy thought disapprovingly, her stepmother had not brushed the linoleum nor shaken out the clothing which hung on hooks behind a piece of flowered curtain. But no matter how diligently she searched, the necklace was not to be found.

Once she was certain it was not in the room, Amy had descended the stairs, meeting Becky who was on her way up to fetch her sister down. 'It's near on time to start the first footing, Amy,' Becky had said excitedly. 'The neighbours are here and Mr Bulstrode has brought a barrel of punch; he says it ain't strong, so we can all have a drink.'

She took Amy's hand and turned to descend the stairs with her, but Amy drew her to a halt. 'Becky, do you remember the necklace Paddy gave me at Christmas? I wore it all Christmas Day but on Boxing Day I forgot. I had breakfast without it and then went upstairs to get it. Only it wasn't on the washstand, where I thought I'd left it. I didn't think of it any more until I was on the tram, heading for

Lime Street, but since I was sure it was somewhere in the house, I didn't worry too much. I thought it might have come off in the bed only I've searched the whole room and there's no sign of it. I suppose you haven't seen it, queen?'

'I saw it on Christmas Day,' Becky said immediately. 'Do you mind that you've lost it, Amy? Only you've always said you didn't like Paddy and Etty told Annie and Annie told me that you were goin' to chuck it away as soon as you got home.'

'Whatever made Etty . . . ?' Amy stopped short, remembering her hasty words to Ruthie on Christmas morning. She felt the heat rush to her cheeks and said defensively, 'Folks say things they don't mean sometimes, Becky. They say them and then they're sorry for them. I . . . I'm afraid it might hurt Paddy's feelings to know that I've lost it – the necklace I mean. Not that he does know – does he?'

'I dunno,' Becky said, tugging Amy down the rest of the flight. 'Hurry up, Amy, Mam's made treacle tart to go with the punch when midnight comes, and Dad's hottin' up the poker and he says I can push it into the punch to make all the steam and sizzle.'

The rest of the evening had passed in a blur for Amy. She could not help wondering whether the loss of the necklace and Paddy's sudden departure were connected in some way. Since she was sure that she had lost it in the bedroom, she did not see how Paddy could possible realise that she no longer had it. However, just in case some other member of the family might have been involved, she waited until all the excitement of welcoming in the New Year was over and then asked Suzie, Bill, Gus and Albert bluntly whether they had seen her necklace.

No one had, but Amy thought that Suzie gave her

a rather strange look and presently, when they were clearing up and the men had gone to bed, Amy asked Suzie why she thought Paddy had suddenly decided to go to sea.

She half expected a snubbing reply, but instead Suzie dried her hands on a tea towel, sat herself down on a kitchen chair and gave the matter her full attention. 'I dunno for sure, queen,' she said slowly. 'In fact, I hoped you'd be able to tell us. Did you quarrel? Because I won't deny it seemed to me that Paddy was sweet on you and had been for a while, only of course you didn't feel the same about him. After he'd give you the necklace he were all lit up, like, happier than he's been – oh, for months, probably ever since Gran died. Then on Boxing Day the pair of you had your heads together, chattering away like magpies and laughing fit to bust, and Bill and I, I don't deny, we thought the old feud betwixt the two of you was over and a bleedin' good job too. We've wondered what could possibly have gone awry after that, because the day you left to go back to Huskisson Street Paddy didn't have a civil word for anyone. He went out without finishing his breakfast, and when he came home he just told us he'd signed on aboard the SS *Frederica* and wouldn't be home again for six months.'

She glanced across at Amy and suddenly Amy realised that it was a look quite without reservation; Suzie was as puzzled as Amy herself over Paddy's defection and was certainly not blaming Amy for one iota of it. Amy found herself warming to the older woman, now that they shared a common anxiety and affection for Paddy. She said musingly, 'I wondered if he thought I didn't value the necklace. I wondered if . . . if someone might have found it

414

and handed it to him, telling him it meant I didn't value him either.'

Suzie gave a little cry and got to her feet. Clasping both Amy's hands in hers, she said roundly, 'There ain't one of us would do such a mean thing, not to you nor to our Paddy. I know I've been against you in the past – I were jealous of you, truth to tell – but I've learned your value now, queen, and I'd be a happy woman if I thought you and our Paddy might make a go of it. He went off very unhappy, there's no doubt of that, but he'll be home again and the two of you can talk it out face to face. He's goin' to write home, he said he would and Paddy's a man of his word, so there's no knowin' – you might get a letter an' all, explaining things.' She gave Amy's hands an encouraging little shake, then leaned forward and kissed her cheek. 'Cheer up, queen!' she said. 'There's worse things happen at sea. Oh, Gawd, that ain't what I meant to say at all – what I meant to say was it'll all come out in the wash. Now you go up to bed, because you've got a full day tomorrow.'

So now, Amy sat at her typewriter, working away automatically and trying to tell herself that she would not worry over Paddy. As soon as they had an address for him she would write to him herself and perhaps then he would write back and she could discover the reason for his flight. Until then she would just have to learn to live without him – something which she had done happily enough for a good many years.

Ella's wedding took place in June, as her friend had prophesied, and Minnie, Ruthie, Laura and Amy were all bridesmaids. Mrs Grimshaw had elegant

gowns made for them in turquoise silk with matching accessories and hats of cream straw, lavishly
decorated with artificial flowers. Ella looked radiant
in a white gown with a long train; her veil held in
place by a coronet of lilies of the valley, and her
bouquet contained the same flowers, as well as the
more traditional white roses and orange blossom.

Amy thoroughly enjoyed the wedding and the
reception, which was held at the Adelphi, so that
Ella's colleagues as well as her friends might enjoy
the party. The only sadness Amy felt was for the loss
of her friend, for Ella was to leave work and become
a full-time housewife in a new house on the Wirral,
which Philip's parents had bought for them as a
wedding present.

Ella had tried at first to say that she wanted to
continue working, but Philip had dealt with this in a
masterly fashion. He had assured her that if time
hung heavy on her hands or she was unhappy, she
might take another job, either in the city of Liverpool
or in one of the villages nearby, but first he
maintained that she should give their home and
marriage a chance.

So now the room in Huskisson Street only had
three occupants and Amy suspected that there
would soon be only two, for Gus and Minnie were
planning a marriage of their own in the autumn, and
even Albert and Ruthie, who still had a deal of
saving up to do, meant to marry when they could
afford it.

Amy had wondered if she and Mary might move
in together, but that was before she had met Haydn.
Having met him, she had been forced to acknowledge that he and Mary were deeply in love and
would be marrying as soon as arrangements could

be made for Haydn either to find work in Mold or to move his family to a house in Liverpool.

Amy, accepting any shifts, no matter how awkward, which the hotel had offered her, sometimes felt so lonely that she could have cried. In the six months that had elapsed since Paddy's flight from Seaforth she had been out with four different young men and had found each of them in turn insignificant and boring when compared with Paddy. A stranger might have thought she had not known Paddy well, but as the months had passed, Amy had realised she had known him very well indeed, but until Christmas had refused to think of him as anything but her enemy. Once the barriers had crumbled, however, she had begun to appreciate him for himself, even to love him, and though he was now far away she could not unlove him.

Letters had come from Paddy whenever he was in port long enough to dispatch an epistle, but none of them had been addressed to Amy and he had given no hint in any of them what had caused his sudden flight. What was more, he had never sent them a forwarding address, saying that his vessel's movements were uncertain so they had best save up all their news for when he returned in the summer.

'Amy, have you finished that report yet? Mr David sent me to fetch it as he needs to read it through before he speaks to Mr Frank.'

Miss Carew's small, bright face, poking round the edge of the door, made Amy jump, but she whipped the paper out of the machine and smiled at her colleague. 'Just finished it,' she said reassuringly, casting a quick glance over the four pages she had typed. 'I haven't had a chance to check it through, though. Can Mr David wait another five minutes while I do that?'

'Oh, I'm sure he can,' Miss Carewe said easily, perching on the corner of Amy's desk. 'Have you heard, Amy? There's been an outbreak of measles – or was it whooping cough? – in Seaforth; ever so many kids have got it. Isn't that where you came from? Oh, I know you lodge in Huskisson Street, but don't your people live in Seaforth?'

'Yes, they do,' Amy said, trying to concentrate on the sheets of paper spread out on her desk. 'Do shut up for a moment, Miss Carewe, or I'll never get this finished.'

'All right, all right, don't snap my nose off,' Miss Carewe said without apparent rancour. 'I just thought you might know a bit more about it, you coming from there. Don't you have a sister still in school? Whooping cough is a nasty thing and measles can be pretty bad, though of course modern medicine does help.'

Amy agreed rather absently, finished reading through her work, pinned the four pages of the report together and handed them to Miss Carewe. Then she picked up her typewriter cover, fitted it over the machine and left the office. Her shift had been over half an hour ago, but she never grudged finishing off a job for Mr David, who was an easygoing, thoughtful employer. As she left the building and crossed Lime Street to catch her tram, she was debating whether to go straight home or whether to pop into Lyons Café for a cup of tea and a bite to eat, which would save her cooking when she got back. She had just decided on Lyons when someone tapped her shoulder, and turning, she saw her father, his face streaked with sweat and his blue

418

eyes anxious. 'Amy! I were just about to go over to the hotel to see if you were there, when I spotted you crossin' the street. Me love, I've come straight from Seafield Grove – your mam's not herself and your sister's really bad. Can you come?'

'Yes, of course. What's the matter with them?' Amy asked, falling into step beside Bill. Once, she thought, she would have corrected the expression 'your mam' pretty sharply, but now she felt that this no longer reflected on Isobel. Suzie had been a good mam to Becky and the boys, and of late had been a good friend to Amy herself, so why not refer to her in future as mam?

But she said nothing of this as the two of them hurried to the nearest tram stop. Bill was explaining that Suzie had suspected Becky of having whooping cough and had put the child to bed, only to wake next morning with a sore throat, a burning head and a voice which sounded so hoarse that he had scarcely understood a word his wife had said. 'I've done me best to see to them both, but it's not easy for a feller,' he explained earnestly as they got on the tram. 'Becky's burning hot and calling for her mam, and poor Suzie keeps struggling out of bed to go to her . . . it all happened so suddenly, Amy. The boys went off to the boat and I meant to make your mam comfortable and then come in to the stall . . . only what with trying to keep Suzie in bed and telling Becky she'd be all right if she'd only keep under the covers . . . and we can't afford to let the fish go bad because there's only young Kenny on the stall to sell it . . .'

'It's all right, Dad,' Amy said soothingly. 'I'll spend the evening with you, make the boys a meal, get the invalids comfortable and then go back to

Huskisson Street. If they are no better by morning then we'll send for the doctor. Why didn't you send for him today, incidentally? One of the girls at work said there was whooping cough or measles, she didn't know which, in Seaforth. Did you notice if Becky had spots? I imagine Suzie probably had measles when she was a kid – perhaps she's got a nasty feverish cold, or influenza or something.'

'In June? Isn't that a winter illness? As for gettin' the doctor, there was no one to send,' Bill said, looking harassed. 'The truth is, Amy, that I've never had to deal with illness before. When your mam was ill there was you and Mary and the nurse always on hand, and the doctor coming in, and when you kids were young your mam saw to you. Last year, when Becky had the chicken pox all I had to do was pop me head round the door when I got home at night, ask her how she was feeling and give her any little treat I had managed to pick up. This ... this is different.'

How different it was Amy was able to judge for herself within moments of entering the house. The fire, which Bill must have been neglecting all day, was dead in the stove and though this scarcely mattered as far as warmth was concerned, for it had been a hot day, it meant that it was not possible for Amy to make the invalids a hot drink until it had been rekindled. What was more, the room was in great disarray, the table covered in dirty crockery and cutlery, the porridge pan on the draining board stiff with dried porridge and the dirty washing, which someone had carried downstairs, piled in an untidy heap before the low stone sink. There was also a stale and unpleasant smell in the room, which caused Amy to fling open both windows and the door before heading for the stairs.

Becky was in the girls' room, alone in the big feather bed. Her face was scarlet and she was breathing with difficulty. She had thrown off her bed covers but was sunk deep into the feather mattress. The bed itself was wet with Becky's sweat, as were her nightgown and her small, burningly hot body. She had appeared to be asleep when Amy had softly opened the door, but as Amy trod across the room towards her she opened large, fever-bright eyes and began to cry. 'Oh, Amy, I feel so ill, I does,' she said in a tiny, hoarse voice. 'Our dad gave me a drink before he left, only I knocked it over and now the bed's all sticky and horrible. I were sick on to the lino and I'd only taken two mouthfuls,' she added pathetically.

'So I see,' Amy said ruefully, gazing down at the sticky patch of vomit on the linoleum. 'Never mind, sweetheart, presently I'll come in and clean you up and change you into a fresh nightgown. I'll do something about that bed as well,' she added, eyeing the sticky, crumpled sheets with revulsion. 'But I must just go along and see how Mam is. She's ill as well as you – did our dad tell you?'

'She isn't as ill as me,' Becky wailed, scrubbing at her tear-filled eyes with small, grimy fists. 'She went downstairs to fetch up my dolly, only she forgot to bring her back. And she said we should have porridge, or a nice rice pudding, only that was *hours* ago and I've not had a thing to eat since yesterday.'

'Mam *is* ill, queen,' Amy said, heading for the door. 'Are you hungry then, Becky? Could you eat some porridge if I made it? Rice pudding takes ages to cook.'

'No, I'm not hungry, I'd be sick if I tried to eat porridge,' Becky whined. 'But I'm ever so thirsty, Amy, ever so ever so thirsty. I could drink a whole big jug of lemonade or even of water, if there weren't nothin' nicer.'

'I'll get you a drink when I've seen Mam,' Amy promised from the doorway. 'I'll be back in five minutes, don't you fret.' She left the child's room, passed the open door of the boys' room, glancing in and seeing with disfavour that it was a tip, the bed unmade and the floor covered with dirty clothing. She reached Suzie's room, tapped briefly on the door and went in. The bed was empty.

For one horrified moment Amy could only stare. Then she remembered Becky's remark about Suzie going downstairs to get the child's doll and a dish of porridge but Suzie, she knew very well, had not been in the kitchen when she passed through. She might, of course, have been in the fish scullery but had this been the case, surely Suzie would have called out or made some sign. Amy turned and was about to leave the room again when it occurred to her to look under the bed. The large chamber pot, wreathed in red roses, was missing. Straightening up with a relieved sigh, Amy realised that Suzie must have taken the pot downstairs to empty it and was probably even now coming back across the yard.

Accordingly she returned to Becky's room and was looking for a clean nightdress in the child's drawer when she heard a shout from below: 'Amy! Come and give us a hand, chuck. Your mam's come over all fainty like and I can't ... I can't ...'

Amy fairly flew across the room, down the stairs and into the kitchen, where she found Bill in the scullery doorway, struggling to get his wife off the floor. Suzie was a big woman and for the first time Amy realised that her father was no longer a big man. She was horrified that without her really noticing he had grown old. Now that she thought about it, she remembered that he was past sixty and the arms that clasped Suzie, though sinewy, were frail compared with her own.

'It's all right, Dad, I'm here,' Amy gasped, bending to heave Suzie up into her own arms. It was no light task, but between the two of them they managed to manoeuvre the unconscious woman to the sofa, where she lay with her head propped at a most uncomfortable angle and her limbs sprawled all anyhow. Amy felt her burning forehead and pointed to the open door. 'Fetch the doctor,' she said imperatively. 'I'll see to Mam and don't go running, because I can't have you ill on my hands as well and you're no chicken, Dad. If you meet the boys on your way, send Albert for the doctor and you come back here. And don't *worry*,' she added. 'It's still maybe only a feverish cold.'

By the time Bill arrived back with the doctor the situation was looking a good deal better. Suzie had recovered consciousness and was sitting up and drinking a cup of cold water, and the kitchen was much tidier, with the dirty crocks soaking in the sink and the washing out of sight in the scullery. Suzie was wearing a clean nightdress, and Amy had her own guess confirmed as soon as the doctor took a look at his patient, for when she changed Suzie's nightgown she had seen the faint beginnings of a rash all over her stepmother's neck and shoulders. 'Aye, you've got the measles all right, Mrs Logan,' the doctor said cheerfully. 'Only fancy a grown woman taking the measles – whatever were you thinking of? I can see we shall be off school for a day or two.'

Suzie smiled rather feebly at this gentle raillery, but Amy could see that she was relieved by the diagnosis, measles being a childish complaint from which the sufferer usually recovers without much difficulty. The fear of scarlet fever had been the first thing that had sprung to Suzie's mind when she had begun to feel so dreadfully ill and it would have meant weeks away from her family, imprisoned in the isolation hospital.

But when the doctor saw Becky he was less certain what ailed her. She had a sore throat, complained that her eyes were hurting her and had been sick twice, but as yet there was no rash. On the other hand when he sounded her chest he told her jokingly that there seemed to be a little orchestra playing down there, and when he and Amy returned to the kitchen he admitted it was possible that the child had somehow managed to contract more than one ailment. 'There's whooping cough about and with her mother having caught measles it's possible, though unlikely, that young Becky has a touch of both,' he said bluntly. 'However, I'll give you a prescription for something which will help the cough and bring the fever down, and you must keep her as clean, cool and comfortable as you can. If the weather weren't so hot I'd advise you to take Becky into her mother's room, but as it is, she's best with the bed to herself. Is it possible to change the feather mattress for a horsehair one? She would be a good deal cooler and very much easier to nurse.'

'Yes, I can manage that,' Amy said. She knew that the single bed in the boys' room which Paddy had once occupied had a horsehair mattress. 'But what about my mam, Doctor? Is she best upstairs? The trouble is if I nurse her in the kitchen I'll be spending all my time running up and down the stairs. And could you write me a note for my employer, please? I don't want to lose my job, but I can't see myself getting away from here for the next week or two.'

Nodding, the doctor pulled out a pad of paper and began to scribble, and presently handed her three notes, two for the chemist and one for the Adelphi Hotel. 'They'll maybe expect you to do without your salary for a few weeks, but I'm sure they won't dismiss you,' he said, indicating the explanatory note destined for the hotel. He looked at her over the top of his pince-nez. 'Have you had whooping cough, m'dear? I remember you and your brothers getting the measles but I can't recall any of you whooping when I came round. Because if you haven't had it, you might become infected yourself – and they're contagious diseases so no hotel will want you back until the three weeks' quarantine is over.'

'What a good thing you mentioned it,' Amy said. 'You're right about the measles, we all had them when I was five or six, but none of us ever had whooping cough, not even the boys. Oh, dear, does this mean they won't be able to go near Becky until she's completely clear?'

'I'm afraid so,' the doctor confirmed. He patted her cheek, then began to pack his stethoscope away into his case. 'Call me if you need me; send one of your brothers if they're at home,' he said over his shoulder, as he strode towards the door. 'Remember, plenty of cool drinks, a light diet and quiet. If you can give them that they'll be right as rain in no time.'

Despite the doctor's cheerful words, Amy had a tough couple of weeks trying to nurse her two patients, for Becky did indeed develop measles as well as whooping cough and had a miserable time of it. Unable to ask for help from the boys because of the fear of infection, she judged it more sensible to move her brothers out into lodgings temporarily, which left only herself and Bill to run the house and see to the invalids. Oddly enough, although Suzie was very sick indeed for ten days, she began to perk up quicker than Becky, whose temperature remained high for far longer. Bill went to the market each day to sell the fish and slept downstairs on the sofa, for he resolutely refused to go into lodgings with his sons. 'I had the measles when I were a young 'un and all us lads had whooping cough in our teens,' he told Amy gruffly when she mentioned the fear of infection. 'I know I'm an old feller and not much use in a sickroom, but at least I can do the messages, bring in wood and water, empty slop buckets and the like. You won't want to leave the house while Becky and her mam are so ill, so you'd best make the most of me. The lads would help, I'm sure, but they've not had the whooping cough.'

Amy was grateful to her father, particularly since he slept lightly and often heard Suzie call out before she herself did. It was hard enough nursing the invalids all day and looking after Becky all night without having to go to Suzie whenever she needed someone.

Amy did her best to obey the doctor's instructions but she reflected it was just her luck that her mam and sister should be ill during the hottest fortnight of the summer so far. When Bill came back from the fish market he carted with him a bucket of ice; Amy used it to freshen the home-made lemonade which her patients enjoyed, but nothing, not even the horsehair mattress, could keep Becky cool. Two or three times every day Amy gave her little sister a blanket bath in cool water and changed her sweat-soaked nightdress, and though Becky was pathetically grateful for the attention and always thanked Amy and said she felt much better now, within an hour she would be hot again, tossing and turning on her pillow, giving the whooping cough which Amy grew to dread and often vomiting into the bucket placed beside the bed for that purpose.

Gradually, however, as the days went by, both Suzie and Becky began to improve. After two weeks Suzie started to get up for an hour or two each day, though Amy flatly refused to let her go into Becky's room – Suzie had never had whooping cough. But if Amy peeled potatoes, gutted fish, or prepared vegetables for a stew, Suzie would put the pans over the flame and keep an eye on them until they were done. What was more, as she improved she began to do small tasks such as washing up, clearing away and laundering Becky's nightdresses and bed linen, both of which had to be changed frequently.

For many days Becky ate nothing at all and a good deal of what she drank came back, including the doctor's medicine, which she condemned roundly as being the nastiest stuff in the world. Then Bill came back with an egg custard, which the baker had made specially for Becky. It looked delicious; but Amy put a small helping into a dish and carried it up to her little sister without very much hope; Becky had turned down so many things with which they had tried to tempt her appetite. However, Amy told Becky how the baker had made it specially for her and how Bill said he had been followed by a group of little dogs, eagerly sniffing the air as he had brought it home, which made Becky laugh and consent to try a spoonful.

With Amy telling her jokes and trying to take her mind off the job in hand, the bowl was scraped clean before Becky fully realised that she had eaten it, and when the custard had not put in a reappearance twenty minutes later Amy dared to hope that the worst of the sickness was over at last.

There followed a few days when Becky was languid but far more comfortable, then she became demanding, wanting Amy to play games with her, to read to her and also to provide any food which she fancied. Bill remarked one evening, when Becky was in bed and asleep, that his older daughter was looking worn out and would, if she did not take care, end up ill herself. Amy pooh-poohed this, but Bill must have said something to Becky, because next day when Amy went to her sister's room with a bowl of warm bread and milk, Becky flung her arms round Amy's neck, kissing her warmly and telling her that she was the best sister in the world and that she, Becky, was a wicked child who did not deserve such kindness.

'Wicked? Well, I dare say you might have been a little naughty in your time,' Amy said, laughing. 'But I doubt very much if you've ever been wicked in your life.' She sat down on the bed and picked up the book she had been reading to Becky the previous day. 'Now you eat up your bread and milk, and I'll continue to tell you about Alice's adventures in Wonderland – won't that be nice?'

'Why, ye-es, only I can't talk and eat at the same time,' Becky objected. Nevertheless she began to spoon the sweetened bread and milk into her mouth with more enthusiasm than she had previously shown for a dish which she considered to be baby food. 'Only I *were* wicked once, Amy.' She looked up at Amy, her large blue eyes pleading. 'It were ages and ages ago – last Christmas, in fact. I did something naughty, something what I shouldn't have done, and then . . . and then I were afraid to tell you. Oh, Amy, it were me what took your necklace.'

Amy stared at her rosy, innocent face. 'You took my necklace?' she repeated incredulously. 'Oh, queen, whatever for?'

'To show me pals,' Becky said dolefully. 'I did try to tell you, Amy, but you said you was tired and I could tell you in the morning. Only you went off early next morning and I thought you'd took it, but when you came back for New Year you said it was still lost . . .'

'Hey, hang on a minute,' Amy said. She was still smiling but the smile was mostly to reassure her little sister. 'When you took it, did you lose it? I mean, did it fall off your neck while you were out in the road, queen? I'm afraid I don't understand.'

Becky heaved a deep sigh, as though Amy were the stupidest person in the world and cast her eyes up to the ceiling, but replied patiently, 'I *telled* you, Amy! I took the necklace on Boxing Day to show me pals – that were why I made you take me off the beach so's I could visit Etty – and then I brought it home with me and forgot all about it because we were playing such jolly games, weren't we? And I knew you'd take me up to bed and help me undress – then you'd have seen the necklace. So I wrapped it in paper and purrit on the mantelpiece.'

'But it wasn't on the mantelpiece; I turned the

whole house upside down,' Amy began, then remembered the haste with which she had left the house. 'No, no, I'm getting it wrong, aren't I? I left the house in such a hurry the day after Boxing Day that I didn't even remember I'd lost it. So go on, there it was on the mantelpiece . . .?'

'I don't know what happened to it after that,' Becky confessed, looking unhappy for the first time. 'I thought you'd taken it, which would have been all right. If you'd been there, Amy, I'd have give it you – I meant to tell you I'd found it on the floor, near where you'd been sitting when we was playing Consequences, only you went early, like you said. And when I came down for breakfast it were gone, honest to God it were.'

There was a pregnant pause while Amy's mind raced. She knew that no member of the family had taken it, but she supposed that wrapped in a piece of paper it might easily have been taken for rubbish and thrown into the fire. She was about to assume that this had happened when she suddenly remembered Paddy's abrupt departure. Was it possible that he had found it? But if so, why had he not simply returned it to her?

Because he thought you'd chucked it away, you blithering idiot, which is what anyone would have thought, a small voice said inside Amy's head. *Remember, you didn't tell him you'd mislaid it and were hunting for it, which any normal human being would have done. But you were too proud and you'd been pretty nasty about the necklace to start with, so you didn't want Paddy to know that you'd been careless enough to lose it. Oh, if he found it he will have been so hurt! And I can't get in touch with him, can't tell him what Becky's just told me. Whatever am I going to do?* She must have spoken the last sentence out loud for Becky, looking puzzled, said, 'Do? Well, you said you'd read me from *Alice in Wonderland*, so you could do that.'

Amy laughed but picked up the book and began to read. Children are so single-minded, she thought. Becky had told her the story of the necklace and by doing so had cleared her own conscience of any suspicion of wickedness. It would not occur to the child that her action might have had repercussions. Once confessed, it could be forgotten, and Becky had done just that.

When Amy had finished her chapter and Becky her bread and milk, Amy put the book down on the side table and stood up. Casually, as though it were of no importance, she asked, 'Why didn't you put the necklace back on the washstand, queen? Why put it downstairs on the mantelpiece? If you had wanted me to find it, you might have known I'd look in the bedroom first.'

'Amy, I *telled* you,' Becky exclaimed. 'I slipped it off me neck while you were in the pantry helping Mam to get us suppers. I didn't think to take it upstairs, I just wanted to hide it so's no one could see. I had me paper from the game of Consequences, so I wrapped it in that and stood on the fender, so's it looked as if I were checking the clock to see how late it was. And I put the crumpled-up ball of paper with the necklace inside by the clock. I meant to come down early next morning, throw the paper in the fire, and put the necklace down by the chair you'd sat in to eat your supper. But when I got down the necklace was gone. *Now* do you understand?'

'Yes, I understand queen,' Amy told her gently. 'Paddy came down before you, didn't he?'

'Yes, 'cos I slept in,' Becky said readily, 'but I don't

431

see . . . oh, Amy! Could that be why he were in such a mood? I mean, would it make him cross to find the necklace wrapped up in a bit of old paper? Why couldn't he have just give it back to you?'

Becky was bright, Amy thought, telling her sister soothingly that it didn't matter because if Paddy had picked it up no doubt he would keep it safe until he saw Amy again. But in her heart she thought that Paddy, if he really had found it, might well have chucked it into the fire and made up his mind to forget her and find a decent girl who would treat him with respect and cherish any gift he gave her.

But no matter what had been, it had happened over six long months ago and was best forgotten. So Amy picked up Becky's slop bucket and carried it and the dirty dish down to the kitchen, and began her day's work.

The SS *Frederica* came into the Crosby Channel and Paddy, leaning on the rail, could see even through the shimmer of the hot July air the Crosby light-house to his left and the Rock lighthouse on the New Brighton point to his right. He had told himself that he would not be affected by his first sight of the city of his birth; it had not occurred to him that passing along beside his old fishing ground would be so full of memories. Every inch of these waters he and the Logan boys had known like the backs of their hands and they had had good times out here, too. Clear, cool autumn days, when the nets had been so heavy that it had taken all three of them to heave the catch aboard; days in winter when they had fished in vain and had had to come home, frozen-fingered and depressed, with nothing to show for their hard work. Other people might not feel that they had come home until they saw the 'Liver Birds' looming out of the heat haze and though Paddy guessed that this would affect him too, it was these waters which had been his workplace for so long, and which he remembered now with a mixture of pride and nostalgia.

When the Liver Birds came in sight, however, half the ship's crew were beside him on the deck, already planning how they would spend their first day ashore. The *Frederica* would be in port for ten days, perhaps a fortnight, while her master sold the cargo he had carried across the wide Atlantic and cast around among those import/export companies who might give him an outgoing cargo for his next trip.

Many of the men, Paddy knew, had no longer got families or close friends living in the 'Pool, and would go straight to the sailors' home on Paradise Street and book in there for the duration of their time ashore. They would spend the first couple of days getting gloriously drunk and throwing around the money they had made on the voyage, picking up Liverpool judies, fighting with anyone who wanted a scrap and buying trifles for anyone who took their fancy. Several of the men, Paddy knew, had bought objects which they would sell on as soon as the city was reached. If they could find a curio shop, similar to the one on Upper Parliament Street where he had bought the necklace, they would find a ready sale for curiosities purchased from South America. And such deals would give them yet more cash to spend ashore.

The thought of the necklace immediately brought a picture of Amy's face into Paddy's mind. He could see her large, green-grey eyes fringed with dark lashes, and the glorious red-gold hair, which he had

433

once rudely called 'carroty', piled on top of her small head. But it did not do to think about Amy, because it brought the whole business back. He had already made up his mind that he would neither visit her in Huskisson Street, nor try to get in touch with her during his time ashore. For over six months he had concentrated on his job as a seaman while they were on board ship. When ashore, he had always chosen girls who were as different from Amy as they could possibly be. This had not been difficult, since South American beauties tended to black hair, glittering dark eyes and, rather too often for Paddy's taste, a dagger slipped into a stocking top. Being spirited was all very well, but Paddy had no desire to find himself on the wrong end of a stiletto and treated such ladies with considerable caution.

He had no doubt that the Liverpool judies who haunted the port, had their own method of keeping unwanted lovers at bay, but since he had no intention of embroiling himself with any local girl, no matter how pretty, he would be safe enough there.

Come to that, although he had mixed with the local girls when ashore in the Americas, he had always made it plain that he was not interested in either buying or otherwise obtaining their company. It was not, he told himself, that he was embittered by what had happened between him and Amy, but he acknowledged that at any rate he had been deeply hurt by it. He fully intended to get married one day and hoped that he would meet the right girl and be as happy with her as his mother had been with Bill, but he thought he would wait a while before taking such a giant step. Bill had been well past fifty before he married Suzie, which was a bit extreme – Paddy thought forty a more suitable age himself – but clearly it behoved one to move cautiously before committing oneself to marriage.

The clatter as the gangplank went down brought Paddy out of his reverie and sent him scuttling down the nearest companionway to pick up his ditty bag. He meant to go straight home to Seaforth, catching a number 17 tram from the Pier Head to the Rimrose Bridge and surprising the family by bursting in upon them just as they were sitting down to their main meal of the day. He imagined, since it was seven in the evening already, that the boys would be back from the fishing and Bill from the market, and he found himself greatly looking forward to seeing them all again. He had brought tobacco for the boys and Bill, a feather boa for Suzie and a hand-painted fan for Becky, depicting a man and a woman dancing flamenco, and a little tambourine made of chicken skin stretched over a frame with brass discs round the edge.

It was a fine evening and as Paddy climbed aboard the tram he had to fight a terrible urge to jump off again and make his way to Huskisson Street. He could make some excuse, he told himself, say he thought Becky might be visiting there . . . but he was firm. Such an action could only lead to more pain, more misunderstanding and was best totally banished from his mind. So he took his seat on the tram, choosing the open upper deck since it was such a warm evening, and watched with increasing pleasure as the vehicle rattled along Great Howard Street. The shops were doing a roaring trade and several times Paddy actually recognised someone, either from his school or a customer to whom he had sold shrimps.

He got off the tram at the terminus without having spoken to anyone and made his way along Crosby Road, whistling a tune beneath his breath and feeling the first stirrings of delighted anticipation. He told himself he couldn't wait to see the lads again, but knew his excitement lay in some strange way deeper than that. You can't be such a fool as to imagine you're going to have a second chance with Amy, he thought derisively, unwilling to acknowledge that the excitement could be caused by such an unlikely event. And presently he put the whole matter out of his mind as he began to recognise the houses of friends and Seafield Grove drew near.

Turning into the jigger which ran along the back of the houses made him think of Gran, and he felt a stab of regret that he would not be able to tell her how his life had changed and his horizons broadened. She would have been interested; the sights, smells and sounds he had experienced, the adventures which had come his way, the new friends he had made would have fascinated her. His mam, though she loved him, had her new family and would not have the sort of interest which Gran would have shown. The lads, Albert and Gus, had their own lives to lead and might even feel a little jealous, a little left out, when he began to tell his stories.

He crossed the yard and pushed open the kitchen door. He stepped across the threshold and glanced around him; the first person he saw was Amy. She was standing by the sink, her curly hair caught back into a knot at the nape of the neck, a large calico apron enveloping her slim figure. She was washing dishes but looked up as he entered and immediately dropped the bowl she held, which crashed to the floor and broke into a thousand pieces.

Paddy had meant to be cool to the point of coldness, should he be unfortunate enough to see Amy during his time ashore but somehow, as he saw the big green eyes slowly fill with tears and a pink flush creep into her cheeks, all his vengeful thoughts disappeared. Without at all meaning to do so, he held out his arms and Amy, with a choking little cry, flew into them.

For a long moment neither spoke nor moved, but then Amy, whose head had been nestled into the hollow of Paddy's shoulder, drew a little away from him so that she might look into his face. 'Paddy? What happened? Why did you go so quickly, without even saying goodbye? And it's been over six months – the longest six months in my life, I should think – without so much as a postcard. Oh, Paddy, I've been so unhappy!'

'I've been pretty unhappy meself,' Paddy admitted. 'But when you flung me necklace into the fire . . .'

'Oh, Paddy, I never did any such thing,' Amy gasped, snuggling close to him once more. 'It was all a horrible accident – have you had whooping cough? Or measles?'

'What's that got to do wi' anything?' Paddy asked, but his arms tightened round her. 'As it happens I've had both. But that doesn't explain why you tried to chuck me necklace . . .'

'It may not explain about the necklace exactly,' Amy said, detaching herself from his embrace and beginning to pull him towards the stairs. 'But poor old Becky's had both – she's still in quarantine – and she's the only person, just about, who can explain what happened to the necklace after Christmas. Honest to God, Paddy, there's been so much unhappiness and misunderstanding caused by what happened – I take it you found the necklace on the mantelpiece? What made you think I'd chucked it in the fire? Not that it matters, because once you've spoken to Becky you'll understand everything.'

'Yes, but I don't want to speak to Becky, not right now,' Paddy said, holding her hand very tightly as they mounted the flight. 'If *you* explain, sweetheart, that will be just fine. Why does it have to be Becky?'

But Amy would not reply, merely dimpling up at him and shaking her head, and indeed, when she ushered him into Becky's bedroom she was glad she had not tried to untangle the web. Becky was leaning back against her pillows, playing rather listlessly with a jigsaw on a tray set out across her knees, but as soon as she saw Paddy she sat bolt upright, sending jigsaw and tray bouncing unheeded across the floor. 'Paddy!' she squeaked, scrambling on to her knees and flinging her arms around his neck in a suffocating hug. 'Oh, Paddy, don't be cross with Amy 'cos it were me that took the necklace. I only meant to show it to me pals ...'

The story came pouring out as Paddy sat down on the bed and settled Becky on his knee, telling her comfortingly that it was quite all right, he and Amy had sorted themselves out and now that he knew no one had intended to throw the necklace away he was quite happy. 'Why, if I weren't happy I wouldn't be going to marry the girl just as soon as I've found us a place to live,' he said, grinning up at Amy with a wicked twinkle in his dark eyes.

Amy took a deep breath to tell Paddy what she thought of him, then expelled it once more in a long, whistling sigh. After all, she already knew she wanted to be with Paddy for the rest of her life, so marriage seemed the obvious step. The fact that he had informed Becky of his intention before so much as mentioning it to her was just typical of him. 'Never take anything – or anyone – for granted, Paddy Keagan', Amy said with mock severity. 'There's a jug of fresh lemonade cooling in the sink, Becky, and just before Paddy arrived I'd taken a batch of scones out of the new oven. Could you do with a little snack, queen? Because I'm sure Paddy would like to have a bit of a wash and a mouthful to eat before the rest of the family arrive back.' She had not said anything about Suzie, but thought she would do so presently and would let Paddy take her the cup of tea, which she usually made for her stepmother at this time of day.

'Ooh, Amy, I love your home-made lemonade and I love scones with butter on as well,' Becky said eagerly. 'Can Paddy come and sit with me while I have me tea?'

'We'll see,' Amy said, crossing her fingers behind her back. 'Now get back into bed, queen, and I'll make you tidy.'

Presently, returning to the kitchen, she found Paddy had had a quick wash and was vigorously drying himself with the roller towel on the back of the door. Amy poured tea into four enamel mugs, sliced and buttered a plate of scones and turned to Paddy. 'I didn't tell you before because I thought you'd had enough news for a while,' she observed. 'But Paddy, my love, your mam is having her afternoon rest because she went and caught the measles and has been pretty ill herself. If you'd like to take her tea up . . .'

But Paddy, ignoring her words, had come round the table in a couple of long strides and caught hold of her by the shoulders, staring anxiously down into her face. 'Dearest Amy, I were so gobsmacked to find you here that I never wondered *why* you weren't at the Adelphi, or in Huskisson Street. Now I come to look at you, though, it's clear as crystal that you've been nursin' Becky and me mam, and you're fair worn out. Why, girl, you're as white as a cod's underbelly!'

Amy tried to pull away from him, but such maidenly shrinking was foiled by Paddy's fingers simply tightening their grip. 'Why couldn't you say my face was white as pear blossom?' she enquired aggrievedly. 'Why does it always have to be perishin' fish?'

Paddy laughed and dropped a kiss on the end of her nose. 'Well, I'm used to seeing you with cheeks as pink as a shrimp . . .' he began and had to dodge the swipe which Amy aimed at him. 'Now, now, no violence, or you won't get the pretty present I've brought back for you from halfway across the world. Look, Amy, just because we're having a bit of a joke, that doesn't mean I'm not grateful for what you've done for me mam, who wasn't that good to you when you were small. Why, you must have risked losing your job to take care of mam and little Becky – you're one of the best, so you are.'

'Your mam and I have been getting on much better for some while and I must say she's done everything she could to help me, once she was well enough to get out of bed,' Amy told him. 'Besides, she's your mother, so I would have done all I could for your sake, old Paddy. As for my job, they've told

440

me to stay away until I'm clear of quarantine, so *that's* all right. Now what was that about a present?'

Paddy dug a hand into his pocket, then held his clenched fist out enticingly. 'Are all our differences over, or shall I find another pretty lady to wear my gift?'

Amy smiled and held out her hand. The next moment she was gasping with surprise and pleasure as Paddy slowly opened his fingers, around which hung the necklace of gold and jade. 'You had it all the time!' she said, her eyes glowing. 'So you really did think I'd thrown it away, it didn't get knocked into the fire like I imagined. Oh, Paddy, you must've thought that I was the most ungrateful girl in the world. Only . . . only why didn't you tell me you'd found it, confront me with what you thought I'd done?'

'I dunno,' Paddy said briefly. 'I guess I was a fool, but I thought you were trying to tell me you didn't want *anything* from me, not my presents, nor my kisses, nor the necklace. So I . . . I berthed aboard the SS *Frederica* and tried to forget all about you.' His fingers were at her neck, fumbling to get the little catch done up and Amy took hold of his shoulders and stood on tiptoe to kiss his chin.

She began to tell him how sorry she had been and how very happy she was now, and how they must never let such a misunderstanding arise again, but she had barely got two words out when she realised that Paddy was lifting her into his arms and that his face was getting closer and closer . . .

Presently they moved apart, both more than a little breathless. 'For a first kiss that was really something,' Amy murmured, gazing up at Paddy with shining eyes. 'All those wasted years, Paddy, years when we spent all our energy in hating one another when we could have been doing ... doing ...'

'First kiss?' Paddy said, grinning all over his face. 'It might have been your first kiss, queen, but I've been practising up and down the coast of South America. Just so that I'd do it properly when I came home to you, of course,' he added kindly.

'I meant the first kiss between us two,' Amy said with what dignity she could muster. 'I've had a feller or two since you went, you cocky Keagan! Oh, I suppose you don't know that one of our room shares, Ella, got married last month? She married Philip Grimshaw, you remember him. And Mary is marrying a Welshman with two little sons – Haydn Lloyd his name is. And Gus and Minnie's going steady, and Albert and Ruthie ...'

'My God, they'll have to call Huskisson Street the marriage mart,' Paddy said, taking the mug of tea and a scone and beginning to climb the stairs.

Amy, following him with Becky's tea, nodded. 'You're right there – and one more small piece of news. Peggy Higgins and that sailor she left our Gus for have split up, and Peggy came round here, sweet as sugar, to tell Gus she'd made an awful mistake and would he have her back? You can guess what Gus said to her.'

Paddy chuckled. 'Just about,' he agreed. He flung open the door of his mother's room and entered, the tray balanced precariously on one hand. 'Guess who's come home from the sea ...' he began and was interrupted by a shriek like a steam train's whistle, as his mother leapt from her bed and charged across the room to throw her arms round her son's neck. Amy stood and smiled as tea, tray and plate of buttered scones flew in three different directions while Paddy, laughing, tried to greet his mother, get her back into bed and answer the questions she was firing at him all at the same time. Amy stole forward and closed Suzie's bedroom door quietly, then returned to Becky. Sitting on her sister's bed she reflected that it was only right Suzie should have her son to herself for a bit after his long absence. For Amy there would be plenty of time – a lifetime, in fact.

But Amy did not get Paddy to herself until quite late that night, for he had to go round to the lodgings, which Gus and Albert still shared, to tell them he was home. Back at the house in Seafield Grove Suzie had come down for the evening meal, as she did every day, and Bill had returned from the fish market. He greeted his stepson with real pleasure, especially when it was explained to him that Paddy and Amy meant to marry when they could afford to do so. 'I always thought you two hid your feelings for one another under all that sniping and disagreeableness,' Bill said sagely. 'What's more, I reckon you're like as two peas in a pod – sharp tongued, quick-witted, but soft as herring roes underneath.'

'Oh, Dad, herring roes!' Amy said, giggling. 'There was Paddy telling me I looked pale as a cod's underbelly when he first came home and now you're telling me I'm squishy as herring roe underneath my quick wits. Still, I know what you mean, and there's a good deal of truth in it. Only in future, Paddy and me are going to be a bit more careful of one another's feelings; isn't that right, chuck?'

Paddy had agreed and they had spent a comfortable family evening, while the prodigal son told them all his adventures and assured them that he would not again take a berth aboard a ship which came into the port so rarely. 'Now that I've had a bit of experience aboard ship, I thought I'd try for a berth on a transatlantic liner,' he said. 'I'd be away three weeks at a time, I grant you, but that isn't like six months. Anyway, that's all for the future. Right now I'm taking a holiday. Besides, Amy and I will want to talk about both our careers, because if I do get a liner then I don't see why she shouldn't try for a job aboard as well. The really big ships employ quite a number of women and Amy's so efficient . . .'

Amy had been enchanted by the idea and intended to look into the possibilities, but right now she wanted to enjoy Paddy's company and talk about their lives together rather than their careers.

So when at last Suzie and Bill had settled down before the hearth, clearly with the intention of making an evening of it, Paddy took Amy's hand and informed their parents that they meant to go for a walk along the beach.

Outside the air was balmy with the scents of summer and when they reached the beach the freshening breeze brought the evocative smell of the sea to their nostrils. Paddy put his arm round Amy and drew her gently down into the shelter of one of the dunes. 'Oh, Amy, Amy, you smell so sweet,' he murmured, smoothing his hand down her cheek.

Amy responded for one giddying moment, then pulled herself free to remark, 'What? You mean the smell of shrimps has faded at last?'

Paddy laughed and held her a little tighter. 'I reckon you never did smell of any sort of fish,' he mumbled into the side of her neck. 'I were just getting at you because you didn't seem to admire me

444

the way I thought you should. But that's all water under the bridge, queen. Now we've sorted ourselves out we'd best get a ring, make it official. Oh, Amy, *how* I do love you.'

Around them the little breeze played in the marram grass and now and then a movement from one or other of them disturbed a tiny, chilly river of sand, which ran down the side of the dune and formed its own miniature mountain on the beach below. But Amy and Paddy never even noticed. Warmly, sweetly, they were beginning to understand what had brought them together. Locked in each other's arms, on the dark beach, with the round silver moon the only witness, Paddy and Amy began to kiss.

To find out more about Katie Flynn why not join the Katie Flynn Readers' Club and receive a twice-yearly newsletter.

To join our mailing list to receive the newsletter and other information* write with your name and address to:

Katie Flynn Readers' Club
The Marketing Department
Arrow Books
20 Vauxhall Bridge Road
London
SW1V 2SA

Please state whether or not you would like to receive information about other Arrow saga authors.

*Your details will be held on a database so we can send you the newsletter(s) and information on other Arrow authors that you have indicated you wish to receive. Your details will not be passed to any third party. If you would like to receive information on other Random House authors please do let us know. If at any stage you wish to be deleted from our Katie Flynn Readers' Club mailing list please let us know.

arrow books

Darkest Before Dawn

Katie Flynn

The Todd family are strangers to city life when they move into a flat on the Scotland Road; their previous home was a canal barge. Harry gets a job as a warehouse manager and his wife, Martha, works in a grocer's shop, whilst Seraphina trains as a teacher, Angela works in Bunney's Department Store and young Evie starts at regular school.

Then circumatsnces change and Seraphina takes a job as a nippy in Lyon's Corner House. Customers vie for her favours, including an old friend, Toby.

When war is declared the older girls join up, leaving Evie and Martha to cope with rationing, shortages, and the terrible raids on Liverpool which devastate the city. Meanwhile, Toby is a Japanese POW, working on the infamous Burma railway and dreaming of Seraphina . . .

arrow books

The Cuckoo Child

Katie Flynn

When Dot McCann, playing relievio with her pals, decides to hide in Butcher Rathbone's almost empty dustbin, she overhears a conversation that could send one man to prison and the other to the gallows – and suddenly finds herself in possession of stolen goods.

Dot lives with her aunt and uncle, the cuckoo in the nest, abandoned to these relatives after her parents died. She feels very alone . . . until she meets up with Corky who has run away from a London orphanage. They join forces with Emma, whose jeweller's shop has been burgled, and with Nick, a handsome young newspaper reporter who is investigating the crime. The four of them begin to plot to catch the thieves . . .

But Dot and Emma have been recognised, and soon both are in very real danger . . . .

arrow books

A Long and Lonely Road

Katie Flynn

Rosie McAllister is waiting for her husband, Steve, to come home. He is a seaman, often drunk and violent, but Rose does her best to cope and sees that her daughters, Daisy, 8, and Petal, 4, suffer as little as possible. Steve however, realises that was is coming and tries to reform, but on his last night home he pawns the girl's new dolls to go on a drinking binge.

When war is declared Rose has a good job but agrees the children must be evacuated. Daisy and Petal are happy at first, but circumstances change and they are put in the care of a woman who hates all scousers and taunts them with the destruction of their city. They run away, arriving home on the worst night of the May Blitz. Rose is attending the birth of her friend's baby and goes back to Bernard Terrace to find her home has received a direct hit, and is told that the children were seen entering the house the previous evening. Devastated, she decides to join the WAAF, encouraged by an RAF pilot, Luke, whom she has befriended . . .

arrow books

ALSO AVAILABLE IN ARROW

Two Penn'orth of Sky

Katie Flynn

Two penn'orth of sky is all you can see from dirty, cramped Nightingale Court where Emmy lives with her widowed mother. Her main aim in life is to escape and she sees marriage as her best way out. When Peter Wesley, First Officer aboard a cruise ship, proposes, she accepts easily.

The Wesleys have a baby, Diana, and all seems set fair for the small family, but Peter is killed and Emmy left penniless. She and Diana are forced to move back to Nightingale Court. Emmy has to take work as a waitress but she becomes ill and when suitors appear, Diana detests them all . . .

arrow books

Strawberry Fields

Katie Flynn

Liverpool, Christmas Day 1924. When twelve-year-old Sara Cordwainer, the unloved child of rich parents, sees a ragged girl with a baby in her arms outside her church, she stops to talk to her, pressing her collection money into the girl's icy hand. But from this generous act comes a tragedy which will haunt her for years.

When, years later, Sara meets Brogan, a young Irishman working in England, she feels she has found a friend at last. But Brogan has a secret which he dare tell no one, not even Sara.

And in a Dublin slum, Brogan's little sister Polly is growing up. The only girl in a family of boys, she knows herself to be much loved, but it is not until Sara begins to work at the Salvation Army children's home, Strawberry Fields, that the two girls meet – and Brogan's secret is told at last . . .

arrow books

ALSO AVAILABLE IN ARROW

Polly's Angel

Katie Flynn

It is 1936 and Polly's guardian angel has to work overtime when her large family is forced to move from the countryside they love into central Liverpool. Money is desperately short and with her mother working and her father sick, Polly is easily led astray by a new pal, the handsome, idle Sunny Andersen.

But soon war looms, and Sunny joins the navy to train as a signaller. After the horrors of the May blitz, Polly too decides she wants to help her country and goes into the WRNS. She hears that an old pal, Tad Donoghue from the Dublin slums, is now in the Royal Air Force. Tad hopes to be reunited with his Polly, but she is in love with Sunny . . . isn't she?

arrow books

The Bad Penny

Katie Flynn

One wild night in the '30s, midwife Patty Peel is called to attend a birth on the opposite side of Liverpool. She pedals off into the storm and delivers a baby girl in a filthy slum dwelling, just as the mother dies. The drunk and violent father tells Patty to get rid of it, so she takes the child away, meaning to deliver it to the nearest orphanage.

But Patty has spent her entire childhood in an institution, except for the frequent occasions when she ran away, and cannot bear to hand the baby over.

However, she has few friends and despises the men with whom she comes into contact with, so how can she hope to bring up the child alone?

She has no idea how the baby will affect the attitude of those around her . . . nor how her life will change as a result . . .

arrow books

A Kiss and a Promise

Katie Flynn

Michael Gallagher is an Irish seaman, fighting with the British Navy. He comes ashore in Liverpool when his ship needs repairs and meets lovely young Stella Bennett on the quayside, searching for her lost kitten.

The young couple fall in love and want to marry but the Bennetts have other plans for Stella and when she gives birth to a baby, Ginny, Michael is dismayed by the child's ginger hair and convinced she is not his.

He returns to Ireland, leaving the sluttish Granny Bennett to rear Ginny. The child accepts her lot, expecting little from life but knows that, in order to escape from the slums, she must attend school. Granny Bennett prefers Ginny to skivvy for her, but when a sympathetic teacher, Mabel Derbyshire, comes into her life, Ginny decides she must better herself and the obvious way to do so is to find her father . . .

arrow books

ALSO AVAILABLE IN ARROW

The Liverpool Rose

Katie Flynn

Lizzie Devlin is an orphan living with her Aunt Annie, Uncle Perce and two boy cousins in Cranberry Court, Liverpool, within a stone's throw of the canal. Lizzie loves her aunt but is hated by her uncle and escapes whenever she can.

She makes friends with Geoff Gardiner, another orphan, and is teaching him to swim in the Scaldy when Clem Gilligan rescues the pair of them from drowning. Clem works on the canal boat, *The Liverpool Rose*, with Jake Piedmore and his wife, plying between the great cities of Leeds and Liverpool.

But Lizzie's situation at home starts to worsen as her uncle grows surlier and more violent. Eventually, the worst happens, and Lizzie is forced to flee from the Court or risk serious injury, perhaps even death. Her first instinct is to make for the canal, but finding Clem is not so easy . . .

arrow books

Order further Katie Flynn titles from your local bookshop, or have them delivered direct to your door by Bookpost

☐ **The Girl From Penny Lane**	0 09 942789 3	£6.99
☐ **Liverpool Taffy**	0 09 941609 3	£6.99
☐ **Strawberry Fields**	0 09 941603 4	£6.99
☐ **No Silver Spoon**	0 09 927995 9	£6.99
☐ **Polly's Angel**	0 09 927996 7	£6.99
☐ **The Liverpool Rose**	0 09 942926 8	£6.99
☐ **Poor Little Rich Girl**	0 09 943652 3	£6.99
☐ **The Bad Penny**	0 09 943653 1	£6.99
☐ **Down Daisy Street**	0 09 945339 8	£6.99
☐ **A Kiss and a Promise**	0 09 945342 8	£6.99
☐ **Two Penn'orth of Sky**	0 09 946814 X	£6.99
☐ **A Long and Lonely Road**	0 09 946815 8	£6.99
☐ **The Cuckoo Child**	0 09 946816 6	£6.99
☐ **Darkest Before Dawn**	0 09 948697 0	£6.99

Free post and packing
Overseas customers allow £2 per paperback

Phone: 01624 677237

Post: Random House Books
c/o Bookpost, PO Box 29, Douglas, Isle of Man IM99 1BQ

Fax: 01624 670923

email: bookshop@enterprise.net

Cheques (payable to Bookpost) and credit cards accepted

Prices and availability subject to change without notice.
Allow 28 days for delivery.
When placing your order, please state if you do not wish to receive any
additional information.

www.randomhouse.co.uk/arrowbooks

arrow books